"A WRITER TO WATCH."
—*The Washington Post Book World*

"An engaging journey into the mystical Far East, the unseemly corruption in the Army, and the mind of a complex man dogged by past tragedies. Lee has earned his stripes as a crafter of terrific thrillers."
—Columbus Dispatch

"Gus Lee is a fascinating writer who keeps getting better and better."
—Portland Oregonian

"Lee uses the thriller form to explore the human condition. . . . Through vigorous prose that writhes across the page, [Lee's] vision—daring, deep, and unflaggingly moral—comes to vibrant life as he takes Kan on a tense and moving journey toward redemption."
—Publishers Weekly (starred review)

"Compelling . . . Captivating."
—Booklist

"A gripping, literate military thriller with appeal to genre fans and readers of serious fiction alike. Highly recommended."
—Library Journal

By Gus Lee:

CHINA BOY
HONOR AND DUTY*
TIGER'S TAIL*

Published by Ivy Books

TIGER'S TAIL

Gus Lee

IVY BOOKS • NEW YORK

Ivy Books
Published by Ballantine Books
Copyright © 1996 by Gus Lee
Map copyright © 1996 by Mark Stein Studios
Excerpt from *Honor and Duty* copyright © 1994 by Gus Lee

All rights reserved under International and Pan-American Copyright Conventions. Published in the United States by Ballantine
Books, a division of Random House, Inc., New York, and simultaneously in Canada by Random House of Canada Limited, Toronto.

http://www.randomhouse.com

Library of Congress Catalog Card Number: 96-94871

ISBN 9780345472793

This edition published by arrangement with Alfred A. Knopf, Inc.

Manufactured in the United States of America

First Ballantine Books Edition: March 1997

146673257

To Diane

Hungry men hunt the tiger,
but brave men pull the tiger's tail.

In Asia, the tiger is America.

Contents

x   CONTENTS

ACKNOWLEDGMENTS

Love to Jena, Eric and Jessica. Gratitude to my publishers, Sonny Mehta and Leona Nevler; my editors, Ash Green and Diane Elliot-Lee; my friend and agent, Jane Dystel, and her VP, Miriam Goderich. With special thanks to Amy Tan, whose magical, literary voice opened all doors and made my present efforts possible. Thanks to Kevin Bourke, Jennifer Bernstein, Suk Park, Celia and Terry Hong, LTC Chuck Buck and LTC Dan McCarthy, for invaluable technical assistance.

To the mad monks in the DMZ law firm of Armstrong, Meinhold, Majers, Ziegler, Reade, Resen, Wells, Gallivan, Lewis, Barbee, Braga, Kirk & Zimmerman, with kudos to Don "Butt Kicker" Meinhold, USMA 1970, whose quiet presence in Korea inspired this tale; to the Big Boy, Colonel H. Jere Armstrong, who miraculously kept most of us out of jail; and to Steve Brown, who remembered more of this tale than I did, and taught me about structure, tension and event.

To the Senate Armed Services' Connelly Investigation JAGCs and their legal counsel, COL Charlie Murray, USMA 62, who uncovered and resolved the largest recruiting malpractice conspiracies in the history of the U.S. Army. To Colonel Lawrence Bell, the USAREC IG, for waking me up every night and for standing tall alongside a puckering, whistle-blower lawyer named Captain Gus Lee.

Thanks to my mentor Charlie Murray who, by sending my Connelly team to cold Korea, provided me with the structure for this book. My salute for his stand for ethics and law, which cost him two stars.

With a prayer to Kim Jong-soon of Soya-san; to Herb Rosenthal, Diane Yu and Mark Harris, for keeping the flame.

As always, with deep gratitude to my covenant brothers, Rev. Paul Watermulder, Frank Ramirez, Barry Shiller, Paul Benchener, Ken Seeger and Phil Knight, who know, as I, where all the thanks are due.

CHINESE MANCHURIA

CHINA

Ch'ŏngjin

NORTH KOREA
(PDRK)

Kimch'aek

Sinŭiju

USSR

Khabarovsk

CHINA

Tsugyuan

Hamhŭng

Hŭngnam

Changchun

Arsenyev

Umariyah

Shenyang

Nakhodka

Vladivostok

P'yongyang

Wŏnsan

North
Korea

Sea of Japan

P'yongyang

I'chon

OUIJEONGBU
CORRIDOR

Seoul

Yellow
Sea

South
Korea

JAPAN

Tokyo

T'osan

DMZ

Panmunjŏm

Camp Casey

Tongducheon

Hiroshima

Osaka

PACIFIC
OCEAN

Kaesŏng

Jungsan Peak

MSR 3

miles 240

Ouijeongbu

kilometers 400

Seoul

Kangnŭng

Inch'on

Sŏngnam

Suwŏn

Han River

Osan

SOUTH KOREA
(ROK)

YELLOW

SEA

Taejŏn

Chŏnju

Taegu

Nakdong River

Kyŏngju

Kwangju

Masan

SEA OF JAPAN

Fizum-do

Pusan

JAPAN

Strait

Tsushima

Cheju Strait

Korea

Cheju-do

한국

Korea

1 9 7 4

PROLOGUE

THE EMPTINESS OF HEAVEN

The elephant grass cut my hand with a clean incision, bright blood following the grayish olive blade like ink flowing from a thick pen. I strained but heard nothing. I sensed echoes of guns, wet boots humping ancient green hills, tired lungs husking wet air, the slither of a fat black river snake. I felt the drumming of my broken heart. I had done everything right and had engineered myself into the worst day of my life.

She was a little girl, no more than ten. Her chest labored; her teeth chattered in the heat. Her eyes flared in childlike hope as she saw me. "Help, Ba," she said. "Help me." My Chinese face reflected her agony as her tiny fingers held mine and trembled with surging nerves. She had run out of the kill zone and I had shot her, and now she thought I was her father.

Her head was weightless, her hair fine and soft. Her eyes shaded as shock took her in the moment of a brave and uncertain smile. The dark gumbo muck stank and grass burned in the shadows of an unkind dawn. Sounds returned like thin smoke struggling through cotton. Flesh-eating insects dropped, making sharp clicks on broad leaves. Moms Bell, my RTO, called the medevac. We were on radio silence except for our own casualties, but he had seen my face and called for a dustoff.

The carrion bugs went to work and a brown leech touched her leg. I brushed them off, not wanting them to feed on my catastrophe. Moms's radio squelched; the medevac was far away.

God, I'm sorry, I tried to say, but no sound came from the hot summer gravel of my throat. *"Doi sin loi,* too sorry," I managed in Vietnamese, and she looked at me, eyes glazing. Blood streamed from her ear to soak my hand, burning the razor cut of the elephant grass. "You are good and strong. God loves you. Please breathe." I could think of no other words in any language. She had a kind face and reminded me of my mother when she was young. Her small hand touched her wounds.

The main body of the enemy lay smoldering in the abattoir of the kill zone. The jungle smoked tiredly with their deaths, like a fire that had lost interest after erupting savagely across a tender field. I had picked the place and the enemy had come, not in silent, well-intervaled file, but bunched, with muzzles down and loud feet in the false dawn, yakking in low swamp country where Americans did not venture. I despised their patrol leader for being blind to what was going to happen. But they were the enemy and very good at killing us. My job was to do them. I always did my job.

I clacked eight Claymore underbrush mines set in overlapping arcs, and five thousand steel balls raked them as grenades crumped. We bared teeth, grunting as we squeezed short, savage bursts of automatic fire, knocking down bodies, flaming the grass, the gunfire proclaiming its own government. An enemy trail party rushed us through the swamp on the right and I fired hot, searching rounds through the thick foliage, branches cracking and leaves floating like green, wounded snowflakes as we emptied magazines and grenade launchers into the fallen enemy and the lime mire with practiced mechanical madness.

The jungle echoed with explosions, the birds long gone, the bugs organizing, the putridity of the swamp smoothed by the sweet acrid bite of cordite and the silence of death. Perimeter security went up; hand signals were affirmative. We entered the muck pools.

The rear party had been women and children. They had run from the fate we had cast for their men. I picked up the girl from the ooze. Beneath her was a dead baby, tiny arms up, slate eyes looking away.

"Jesus Christ." Moms Bell stared at me. I was Magic Marker Man, a company commander who taught men of all colors to move silently like Chinese ghosts through bush, the man who never swore, who taught the frightened to breathe slow instead of curse hot.

We did not blow away dinks, gooks or zipperheads. As a family at war, we had no cherries, crapbirds, dipshits or slackers counting down days while walking trip-wired trails. My men constituted the largest job God had given me and the most remarkable assemblage of men I would ever know. We lived the resilient comedy of professional immigrants. I had laughed with bright teeth at hard times, but was not prepared for this.

She wasn't breathing. I pinched her nostrils, bent back her head, covered her mouth with mine and puffed air into her, my head filled with bad-luck screams, my helmet rocking emptily in green water, Moms Bell calling for Doc. I heard Doc cluck his tongue, issuing his sad, clinical assessment for body bag fill while I blew air, smoothing wrinkles and creases in her wet, black tunic.

"She's dead, Urchin," said Law Man, Lieutenant Colonel Carlos Murray, the battalion commander with a law degree who humped with us. Her chest inflated. Murray had a hand on her neck, the other on my shoulder.

"They're dead. *Lo siento, compadre.* I canceled the bird."

He had not shot her. I hated the wet heat of his hand on my shoulder, near the steel hilt of my knife, offering solace. I flicked it off, breathing harder into her, all my will at work, the taste of her death in my mouth.

You are good and strong. You will live. Please live. God, make this a bad dream. I prayed with all my soul to the One True God, using all that I had been or could be, leaving nothing for tomorrow, god or ghost, spending all my *yuing chi*, the world collapsing.

Blood came from her slack mouth and her last breath rattled into my throat, a glaring neon sign that illuminated the emptiness of Heaven. For a moment, I glanced at the stone vacancy of her tender face. I felt bitter truths: there was no god that heard a firstborn's gut prayers and cast light through breaks in the rain forest. My audience was a host of carapaced bugs and a brown leech. They were not interested in my soul or in the hopes of bloodied mortals; they sought the flesh of an innocent girl in a world ruled by heartless insects and helpless men.

I blew harder into her quiet lungs.

1

GIRL

It was number-one-best *ding hao*, good fortune, the magic of Chinese river fogs and BaBa's bright-red good luck, that made her eyes open. She was alive, and I'd take her to Disneyland to ride the teacups and tell knock-knock jokes. I would grow full on her happy laughter.

She was above me in a sky-blue kimono. *"Anata, anata!"* she cried—Sir, sir!—small hands trying to lift me. A stewardess. The Dong Nai had been six years ago. No snakes, no swamp, and the girl was dead. I blinked in a cold sweat, on the floor of the first-class cabin, holding a crushed can of Diet Pepsi.

A pillow, Ma's salted fish, a Korean dictionary and Frigault's *Psychology of Nightmares* lay like casualties. My head ached. I fought for air. I looked at my bloodless hand.

January 14, 1974. I was following the sun across the Pacific on Japan Air Lines Flight 001 to Tokyo. I had fallen asleep and entered the old nightmare like a lamb to slaughter.

"Yoroshides." It's okay. I collected my gear and stood. The other passengers were Japanese, standing solemnly like honorable men watching the failing of a family bank. I bowed to atone my rudeness. They bowed lower. It was one thing to have a big, deranged Chinese with them. It was another if he was going to cry all the way to Japan, trying to resuscitate a pillow.

The copilot watched a stewardess place cold hand towels on my forehead as another gave me slippers, eye covers, nail clippers and playing cards and a doctor slid a stethoscope under my turtleneck. A small girl with a one-eared stuffed rabbit gazed at me and my missing ear. Tourist-class passengers gawked from the curtains. I laughed—I had been booked in first class on a foreign air carrier to allow me quiet and unnoticed entry into Asia.

I was returning to the Far East, the land of my birth and my error. I was going to rescue an old friend and investigate a fading memory of a prior self, hoping I wasn't too late for either cause.

I am Jackson Hu-chin Kan, the firstborn, accountable for the clan line. My veins run with the memory-rich blood and river silts of China. They bind me to Ma, to BaBa, to our *jia*, our household, across the sea.

From the Golden Gate, I speak to family graves on the Long River and our thousand generations of black-haired men.

I pay all debts. I perform honorable labor and will do so for all my days. I am son of a *laoban*, a sweaty, hard-faced Chinese junk captain. I am no stranger to hard work.

I obey the currents and accept the risks of the river. Beneath our hull and wind-chopped waters lurk slimy river demons who would hold us facedown for the price of a small fish.

The risks do not matter. I do my job, honor my parents and all elders, and remember the before-borns. I close all files.

Until he became Christian, BaBa was a drinking gambler, a cursing shamanist sailor who had me beat a gong to the fast pop of firecrackers each time we left the quay with good cargo.

"Hu-ah," Ma had said, holding my face to keep my little boy's mind from wandering. "The gods promised you to me.

"You are Hu-chin. *Hu* means the tiger—and danger and courage.

"Aiya! Tiger! Bad name for my laughing son! Your father's father named you after drinking two black jugs of rice wine for your birth.

"Hu-chin-ah, you were born in war and named in his drunken happiness. *Chin* means 'gold' or 'precious,' names to protect the clan in sad times." Ma later said this made finding a wife difficult.

Mrs. Wong, meet my firstborn son, Precious Danger.

Kan, my all-important clan name, means "to find the good, to cast out evil," suggesting a perpetual opportunity for work.

I was seven when hard-boned BaBa brought us to America. BaBa talked to stars and loved America's familiar nautical skies. He had no fear of soldiers or bandits on foreign land; my two younger brothers had died in China, not in America.

Disliking my name's feral hostility and its American rendition—Urchin—he called me "Jack" after the comic Mr. Benny, adding the "son" as a good-luck bonus.

The sound of my American name gave my father pleasure.

My names described the objects of my character. It was my *yeh*, karma, to be the firstborn male on the river side of the Kan *jia*, to be educated by the U.S. government to become a soldier, to have a doting mother and a father who loved laughter, to be a man who was always a friend to danger.

I climbed the circular staircase to brush my teeth in the lavatory of the upper-deck piano lounge of the new 747 jumbo. A tony crowd of sophisticates in open-necked earth-brown shirts drank costly scotch and smoked thin cigarettes. I sat at the Yamaha piano and watched the endless blue expanse of the Pacific, en route to 180 degrees west and the Far East, the border between two worlds.

Immigrants feel a levitating happiness while sailing homeward. We remember all that is good. But arrival in Asia never matches that high expectation of return, while the backtrack to America reeks of survivor guilt and the musts of alien melancholy.

A square of cold, bright sunlight warmed my face. It was like the Vietnamese sun, full of hard copper and wet heat. The piano reminded me of Cara, filling me with painful longing and regret. Softly, I played Porter's "Night and Day" and the Bergmans' "Like a Lover" for her, closing my eyes when women sat closer.

I was bound for an unknown challenge, sent by Carlos Justicio Murray, a man loved by some and hated by others. I had been altered each time his life had crossed mine.

He had taught me law at West Point. "Law school," he

had said, "is to free thought as foxes are to hens." He was
a big-fisted, broken-nosed El Paso street fighter who had
graduated from the Academy and Yale Law and had
fought in Korea.

Murray had imprinted memories of his humorous
charisma on our psyches with the adroitness of a Navy
tattoo artist. He loathed tranquility and detested dis-
honesty. He inspired heretical thinking, occasional il-
logical acts and steady followings of the young and
innocent.

His logical assaults on our presumptions of Perfect
American Justice led some of my classmates to mistake
his realism for communism. He had a rash, Irish streak of
humor, an irresistibly contagious *yang* male laugh and
the romantic grin of a Mexican knife fighter. He had
made me think and he had made me laugh, and I had
always hoped to see him again.

I was playing a piano at forty thousand feet because
this idle hope had been realized in full.

Five hours ago, he had said, "Today, you go to the
DMZ."

BaBa's heart beats to the tune of the Yangtze's iron
currents. We have sucked our own wounds and tasted
China. Carlos Murray's will had been forged in the hot
flats of West Texas to the tune of honeyed Mexican gui-
tars and the cadence of angry Irish hearts.

He was a stout, muscular stick of human dynamite,
amusingly insouciant with a homicidal *bon vivant* touch.
He pulsed ethics with the fever that drove most men to
common sins.

I played the piano for Cara. But all the chords led to
Asia, where I had been born and where I had died.

In the spring of 1966, I was Bravo Company commander, 2nd of the 502nd Infantry, 101st Airborne,
Vietnam. I believed in God, the rational use of force, the
sanctity of the free world and the beauty of children. My

yeh, karma, was good, and my battalion commander was my old professor Lieutenant Colonel Carlos Murray.

At Dak To I lost two platoon leaders, Curt Tiernan and Cyril Magnus. We inserted into the Iron Triangle and set the Dong Nai ambushes, denying to the NVA a key swath of the Ho Chi Minh Trail. We killed hundreds of the enemy; I slew a family of women.

I had prayed over the girl's grave as Murray recited the Twenty-third Psalm. I stared into the soft, pungent, fertile, violated earth, our entrenching tools heavy with wet, adhesive mud.

Foul-luck demons swarmed out of the dead.

"Urchin, there's a purpose to our losses." His voice lilted in a dark, Irish moment in equatorial Asia.

"Bullshit," I said, spitting out my bitter *yuing chi*, my fortune, the girl's blood in the pores of my soiled hands, changing my chemistry and the honor of my clan. My hands touched frag pins, knife, ammo packs, compass, canteen, notepad, inventorying the familiar. I observed the ruin of me in the shallow ditch; I could crouch motionless at ambush for a week, but now I could not stop my hands from fretting with the memory of the shooting.

Josh Lott, exec, had the company on perimeter. Top Sergeant, Moms, Doc, Murray and the battalion sergeant major stood with me at the graves. We had made forty men and six females disappear. Murray stood closest, unafraid of the mental unhinging that flared in my unfocused eyes, trying to carry a portion of my loss, to annul blame.

But there are losses that defy words and the passage of time. In that moment in the mud, I felt revealed as Asian, my American cloak falling from me like a reptile's dead skin. I spat like a Chinese *yaofan*, a want-rice beggar, rich with ill fate.

"She's your angel, Urchin. She's made you a force for the good. You'll let no harm befall the innocent." He spoke as if I were the person I had been, as if we were walking up to Michie Stadium above the Hudson. It would be a crisp autumn day with Gaelic drums, emerald fields gracing the Corps like the enchantment of first love. The granite forests of West Point would be turning gold, yellow and orange, the river a deep, calming, pristine blue with soft currents and no gorges, each lap of the river against the rock restoring my youth in bright and blooming innocence, and all the odds in Heaven canted in our inculpable favor.

I had played the Chinese blood game. Kill the enemy and make them disappear, facedown in foreign mud, beyond the reach of Taoist honors and the ritual talks with their descendants, unable to hear reports on the health of the clan's firstborn sons, burning in the silent eighteenth level of a lonely Eastern hell.

Do not flinch when you kill them and bury them like animals, even if they look more like you than the men you command, the American men you must keep alive, who look at Asians as things.

I looked out the window of the airplane into the Eastern sun. I drank a Virgin Mary, toasting the girl as she flitted, unbidden, from the deep recesses of an obsessed memory. I felt her fine hair in my hand and tasted her death in my mouth. I left the piano.

I wish you good things, *bohbooey*, Little Precious. For you, I hope there really is a Heaven, filled with good and tender white rice, fresh and crisp long beans, the warm chatter of the *jia* on winter nights, kind men and grandmothers with big hearts.

Murray had been wrong; the girl was no diaphanous angel with wings of down, rouged cheeks and gilded halo. She had become a cross, all dead iron and coarse, splintered wood stained with old brown blood on a path with no end. She had joined the swollen ranks of the premature dead, a sad society to which my parents had donated two sons.

Only Cara Milano, the woman with too many men, the woman I had promised I would never leave, had been able to chase away the bloody girl.

I shut Cara from my mind.

I had a job to do.

2

BITTER AND SWEET

The mission packet held orders and a Richelieu letter—a sweeping authorization from The Inspector General that would open most doors in the military world. I studied the glossy Official Military Personnel File photo of my target.

Colonel Frederick C. LeBlanc. Noble features, clear eyes, heavy jaw, creased cheeks, a compelling gaze. A man with dislikes and grooming, nicknamed the Wizard, suspected of high crimes, drawing me to the East. In contravention of standard operating procedures, I was about to investigate a superior officer, and in questioning an elder, I was offending a fundament of ancient Chinese propriety.

Carlos Murray's call began with conventional solemnity. "Urchin, *¿cómo dice la buena vida?*" What says the good life? "*Amigo,* I have good news and I have bad news."

Law Man. I knew the voice but I smiled anyway. "You find me, as always, in quailing fear of you. I'm happy to hear your voice, despite the fact that I know who this is."

Murray was the most powerful staff lawyer in the

U.S. Army. He was staff judge advocate for The Inspector General—TIG. Carlos advised the Joint Chiefs of Staff and played hangman on bad officers. Rotten lawyers hated him for his lack of professional courtesy while victims named children after him. He was a Thomas More, attended by raving affection and bitter enemies.

TIG was the ultimate police authority in the Army, and law was the new faith; TIG lawyers were the anointed high clergy, bearing badges to cleanse fraud, correct wrongs, repair faith and ship defendants to speedy trial for maximum punishments.

"Ah, Jackson, my favorite son in a raggedy band. A black Irishman of the Chinese variety. Scramble your line." I punched the button that made our conversation secure. My heartbeat went up.

"You go to the DMZ. Now. That's the good news."

He had said what my soul needed and what my heart feared. It was a Chinese moment, full of sweet and bitter. He was offering me a chance to leave the woman I probably loved, to work on a debt that worked on me like an angry cancer. There was a relief in his mission call; Cara had repaired parts of me, but her intimacy was an unknown threat to old demons.

"The bad news?"

His jaw cracked through my earpiece. "Jimmy Buford is missing in Korea. He has been out of net six days. Local ROK authorities have found nothing. I have ruled out accident."

Jimmy lost in the ROK. The Republic of Korea.

"The man he was to investigate has taken over the search. I trust no one. I cannot call there without knowing who is who in the zoo. I am not screwing around anymore. You are going in."

My big brother, drawling, indomitable James Thurber Buford. He and I had been the lead neurotics on a workaholic legal team at Bragg. After I left for the Presidio, Jimmy, Beth and the three boys had gone to the Pentagon to work for Murray's low-profile, high-octane ethics unit on the second floor of the D Ring of the Pentagon.

Jimmy had gone to Carlos on my recommendation.

He had become Murray's best solo hunt dog, returning with bad judges, defense counsels and prosecutors between his fine, legal teeth. Jimmy had never been in combat but had the courage of lions; he had set the precedent of captains hunting colonels. He used the Uniform Code of Military Justice and the Fed Regs like Sinatra used a mike. He called up the most obscure opinions at will. Jimmy was two times the lawyer I was, and I wasn't half bad.

I pulled out a mission notepad. "Give it to me."

"Jimmy," said Carlos, "went in the military replacement flight. His target was the Second Infantry's SJA"— Staff Judge Advocate, the top lawyer for the lonely, forgotten American division on the DMZ.

"Urchin, you go in-country as a U.S. attorney. Deep and dark, civvies and foreign airlines into civilian airports. Jimmy went in uniform, grinning at strangers and kissing babies. So you go quiet, in a suit and tie. Trust no one.

"Inform *no one* of your mission. Your alibi is sick call. Your SJA will be told you are at Walter Reed for back surgery and that you are not to be contacted. I will take care of your case load. All you need is shots. A medic is on the road."

The attorney general, John Mitchell, had sworn a few judge advocates into the Justice Department, making me an Army prosecutor and an acting assistant United States attorney. Carlos was picking me for my federal badge, my Asian face, my Irish sympathies, my loyalty to his lonely causes. My laughing at his bad jokes.

"Once at Camp Casey on the Z, put on the uniform.

TIG will not let you go completely incognito; once there, show the IG flag.

"Port of call is San Francisco." He gave me flights. Japan Air Lines to Narita at Tokyo, Korean Air to Kimpo in Seoul. The place names were music, heavy on the bass and elevated pulses, on the far side of the second meridian, full of sudden death and second chances.

"At Kimpo, wait for your contact. As we speak, I do not know his identity. He will find you by looking for the big Asian at Korea's largest airport. I presume you will stand out, like you did in the highlands and the Triangle."

Except in the bush, I had not merged quietly into Vietnamese society. I had drawn mobs.

"Tell me about the man Jimmy went after."

"Colonel Frederick C. LeBlanc, a.k.a. the Wizard, West Point '53, the DMZ's SJA. He has been in Korea since Peter caught fish in the Sea of Galilee. The community worries about him." The Pentagon. I wondered why.

"His Defense section has the lowest acquittal rate in the Army. JAGCs get assigned to him and volunteer not to come home, violating the one-year DMZ rotation policy." JAGCs were Judge Advocate General's Corps lawyers. Carlos had left something out. A mystery.

"Estimate how long the Wizard has been out there, on the line, sniffing Manchuria's rear and staring down the Mongol hordes."

I hated to guess at anything, and particularly something so described, but Carlos was my superior officer. "Three years," I said.

"Nine." He was silent. He wanted my imagination to engage. Too much power and too much tenure—too much like Congress. Branch Assignments had tied up, leaving a man in Siberia too long.

"What's he doing wrong?"

"Urchin, the man does not love God."

"Maybe you could be more specific?"

"I cannot. That is why you are going. Cuff him or kiss him. *Cuidado*—Casey houses a private American army of renegades who prefer Asia to the States. The Second is a bad cluster of angry trained killers. And the weather sucks." A pause. "And the Reds are pissed, utilities do not work and the food would make dogs barf.

"You will have a carte blanche Richelieu letter that declares your actions to be in the name of the Army Chief of Staff and the Republic. You will have a firearm with ROK and Japanese permits.

"Your cover is race relations. Do not report to the Wizard. Jimmy went in straight and the Wizard did him. Now they are lying in wait. Keep out of grenade range of LeBlanc until you get Jimmy. Then, get me evidence on LeBlanc. Or clear him."

"Carlos, why'd you wait six days?"

I heard the big hand slap the artificial leg. A month to the day after the Dong Nai ambush, I blew out my back pulling men from the bush and was shot in the head, losing my left ear, and in the gut, losing some small intestine. Two days later, a mechanical ambush on the Rat River ripped off Carlos's left leg. We had been profiled out of Airborne Infantry into the harsh ambitions of the Army practice of law. Carlos's annual ability to charm docs into accepting his prosthesis as a true limb became the lyric matter of Army legend.

"Got messages from him in Korea," he said. "Bogus."

My stomach soured. No accident. "Foul play."

"My nose says it's LeBlanc." I heard him sip hot coffee.

"Sir, what's your working hypothesis?"

"Something is rotten as pig crap in Korea."

"That's so descriptive, I don't know why I have to go."

"I'll commo you as 'Hu.' You call me 'Justicio.'"

"Why's the Pentagon worried about LeBlanc?" Criminal defense failures didn't keep generals awake at night; they worried about *not* getting convictions. They detested thieves, dopers, rapists and killers. Murray had left something out.

I lifted my pen.

"Marker Man. Forgive yourself yet?"

I said nothing.

"This mission. It will help. I know you can feel that. Going back to Asia. *Culero*, you sound good, like you quit the gin and are sleeping like a rear-area professional."

Cara's face, her stubbornly curly auburn hair on the pillow, the soft rhythm of her breathing. I would awaken to look at her, her beauty, to feel her trust, salves on my past. Sometimes I felt this was my *yuing chi*, my good fortune, to share her bed, to see her innocent sleep, to merge our opposite pasts in love. She had come to me like an answer to an unknown prayer.

"I do Diet Pepsi now." Saccharin was like rodent poison, but I never drank gin for the taste. Pepsi made me grimace like Bogart and spared me the side effects. "Met someone. I promised I wouldn't leave her. You didn't answer my question."

"*Hombre*, good for you. Happy for you. But you are the man and you have the duty. You cannot tell her you are going. I picked you because you are a perpetual bachelor with no dependents."

If I owed him money, I wouldn't be on this mission. Telling Cara I was leaving would be like telling Abélard it was just a knife. "Not telling her's unthinkable."

Silence. He had given an order. I heard BaBa whisper that our before-borns watched us, always. Do your job, Hu-chin.

In that moment I knew what I needed to do, more than tell Cara that I wasn't coming home for a while: return to the site of the Dong Nai ambush, reverse azimuth to the villages and give solatium money to her clan. I didn't even know her name. I spoke fifty Vietnamese words poorly and had a lot in savings. I could do it.

"Urchin, do not be thinking that. You go back to Vietnam, as the last crap hits the fan, you will not come out. *Hermano*, the girl is dead. Let her be. Save Jimmy."

I put down the phone, my unanswered question forgotten.

A knock. A long-faced medic entered, tired from seeing too many bodies. He closed the door, checked my ID, laid out inoculation needles and antiseptic swabs and punctured me.

I signed for the mission packet: Far East Theater entry authorization, tickets, a civilian passport smelling of fresh glue and a black padded nylon bag with ROK Korean and Japanese government weapons permits. Inside the bag was a 9mm Browning automatic High Power with a four-inch barrel, ammo boxes and extra magazines.

I looked out the window at the Golden Gate Bridge. Cara, Jimmy's missing in Korea. I am going to get him. Don't sleep with anyone while I'm gone. If there were a God, I'd ask him to watch over you, to keep your smile bright.

It's a short trip. I'll be back.

3

Gu-Gu

Jimmy the Bee Buford had spent his youth killing fish, playing with lizards and feeding stray cats. At Bragg, where I had come as a lawyer after med rehab, he had attacked my moral ills with the pleasures of his family, the soporifics of Methodist chapel and the spices of Carolina Frogmore Stew.

He was a bright, hyperactive, slow-spoken gentleman with a Duke law degree and the slickness of an Everglades water snake. He had graduated with a four-point and Order of the Coif and pretended to be as stupid as a tree branch in the dead of winter. He was masterful in fishing and lousy at sports and had the naturally slick hands of a professional pickpocket. A client had taught Jimmy the art.

Jimmy the Bee was an honest man who employed slowness to relax the opposition and to pry truth. He reminded me of the deceptively bumbling detective from *Crime and Punishment.*

I had developed my inscrutability, but Jimmy had read my combat fatigue like a book.

"Hey, buddy. Y'all a little sick in the head, ain't ya?"

I looked out the aircraft window at the endless blue Pacific. I had stood as godfather to his youngest son and became a brother to Beth, his wife. In a sentimental moment full of *ganjing*, the emotionality of pure human relations, he had asked me to take care of his family if anything happened to him. I had said yes.

18

I traced a finger across the condensation on the cocktail glass. In the summer of 1973, the Bee and I convicted Private Johnson Joe Spheres for the murder-rape of a nine-year-old girl. Spheres got life at hard labor at Leavenworth; I got recurring Vietnam nightmares.

I would wake up in a Carolina night sweat, blowing breath into dead girls, accidentally shooting civilians and shaking cold, clinging kraits and bamboo vipers from my legs. Shuddering, I covered my good ear to block out the sounds of low-whumping choppers and distant rolling artillery, unable to separate actual installation sounds from triggered memory. I had become a man filled with holes, trying the military panoply of cures: bourbon, scotch, gin and vodka. Gin, a Chinese word meaning "war," had my name on it, but the sleep it purchased was painfully counterfeit.

I hated my job and disliked juries and judges, triggering all my Asian cultural alarms. I requested posting to the Presidio, where Letterman's psychiatric staff had expertise in treating brains that were still mired in Southeast Asian muds.

The Bufords drove me to Pope Air Base. Bee's bearhug. "Get some shut-eye. Find your smile. God bless ya, Jackson. He shorely knows Ah'm gonna miss ya. Got places ta go, thangs ta do."

"People to see," I said, kissing Beth and hugging the boys. He and I were the same age, but Jimmy had been my *gu-gu*, my older brother, who had helped me morally when help was needed.

I had given them an immense mural-like portrait of their family, a conventionally ostentatious and sentimental Chinese gift. They gave me a wood-carved model of a Chinese sea junk.

I gave the model to BaBa, who smiled and blinked.

In the Presidio and federal court, I prosecuted drug dealers, experiencing all the joys of turning a hamster wheel. I saw Doc Benton, a quiet shrink who regarded my rage as normal. At night, chronically fatigued, I kicked out of uniform, loathing myself for having become a professional Nam vet, full of fecal dreams, alkie sweat and the screaming dead, a member of a growing leper colony.

I felt cored out. I was uninterested in sex and was overcommitted to killing insects that buzzed. I would sit in my Q, a dark, defurnished one-room World War II quarters in Building T-41, across the street from the Spanish iron cannon of the Officers Club, reworking the ambush so the trail party would not die. But all solutions endangered my men. In these undressed hours a long-suppressed Indochinese gut fear swarmed over me like live, steaming entrails, and I would hurl the Randall knife into the splintering desk, trying to silence the unseen devil that gnawed at me from within. Hating self-pity and the bottle, I kept the emotion and quit the juice. But I could not manage neatness.

"Uuuoh," said BaBa, looking at my Q, his teeth bared, Ma squeezing his big arm. "So very bad, Jackson. What Master Wong say to you? So bad messy! Hey, you have broom?"

I put away the Wizard's photo and read the memo.

In 1964, Frederick C. LeBlanc was relieved for meddling with client finances. He was sent punitively to the Second Infantry, Camp Casey, DMZ, his military career effectively ended.

But at Camp Casey he earned max evals, extended and was twice promoted. He has been Staff Judge Advocate on the Demilitarized Zone for four years and in-country nine. DMZ troops serve twelve-month hardship tours, so there is no institutional history on him.

Major General Michael Peters became CG at Casey two weeks ago and can be expected to know little about his top lawyer. But CPT Richard Johnson,

Military Police, just returned from Casey. Now with TIG, he described a moral reign of terror in the police establishment and a *cosa nostra*–like atmosphere in the JAGC office. He said there was one straight senior MP, a Major L. Foss, and that the Provost Marshal has been in Casey for eight years and is as suspect as LeBlanc. His suspicions sent CPT Buford to Korea.

The map showed Camp Casey adjoining Tong-ducheon, a village on the DMZ and the North Korean border. To the south was Seoul, the capital, where I would land. Below it was Osan Air Base, where Jimmy had landed in a military bird and disappeared.

The memo reminded me that we had split Korea with the Soviets after World War II and then invited the Korean War when Secretary of State Dean Acheson announced we would not defend Korea against Communist aggression. The North Korean People's Army, the Inmingun, promptly invaded the south through the Valley of War, fighting for reunification.

Joseph Stalin was going to commit the Soviet Army against us in Korea, but he died. Had the Red Army engaged us, President Eisenhower would have nuked the Russians, giving us World War III in 1953.

Korea is the most dangerous place in the world, where global thermonuclear war could erupt between four nuclear powers. An accident there could light the planet.

A beautiful woman looked out expectantly from the Korea Travel Bureau brochure. "We love you to visit us. We pay attention to you. Please visit Korea, Land of Morning Calm."

It was the Land of Morning Calm to which I flew for Jimmy Buford. My orders were cut. I had aspirins, a text on nightmares, several Forms 15-74 to cite the guilty, good pens, a notepad, my knife, a sidearm, a Korean dictionary, a bag of cigarettes and gum to encourage interviewees, warm clothes and high hopes. Ma's modestly smelly, dried *kwei-yu*, good-luck-long-journey fish, was in my briefcase.

I wore a crisp military haircut, my class ring in my pocket, pretending to be a civilian. I would try to persuade Colonel LeBlanc that I had arrived in Casey to investigate racial problems, and not him.

Normally, IG brass on the collar brought latitude instead of a kidnapping. I finished the tomato juice.

I would enter LeBlanc's law office and his private quarters and use my Asian face to best advantage. I would restore Jimmy to his clan and convict the guilty.

What crimes were worth the kidnapping of Carlos's top IG? The cost to Beth and the boys could not be measured. I feared it was costing me the love of my life. Cara.

Even now, I couldn't recall the moments of our first meeting with my customary clarity. The bright afternoon in which we met and the first evening of our love did not fall into niches to be retained in the manner of my training. There were no evidentiary signposts, military log or historical chronology, no courtroom logic, only moments forever held, a sensation of never-changing lights. A lawyer's nightmare, a poet's dream, an entry into another world. Standing there, I had already fallen for her.

Knowing green eyes; bright words in a soft and husky voice; her disturbing, stupor-creating contours; a hint of vulnerability amidst a sea of admiring men; the quick and elevating humor. I disregarded the low coin of her popularity, the chasms in our backgrounds, the warnings of her blatant sexuality. I forgot my own expanding, insidious problems; I saw only her face.

Her eyes as she accepted my invitation to dance. The

artistry of a lovely face, her laughter merging with the distant tinkling of champagne glasses, the murmur of an unimportant world. Her allure, her voice, full of lightness and hope, tinged with wounds well worn, a persona otherwise unchanged in so many ways since an earlier day.

We danced, the soft jazz flowing from her rather than the band. Accustomed to control, I kept a distance; mirthful, she moved closer. The pleasure of her face surpassed the warmth of her body and the invitation of our fit. The small channel between nose and sculpted upper lip had been fluted by Michelangelo; her soul was palpable, coming out of her bones, her allure mesmerizing, but elusive of recollection.

"You feel good," she said. "And smell good." A slow, lazy smile. "Can you talk?"

I shook my head. "I am no longer of the earth. I have the feeling that this day is mine. I haven't felt that way for a long time." I tried to smile, and nothing showed. She studied me.

"So you don't use pick-up lines. And you're very attentive." She licked her lips. "I like how you look at me."

The aircraft bounced in turbulent winds as it crossed into tomorrow. Calm seas, BaBa said, do not make good sailors.

BaBa would turn the tiller toward Kiangsu Province. He would say: Hu-chin, find your grandfather's grave and find the mud graves of your younger brothers. Put them in fine thousand-silver-piece *guan ts'ai*, red ironwood caskets, face-up. Get very smooth wood. Say the Jesus prayer for them. Hu-chin, thank you.

Grandfather and my brothers had been buried in haste along the riverbank, without good wood or paper money, in the middle of a bad-luck war.

On the western horizon, beyond the great, endless

ribbon of pallid clouds, was Asia, beckoning, patient, ancient and ominous with old debt.

4

A WARMER SEA

Tuesday, January 15

Thick, imperfectly straightened auburn hair framing a rich, smooth complexion. She was not of the cool Pacific, sailing instead from a smaller, warmer sea that would smile on olives and palms and kindnesses toward children. Her eyes were magnets, free from grand error, witnesses to life's frolics, gently overseeing a fading scent of a secret and distant sadness. We were at a Stanford wedding in which she was known and I was at the outer margin. Her name was Cara Milano. She was an associate at Craig, Hofer & Tyler, a City firm that was giving women a chance. She earned three times my salary and drove a cream Alfa Romeo, a car I couldn't afford to insure. I could organize work, but not my life, and had no wheels.

I tried ignoring her. Then I asked her for a ride. We ended up at North Beach. The gods smiled and gave us a shadow of a parking space for Club Sport, where gaunt, unshaven Sicilians pitched curses and dishes like underpaid zookeepers.

"You could've left with any of fifty men." A waiter jostled me, losing a tray. "Or all of them. Why me?"

Crockery crashed. Her hands steepled. "A herd of cute, moneyed Protestants. I know them. And there was you."

"I know there's a compliment in there somewhere."

"You have a darkness. It's almost beautiful. What is it?"

A rash of Sicilian curses. "My past. Then, I saw you."

I brought up Watergate and avoided mention of Vietnam, Carlos Murray, Moms Bell and his radio, Doc and his fatal, clucking diagnoses, Curt Tiernan, Cyril Magnus or the fifteen plastic-wrapped riflemen I had lost, the Greek chorus of grieving mothers and widows and six bloody Asian women, my regimen of nightly epistles to the survivors. I didn't mention the Bufords, who had cared for me in my phantom days.

The withholding wasn't dishonest. It was *ji hui*—inauspicious talk—to speak to strangers and the innocent of bad times, of death and slaughter, of the secrets that expose the *jia* to criticism and risk.

She had loved, perhaps too much, and had known many somehow imperfect men. She loved knowledge. The television game show *Jeopardy* was a warm-up for a fertile mind that knew the architecture of Arnolfo di Cambio, the durable flora of the Kalahari, the wages of cholera vibrio, the contents of the *Index Librorum Prohibitorum.* Her curiosity was aroused, making her voice a caress. We were lawyers, each wanting the other to speak. Her eyes said: IF you want me, talk. I spoke, animated by the riches of China, driven by soulful desires, risking unfamiliar shoals, propelled by winds of unknown origin.

She listened as if I were a Shanghai storyteller with a drum, an empty stomach and ten voices. I described our thirty-foot, high-sterned, crimson-sailed, night-eye-painted *ma-yang-tzu yan chu'an* salt and tung oil junk, built by hunchbacked Hunanese and manned by lean, long-haired empty-stomach-men.

I told her of the emaciated *k'u-li* bitter-work-Wushan trackers who pulled our junk through Three Gorges.

Her eyes misted. "You know, I want law to be Christian, caring for the poor and weak. I prefer *pro bono*s to the big clients." She practiced a profession she did love, and was a junk-puller in her heart. I learned she was loyal to a Basset named Noah, disliked silence, was pursued by most of the City's male heterosexual attorneys, and inspired in me a humor and a mirth I had not known since childhood.

I laughed as she weighed me on a complex scale for an undefined but highly sought job, threatening me with probes, urging me to be emotional, intriguing me with her attention.

Our talk was a soft fencing of backgrounds. I paraded my Chinese ways in food, family and traditions as warnings of difference, finding that they beckoned rather than deterred.

Another night, at Ondine's, she studied the fog. "It was a sweet childhood. *Cannoli, sautagostino, pasta frolla*, living for Columbus Day. Operatic shouting. Passion. Family everlasting. Then Papa left." She shrugged, touched her lower lip. "It made me . . . professional. Tell me about your family."

I was the firstborn, responsible for the clan line. I described the eccentrics, the comic and petty tragedies, omitting real ones like the deaths of my brothers, the demise of China and the woman who died on our deck.

I smiled with her quick laughter. She uplifted me, filled dark, humid holes with clean, sweet pleasure. The easy warmth of her eyes was an inoculation against my disease. There was pleasure in her ideals and in our shared days as she chipped away at me, teaching me about myself as I asked about her.

Ma stood in an ancient cardigan, next to the odorous fish, hair untouched, a run in both stockings, shouting silently about her only son spending time with a foreign woman.

Cara stood at the appropriate distance, bowing slightly. *"Kan taitai, nin hau ma?"* Mrs. Kan, how are you?

"Ah, ha," said Ma, smiling in surprise, returning the greeting.

"Do you like her?" I asked later, meaning, Do you

mind that she's not Chinese, and will have trouble cooking black-bean *chow fun* rice noodles and arguing endlessly about best stock, best dish, best bank, best girl to marry, and passing the same unopened bottles of Johnnie Walker around as notoriously insincere social gifts? And that eyeballs will be pulled by the *low fan* foreign women?

Fullface, Ma was salty and quick-tongued, worshiping all gods, laughing at her sons and chiding a good husband.

In profile, she was noble winter, cool ice on a hard river, remote, a modern Chinese woman hewn and shaped by continuous and unimaginable laments. She showed me her profile.

Chinese mothers own the bodies of their sons. My hurts were her wounds.

"Hu-ah, I happy you date *anyone.*" Ma loved Cindy Chew and had lost *guan shi*, face, with the Chews when I broke up with her from Vietnam. Ma knew Cindy was a casualty of war, a demon too big even for Ma to fix. War had undone China and a million *jia.*

"Even if she talks like foreign-country person."

"Ma, she *is* a foreign-country person."

Patting me. "Hu-ah, that what I say!" She often saw my feelings before I did. She sensed my guilt, misreading its cause. In the high pleasure of seeing Cara each day, I was not worried about my ultimately tolerant and loving parents; I was betraying a virulent loyalty to sadness I had brought home with me from Asia. It was the one thing Ma had hoped we had left behind us.

Cara insisted on seeing my Q. I had tried to clean it. It would have been easier to sing Puccini in Yiddish. "Enter and abandon all hope," I said.

Her eyes opened wide. "It looks like you had a fire."

"Almost. It *needs* a fire."

A sigh. A change in the atmosphere, a fine French perfume in a moldy Q. A smile. "That's what this country needs. A return to naked lightbulbs."

I scratched. Cholera, typhus, tetanus, tine test, Asian tariffs. At Tokyo's Narita Airport, beneath haunting flight announcements, I caught the Korean Air shuttle to Kimpo. The single-class cabin stared at me in unison. A disastrously thin American with an Infantry haircut and old Indochinese pallors, dressed in head-to-toe burgundy polyester, sat next to me. If a fire broke out, he'd melt.

He saw I was Army. Short hair, eyes that had seen worse than bad cabin food, a practiced bovine gaze. "Henry Jubala," he said in a high, tired voice.

"Jackson Kan." We shook. I recognized the name; he was the Army marathon champ, a narrow knot of gristle and guts. A blue, tattooed snake head with a questing tongue slid sinuously from his right cuff.

"Enda mid-tour leave," he grumbled. "Back to Korea. Damn ROKs'll probably blow us away with friendly fire." The light-triggered, security-conscious ROKs—not to mention the North Korean Reds—had fired at our inbound aircraft. "Crash, burn and die."

"Well, Henry, that will probably ruin the whole flight."

Over the horizon was Chinese Manchuria. My past, as we Chinese say, was in front of me. Jubala's gaze was terminally bug-eyed.

"War's gonna break on the DMZ. The dead'll draw maggots."

I grinned. "You always this cheerful?"

"We're outgunned twenty-five to one. A million Inmingun led by thirteen-man Tiger Tails who'll slit our throats."

"That would ruin my whole trip." Inmingun, North Korean People's Army: fourth-largest, and angriest, army in the world. "What are Tiger Tails?"

His thin face scrunched. "Inmingun special-op raider teams. Sappers, snipers, spooks, terrorist night-crawlers.

You know—Nam drained the crap outa us. Tiger Tails'll
hit us first. Then the Inmingun'll cross the border. We'll
be maggot chow, cuz with the Nam, America ain't gonna
fight no two-front Asian war. We'll dangle in the suck of
a minus-seventy windchill factor. Shit, now, that make
you happy?"

I gave him a stick of gum. Juicy Fruit, to sweeten him.

I imagined Cara worrying what had happened to me.
Being told I had gone to Walter Reed Hospital without
telling her. The remembered promise. The hurt. The
anger. The other men.

"Might make someone happy. Know any more jokes?"

"Yeah. I'm going back to Casey." He popped the gum
and put the wrapper in his pocket.

In a world infested with decrepit posts, Casey was the
clear, algae-green victor of the dog pool at the butt end of
the American pipeline. It was a reminder that defiance of
the massed Inmingun, and low-quality life in the modern
age, were not outmoded concepts. Casey was proof to the
ROKs that the Yankee Tiger—the symbol of America in
Asia—would not ditch them as we were at that moment
ditching South Vietnam.

The U.S. Army had exported the horrors of urban
America to Korea, creating the Army's worst violent-
crime indices in homicides, rapes, robberies and assaults.
I had met defendants at Fort Ord, where I interned during
law-school summers. I smiled brightly at my first client,
a hard case up for manslaughter.

"Morning," I said, my back stiff from the surgery that
ended my Infantry career. "How are doing today?"

"Fuck you," he said.

"You Infantry?" asked Jubala.

"I'm a JAGC. Tell me about Casey."

He whistled. "Thought you were part of a Peregrine."
A Peregrine was an Asian-American hunt-kill team.
"Seen characters like you at Casey. You're not one a
them? Big sucker like you, a rear-area lawyer?"

"Paper's gotten heavier. What's your job?"

He didn't answer. "The SJA, the Wizard, he's a different duck." He snorted. "Casey's a proctology test. Smells like crap." He rubbed a long, crooked nose. "Sits under Jungsan Peak, mouth of the Ouijeongbu Corridor. Old Valley of War.

"Valley's the invasion highway of the Bando, the peninsula. North Korea to Seoul." He formed his fingers into a blade and thrust them forward. "Where the Inmingun crossed the border in 1950. Bastards are still up there, ten klicks from Casey. We sit like a damn tin can in front of a freight train.

"If the Inmingun come, we're top dead center in the kill zone. We'll all be red meat, dead kids stacked in alleys."

The images went into focus with colors, my sense of purpose evaporating in the hot, ignited air. The girl. Help me, Ba. Oh, baby, I can't help you. A hundred crying or dead, ninety percent of the officers down. Men shot themselves or tossed chloroquine to contract *genus Plasmodium*, riding self-inflicted wounds and malarial fevers to avoid the rivers. Cyril's baby girl. The rounds went through him and the photo, turning it crimson, the picture weeping red tears. I put my head down, focusing on his snakehead tattoo. The tongue was fading to pink. Two flights to Asia. Two breakdowns.

"Hey, buddy, you're cool. Crap, man, didn't mean to trigger it. I'm such an asshole, talking it too much." His voice dwindled. "Yeah, I miss 'em, too. Not our fault we made it out. Goddamn, that was a shitty place."

5

LAND OF MORNING CALM

I had gone to the Q to pack. Ma vigorously swept my room. Her gray hair was tangled and she still wore her cotton coat, evidence of preoccupation. The dust made me sneeze.

"Hu-ah, Fan *taitai* call me phone, say you go long trip."

Mrs. Fan was a Chinatown *I-jing ba-kua*, horoscope seer, known for penetrating insights and prophetic powers. I was seven when she told us that I was to be an American officer. Fan *taitai* had averted her eyes; she detested soldiers.

Seven years ago, she had demonstrated a loss of prowess by predicting I would have a wonderful time in Vietnam.

BaBa disliked Mrs. Fan's predictions and Ma never doubted them. "So *is* true! Fan *taitai* say you go faraway mountain. Meet *wu* lady"—a shaman. "She help you get *jen* back." *Jen* was Confucian benevolence, which I had lost in a rain forest with three rivers. "Hu-ah, you come back, you give her gift.'

"Then I smile, so happy my son can live with lady!" Ma and her focus on a society of women. "Make lady happy, make happy son. You know Fan *taitai* say you meet foreign white lady who love you? Yes, true! No tell you, *ji hui*, make it happen!

"How your back? Here, for you." She pressed salted

31

gwei-yu, Mandarin fish, into my hand. "Eat upriver, like old days."

Nodding as if I had answered, she tried a smile, weights on her words. "Hu-ah, you want marry Cara?"

I was leaving Cara without a word, inviting disaster.

Ma's eyes darkened. "Hu-ah, you sleep her bed, you marry her." She pulled hard at my cheek for good *yuing chi.*

"Murray *syensheng* say shoot gun, you say *no.* You thirty! We need grandson! You *lu-shih,* not *k'u-li.*" Lawyer, not worker.

She wept, in profile, as if I had died. "Hu-ah, you have my heart. Moonrise, I think, is your lantern. You come back, then I sleep. And smile." She smiled, then sighed. "Your father, he not worry, he talk to God like man smoke opium."

Fiercely, she hugged me, fingers searching, feeling in me the lost futures of my two brothers. "Hu-ah, you close to river, light joss for Hu-hau and Hu-chien." Good Tiger and Strong Tiger. "Okay?"

"Okay, Ma." I slowly dried her tears.

"Hu-ah, oh Hu-ah." She cried again. *"Manmanlai,"* she whispered. Go softly. Clutching me like a Chinese mother, so I could not move without hurting her.

We landed on an icy runway with three hard, leap-frogging, bouncing touchdowns at Kimpo, southwest of Seoul on the south side of the frozen Han River. Korea looked like an icebox. I had gloves, longjohns, a heavy cashmere overcoat and no fondness for Arctic winds. Snow fell past the bulkhead windows. It was Tuesday afternoon, 15 January 1974.

Customs was cold and filled with tension as agents rototilled luggage. One studied me, my civilian passport and packed uniforms. I offered the blue Department of Justice ID folder and he bowed low. I gave him the Browning and the ROK Ministry of Defense Permit, which brought more bows. After a conference, he bowed again, returning the weighted weapons bag and the letter.

"See you, Jack!" shouted Jubala. "Take care a yourself."

"Where do I find you at Casey?" He left.

A ROK national policeman in a dark blue uniform pointed at an elevated counter where sat an American soldier.

"Orders, sir," said the troop, a Spec Five in class-A greens. He wore JAGC insignia, a Second Infantry Indian-head shoulder patch and an Army union-leader, I-like-drugs center-part in a longish blond mop. He was from Camp Casey, and all legal personnel there were assets of Colonel Frederick C. LeBlanc. The Wizard's point man. He smelled of stale tobacco. I gave him the U.S. Attorney ID.

"Army has no jurisdiction in Korean customs," I said.

Korean passengers stopped to stare at us, and mostly at me.

"Sir," he said, froggily, "how come you got uniforms?"

"Answer my question."

He stiffened. "Sir, I'm just doin' my job."

"Which is?"

"I log in all officers comin' in-country."

Not a job of an Army lawyer or legal staff. "What if the uniforms are for someone stationed here?"

He thought about that and nodded. "Oh, yeah. I dig."

He had a black Army telephone.

"What's this for?" I asked him.

"Sir, none a your business."

"Think again. I'm a federal prosecutor."

He considered that. "Well, sir, I call Casey if any JAGCs or IGs come in-country. Uh, that's Army for judge advocate general's corps officers—lawyers—and inspector generals. IGs are kinda like cops and the FBI."

I looked at the phone. "How'd the Army get you in this room?"

"Wizard, he has ROK Army generals as drinkin' buddies."

"Do U.S. attorneys count as—what'd you call them?—JAGCs?"

He shook his head. "Negative, sir. You're civilian."

I gave him a pack of spearmint gum. "This is better than smoking." He admitted me to Korea, where spirits of four million war dead were remembered in shaman rituals and American wizards played tricks across jurisdictional lines.

I entered the terminal and its deafening din. It was like the fall of Rome, citizens at the back door and Visigoths coming fast with axes. We snaked through the building, where two thousand people screamed and raged at each other in a space designed for a quiet family of ten. All sought to locate dear ones by screeching hysterically in a place packed with people of uniform height and black hair. I didn't like the screaming.

Outside, the icy wind hit me like a two-by-four. Mobs fought for cabs. No one offered me a ride. I waited, my blood thinning.

A short ROK Army corporal ran to me. He slipped sharply on the ice, crying "Ai-guuuuu!" as he sailed upward and then fell square on his rump with an ice-cracking thump. He struggled up to render a pitiful, shuddering salute. "Kan *dae-wi*?" Captain Kan.

I returned the salute. "Corporal."

"*Dae-wi*, I Corporal Min Oh-shik, KATUSA." To Americans, he would be Oh Shik Min. He struggled to form the words: "Ko-rean Army, attach-ee to U.S.-ah Army, K-A-T-U-S-A."

I had heard of KATUSAs—ROK troops lent to the American Army for driving and translation services.

He rubbed his backside. "I drive you and other *dae-wi* up Camp Kay-shee, *neh*?" He peered at my coat. "Oh! numbah-one coat, *dae-wi*!" He fondled it.

Other *dae-wi* meant other captains.

He wore thick, black-framed fright glasses and smiled hopefully with two of the largest front teeth this side of Bugs Bunny. He reeked of garlic. He seemed constricted, skinny, genderless and stupid, had trouble breathing, and seemed to be mostly head and huge feet. He was the cruel Hollywood stereotype of the neutered Asian male which Jerry Lewis and Mickey Rooney had turned into bigoted art forms. He blinked. He was all I had tried not to be in an America defined by movies.

"Your ID." I couldn't be sure, but it looked good. He took my bags. I checked out the staring crowd. A man in a dark suit observed us.

I moved for him and he barged into the terminal, shoving desperately, making people cry out.

He disappeared. Medium height, short haircut, athletic, quick. Tall for a Korean.

Corporal Min sucked in breath, fumbling to give me a TWX, a military cable communication. It had already been opened.

"Who opened this?"

"*Molla-yo*, do not know, *dae-wi.*"

CPT HU KAN: CPT B.K. MAGRIP, JOGC USMA 1968, YOUR ASSET. MEET KIMPO NOW. CPT P.K. LEVINE, JAGC, TO FOLLOW. MESSENGER IS ROK ARMY AND IS YOUR DRIVER. TRUST HIM. GOD BLESS AND GOOD HUNTING. JUSTICIO.

Murray had given me a team. And a driver who read my mail. If Captain B.K. Magrip landed now, he would run into Colonel LeBlanc's customs gate watcher, who would pick up his phone and tell the Wizard we had come. A bad start. "Wait here."

I pressed into the masses. A stout woman elbowed me in the ribs and climbed over me, screaming at the file of escaping passengers. She punched me in frustration. I smiled, but there was no winning her favor. The din elevated as I headed into the maelstrom. I looked for the tall, dark-suited Asian who had crashed into the terminal. I didn't see him.

Murray had sent me B.K. Magrip. Three years behind me at the Point, a Wisconsin farm boy and a vicious killer in close combat, known for a vast anger and poetically called the Butt Kicker. Now, a rookie JAGC. Carlos had not sent him for his legal skills.

Using my size, I made steady progress, twenty meters in four minutes. I had never heard of Captain Levine. Murray had assessed the Wizard as a team project. I felt like spitting; I didn't want to risk any more losses or add to my correspondence list of survivors. I hoped Magrip and Levine were bachelors.

But Magrip would be an asset. We needed to be a team, and West Pointers majored in that stuff in college.

Too late: a big American emerged from the demented mob as whistles blew and police used nightsticks to fight their way into the terminal. He struggled toward me, his big body parting the short crowd like a downhill bulldozer. B.K. Magrip. I knew him from the *Time* cover.

I saluted, the drill for Medal of Honor recipients.

He spat, making pedestrians whine and jump. "Can that crap."

"What do you do when people try to shake hands, shoot them?"

He recoiled. "Aw, shit on a Hershey bar. Jackson Kan. Murray didn't tell me *you* were team chief. Screw me to tears." He was pink with sunburn and wore a garish red-and-yellow aloha shirt with skewed collar under an ugly brown, collar-up overcoat, tails flapping in the cold, biting wind. The crowd jostled us.

"Damned Oriental people." He gritted teeth.

"Glad you can discriminate."

Magrip tossed me a black telephone with a dangling cord. I caught it. "That asshole in there," said Magrip, "calls no one."

It was the GI's phone from customs.

"He kept dialing. I took it. He went batcrap so I stuck a grenade in his shirt. Cops took him in custody." He plunked a spearmint; he had the packet I had given the sentry.

My new colleague had just committed destruction and larceny of government property and ten federal weapons violations. "I felt better before you explained." I studied him. "Magrip, you just cross the Pacific with a grenade in your pocket?"

"Don't get your panties in a bunch. Got two left." He glowered. "Dumbwad, this is Korea. Wanna use bare hands? Listen, Captain Kan, Pentagon boy scout, I like area weapons." He smiled sickeningly. "They don't discriminate."

"How'd you get grenades through security?"

Magrip flashed a brown box. "Plastic demagnetizer." A mob stared at our quiet entry into Korea. So Jimmy had been snatched because he had left home without his grenades.

Cops emerged with the Wizard's Spec Five on a stretcher, his long arms dangling. Magrip shook his head. "Only hit him once."

Add battery to the list of federal and international offenses. "Magrip, we're supposed to be covert."

This amused him. He lifted his chin. "Ha ha ha!"

I introduced Magrip to Corporal Min. Magrip spat; Min saluted and bowed. Corporal Oh Shik Min took the phone and luggage and led us to an olive drab Willys M38A1. As senior officer, I sat in the front, responsible for all accidents. We lurched as the tires spun and the jeep sped wildly into thick afternoon traffic. The flathead 134's heads yammered under poor maintenance.

The congested traffic was predatory—midtown Manhattan on St. Pat's Day after a garbage strike, a snowstorm and a Presidential visit.

Min drove indifferently, as if blind or already

pronounced dead. Magrip was my height, six-two. Over-
hung brows, modest nose, a wide gap between front
teeth, light blue eyes, a buzz cut, and the kind of mouth
dentists see when they do root canals. He cursed Min, the
traffic, Korea, Carlos Murray and all Korean drivers
while we dodged death. A truck filled with hippolike pigs
avoided a head-on collision with us at the last instant.
Horns blared like wounded beasts.

"Magrip, I'm glad you're here."

"You're the fucking Lone Ranger on that one,"
he said.

"You ever smile?"

"I am smiling, asshole."

Horns blared as we skidded in and out of a traffic
circle. Crunching collisions were occurring with each
light change. Some angry drivers brawled on the street as
traffic zoomed past them. Corporal Min seemed unperturbed and unskilled.

"Crap," declared Magrip. "Can't fucking believe I
came back here to die."

We rode the traffic as if borne by an intoxicated,
enraged water buffalo. In a crazed herd of smog-spitting
vehicles, we passed the European-styled Seoul Railway
Station and immense crowds of understandably concerned pedestrians. Buses and taxis fought each other for
inches of advantage, as if each driver had taken a pledge
to die horribly in traffic, taking with him an optimum
number of cars and pigs. The presence of another vehicle
was invitation to a passing game of suicidal Chicken.

We escaped Seoul for the frenzied vehicular combat
zone of the MSR, Military Supply Route 3, the north-
south artery that led to the DMZ. I had a chain of cardiac
arrests as taxis, buses, head-on drivers, tanks, yapping
dogs and fleeing pedestrians formed a kaleidoscope of
absurd death while Magrip cursed me.

"Not happy to be here?"

His square features shifted. He opened his mouth and

shut it. Deadly blue eyes and a bad shave over sunburn. "Hell, no. I'm back with a million Inmingun on a Carlos Murray TIG carnival for the dumb and stupid. I *did* my goddamn tour. *Ate* the Korean crapburger and did two sucking Korean winters and—AW SHIT!"

We jolted hard in a sharp crash of metal that made us grunt like a single beast. Steel screeched and snow was in the jeep. A big ugly truck with teetering crates of frantic, flapping chickens bounced off us, wrenching off our side mirror and catching the roof. With a loud, wailing tear, it ripped away our canvas top.

"Crap!" bellowed Magrip as the top whipped away and the wind blew maps out the back in a feathered jet stream. Wet snow pelted us. A mass of chickens squawked at the tops of their little red combs, their fluff filling the jeep and our gaping mouths, coating us. We sputtered blindly in sleet and chicken debris.

I remembered the brochure. We love you to visit us. Welcome to the Land of Morning Calm. We pay attention to you.

The good news was that Magrip had been here before. The bad news was I had left Cara to die in a pointless Korean highway accident, for which I would be held posthumously accountable.

With a jarring crunch, we rear-ended the chicken truck. It popped backs, whipped necks, and blew out air. We caromed, skidded, plowing thick snow to swerve back onto the road, chassis and axles groaning, heads bouncing like dashboard figurines.

Magrip sputtered feathers as they covered his big body.

"DAMMIT! JUST SHOOT ME NOW, YOU SICK TWISTED SONOFABITCH!" He shook Min violently in his big hands as the jeep nauseatingly swayed. Min, awash in feathers and snow, cried "Ae-ae-gu-uu-uu!"

"Let go!" I shouted in the wind. "He's got the wheel!" Magrip was engrossed in the Academy axiom of undertaking positive action in a negative environment. He was past listening. We swerved badly.

I bent Magrip's fingers until pain defeated rage. He released Min, who, like a snapped rubber band, smacked his head into the wheel. He moaned but kept to the road. Snow fell more heavily and we spat feathers.

"GOD, WHY ME?" bellowed Magrip.

"Because you tick me off," I muttered. He was bad *yeh* in two boots.

We used the Braille method of driving, hitting the truck with a resounding crash. Magrip flipped me his pinky. "When you don't care enough to send the very best."

Nice team, Carlos. We jerked as we hit the truck again, jolting my bad back with white-hot, incandescent pain. A crate hit my head, splintered into planks and whipped into the wind.

Flying slivers, flaky chicken flotsam and a cascade of live, miserable, kicking, stinking, screeching, flapping birds with sharp little claws and beaks rained into the jeep compartment. Most of the debris ricocheted off my cashmere coat to land on Magrip, who roared as he shredded the poor chickens as they wildly shrieked and scratched to escape him.

I knew how they felt. My back ached and I needed a drink. I popped five Army APC aspirins and opened a warm Diet Pepsi. I tilted it to my mouth as Min rammed the truck.

6

CASEY

We entered a mountainous, snowbound valley with a remarkable number of black-hatted elders ambling innocently down the dead center of the military highway. It was five P.M. Eight more minutes on the icy macadam and we would be at the DMZ, having tea with the Inmingun.

A moldy slice of America lay beyond a faded green security kiosk. At a sad angle hung the division's Indian-head emblem. Rusted concertina lay like steel tumbleweed below snow. An old U.S. flag whipped in storm winds. Sentries emerged to stare at two men in civvies, casually touring Korea in January with the top down, driven by Chicken Man.

"God," intoned Magrip, "I am sorry for whatever the fuck I did to be sent back here." We looked like we had been tarred and feathered. Magrip seemed cheerful; I looked like a politician.

"Why me, God?" he sighed.

"Holy cow crap," said a worried MP, unsnapping his holster.

"We're on your side." I gave him military ID. "We're in disguise. We need to move on ASAP." I waited for his salute.

"Say again, sir?" he asked, molasses in January.

"The Three fuckin' Stooges are here," said Magrip. He had included Min. "Gimme a scotch and no one gets hurt."

Moe, Larry and Curly were not on the guest list; the MP licked his pencil and slowly took our names and rank. I said we were going to headquarters for showers and rabies shots.

A Sergeant Myers emerged, banging his gloves. "Sir, you gentlemen TIGs?" Everyone worked for the Wizard.

"Right," said Magrip. "We look like peckerwood IGs?"

He laughed. "Check." He looked hard at us. He pointed at Min. "Pull over to the interrogation hut."

"Fuckin' A," said Magrip. "Here, IGs are the suspects."

We shook ourselves and stiffly entered a gray hut with clanking heat registers, a radio playing Armed Forces Korea and faded safety signs that looked like old bullfight *corrida* posters that covered the GI bars on the Mexican border.

A stocky, mustached MP major in a small, worn, brown watchcap looked up from his incident and blotter reports. Coffee steamed from a heavy, chipped mug that said, "Don't Ask." He peered, as if we were in a blinding Arizona sunrise, with a tired poker face that had seen far worse than us. His name was Foss and he was quietly filing our features into memory, an accountant forming suspect sums for later audits.

Through his stained and grimy window was a slow-moving jeep. The driver was Korean. He resembled the man who had surveilled us at the airport. I moved but couldn't read the bumper stencils as he sped away, banging gears.

Foss snapped fingers. "Don't be dumb. Gimme orders."

They showed we were TIGs; we were now on the radar screen. Small ears moved below the cap. "About time." He frowned, stood and patted Magrip, linebacker neck swelling.

Then he recognized Magrip and saluted. "An honor."

"C'mon, man," said Magrip, "can that crap."

" 'Can that crap, *sir*,' right?" he growled. " 'And please to hell excuse the grenades in my armpits, *sir*,' *right*?"

Magrip nodded and slowly returned the major's salute.

Foss cocked his head at me and then at the door. "In there." To Magrip, "Honor Man, you stand fast. Keep your frag pins bent."

It was a concrete cell with a lightbulb on a ceiling wire. It was like my quarters in the Presidio, only colder.

"POB and gimme your green card." Birthplace and immigration legal resident papers. Welcome to New York.

"Shanghai, China. Naturalized citizen," I gave him my card.

He looked at me, up and down. "Who won the first Super Bowl?"

"Green Bay. Me, I'm a Niners fan. Getting infiltrators?"

"Don't fart in *my* barn. You a Peregrine? With some of you shamming as Seventy-six Yankees?"—76Y, supply clerks.

Murray and I had been in the Bien Hoa snake pits, lousy with Nam dust and Okie avgas, when he said he had extended for another year. "We're forming a Peregrine": an Asian-American strike team of paratroopers, Rangers and Special Forces, a rich Eastern blend of Chinese, Japanese, Filipino, Samoan, Tongan, Hawaiian, Vietnamese, Thai, Campuchean, Okinawan, Laotian, Nien, Fijian and Hmong killers.

"Old Man wants you to head it. Do you want it?"

Do I want it? I had begun to count the days. I feared wrongful deaths of children. Peregrines operated behind the lines and killed witnesses. I shook my head. "It's not for me."

"Negative," I said to Foss. "Not aware of any such operation."

He hitched his head toward the door. I returned to the relative warmth of the main room. Foss followed. "You must be grade-one hot shit ass-kickers to roll in here in civvies with Colonel Sanders overcoats."

"I screwed up," announced Magrip. "I'm being punished."

I nodded. "We pluck chickens. It's not as easy as you'd think. The chickens have figured out why we pluck them."

"Ha. Wait one. I gotta call the Wizard."

"Major Foss," I said, "The Inspector General, capital T, does not want the SJA or his JAGCs to know we are here yet. You will not inform him. I am on record giving you that advice."

I pulled out my pad and made the note. "Captain Richard Johnson said you still worked for America."

Foss dropped his hand heavily from the phone, fingers moving like crab legs. "Well, crap, ain't *you* a piece a work? Freak my guards and drop names. Well, Mr. Shanghai Hot Pants, Wizard left orders to let him know if TIG shows." He scratched his head through the cap. "You're dropping feathers in my office."

"Major," I said, "we're IGs. Stay out of our road."

He held his head. "Damn lawyers. You give me a case of ass."

Magrip puffed out his chest. Foss nodded, jaws tight. I trusted him to stay quiet about us. We left and got in our jeep. The guard saluted. Min popped the clutch, whiplashing us violently as we jerked into Casey, feathers floating in the icy wind.

"Nyuk, nyuk, nyuk," said Magrip. "Crap. Guard's on the phone."

"Stop, back up," I said to Min. Weaving nauseatingly in reverse, Min banged into the kiosk, knocking snow from its roof, busting brake lights, stressing backs and snapping our necks.

Magrip cursed. "Just our luck. We got a North Korean driver."

"Hang up," I said. The guard hung up. "Who were you calling?"

"SJA, sir." He studied the huge dent in his kiosk.

"You call," I said to the sentry, "I'll extend you in Korea."

"Hey, sir, I ain't callin' nobody!" He saluted. I saluted and our lumbars popped as Min hit the pedal like it was his enemy.

"Once LeBlanc knows we're here," I managed, "the evidence will disappear. We approach him smart and indirectly."

Magrip spat out the jeep. "Like your style, Kan. Lots of guts. Stud IG. Hide your badge and run from the suspects."

Casey was as Henry Jubala had described it: an east-west camp of tired Quonsets astride the valley invasion route, a hobo rest home and a bull's-eye for a wrecking ball.

I told Min that we needed TA-50 winter gear, a janitor's uniform and a civilian overcoat, all extra large, and a new jeep top and maps. If he followed orders like he drove, he'd bring us a silk bathrobe and a Volkswagen hubcap.

Headquarters, Second U.S. Infantry, was a long toolshed that looked like the casual work of angry orangutans. In the snow-covered lot stood a miniature gray stone, six-level *torii* pagoda tower surrounded by dead shrubs. The HQ jeeps were parked noses out; the staff was ready for incomings and a quick emergency exit.

The interior had the charm of a refugee center. The sentry stared at me, Magrip and Min, then stood and called the SGS, the secretary of the General Staff. I gave him our orders and asked to see the commanding general.

"You smell," said Major Young, "like saccharin. We're groady on the Z and we live in grutch, but you're pushing it." He checked the time. "CG has a commander's Tac briefing in zero-niner. I can get you in."

General Michael Peters was short, immaculately hand-some, and black. Alert and tired eyes, stupendously large forehead, his voice soft and measured. Hanging from a coatrack was his sidearm.

"What do you need, Captain Kan? Besides a chicken coop?"

"Housing, sir, and run of the post." Major Young scribbled a note on the CG's red-flagged, two-star stationery.

"Done. If we have a race problem here, I want to know ASAP. How's our one-legged bandit, Law Man?"

"Sir, Colonel Murray is sarcastic and warmer than us."

The CG signed the paper; the SGS passed it to me. "All courtesies, no limits, by my order, LTG Michael Paul Peters, CG 2X." "2X" was short for Second Infantry. This was a Disneyland "E" ride ticket, good for all concessions, parking and rides.

"I say he needs a shower," said the CG. "Let them use the gym."

Something passed across Major Young's face. "Yes, sir. Gym showers below, Captain. I'll arrange quarters. Need office space?"

I declined; we would work out of our Q.

Major Young led us through a bomb shelter tunnel to a dark stairway. Min slipped, jettisoning our luggage in all directions as he lost his balance, windmilling his arms. "Aiguuu!" he cried, grabbing an overhead pipe as he fell, tearing it from the wall. He thumped down the stairs in an avalanche of rotten clay-pipe fragments into a small, dank, concrete weight room, colliding with rusting stacks of weights that fell, crashed and rang like an OSHA catastrophe.

"Bleeding human banana peel," said Magrip.

Min brushed himself and wobbled away. He was embarrassing me.

"Kan," snapped Young, wincing at the wreckage, "out of here ASAP." Magrip and I showered for two minutes,

when the tepid metallic water ran out. We cleared
feathers from the drain, put on long johns and double
winter socks. Magrip gave me the imperial sword-and-
fasces IG brass for my collar and got into uniform.
Min returned. The janitor's rig felt like a small.

"It's you," said Magrip, shaking his head as he eyed
my ill-fitting clothes. Then he mocked an evaluation
report: " 'This officer sets unusually low standards for
himself and fails to achieve them.' "

"Guess who'd be wearing this if you could pass for a
Korean janitor. Get the housing from the SGS, then
check the gate. See if Jimmy entered or left Casey. Use
the CG and IG carte blanche letters."

Magrip pulled out a notepad. "Wizard's got twelve
lawyers, five of them for six years. The five were rated at
the bottom of the Corps before coming here as boozers:
Nagol, McNallum, Willoughby, Wilperk, Remca. I
wouldn't turn my back on 'em."

"Thanks," I said. "Enough playing house. Let's find
Jimmy."

It was like any other staff judge advocate shop on an
overseas shantytown post: cold and open until eight P.M.
The wind whistled as I shut the door. Clerks and Korean
civilian staff banged typewriters in a big bay. Those on
break huddled around clanking, red-eyed heaters,
sucking odorous barley tea and smoking. Lawyers'
offices ran in a long row down the right wall.

A big, freckled, red-haired specialist fourth class with
a pug nose looked up. My entry had hit him with frigid
air. He wore a sidearm, which was highly unusual for a
JAGC office. He looked like Howdy Doody after
puberty.

"Hey, slick! You bad numbah-ten janitor! Bad slicky
boy, bad!" I resisted barking, rolling over and waiting for
him to throw a ball. "Hey, craphead, close that door mos-
tic! Cho-gi me java ricky-tic, chop-chop, slicky boy, and

ask me how I like it!" He was angry; my size had disoriented him.

"How you likee java, boss?" I asked in a high voice. Sugar, no cream. I grounded my gear, bent over and employed every obsequious move employed by Asian bit actors in American films to get his coffee. I was captured, in Korea, by an American presumption of the servile nature of colored people. He was the reason Cara had a political viewpoint. I wanted to lift him by his throat, ask him about Jimmy Buford and pinch his head off. If angry, said Master Wong, breathe as if air is gold. I breathed slow and deep.

He sucked java. "Unass my AO, slick." Korean GI talk. Units of the Second Infantry had been here since the end of World War II and had spawned "gook" from the Korean word for country, "unass" from the anal nature of the DMZ, and "in-country" from the prepositional failures of three generations of day-counting, hip-jive Army clerks.

This jargon had given birth to the lexicon of Vietnam.

Ears hot, I entered the Wizard's den. A shrine to knocking ducks, elk, deer and golf balls. Shotguns lined the walls. One rack was empty. Golf bags leaned against walls like soldiers after a hot march. A teak desk was bare but for dust and an ivory nameplate:

COL F. LEBLANC JAGC
THE JUDGE
BE ALL YOU CAN BE

Empty waste can. No unit photos, Academy sheepskin or bar placards. He didn't work here very often. He liked guns.

Major Thomas Nagol, deputy SJA, the number-two man, had an office that was culturing morgue mold. His desk was a ruin of undone work. Cigar ash coated unopened mail and paper bins like Vesuvian dust. Pill bottles lay like empty cartridges on a battlefield. No court calendar. He was not an organized man overcome by demand; he was a slob who had been defeated by it.

Without a search warrant, I could look only at the debris in plain view. An unread phone message said:

URGENT RED FLAG: 1315 HRS 8 JAN   TO: MAJ NAGOL: LTC ARMSTRONG 8A SJA CALLED RE: CPT JAMES T. BUFORD, INSPECTOR GENERAL, MISSING. FIND AND CALL ARMSTRONG URGENT AT YONGSAN 4511 OR QUARTERS 6743 ANY HOURS. WILLOUGHBY

Carlos had presumed a sinister presence in Jimmy the Bee's disappearance. He hadn't thought of blaming negligence. Carlos said he had waited six days to send a search party because he had gotten messages from Jimmy. But they had been bogus. Someone had faked us out.

I emptied Nagol's wastebasket into a sack labeled "N," and threw the sack into my utility can.

I found the chief prosecutor. The sign said: CHIEF OF JUSTICE, CPT MILES ALTMAN. So Pig Breath and his war cry for convictions *über alles* had come to Casey. Pig advocated military flogging, cruel and unusual punishment and hostile, jumping halitosis. He would be as helpful as a German invasion.

Pig Breath Altman was in the library, sitting at a battered, stained table that probably had been a MASH surgical surface twenty years ago in the Korean War. The library was unstocked. Pig still bore the trademark Prussian flat top. A bulbous, cauliflowerlike nose dominated a weak face made worse by the absence of a chin. His chicken neck was the handle to the frying pan of his Southern-fried-steak gut and old truck driver's flat bottom. He was prematurely farsighted, holding the case reports at a distance in the coldly unpleasant library. He took short, sharp notes while clearing an active throat. Intent in all he did, he had no idea I was there.

His office was psychotically neat. I dumped his waste can into a paper sack. His clerks' desks were orderly. Pleadings, sentences and summaries seemed normal, heavy on assaults and larcenies. Pig Breath's three trial counsels worked in their offices.

The two Defense offices were in a cold back corner and empty. Their clerks' desks were overloaded and smelled of dank defeat. The trial calendar was anemic; convictions were by guilty pleas. JAGCs rotated into Korea for one-year hardship tours, did their jobs and returned stateside, grateful for Chicago winters.

But five of them had made Korean service a career. One was Nagol. The other four were in claims, a job normally done by one JAGC. If a GI lost a rucksack or a mortar tube, he'd have to pay for it, unless he could convince the claims officer that the loss had been line-of-duty and act of God—like a monsoon or a lightning strike.

The claims paperwork suggested a massive payout for lost gas masks, rifles, rucksacks, entrenching tools and radios. For confirmation, I needed a cumulative computer printout from Seoul.

"Hey, slick, what the hell you doing?" A man with an automatic in his hand, the hammer back, muzzle down. His name tag and rank: Captain Willoughby, JAGC, one of the Wizard's own.

I had a broom and a garbage can and remembered Ma's admonition to be a man of letters. I threw the claims papers in the air, punted a waste can, tossed the broom and cried "Aie-guuuu!" and dropped, hoping my Min imitation wouldn't startle him into shooting me. Captain Willoughby jerked with my shout, ducking the flying papers and clattering broom as he backed out the door, his gun arm up as a shield.

On the floor, I scrambled to pick up the papers,

keeping my face turned while retrieving my cherry-picked garbage collection. I left with my head down, grimacing in a Jerry Lewis forced smile, banging into walls and doors, working for a laugh.

"Meeahn-hae-yo!" I hissed—Sorry!

"Goddamn douchebag janitor!" shouted Willoughby. "Asshole! Jerk! Scared me to death!" He clumsily unhammered with both hands and I winced as he almost shot himself; I had been in greater danger than I realized.

This was Korea, where crooked JAGCs majored in graft and even janitors were at mortal risk. Nice place, Carlos. Come and visit sometime. Bring the kids.

7

ICE PALACE

The sun was down. Our Q was north of HQ on Hill 340, charitably called the Ice Palace and uncannily sited to take harsh Manchu winds in the shorts. The wind howled around its walls. The room failed prison standards. "Club Med, I presume?"

"House of Usher," said Magrip. Space heaters ran futilely at max strength in the paint-peeling room. One metal bunk bed with bayonet-scrawled graffiti, one desk and two metal folding chairs constituted the decor. The naked, glaring lightbulb buzzed angrily, surrounded by dark fly carcasses from summers past that dangled thickly from the cracked, sagging ceiling. I didn't like the buzzing.

It was Spartan, like West Point before it was founded.

"Rat crap," muttered Magrip. "Honeymooning on

Waikiki and a Pentagon scumbag does me. Fucking
Korea. Again." He hurled jump boots against fading
paint on defaced, hole-punched walls.

Honeymoon? "Sorry, Magrip." Cara, abandoned by
me for a covert government mission while detectives
chased the President of the United States for Watergate. I
threw my bags on the lower bunk.

"I want the low bunk," muttered Magrip. "Got a bad
back."

I was about to give it to him when I saw, in my kit, a
photo of Cara I had taken at a Mendocino coast cabin.
Her dark hair was highlighted by the fireplace, smiling as
she lifted a glass of Merlot. Her memory warmed the
room and made my guts flutter. I sank into the photo, into
her eyes, her mouth.

We were at her door under a canopy of stars. Tenth
date, and we had never kissed. With women, I had been
very careful; each one could be a wife. After Vietnam,
care had been replaced by withdrawal.

Her eyes closed. Our lips touched, grazed, caressed.
We kissed, her lips parted, her breathing the sighs of
female gods who could stop time. Her mouth was heaven
and the world rushed like the Yangtze in spring.

It was exquisite in a boundless, private universe of
two, the possibilities of us summoned in our hearts into a
promise, as if Guan Yin, goddess of mercy, had designed
our lips, our bodies and our lives from a central poem. I
held her close. Her hands swam over me, touching,
caressing, her body warm and full. She pressed in an
urgent, endless kiss, moaning as I broke from her. "Oh,
God."

I spun in her excitement. She hungrily covered my
mouth, her passion restoring, reconstructing the persona I
had once been. The pleasure of her was like a narcotic of
the gods.

"Your girl?" asked Magrip.

I put the photo away. "Sorry about your honeymoon," I said.

"Yeah? Then get me the fuck outa here."

Three mounds capped by helmets showed Min's good work: he had pulled our TA-50 winter military gear. The third was for Levine, whenever he got here. Three captains to find Jimmy and trick a Wizard.

I got into uniform. Down the hall, two Korean men scrubbed uniforms in the shower that would service thirty officers after the dawn reveille run. A sign said we owed them twenty cents a day.

"The Wizard's boys are the deputy and in claims. Doing fraud."

Magrip spat in the waste can, making it ring. "So bust 'em."

"First, we get Jimmy. You know why the Puzzle Palace is worried about LeBlanc? I asked Murray and he didn't say."

Magrip shook his big head. My stomach growled.

Min knocked and entered the Q. "*Dae-wi*, you want food?"

"Get the crap outa here!" bellowed Magrip. Min skittered out.

"Magrip, a small military secret: Min's on our side."

Magrip sat up, feet on the floor, old cot springs creaking. He ran a big hand over his cropped scalp, flexing the fingers I had bent in the jeep. He smiled crookedly. "I heard a you. Pentagon poster boy. Jackson Kan, always gets the job done. Snag the medal."

The downside to overwork.

Magrip's Vietnam War wasn't over; blood and mud were still caked on his personality. He fought it by inviting conflict with anyone he met.

"Min's on our side and Murray called you for a reason."

"Yeah, I musta run over his dog and liked it too much."

"Jimmy's in trouble. We'll need you to get him out."

I saw Cyril and Curt, laughing on the day before death.

Magrip's two tours with the Twenty-fifth Infantry's main body at Cu Chi led to a *Time* cover story on his Medal of Honor. He was the last man Murray would invite to a banquet, and the first he would stand next to in a firefight. Butt Kicker had lost his sense of teamwork.

He squinted. "Kan, you make Brutus look unambitious."

"Brutus was a premeditated killer. I would've busted him. I'm sorry about your bride, but I'm sorrier about Jimmy Buford."

Magrip closed his eyes, bored.

"Magrip, why not bail out? I'll get a grad who'll serve."

He snorted.

"Stow it," I said slowly, anger coming, "or you are relieved."

"Good pep talk. Enjoy farting in the wind?" He yawned.

I hurled my chair into the wall above his head. It crashed and stabbed through the cheap drywall and sagged like a dead metal insect. He made a noise in his throat as he jumped up, hands out low. I put my face in his so he could hear me.

"WE GOT A GUY ON THE LINE! PULL YOUR LOAD OR STRAP OFF!"

He glared, panting, his blood up. Good. No more eyeball rolling while someone had Jimmy by the nuts. I took my face out of his. "Glad we had this chat. Now tell me about Jimmy and the gate."

Magrip's barrel chest heaved; his face was red, his pupils pinpoints. He looked at the imbedded chair, rubbing his face below the nose. He hated Asia. Asia was flop sweat. His devils were here, playing Oriental pitchfork with mine. Once we were young and innocent and could have killed a sixpack after the Navy game and told tales about the Tac Department. He looked at me, his eyes small, nodding to himself. He yanked the chair from the wall and threw it through the window, knocking the fragile wood frame and shattering old glass into the piles of snow outside. Plinks of glass bounced into the room as gusts of cold wind and snow burst in, sucking our heat.

He sat and pulled out a notepad, his breathing irregular. He probed an ear. "Think you can take me?" he asked in a high, thin voice. He chuckled, lifting his chin to me, his teeth out. "No way, you dirty twisted sonofabitch." He smiled like a cat, his chest working. He pulled out a Camel and lit it, hands steady, the bitter wind rippling his notepad. "Kan, I'll fucking kill you." He blew smoke in my face.

"Okay. You talked me into it. You can have the lower bunk."

Wet wind gusted and blew out his cigarette, rocketing papers around the room. "Primo number-one Asian suck. Okay." He opened the pad. "Buford got here 1130 hours, Sunday, 6 January."

Good. Jimmy had made it to Casey, improving chances for a quick rescue by limiting the area of search and eliminating the fear that he was lost somewhere in the reaches of North Asia in winter.

Boots crunched. I picked up the knife. A sentry, rifle at port arms, stuck his head through the hole, watching snow fill the room.

"Jee-sus Christ on a stick! Y'all know yur window's broke?"

I used my knife to knock out the pins from our Q door. I rested the door against the window. I pushed the bunks snug against the door and the snow stopped. "Y'all have a nice day, now," came the guard's muffled voice.

"Thank you," I said. "Go about your duties."

Magrip shook snow from his hair. It was too cold in the room to melt it. "Two hundred two vehicles and nine full military convoys checked out since Buford came in on the bus."

Any of them could have taken Jimmy off post. Whoever called the Pentagon pretending to be him was trying to buy time. Toss evidence. Cover up crime scenes. Burn witnesses. Wait for apathy to take over and for incompetence to assume control.

I gave Magrip the nylon bag. He pulled out the nickel-plated Browning High Power. He cleared the action and put it back in the bag. "How the hell you get this in-country?"

"Eastern Theater weapons permit, ROK- and Tokyo-approved."

"You're shitting me. I thought JAGCs killed with paper."

"Then why the grenades?"

"Frags take out all kinds of people." He smiled falsely.

"Forget it, Magrip. The paperwork on my death would take the rest of your life." I put the Browning in my briefcase.

Murray had sent me a warrior, more interested, perhaps, in killing me than in killing the enemy. Maybe if he took me out, he'd smile.

Corporal Min stopped the jeep at Pork Chop Hill and Heartbreak Ridge roads. Traffic was heavy with troop patrols in trucks.

"Up there, *dae-wi*," said Min. "Wizard Q." Wizard quarters, Colonel LeBlanc's hooch. The moon was rising, swollen with light, a traditionally good omen for authorities seeking bandits. It illuminated a gray two-story house with a smoking chimney.

Oz of the East, comfortable and warm, the lights bright.

Jimmy, you be up there, recording events, charming the guilty with tales of Southern belles and Carolina shrimp recipes, pickpocketing watches and the laughter

of your boys. Your faith in all tomorrows intact, sharp
eyes clear, dog tags dry and warm against a breathing
chest, the father in you preserved for the future of innocent children.

I'll come back, Jimmy, tonight, when dogs curl up
near heat vents and frostbitten riflemen stack rifles.

Then we'll see how soundly the Wizard sleeps.

8

THE LAS VEGAS

We reconned Casey's rows of dismal barracks and old
Quonsets. Choppers whumped across camp, the rotors
raising my pulse. Six P.M. and getting colder. "Corporal,
take us to high ground."

"Hill 902," said Magrip. "Radar peak. Good view."

Min parked at the top. A concave radar dish turned, the
generator hum loud. I got out. "Please get grub. Come
back fast."

Min handed us old copies of *Stars and Stripes*, the
Army newspaper filled with ads for throwing knives,
used Chevies and Philippine rattan furniture. "Use in
jacket, *dae-wi*." We opened coats and inserted newspapers around torsos and zipped up.

The jeep rumbled away. The view was good and the
wind caustic. My eyes teared and my bones and innards
felt brittle.

Casey, home of the Second Infantry, the only Pacific
Theater combat unit not to go to Vietnam. But the smoke
from that war worked like a depressant on all American

soldiers. Here was a village of GIs, living on booze and danger, counting down days.

To the north were forbidding, hard-spined mountains that formed an encircling horizon against a darkening sky. Five snow-capped peaks stood sentry over the leprous valley, the wind whipping the ice pack on the higher ridges. To the south was a taller, darker mountain.

The mountains formed a channel that led from the DMZ to us. It was an Inmingun attack highway. It was not a pretty sight.

"Shit," said Magrip. "No way we can defend this damn valley."

Indefensible. "We're a North Korean speed bump."

"Yeah. Pearl Harbor, they blow us away—America avenges Casey."

Not the best tactical posture: kill me and my daddy will beat you up. It was the Alamo and the *Maine*, stuck on the dark side of the moon. I felt something missing in the equation.

"Tough to find one missing guy," said Magrip. "Everyone here's a transient. Winter or a commie sniper could take you out."

"Where would you hide Buford?" The wind howled.

"Under ice. Find him in spring." The weather invited irritability. Casey was like Vietnam, with numbing cold in lieu of sweat tropics. Maybe Jimmy could see tonight's sky. He would know that Carlos had assembled a team, and that I would come looking.

Min returned and we got in the jeep. The Q was merely cold, an improvement on what whistled around the building. I blew on my hands. The battalion mess halls were closed, so dinner was snack-bar Gainesburgers, nine-tenths grease. Min ate rice from a small tin. I paid him for the meal and took the paper from my chest. I took a bite; it was more than enough. I put the knife in my boot and gathered the Browning and magazines.

"Time to climb in a window in Wizard Q. Tell Jimmy the Bee to wash his hands for dinner."

Magrip stood, smiling like a pirate, happy with the prospect of hurting someone. He put a Gerber knife in his boot.

A knock sounded; I stowed the gun. A fine-featured man in a black turtleneck, a double-breasted gray blazer and a fur-lined overcoat, George Hamilton on the town. I knew him. The question was, would he recognize me?

"Gentlemen, Gary Willoughby, claims." He had taken the phone message about Jimmy. He had pulled an automatic on me in the SJA shop, almost shooting himself.

"Gents, welcome to Frozen Chosen, home to the Fighting Second Infantry and five thousand comfort girls." It was rehearsed. He thrust his hand at me and shook heartily without a hint of recognition. He saw Min.

"What's a garlicky craphole KATUSA doing in the Q?"

"Funny," I said. "I thought it was *his* country."

Min kept his eyes down, big boots twitching.

Willoughby shrugged. "Get civvies. I'm going to the Ville."

"I'll alert public affairs. How'd you know we came in?"

"DMZ rumor control, light speed," he said. "Oink, oink."

"Oink oink?" I said.

"O-I-N-K—'Only in Korea,'" he said. "Where the sun never sets on the American Far East empire. C'mon. I'll show you around."

"Seen it," said Magrip, eyes shut. "Prostitute country."

"C'mon, guys," urged Willoughby. "It's Disneyland for men!"

"I'm married," said Magrip. "Or I was."

"I'm not doing women right now," I said.

Willoughby looked at me in shock. "Wrong place to quit! Guys! Just a beer! Any of you like military history trivia? I know a lot. Look, I'll buy. C'mon, Jack Kan—be a pal!"

A lonely, friendless man offering a chance at recon and the unknown. "Corporal, you want to join us?"

Min shook his head, his jaw flexing. My knife was in my boot. Magrip checked his armpits and belched. My team was ready.

Strobes blinded us. A mob was roaring. We were in the Las Vegas Club, fifth hellhole from the first corner of the Strip of the Ville and two klicks from the gate.

Willoughby slapped me on the back, grinning wildly. He was happy. You could see the caps to his dental cavities and the girth of his tonsils. "Is this sweet, or what?"

"It's cute as leaping crap," snapped Magrip.

"Luke, you're bad-mouthing Heaven!" cried Willoughby. In civvies, we looked like sailors come to shore.

"Don't call me Luke," said Magrip.

The Ville, said Willoughby, was Tongducheon, a farm town of fifty thousand centered in the Inmingun invasion route. It had three markets, a drainage canal, five thousand hookers, an overburdened VD clinic and an American GI ghetto of unredeemed whorehouses, knife fights, regimental inebriation, American projectile vomiting and a full company of U.S. Military Police. This to arrest a random few and provide a political suggestion of civil order.

The Las Vegas was like last year's birthday cake with the candles still burning. The Rolling Stones screamed "Satisfaction" the way dying men cry at fate. Ill-timed strobes blinded us, lending disorientation to our jet-lagged sense of moral defeat. Garish murals adorned concrete walls. A worried MP scanned us, adjusting his nightstick, service automatic, cuffs and CS gas canister as we stomped on icy, muddied sawdust.

GIs danced with Korean waitresses, doing the frug

and western swing in a floor space bordered by a mirrored bar where five Korean bartenders in red vests and white bow ties spilled booze for steady queues of drunks. A cigarette-dangling DJ spun platters inside a smoke-filled cubicle on the right wall, leaning on the Stones.

Racially and morally, I had loathed such institutions in Saigon. Later, jittering on the steel bed of the vibrating medevac, my brains scrambled and back blown out, I regretted not having seen the Amazon, the Nile, the Irrawaddy and the beautiful Asian women who danced in the bars on Tung Heng Dai Do, inspiring febrile memories in my men.

Now I was here. There was a concealed rear area. The front was astream with long-haired waitresses carrying beer pitchers with the care it takes to fall from a bridge. Miniskirts revealed pink underwear. Little plastic blue hearts adorned each left breast. "Hey, little Blue Heart!" cried a GI.

A waitress with hip-long hair, tiny waist and over-advertised legs looked at me over her shoulder. She tapped a friend and pointed. She approached, smiling, warm from her work. She brushed back her hair, lips parted professionally.

"Officer man, I think I love you too muchee." Breathless. "You big honcho man!" She was pretty as a picture, hard as a tank hull, panting like Marilyn Monroe in front of the camera.

"I'm married," I lied. "We have six kids."

"Eh, you like-ee good time! I here for you, sweet time!"

I smiled. "No, thank you very much."

She leaned into me so sincerely I felt her folded money.

I backed up. She curled her lip, turning her pretty face into something quite different, and left with angry heels.

"Tina digs you!" shouted Willoughby. "Her stuff

makes my teeth ache! An overnight with her is fifteen bucks and she screams!"

We followed him deeper into the club. Blue Hearts stared.

Willoughby screamed like a rebel at Bull Run, making my skin crawl. "I'm a consumer in the supermarket of love! If I do a Blue Heart a night, I'll do them all in thirteen years. Every one of these girls trying to get a ticket to the Big PX in the Sky—using hum jobs on Mr. Happy." The Big PX was America. Mr. Happy was probably Willoughby's cause for life.

He nodded. "Guys." Six GIs nodded back. Their table lacked Blue Hearts offering wares. Six men with empty beer pitchers, nervous as they studied me and Magrip. One was a big man with a broken nose in an acne-scarred face, a hand out of sight. He wore the longish center-cut. They looked like Leavenworth cons or recycles from the disciplinary barracks of the Retraining Brigades.

"This," said Magrip, shaking his head, "turns men into jumping idiots. Whores who set up murder. Hundreds of whores."

"Five thousand," corrected Willoughby. "Tell a bad joke, they still hum you all night, all you can take. Luke, you'll love it."

"And some," I said, "dare say romance is dead."

"No one calls me that," hissed Magrip to Willoughby.

"What do you want me to call you?"

"Nothing," said Magrip. "Unass my life."

Willoughby shrugged, accustomed to rejection. "Guys," he breathed, "this is sweet paradise on high heels."

"You're full a crap," snapped Magrip. "Kan, you had enough? This stinks." He grimaced. "Let's bag it. I was here before."

"He led us here," I said quietly. "Check out the back."

Magrip sighed. "I can see brains aren't everything. This is a whorehouse. You look under the sheets, you find whores."

At a table on an elevated mezzanine sat a woman in white. Through the bad, explosive lighting and the world of noise, she looked at me with large dark eyes. I sensed her sadness, the hints of dignity or clinical depression. Then, a tug of superstitious, boyish fear in my gut, a warm breath of the unknown in my throat. She did not wear a heart. I wasn't sure what she was or what she represented.

"She is checking you out, big-time," said Willoughby. "Ice Queen. Bitch plays hard-to-get in a whorehouse. You love that? There's a pink pot on her. Put in and score, you get the pot. Hey, man, your chances are *excellent*. She digs you!"

A small, rotund woman in a flowing, floor-length lavender robe arrived in a swish of satin. Willoughby introduced us. Mrs. Cho, proprietress. She grabbed us, taking my arm.

"Too muchee big Chinese man! Come! No, *dae-wi*, no lookee her—Ice Queen, michaso, crazy, no-good numbah-ten! My good girl make you happy. Bambi, Boom-Boom, Shanghai Mary, hum-job you, make you feel Heaven! Aeguu, *dae-wi*, I likee your arm too muchee! Big Man, you pickee!"

"Diet Pepsi?" I asked. Mrs. Cho blinked. The women gazed at Magrip, drawn by his raw *yang* scent. Magrip scowled and curled his lip, causing swoons.

"Elvis," breathed one.

You ladies see Jimmy Buford? I wondered. Not his kind of place, but he was an IG, and Willoughby was the tour guide.

Mrs. Cho lambasted Bambi, who changed chairs to press her chest on me while she poured a beer with a cardboard smile. It was a big chest. I may have coughed. "No, thank you," I said, and Bambi leaned back, relieved. The beer smelled like radiator antifreeze.

Mrs. Cho shook her head, then spoke above the music. "My girl not used to Chinese soldier. My girl, she see your honcho face, see Kong-ja, Confucius. See father. Get muchee *pukurom*—shame. Their family hate them too muchee. You no hate my girl, *neh*?" The Marcels began to sing "Blue Moon."

I said that I didn't.

A statuesque, improbably proportioned woman arrived, her chest working. She wore buckskins and tassels and hair past her waist. She hitched her head and Bambi leaned both hands on my privates to stand, leaving with a smile to match my raised brows.

"Crap," said Magrip. Miss Buckskin sat and gazed at him, eyes bright, lips parted, chest heaving, her hard, angularly handsome face alight with carnal or monetary fantasies. An entourage of panting GIs regarded her as if she were Ann-Margret.

"Ma-grip-ee! Is you! Oh, *yobo*!" She took his hand and molded it to her breasts, moaning as she sucked the fingers of his other hand.

"I think she likes you," I said.

"I love you best," she breathed over Magrip's digits, the blinking of ponderous false eyelashes sounding like the rabid beating of happy puppy tails. "I love you too muchee!" Sucking harder. "I miss you too muchee in my heart, Ma-grip-ee!"

"Brigitte—no. Stop. C'mon!" Magrip, eyebrows up, tried to extract his fingers. They were stuck. He freed his hand from her chest and looked at me. "Of all the fucking gin joints in Korea, you bring me here." His eyes burned like flares. "Lemme tell you something. If I get laid over here, I'm killing you."

Gunfire erupted and Magrip and I went flat as Brigitte squeaked. We looked around and jumped up. My heart hammered, selector switch on auto, ready to shoot at movement. Sharp fear adrenalized me. I felt death knocking, taking names and dealing cards, my heart doing the beat.

The troops in the club were up in a cresting wave,

pounding tables and roaring cacophonous, whooping cries. The galvanized mayhem and shattered glass were focused on the door. One group led by throwing beer mugs and pitchers. No guns—only a brawl cheerled by Willoughby's friends, the six GI thugs at the isolated table. Magrip, teeth bared, took his hand out of his armpit. A finger bled; in the uproar, Brigitte had bitten him.

I smiled. "Lucky it was just your finger."

A Caucasian woman had entered the Vegas and the lone MP was up with his nightstick, clubbing her fans as they closed on her and beat him with grimy, outstretched hands, chanting "ROUND-EYE! ROUND-EYE!" with charming anatomical modifiers. The MP was being beaten as he desperately tried to blow his whistle for help.

"Americans," sighed Willoughby. "Do we love women or what?"

Magrip and I forced a path. I took off my ring. Someone kicked me, shooting nervy signals up and down my lousy back. Glass shattering, the club rife with chaos vérité.

We pushed and waded our way to the MP and the woman. She was tall and swinging back. Magrip hit and dropped two men in rapid sequence and grunted happily as he knocked gaggles of troops away from the woman with his big body. I pushed the stunned, bleeding MP behind me, blocked wildly thrown punches. I shouted for order in the wild, flickering light; it didn't work. A man rushed me and I punched him in the nose in a burst of blood. More came and I had to kick two men in the groin.

A fellow with a big florid face rocked me with a punch to the jaw and Magrip decked him, making a deep sound of pleasure as the man flew backwards, arms out. I spat; no blood or teeth. Magrip was better at this than I; he liked it.

"AT EASE!" I cried as a trooper threw his body at

Magrip and I turned and side-kicked him into a table. It cracked like a log under an axe as the halves fell on him. I had a big voice and was accustomed to people listening to me. This mob had a purpose.

Find the rhythm—hard in a brawl. I punched and missed, then kicked one in the face as a small, wiry trooper ducked Magrip's swing and thunked him viciously in the chest with a beer pitcher. Another pitcher shattered on the back of my head, making it sing. My vision blurred and a huge black man held me up with one hand.

He was a monster with a Mohawk and a mustache, a wall-to-wall-shouldered behemoth of iron banging and unrestrained steroid abuse. I shook my head. He snapped a thug's arm like a twig and threw the screaming trooper into the mob. Breathing easily, he destroyed the face of another with one snap punch.

"I'm on your side," I said. I marveled as he lifted a trooper at neck and crotch and hurled him toward Alaska with good follow-through. I sidestepped a wild swing and snap-kicked to the face, getting eyes and nose as the woman behind me shattered a bottle on his head.

Someone screamed "Fuck the chink!," the epithet galvanizing others to come en masse. The Marcels sang "dinga donk ding Blue Moon" and one stool bounced off me while another crunched the ironmonger in the skull with a blow that would have made a house shake. He shook his head and threw a running punch that landed like a truck ramming a picket fence. A man swung at me with a knife and I jerked right. It was the acne-faced, broken-nosed thug, wild with fear and hate and bad aim.

The hell with this. I screamed as Master Wong had taught me when I was a little boy, my lungs reaching to the heavens while I spun, jumped, coiled my thrust leg and emptied my *chi* in a jump-kick that caught Acne Man mid-body, took his momentum and punted him through the air, both of our howls echoing in the club.

"Three points!" cried Magrip in a blood frenzy, punching a stubborn GI with jabs and crosses, then raising his arms in a field-goal sign, laughing and hungrily waving for more victims as I kicked three men rapidly, aiming for heads but hitting throats—jet lag. Magrip and the huge bruiser were in rhythm, and the thugs in front cursed and scrabbled away, pushing against those behind.

A big man charged with a stool. I kicked low, crushing his knee, and jammed the stool into his throat. He screamed, fell, choked and doubled up. It was Howdy Doody, the rude, freckled SJA sentry who had scolded me for keeping his door open. I had wind, my back was covered and I had no injuries.

No one wanted to play.

Boots tramped in the street. A wing of MPs burst into the club, helmeted and armed with baseball bats, fanning across the room and soliciting the retreat of the mob. A last pitcher exploded on Magrip in a shower of glass as he debrained a victim, using the man's head to reseat floor nails, his eyes bright in combat delirium, looking around and chuckling. The strobes quit and the ear-splitting music stopped in the new order of pine versus flesh.

I threw beer on Magrip. He spluttered. Impervious to pain, he disliked moisture. "Cease work. MPs are here." He stood, dropping the head in his hand on the hard, dented floor, shaking sweat and beer like a bear in a downpour. The amusements were shutting down. No more cotton candy. His mouth turned down.

The bulls sealed doors and began arresting. "Him," said the sentry, chest bellowing, blood pouring from lip and nose. "Him him him. Battery. This guy, sex battery on the lady. This guy hit me with a pitcher—ag battery, weapon. Acne Man here, throwing up—he was like a leader, inciting. Hey, whaddya know. It's dirtbag Fleeg."

If we had been doing what Casey needed—criminal

defense—they'd be tomorrow's defendants. Not the best thing, JAGCs thumping their own clients.

Hello, I'm your lawyer, take this.

The MPs looked warily at Magrip and me. "No—good guys."

An intuition. I searched the supine for Howdy Doody. He was out, his leg awry at a bad angle, his knee blown out.

I lifted him, his leg spasming. "Who's this?"

"Muldoon," said the MP. "Legal clerk. Two-bit bully."

I looked at Magrip and made the snapping hand motion for talking. He took Muldoon, seating him softly, easing his head onto the table. Magrip gently poured beer down Muldoon's head and then slapped him hard, jolting head and torso, drawing blood and almost knocking him out.

"Muldoon," said Magrip sweetly in his ear, a buddy. "I think I killed one a them. I forget. We supposed to kill 'em?"

Muldoon wheezed. "Aw crap, no," he croaked. "Tol' you . . . jus' whale on 'em." Belch. "Fuck 'em up." Bingo, as I suspected.

He choked. "Ahhckkkk!" He vomited zealously on Magrip.

Willoughby was still at Mrs. Cho's table. My head ached. My head, mouth, hands bled. Get the chink. Screw up my team. I wanted to punch Willoughby in the face until he had a different personality.

"Life," said Magrip. "The contact sport." He snapped vomitus from his hands.

The monster who had come to our aid wiped blood from the back of his blocky head, hawked and spat, breathing smoothly, energized from the fight, twitchy with adrenaline, worried about consequences, eyes darting. He was leaving.

"I'm Captain Kan. Who are you? I want to thank your

CO." Commanding officer. We shook. His palm was all dead gristle.

"You didn't see shit. I ain't here. I ain't got no name."

He showed his ID to the MPs at the door. They let him go.

I showed my ID. "Sergeant, who was that man?"

"Sir, Sergeant Barton's red CG sticker gets him through MP lines and crime scenes."

A commanding general sticker. I said I had never heard of such a thing.

"Well hell, sir, oink oink." Only in Korea.

The woman in white was gone. I didn't blame her. GI arrestees whined as handcuffs were ratcheted down.

"Captain Jackson Kan," said a woman. "You think it was something I said? I'm Levine."

I turned. She had eyes like fine lights in San Francisco Bay. Captain Levine, the third JAGC, jumpy from spastic illumination and male madness, chest heaving in a black overcoat with a missing button, her short brown hair in good order, licking her lips.

Murray had given me a suicidal driver, a homicidal grenade thrower and a woman who caused sex riots. She removed an old leather glove and offered her hand. An empty Crown beer bottle was in the other. We shook.

What the hell was Carlos thinking, sending a woman here? He had a nuts sense of humor, but there was no joke in pitching a female to the DMZ to test her reaction to gang rape.

"Thanks for your help," she said. "I am happy to work with you. It's an honor to be with someone focused on mission." Levine then set her face, preparing for rejection.

I was a West Pointer, trained to take the worst member of any team to the designated objective. I was also the firstborn son of a Chinese Christian *laoban* and a Taoist Long River woman. You ride the current the gods give you, carrying the cargoes reddened by your father's blood mark. You do not argue about leaking wood-oil ballast or complain about starving pirates who smile at the screams of women. You do not curse the winter wind god or the red war god, who killed your *gung-gung* and *didi*, your grandfather and younger brothers. You obey your father and all elders. You marry the merchant's pig-tailed daughter BaBa picks for you.

You do your job.

If you must, you work with women, even if they can get killed doing it, their blood on your hands forever.

9

CAPTAIN LEVINE

For some reason, Magrip and I looked like we had been in a cathouse brawl.

"Captain Levine, this is Magrip. Magrip, Captain Levine. We have a high standard of Dignity Under All Circumstances."

Chunks of glass fell from Magrip's stinking clothes.

She laughed loudly, a honking goose, offering her hand. Magrip took it as if it were the palm of a herpes patient.

"Got held up. Fog in Frankfurt. The taxi ride up MSR-3 was a kick. This . . ." She waved at the Vegas, the staff picking through the wreckage. "Surreal. But not fun." A distant breath of New York. "Kan, I got your note to meet you here."

I shook my head. "I left no note. We were set up. Looks like the Wizard's welcome. Not homicide. Just a sincere beating."

She digested that. "You do this often?"

"This afternoon, we imitated chickens doing the Grand Prix. You been briefed?"

She had. I pointed with my eyes. "Willoughby works for the Wizard. I think he set up the riot. Say nothing."

The madam stared at the Caucasian female in her factory.

"Kan *dae-wi*," hissed Mrs. Cho, "is she prostitutee?"

"Ma'am, she's a captain lawyer in the American Army."

Mrs. Cho swooned. Blue Hearts ran to her, fanning her face with cheap paper napkins that once had been in Army inventory.

I introduced Levine. Brigitte aimed her chest, her only weapon, at her. Levine nodded. "So that's where they went."

Mrs. Cho hissed an insincere welcome. A round-eye woman lawyer would inspire thoughts of unions, health plans and night school. GIs would remember mothers, sisters and wives. Levine represented recession, even depression.

Willoughby had a different idea. He approached Levine with the subtlety of stallions in spring. I tried to count the reasons I despised him. Too daunting.

Mrs. Cho waved at her DJ. The lights went out, the strobes flashed and "I Want to Go Stateside" began, allowing my ear to ring once more while I went temporarily blind. Every American officer in the club, none of whom had helped us, gathered around Levine like bees about the queen. Even Brigitte's loyalists changed flags. The Blue Hearts left huffily. For the officers, I made a slicing motion across my neck. Remembering Magrip and the Mohawk hulk, they left.

Levine removed her overcoat, wanting no help. Willoughby studied her as if she were removing everything. She wore a gray wool pants suit. Dark, thoughtful eyes studied us as I sat up, for reasons not entirely clear. Snow melted in her hair.

I had seen Caucasian American women two days ago, but the cultural curiosity of Captain Levine in this place made us gawk. I pushed my beer mug away from me. It was as if one of my sisters had arrived, and I didn't have any sisters.

She had short, thick brown hair above a narrow and muscular neck, a softly curved nose, a wide and generous mouth and a natural, sharp intelligence that rose from big observant eyes like morning mist. We could use that. We could dispense with the woman part. Magrip would like her because she invited brawls, but we needed to get the Bee.

"Where did you come in from?" I asked.

"Twenty-First Support Command, Heidelberg, Chief of Justice." She narrowed her eyes. "Are DMZ troops psychotic, or is it the water?" A strong voice, casually employed.

She observed us with a fine exactness. The moral, confident prosecutor, operating on brains, reliant upon insight, friend to humor, no stranger to courage, and better organized than most men. She rode subways and knew New York at night.

"It's the weather," I said.

"I'll be careful." Tough, but in need of guarding. Magrip would hate the duty but would love the friction, which ought to make him happy.

"Why's the IG here?" asked Willoughby.

I faced Willoughby. "Who's an IG?"

Willoughby frowned. "You telling me you're not?"

"I'm here for the sun. Get a tan and truck home."

Willoughby, doubtful: "Dogface Nagol wants you at 0800." The Wizard's deputy calling the tune on his own investigation.

"Where do I find Nagol? Right now?"

"Shacked up with his *yobo*. Hey, wait till you see

him." He shook his head and sucked air through teeth, Korean style. "You'll witness the power of the almighty greenback over the judgment of Oriental snatch."

"Watch your mouth. Where's his hooch?"

He shrugged. "None of my business."

Pig Breath would know. "Where's Pig Breath Altman?"

"Library," said Willoughby. "Book farter. Probably a fag."

I leaned forward. "You got a mouth problem. Fix it."

Willoughby tried to smile, wondering at my joke. Magrip returned and shook his head without a suggestion of subtlety; no Jimmy. Brigitte stood, wetting her lips as she leaned on Magrip, settling on him like tapioca on a spoon. She closed her eyes, hips undulating, pressing assets into him. "Ma-grip-ee, too long stay 'way," she breathed. "You, me, go have love."

"I'm married, now," growled Magrip. "Buzz off."

She tried to change his mind. Magrip pushed her off. She looked hurt. She had an old crush on Magrip. Bad choice. She left, injured, still managing to look like Jayne Mansfield absorbing admiration on a klieg-lit, male-convict-infested runway.

Willoughby examined her as she left. Then he turned to Levine. "Been here a long time. Seen stuff. No one as good as you. Lady, you're a stone fox and you knock me out. Not because there are no American round-eye chicks here. It's you. You're really beautiful. Got a great body. I mean that sincerely." He laughed easily. "I like long-legged women with small waists and good hips who still got it upstairs."

"Don't stop," I said. "What do you think of her pancreas?"

He thought about it for a moment. "Where you bil-leted?" He smiled with white, straight teeth. "Jewish, right? I *love* Jewish women. Lotta guys don't. Think you're all too neurotic. Not me. You're all sensualists! Let me escort you. Hey, lady, I'm smitten. Big-time."

She looked at her well-formed hands. Attempted gang rape, and now Willoughby. If she looked up, a hundred strange men would propose marriage for the benefit of the honeymoon.

"Let me make this clear. I understand male hormones. This understanding fills me with pity, but not kindness. I'm not here to play bull's-eye for your testosterone overload."

She interlaced fingers. "Captain Smitten, I am not here to see who can score." She looked at us, the prosecutor assessing a new grand jury. "I am here to do my job to the best of my ability, under the provisions of the Constitution and the Uniform Code of Military Justice."

Tight jaw. "All I ask is that you keep your personal problems away from me. Use whatever discipline you have as an officer and a gentleman. Please take your eyes off my chest."

Willoughby tried, his eyeballs becoming elliptical in an effort to comply. He moaned in the grip of the moon. "I'm in love."

Magrip scowled: women on the DMZ.

"You're going to be a lot of work," I said quietly.

A New York shrug. "Love your support." She ignored me and Willoughby's brainless, doelike gaze.

I stood. "Levine, see you later. Magrip, with me." I looked at Willoughby. "For a moment." We stepped away.

"Proud of you. I know it was an accident, but you left some people alive."

He lifted his big jaw and laughed. "A sweet fight. Ended too damn soon. I owe Willoughby for starting it."

So did I. Magrip was Scarlett O'Hara after a warm kiss.

"Magrip, how's your sense of humor?"

He paused. "I'm the funniest goddamn man you'll ever know."

"Good. Protect Levine. Get her housed and stay with her."

He recoiled. "You're shitting me."

"I poop you not. Your shorts too tight? Stow that anger."

He pushed my shoulder. "Who the fuck says I'm angry?"

I stiffened. "No one. It's a vicious rumor being circulated by the fifty guys you just beat the crap out of."

He faced off, nose near mine. "I'm happier than shit. I'm married." His eyes went through me. "Hell, I'm learning how to cook and like it. I'm a lawyer now, so I won't see any more HQ Infantry cluster fucks." He squinted. "I'm like *real* glad you can bar-fight, but if I call Immigration, they'll probably send your ass back to China. So I'm big-time happy. *Got* it?"

"I'm real pleased for you." I pointed at him. "Stay close to her. She's your partner."

At the door, I saw Magrip say something to Willoughby, who quickly moved his chair away from Levine. Magrip spoke again and Willoughby nodded emphatically and changed tables.

Meat wagons were hauling off perps like midtown taxis on a rainy day. I stuck my fists in the snow, cooling my torn and offended knuckles, turning the snow a light, candied pink. I had trouble sliding the class ring on my swollen finger.

Time to find Major Nagol, the Wizard's right-hand man and poster boy for dust, disease, disorganization and the ambush bashing of IG investigators.

10

Pig Breath and Ghoul

Officers and a third of the Second Infantry's enlisted men—five thousand souls—had passes into the Strip. Fellini could have set the stage through which I walked. Troops cursed excessively and drank too much. They played craps, poker and pool, argued over fees and bargained with the devil while cold, underdressed squadrons of unlicensed street hookers counted money, taunted, flirted, invited, cackled and waved. One hailed me by jumping on my back. I pulled her off.

Later, there were footsteps—a man. I chased footfalls into an empty alley. Nothing. My short military hair felt electric, my adrenaline up with nowhere to go.

The lights in the office of the staff judge advocate burned brightly across the fields of snow. Casey's chief prosecutor was still in the library, daydreaming of mass Sunday hangings.

"Hello, Miles Altman. I'm Jackson Kan."

He kept writing, irritated. He didn't point his mouth at me, showing that diplomacy was alive on the DMZ. "Screw off."

"I need to see Major Nagol. Where's his hooch?"

He snorted at me but I didn't faint. "He's an idiot. Wears a gun. Bigger asshole than me, king of all gaping assholes."

"There's a closing argument to live by."

He faced me. Baby-blue eyes in an unpleasant face, the

nose and chin looking like they had been punched by experts.

"Hear you're an IG now and you brought Butt Kicker Magrip with you. The freaking odd couple. What are you after, Kan? The Wizard?"

I coughed, hating to lie. "Race relations."

His lips fluttered. "Yeah? I hate Asians and Medal of Honor winners. Your mission's done. What crap! Fix claims and recruiting and make the cops do their job!" Spittle flew.

I blinked, my eyes watering. "Duly noted." I made the note.

"So eat me."

"You're too kind." I gave him the Richelieu letter that proclaimed I had the powers of the Pope, and backed up.

"You asshole. Shitting Pentagon turds on my desk." He sighed, surrendering. "Dogface's world-class super-snatch clap boiled up. Grounded at the CG's mess." He exhaled. "You owe me now, Kan."

I wiped my watering eyes. "You're right, Pig, I do. Be patient."

His ears perked. "You sonofabitch—you got something cooking?" He smiled, caressing his pen, exuding swamp gases, smelling blood. Pig stank like hell's death, but he had the heart of a prosecutor, loving to bust the bad and the strong.

The sentry was a scar-faced British Army Gurkha with a curved kukri dagger in his cummerbund. The UN was here. He stopped us. "Sorry, sir, only field-grade officers"—majors and above. He had a charming accent, cold eyes and a stone mouth.

"Chief of justice to see Major Nagol," said Pig Breath in his face. The Gurkha staggered back, blinking desperately. I flashed the CG letter before his watering eyes and we went in.

A pistol belt hung from the coatrack. A lawyer was here.

I knew bars. They beckoned darkly to proud liars, shameless confessors, the great, cantankerous adult orphanage of the military. Army watering holes served warriors, alkies and chair jockeys. There, officers who fought staple removers rapped in the hard patois of killers, and at the bar, "fucking" modified some verbs, many nouns and most thoughts.

I had never fit in the O Club subculture, where booze lured waste from guts and souls and summoned men to spend years of sour eves in oblivious communion. When I had been a practicing drunk, I had gone to the Club for the gin.

The commanding general's mess was a low stone cottage with a mirrored, mahogany bar, a tablecloth dining room and white-jacketed Korean waiters. Picture windows showed snow, a frozen pond and a flood-lamp-illuminated white-out. We were leaving the lights on at Pearl Harbor. I imagined what a hard-hearted North Vietnamese sapper could do to the mess and our command staff.

This was Korea, beyond the conscience of families. A woman could be purchased for pocket change, the weather was lethal, North Koreans could slit your throat and a large number of men drank for a living.

Dogface Nagol looked like Dracula in the morning, his sallow, ghoulish features troubled by the challenge of unkind bar lighting. I halfway expected the mirror to not reflect his image, but it was there. Broomstick arms, sunken chest, bony shoulders, the effect of malnutrition interrupted by a bowling-ball gut that shadowed thin hips and scrawny legs. He wore sharp civvies, looked half dead and faced six whiskey sours.

Two obese majors bracketed him, working cheap cigars. There was a time when the sound of gin hitting the bottom of a greasy glass could have invited me to stay for a week.

Pig Breath coughed; a chubby major gasped, elbow slipping. "Sir, this is Captain Kan, IG on race problems."

Nagol flinched; I was supposed to be battered in the Ville. The majors turned, too fat so close to the enemy.

Nagol slowly rotated the stool, conserving energy on low internal batteries. He had a cadaverous face. Death had taken his pitted complexion; his eyes were shrouds for things that go bump in the night. His hair was brush-cut and clumps of it were missing, leaving in their place greasy pink patches of necrotic flesh. His lips were thin and purple, highlighted by four bright-pink and gray pustules rising from a stubby field of poorly shaved whiskers; the nose was a pockmarked, burst-veined, puce-hued exhibit for temperance. His nails were dimpled and broken and he smelled bad. He was a ghoul who made Pig Breath Altman look like Robert Redford.

I felt sorry for him, but that wouldn't help either of us. He had charted his course, taken chronic blows and passed the point where he could recognize kindness or respond to it. Looking at him made my teeth ache. I wondered if he shaved with a mirror.

Narrow, shadowed eyes squinted as if he saw me through shimmering heat waves. I expected visible formaldehyde fumes, and avoided looking at any single facial feature.

I smiled brightly, knowing he would hate mirth. "Good evening, sir."

He shirked. "What the hell do you want?" Each word a physical pain. "Stud Book says you're a Sixth Army trial counsel with dual U.S. attorney duties." The Stud Book registered all JAGCs by assignment. "What the hell you doing here for the IG?"

I smiled charmingly. "I'm a race expert."

He grimaced as if my jump boots were stomping his bare feet. "Then go fuck yourself, expert," he snarled in his busted voice, hampered by booze, tobacco and the wages of vices. "Report at 0800 or you're under arrest.

You're a JAGC in Casey, so you report to the SJA. He's top lawyer. Captains aren't allowed in here. Fart off."

"Here, here," burbled the quartermaster officer.

"Sir," I said, "the IG outranks you. You persist, it'll draw attention, and then you will get spanked until it hurts. Not like that amateur job at the Las Vegas. We do it right. We use judges, juries and the UCMJ."

He turned back to the bar and downed another, cigar ashes floating. So the law didn't work in Korea. Oink, oink.

It'd be fun to play poker with him. You could knock down gin and ask him how he had come to attract heart failure, alcoholism, nicotine addiction and tertiary relapsed Indochinese syphilis in the same lifetime. I forgave him the alcoholism; I wanted a drink. I went to the latrine and washed my hands in scalding hot water.

I sensed Jimmy had met that man. Jimmy was missing.

I listened and watched for phantom trailers or flankers on the way back to the Q. Nothing. It was midnight of our first day.

Drunks crashed into walls, playing the Doors too loudly and heaving in the shower so others could use the heads. I entered the Q, bone tired. Someone had moved a second bunk bed into the room.

Levine was at the desk in bulky white sweats, emblazoned with black letters: MEN ARE NOT POND SCUM. POND SCUM IS A HIGHER LIFE-FORM. She bit from a candy orange slice, looking at me.

I was as happy to see her as a canker sore. I thought, at first, it was because I couldn't belch, spit or walk about with equipment uncovered. I realized, with instant nausea, the truth: here, at the DMZ, where someone had taken down Jimmy the Bee, Captain No First Name Levine could get blown away.

"Hello, Kan."

"Hello, Levine."

She offered candy. I declined. Magrip, fully dressed, snored like a busted lawn mower on the unmade cot, hands crusted in dried blood.

I started making the other lower cot. She stood. I wondered if she was okay after the riot. She'd tell me. I wondered where she was going to sleep. She'd tell me that, too.

"No quarters for women," she said. "May I crash here?"

I sat heavily on the cot. I knew Tongducheon didn't have a Ramada; I hadn't foreseen that nothing could be made available.

Without quarters, she'd be tuna in a shark pool.

"Yeah."

"There's a warm and toasty welcome." Magrip's snoring rattled the bad paint.

I coughed. "Which bunk do you want?"

"In a lower one, I could hang a curtain and change behind it."

I nodded and started making the upper bunk. "Take one of us when you use the latrine." I folded a hospital sheet corner. "Levine. Why'd Carlos send you?"

"What do you mean, exactly?"

"We're supposed to be covert and you show up like Goldie Hawn at Fleet Week. You got something worth the attention."

"I speak Korean and know computers." She took a breath, speaking to herself. "I *will* be nice." She looked up and took another bite. "Captain Kan, my skill is the ability to endure men. In real short bursts." She brushed sugar from her fingers. "You should know: dogs are smarter and more loyal."

"Ha ha," I said. Cara's thoughts about me, now. She sensed blood in my laugh, and liked it, her eyes bright.

"Levine, claims looks sour. I want a full historical claims printout from Eighth Army in Seoul. Can do?"

"Roger that." She crossed her arms. "Three things: I

don't lie. I don't plea-bargain. The third is classified. Colonel Murray directed me not to reveal the skill. He did not tell me to conceal its existence."

The mission was undulating like rope from a sunken ship. I liked tight knots. "I don't like playing twenty questions. Give me an idea of what you're talking about."

She smiled. "I'd have to kill you."

Against my will, I smiled back.

"Kan, can you sleep with me here?"

I rubbed my chin. "That's classified; if I told you, I'd have to kill *you*." I looked at her flatly. She laughed with great honks, making Magrip moan and making me grin.

"Levine, sleep's overrated and we stand guard. I don't want Willoughby coming in here any more than you do."

She shuddered. "Willoughby! God forbid! Kan, I asked not because I'm attractive or anything. It's because I'm a woman and you're men and you have control problems. Your reproductive impulse puts male rabbits to shame."

Magrip said something that sounded like "Gnorffph?"

"What's our plan?" She stretched, then rolled up her sleeve to look at the time. It didn't matter. We were in Asia, and all we would do is work against Eastern odds until the job was done.

"We presume the Wizard knows we're after him, so shields up. Someone's been following me." I took the automatic from the nylon bag and slid the magazine home, racked a round, safetied it, and slipped it into my belt. "I'll take first watch, to two. You got two to three. Best time for the Wizard to do us is from three to five. That's Magrip's. Wake him easy."

Levine's look: anticipation, excitement, anxiety.

"Tomorrow, study the trash I got from the Wizard's workshop." I pointed at it. "Magrip'll check out the vehicles on the gate log that could've taken Jimmy out of Casey."

"Roger that," she said.

"We got a ROK Army driver, a KATUSA—Korean augmentee to the U.S. Army—named Corporal Oh-shik Min. Kamikaze driver. Something about him. . . . Anyway, I'll ask him to wire a phone so you can call in your computer run. Then I see the Wizard."

"And follow the yellow brick road. For a heart, brain, courage, or ruby shoes for a trip back to Kansas?"

"I get Jimmy or the Wizard goes to jail." I left, toothbrush loaded, Browning in belt, knife in boot, with thermals, field jacket and an old gym towel.

I turned out the hall light. I brushed my teeth and pulled glass from my hands and my head. The towel around my neck, I put on the winter forage field cap and stepped outside. I moved from the building and walked the Q perimeter, shivering in the wind, listening, all my antennae up.

Nothing but frostbite and a hollow, absorbent silence. I walked a wider perimeter. Something moved and I sprinted to a low hill, the automatic out and safety off. . . . No one. Medium-sized boot prints in the snow.

I had left Levine.

I raced back, banging doors. Levine was breathing softly behind a makeshift curtain. I turned off the ceiling light and sat in a bad chair, the Browning on my lap, my muscles relaxing, my heart still slugging. I felt every blow I had taken and given in the Vegas, my back aching from the brawl and the poultry odyssey.

Cara would have called both my Presidio SJA, Jonas Brent, and Walter Reed Army Hospital, where I would be declared unavailable. Under a flashlight, I wrote poetry to her, the crossouts louder than the composing. I changed into sweats. At two, I awoke Levine, gave her the gun and flashlight. She was tired, emotionally vulnerable in the cot and slowly alert.

I lay down and closed my eyes. There was no sleep for me. I thought of Cara's darkened bedroom.

I had imagined it as a room unlike any other, a kind pastel, rich with flora, a sumptuous bed, a table with fruits and wines. A space of doves and hushed beauty.

I had carried her easily to the bed, one hand near her breast, holding her legs. Her eyes were the colors of my heart, and I lifted her beautiful face close to mine. Say yes.

"Yes," she said. The heat in her eyes flowed into me, a balm. Our lips met and I moaned with the opulence, the strength and draw of her mouth, full of wings and songs as it opened for me. The kiss was without measure, free of margins. The loveliness of her, breathing as if we had escaped death and stepped into the first mist of mythic paradise, a gentle dew already on our skin. I put her down and kissed her neck, finding a sweet place, and she helped me, twisting, "Yes. Oh yes. Oh Jackson, oh *caro, caro.*"

I kissed more, wanting more as I followed her hints, our fires licking at each other in a warming room. Her honeyed mouth, her reckless heat, her beauty, my need. She touched a switch and light came from small ceiling lamps, casting soft light on a table with oranges and nectarines, shining on her as if it were of the moon. I was in a place of which I had dreamed.

I wanted everything to move like an eastern sail in a summer breeze, wanted to remember all of it, to absorb this time into deepest memory, into the levels of recollection that embrace the scrolls of old emperors and the poetry of the Sung. In this way I loved her, undressed her, adored her, held her face, kissed her long, deep and knowingly, sensing the possibility of all. I touched, caressed and trembled. In her bed I marveled at the impossibilities of her beauty and I gazed at her face above the pillows, knowing I would always remember this, my soul in her heart, there, never to be retrieved. I kissed her as if life itself were in her mouth. "Now, *caro,*" she breathed.

Not yet. Let me pleasure you. It was not what she wanted, but she indulged me.

Later, she pulled me to her with words and movements, short and hissing. There was neither memory nor future, only the closeness, the oneness, the hot dance of circles and lines of spreading, urging, caressing, beckoning, rising, lifting, cradling, entering, retreating, all fury, love, heaven and languor.

Cara. How many times did I kiss her? The sands of Egypt. How close were we? Too close to ever leave. How much did I love her? I could not say. We kissed, our eyes open in nameless petitions, Cara guiding with her hands, crying as I licked and bit, my patience swept away in her currents, her shuddering sob more than I could bear as we soared and cried and coasted in sweet demise above salt waves, intimate, one, trembling, joined, her face wet with my tears.

"Never leave me," she had whispered. "Promise."

I had. In a play of whispers and admissions, I held her, caressed her face, her hair, her neck, squeezed her hands. She smelled of peaches and salt and was more delectable than the greatest foods of China. She wanted me to remain awake with her, to call her "Cara" with an Italian trill on the "r," to talk into each other's mouths until the sun replaced the moon. But I faded, sleeping dreamlessly as in youth, bathed in her scents while the river caressed the boat hull and the gaudy orange-berobed *gwei yu*, Mandarin fish, waited lazily at the bend of the river.

I awakened to find her gazing at me as she traced raised, finger-wide scars on my abdomen. The scars itched and were prone to sunburn.

She touched my ear, the scars on my back. "Baby, what happened to you?"

I smiled. "I was in a knife fight. Only the docs had knives."

"No, *caro*. Tell me."

The buzz of the rain forest, the click of carrion. I closed my eyes and held her, trying to make her reality greater than my past.

Every day I held her beautiful eyes. Time and outward duties began to fade as pieces of a puzzle assembled of their own accord. I owed, lived, thought only of her, my table of Confucian accountabilities of *gahng, lun, ganjin, guan shi* relational duties whisked away by her magic, with only hints of my ponderous and ancient past remembered.

I jerked as the girl's blood ran down my chin. I rubbed it away. Magrip moaned. I was in Korea.

I asked the girl to let me sleep and closed my eyes. She came to me instantly, running, arms open, black hair streaming in a warm wind. Help me, Ba, and I knew she had never left me.

I had learned this on the Japan Air Lines flight to Tokyo.

While I was in Mill Valley in Cara's peach-scented bedroom, the long-tressed girl of my nightmare had vacationed at the River Styx. Now she was back, tanned, rested and ready to die a thousand deaths in my mouth, leaving spores of sour ruin everywhere. I closed my eyes.

"Wake up," said Levine, shaking me. "Bad dream."

I sat up. Levine was in the pond scum sweatshirt. She was saying that her grandpa was a confectioner's son and grandma a lawyer's daughter. They had come alone as small children to Ellis Island from Munich, a year after Hitler took power, never to see their families again.

Levine's mother was an Arthur Murray dance instructor who married her best student. Wanting sons, they had five girls who, between them, performed fifty years of ballet and tap. Levine, the firstborn, had supplemented pliés with track.

Mr. Levine was a diligent, loyal, rather comical man who hated music, loved fabulously corny jokes and worked on the Cracker Jack assembly line, giving his daughters a yen for sweets. Once, he had survived a Niagara Falls barrel dive to win a bet.

Levine had loved men until she discovered the distance between them and Dad, an empirical undertaking with a fairly large *n*. "Bored to sleep yet?" she asked.

"After that story, I'll probably never sleep again."

"You *already* weren't sleeping. Your girl must be some character. You always have nightmares about her?"

I wiped my face. "Not about her." I jumped off the bunk. Levine sat in a metal chair, legs extended.

"She have a brain?"

"Fearsomely endowed."

She nodded. "So. What's her thing that gets you."

I thought for a while. "She's fond of me."

"Well, that's honest. Her worst?"

"She likes men too much."

Magrip snorted. Levine thought. "Sounds like a woman who'd inspire a purely physical relationship."

I nodded. "That's a lot of it. She's a very good woman. I wonder if her goodness is the driver in the relationship. You know, if she'd be that good to anyone, and not just me."

"This what guys think about. Thurberisms?"

"I don't know. It's what I think when I can't sleep."

"Which is, like, always."

"Levine, give up sleep and you get more done."

"Give up sleep and you get nothing done. If you were capable of thinking, what would you look for in a woman?"

"What do you look for in a man?"

"Pshaw. I don't. They don't have it."

"I know I'm going to regret this. What's 'it'?"

"Intelligence, humor, moral principles, loyalty. Caring, compassion, understanding, sensitivity, generosity, thoughtfulness. Kindness. Tenderness. Mercy. Faith. Insight."

I nodded. "Doesn't sound like a man."

She looked at me. Lacking insight, I couldn't read the expression. But she looked like a woman who wouldn't shrink from rolling over Niagara Falls in a barrel.

11

Dr. Death

Wednesday, January 16

Levine roused Magrip. He catapulted out of the bunk, knees bent, arms out, eyes searching wildly. "What the fuck?"

"You're at Casey. It's three. You got the watch."

I got up. "I'm going to work out in the CG's gym."

"Is that safe?" asked Levine. Frowning: "Don't do it. In fact, I insist you don't. It's so unsmart, it's moronic."

It didn't matter. The girl was back and I was going. The night was black and impenetrable. I stood, listening. Nothing. I stretched, my lungs adjusting, my blood scurrying for cover in the shock of acute windchill. I quietly jogged and wind-sprinted under a flat, ebony, starless sky to HQ. The Inmingun were to my front. I hoped the Wizard's agents were asleep.

I had lifted weights at the Academy, but had begun the sport as a boy, helping the Wushan *ku-li* trackers pull our junk upriver at Three Gorges. My muscles ached for activity.

Thick winter ground fog rose from the floor of the camp. Hints of the yellow halogen lights of the HQ shed structure.

The sentry was a young private who looked like a

Malibu surfer. He had a riot gun on his desk. I coughed; he jumped. I gave him ID and the Richelieu letter.

He read it slowly, then nodded. "Good to go, sir. You're in."

It was 0320, two hours before dawn, and the bomb-shelter tunnel rang with the clang of heavy iron. The tunnel descended and turned to a flight of stairs. I went down, stretching.

"Go, Dr. Death!" came a high voice. Then a chorus. "Ironman! Do it! Do it, Doc! Strong!" "Push!" "Go, 'Shroom!"

Two men spotted a third on the bench. He was cheating, arching off the bench with ten 45-pound plates. With the bar, he was benching four-ninety-five. Men in sweats and tank tops paused with weights to urge the lifter to bang the bar.

Six steroidal professional-looking weight lifters with old, wide, sweat-blackened weight belts, finger-cropped gloves, yellow headbands and wartime Mohawks. They had the look of years of popping sinews in Uncle Sam's funky, smelly, unventilated, steam-piped weight rooms.

Something else. They weren't acquaintances; they were a squad and knew each other down to individual body odor.

A noise behind me. My stomach fell with a sound from the land of the dead: a Remington 870 boonie-point-man pump gun racking a round into its chamber, ready to take my head off. There were seven of them.

Weights and bars dropped from one corner of the room to another, making the floor shake and my good ear whine.

Six men moved fast, creating spaces, and there was a small, simultaneous click of selectors coming off safety, and two had 9mm Uzis pointing at me while a third Uzi-bearer sprinted up the stairs I had descended. With Shotgun Man downstairs, topside was uncovered.

I saw a camo tarp covering lumpy gear on the far wall.

It was six to one with a seventh upstairs, one dumb Chinese immigrant facing several methods of quick death.

The Randall knife in my boot was lonely. Behind me, on the stairs, a Hispanic in sweats and tennis shoes looked like the San Francisco Public Library with shoulders. He held the gun muzzle at my head, and would cap me for a twitch or a bad thought.

"Move." I stepped forward as he cautiously circled me, the muzzle steady, his intent as lethal as the Uzi men's. He knew I was American and didn't care.

"My fault, Death," said the Shotgun Man. "Went to the latrine to bleed my lizard and that slick rookie sentry passed him. I figure this asshole knew my routine, cuz I was gone thirty seconds."

A massive man, black and painstakingly muscled, pointed a heavy, tree-trunk arm. "Who *are* you, man?"

I smiled. "I'm Albert Schweitzer. Can I work out here?"

"I know the dude." The bruiser from the Vegas honky-tonk brawl, the black man with the mustache and the shoulders and the red CG dot on his ID card, the man with no name who said he hadn't been there. "Dude's an officer. Karate man. Check?"

"Nice to see you. Captain Kan, IG. Maybe your friend can move the muzzle from my ear. Doesn't take loud noises well."

"No, sir," said the gunner. "Not til Doc Death says so."

The bench presser moved. He was a behemoth, a spectacularly built Samoan, six-four, two-sixty, slightly balding, with tired eyes that drooped at the corners, a square face, and the demeanor and knowing musculature of an old Silesian coal miner.

"Captain Christopher Sapolu," he said in a voice that came from the cavern of a mighty chest with a soft island beat. His great arms were swollen from the insult of muscle-bombing reps with enormous weights, the veins like the flooded rivers of inner China.

"Jackson Kan."

"Jackson Kan, wassamattayou, *pake*? You can't be work out here. Is *kapu*, off limits." Fast island pidgin. *Pake*—Chinese. "Now, brah, I gonna pat you down." Uzis moved to allow the frisk.

"I don't think so. Who are you?"

"Hey, fool. Gonna do it, total out. Dead or alive."

"In that case, I'd be honored."

He took knife, ID and papers. He read them. "Clear," he said.

Shotgun Man lifted the pump gun and ran up the stairs, shouting, "Canizales on trail!" An Uzi man moved to the door, replacing the pump gunner, moving smoothly, a massive iceberg on roller skates. The third Uzi man came down the stairs.

"Barton," said Sapolu to the man from the Vegas, "you flash DTOC"—Division Tactical Operations Center— "we got a unknown in our AO"—area of operation. "I want the story on this Chinese man five minutes ago." He held out my papers. "Run top speed limit, man."

Barton took my papers and ID and sprinted up the stairs, shouting, "Barton on trail!"

All I had wanted to do was bang some iron. Instead, I had caused a sensitive tactical unit to sound an infiltrator alert.

"Cool," said Sapolu, feeling the knife's edge.

"Thank you. That mean I can work out?"

"You mostly mental, Captain," said Sapolu. "Dis our business. We the Army weight-lifting team, dig?" His eyeballs bulged. "We tight. I push Samoan *matai*— family system—on dese boys. Tha's why you think we funny. But you *pake*, you unnerstan'. I die for my boys."

The weight-lifting team wouldn't be in Korea, toting Uzis. Sapolu wanted me to believe, but if they were who he said, I was the Armenian Easter Bunny. I looked at him askance.

"Hey. What you think don't matta. Now you go topside." Three men moved as one. I wasn't sure what would happen next.

"I think you're making a mistake."

"Uh-uh," said Sapolu. "No think, brah. No ask, neez know nothin'. I see you big man on campus, plenty *akamai*. Down here, you bug crap. Now peel out." He moved his head. I went up. He followed.

We waited in the hall. Barton returned from the HQ com center and whispered a while to Dr. Death. Death whispered to me.

"Okay, cool, brah, you give generals hard-ons. You a kahuna used to own the road. Captain, we classified. You sneeze funny, I shackle and gag your IG ass forever. Believe me, man, I got authority to disappear people who stick nose in our locker.

"You hear 'bout GIs get Vietnam black-ball VD, no go home? Man, you fuck with us, you get ROK black-ball VD profile, finest kind, go like permanent forever-time, Pigum-do Island, Yellow Sea."

His unit was worth a lot of protection, shrouded by a covering myth of incurable genital rots.

"Listen to me now, *pake*. You got no business with us. You tripped on us cuz I slacked. My fault, man, not yours. But Kan, you give word you stay off our road. You *never* come back. You tell *no one* what you see. I serious as a heart attack." His eyes worked into mine, hot, motivated, prosecutor-style.

"Sapolu, we lost an IG somewhere in Casey. That's why I'm here. You disappear one of our guys?"

He shook his head. "Man, sorry about that, but negative. Now is your call. What you gonna do, brah? Be smart today, or stupid?"

"I always vote for smart." Sometimes, I get stupid anyway.

He returned my papers and knife.

"One question. What do you know of the Wizard?"

Sapolu pursed his lips, then relented. "He our lawyer. Do us out of trouble." He looked at Barton. "You know. Like when *poho*, fool, trip on Doctor's orders, bust my law, and go poke squid on some illegal pussy in the Ville."

Barton came stiffly to attention, eyes a thousand meters away. "Ah got no excuses. Ah was a bad troop and Ah let you down but Ah paid mah price and learned my lesson good and there ain't no call to be poundin' my black ass big-time in front of this IG. Sir."

"I was happy," I said, "that Mr. Barton was there last night."

"Yeah, yeah. Aloha, Captain Kan. You know too much. No more stinking questions. Peel out, man."

I nodded and left, then stopped.

Barton and Sapolu separated from each other, taking slow and steady breaths, ready.

"You guys know of a good gym around here?"

12

Wizard Q

Dawn. We stood in the wind as the companies of the Second Infantry ran three reveille miles in the dark. No spirited singing of Jodies, chants to keep step, just the steady trudge of thirty thousand boots pounding sludge, the wheeze of lungs passing ice. Men constantly slipped and fell.

Korea, where the conditioning could kill you if the

enemy didn't. My Presidio vacation was over; I was back in the Army. I did push-ups, sit-ups, *wu-shu* kicks, blocks and punches. The men below were tired from patrols and booze, sullen and hung over in the frozen tundra. I went down to run with them. Magrip came with me.

Magrip and I passed running companies at a seven-minute-mile pace. Levine passed us in a long wind sprint. We tried, but there was no way we were going to stay with her. When we saw the Q, we slowed to a fast walk. She could not be seen.

"Good runner," I gasped, leaning over, hands on knees.

"No shit, Sherlock," huffed Magrip, exhaling clouds. "And she's still a woman." He took deep breaths. "You're such an idiot—you were gonna send *me* back. When is *she* outa here?"

"She's not. Murray sent her for some covert skill."

"Yeah. *Real* covert. Kan, she's trouble and she's gonna get us killed worrying about her." He spat. "I can see good grades aren't everything. You're using a Kotex to think."

"I like that about you, Magrip. When you talk, it's poetry."

A ring of mountains surrounded us. I had inspired the troops and collected the Wizard's garbage. Time to do his quarters.

Thirty minutes later, I entered Wizard Q as an invisible janitor with a broom and utility can. No windows, a low ceiling, double doors leading to the main area, walls earth-tone browns and orange, like current decor in the States. Central heating. An armed sergeant named Smith faced me behind a table. I got his coffee. Wizard Q not only housed the SJA; it served as a functioning office.

"Good, slopehead," he said loudly, so I could understand.

I went through the doors. A marbled girl poured water

from her skirt in a fountain. A conference room and two offices in basic white, a somber Christ on a wall.

Colonel Frederick LeBlanc was in the center office, reading a large gold-leafed Bible while Chopin played from a Matsui sound system. His desk was fastidiously clean, his reading focused, the music peaceful, as if this were the garden chapel behind Grace Cathedral on Nob Hill instead of a shack in Tongducheon, Kyonggi-do Province, looking over the fence at Stalinist North Korea. He saw me without having seen a person.

I swept away. LeBlanc looked as good as Major Nagol looked bad, as if LeBlanc's sins had been visited on his deputy.

Alcoholics Anonymous documents sat on the table like chess pieces. A door led to a garden of stunted pines. Something protruded. I stepped out and cleared snow.

SGM PATRICK TREATY MCCRAIL U.S. ARMY
BE ALL THAT YOU CAN BE
1927–1966 [Buried in Arlington]

The lettering had baked off in seven Korean summers.

I went back in. Stairs led to an austere bedroom and private bathroom equipped with modish brown sinks. No sign of Jimmy; the Wizard was dumb enough to kidnap and assault IGs, but not dumb enough to store a hostage in his own Q. A Mossberg shotgun in a rack over the bed. Downstairs, I entered his office, sweeping.

The colonel was composed and compact. In the warmth of his Q, he wore short-sleeved, ribbonless summer khakis, a bold fashion statement in Manchu climes. His once wide-screen handsomeness had been compromised by a fine burst of broken blood vessels lacing nose and cheeks. In Army parlance, he had seen the elephant without losing his nuts in the admission price. He drank from a green porcelain soup bowl. It smelled like beef broth.

Above him was a map of Korea, the pink DMZ the highlight. I swept; behind his heavy door was another map, covered by both an acetate tactical overlay transparency and a roll-down Korean silk decorative sash. I wanted to see the map.

I went behind his desk for the waste can and jerked, my heart swelling, engorging my throat without taking a beat.

On the floor was the girl I had killed, her long hair below her shoulders, the pretty face clean and healthy; a cold sweat filled my eyes, armpits, my feet and hands. She looked at me without recognition. I was sputtering screams and crabbing hands and I shut my eyes, a child before the night monster, chest collapsing in the agonized implosion of a sick heart. Jesus. I was hallucinating in full daylight, in front of the enemy.

I opened my eyes: a Korean girl, kneeling on the floor. She looked at LeBlanc as she watched me through the corners of startled eyes, shivering, as if she had felt all my fear.

Hands shaking, I emptied the garbage can. God, she looked like the girl! My heart slugged, its chambers, its tissues afire, wet cold sweat all over me.

The colonel snapped his fingers. The girl jerked and stood, removed the bowl, replaced it with a platter of rice, vegetables and beef, and bowed, backing away, her face down, and knelt. She looked about fourteen and wore a red silk robe, old, brown corduroys and white socks, waiting with the tea.

The intercom rang. The colonel hit the speaker. "Yes."

"Sir, Major Nagol's here. With CID agents Haley and Holt." Criminal Investigation Division: Army detectives.

A pause. "Smith, send them in." His voice did not hark back to the peaks and valleys of youth; with four simple words, it offered calm harbor to those in human conflict. His voice was grandfatherly, congenial and kind, projecting in the middle registers, given to the quiet reading of soothing stories to small children clutching stuffed animals, blankets pulled to their chins.

Nagol might recognize me from our chat at the CG's mess. I scuttled into the vestibule, where I used paper towels to clean the base of the fountain.

Nagol walked with painful, angular fragility, one bone at a time, bearing his sins. No one noticed me. I saw the Wizard look up. his blue, purposeful eyes mystic, unreadable. "Please leave us." A voice with a halo. The CID men left.

Nagol said, "Colonel—"

"Be silent!" The Wizard's face was down, arms laid across the desk as if to keep it from rising. "That *you* would defame my trust, disgrace my office, and humiliate *me*—after *all I have done for you*—is unspeakable! Monstrous!" He stood, unable to look at Nagol, who trembled and swayed on the edge of collapse.

"Sir—"

"Not one word! Good Lord! I *asked* you if anything was irregular in claims and you *assured* me all was correct."

LeBlanc lifted a CID two-prong vertical file. "*This* says our claims are bogus, frauds, fabrications. And authored by *you* while our JAGCs had no idea what you were doing."

The Wizard trembled. "Do you have *any* idea what you've done?!" He threw the file at Nagol, and it exploded into a cascade of paper, knocking Nagol into a chair; his head bounced backwards, then forwards, into his hands, shoes covered in falling paper.

"Jeez—"

"Yes, Thomas. Pray! I gave you life and you chose larceny. You're a disgrace. And you still smoke cigarettes, inhaling nicotine, and you drink and whore with—with, with—whores."

Nagol's shoulders trembled. The Wizard sat heavily in his chair. I rubbed the fountain base.

The Wizard hit his buzzer and the CID agents returned to stand at attention in his office.

The soft, beguiling voice: "Put him in D Cell, excommunicado." Detention blocks. Colonel Frederick LeBlanc waved dismissively. The agents lifted Nagol and took him.

I put down the rag; the fountain base sparkled. At first, the Wizard had spoken like Grandpa Walton; but in hazing Nagol, he had used the voice of old Master Wong, our fighting junk passenger, whose anger seemed to grow rather than dissipate over the years. Master Wong's spiritual fuel was rage: rage at war, at the river, at the Japanese, the Communists, the Nationalists, the fishermen, their wives, and their small, unteachable sons who were his students.

Master Wong, the short, grizzled *wu-shu* teacher with iron hands. He had taught me the *wing-chun* way of the Chinese fist, the path of the Chinese foot, the power of the Chinese hip in hand-to-hand combat. In return, we took him between Changsha and the White Gorges, where he visited his second wife, a young Mohammedan woman with black teeth and a body composed of river-like curves.

"*Ma*—horse position—lower!" he would scream, hitting me into the correct stance with a blow that knocked out my spit. Punching him in drills was like hitting stone.

The Wizard had softly closed his door. A sheet of the CID report had wafted into the vestibule. I took the paper and folded it into a pocket, took my gear and glided to the door.

The intercom buzzer sounded.

"Smith, ask Captain Kan to join me. Bring coffee."

The sentry looked about. "Sir, ain't no captain here."

"Smith," said the disembodied voice, "Captain Kan is the big janitor with the broom. Ask him in."

13

LITTLE TIN HEROES

Colonel Frederick LeBlanc glanced up, the gaze holding me, the stern principal with the delinquent. His eyes were a stellar blue, the left larger, the right brighter, each feature unique in angle, the sum forming a face more compelling than the one in the OMPF personnel file photo.

It was in the eyes: the burden of lesser men and the comfort of their shortcomings. His face was translucent, androgynous, the long nose not male but universal, the aspect genderless, textured by ambiguous sphinxes and hardened sandstone, the mouth a weapon, the hair white and patrician. He smiled and he was BaBa, the kind father. The cast of his gaze seemed more Asian than Western; his face was free of European precipices and hard Alpine turns.

He had looks not to envy but to admire. His gaze sought quiet prisoners, all who might be uncertain in an alienating world. He was a bodhisattva—serene, transcendent, sexless, not of matter and its pains, a rock in a quiet stream described by music of gentle waters. West Point was not a zen place, and here, on the welcome mat to the DMZ, he had made a bandit's stand with the demeanor of a Gregorian monk.

All this was made clear in only moments. I sat. The sentry brought hot coffee. The girl who had come from my nightmare to kneel at the Wizard's feet was gone. Time to play the prescribed role.

"Sir, units from the Panama Canal to Berlin Garrison have had race problems. The Second Infantry hasn't. TIG wants to know why. I was to merge into Casey society and make my report. I'm sorry for entering your Q without more candor."

Colonel LeBlanc crossed his legs, his gaze neutral. "Captain Kan, everyone's looking for Buford, the missing IG. I have better ROK Army contacts than any American officer in the field, and I think it helps in this regard that I understand the Oriental mind."

I nodded affably.

He interlaced his fingers. "Captain, I dislike your type, sauntering in like little tin heroes. You are better fit for the Gestapo than the U.S. Army. You threaten liberties. It is hard not to take that personally." He gestured dismissively. "That is why I cooperate, giving you everything, so you will leave. So we can return to our work. Buford is not here."

A captain would now run for cover. "Sir, I'm just doing my job. You think I *want* to be chasing race relations over here in winter? I don't think so. I was ordered here. If you think your work is beyond the concerns of the IG, don't bust *my* chops. Pick up your phone and call Carlos Murray. Tell him, Colonel. Not me."

Colonel LeBlanc sighed. "All right, but know this: had your Captain Buford come to me, I would have refused him nothing. An IG officer masquerading as a janitor is offensive. To snoop and pry as if my men were the enemy . . ." He scratched his scalp. "Lord knows we have problems here. This is the moon, and lunacy even affects good officers, like Thomas Nagol."

Nagol's castigation had been good theater. For me. Carlos had said of the Wizard, "The man does not love God."

Light reflected from the Wizard's golden-edged Bible.

I was better at prosecution than at acting. Now, for both.

"You know, an IG who's disappeared would be dead center in the IG mission statement. Let me ask you some questions about that, sir."

A pause. "By all means." A flourish of a manicured hand.

"Why have you extended here for eight hardship tours?"

He rubbed a thumb against an index finger. "It's a matter of record. I failed to impress my superiors stateside."

"How do you encourage JAGCs to extend with you?"

"They didn't do very well over there either. Here, they do."

"Why is that?"

He smiled. "I give them God." He interlaced his fingers.

"What, sir, are you going to do about claims?"

"Personally prosecute the guilty for max sentences."

Wrong. He would have to recuse his office, since Nagol was in his command. "What, sir, is on the map, behind your door?"

Interlocked fingers tightened. "None of your business."

"Is that what Jimmy Buford asked you?"

"I dislike the insinuation."

"Sorry. I asked, sir, is that what Jimmy Buford asked?"

"No."

"Who knows more about American criminal law here than you?"

He hesitated, licking his upper lip. "Frankly, no one."

I studied his eyes. "What's your best guess to explain Captain Buford's disappearance?"

His eyes glittered. "Whores and lust, Captain. There are more comfort girls, business girls, harlots, prostitutes and fallen women in this community than there are mountains in Korea. They cluster here and take down our troops. You asked; I will tell you. Captain Buford visited a honky-tonk bar and—"

"Was jumped by Specialist Muldoon's five idiots and Captain Willoughby?"

He took a breath. "Your noble friend fell victim to a mugging."

I opened my notepad. "Batteries on ROK civilian females by U.S. troops, 1973: one thousand two hundred twelve." I looked up; no argument with the civil character of the new volunteer, non-draft Army.

"Batteries *on* GIs by ROKs, same period: four. Number of those determined to be self-defense: four." I looked at him with hope for an explanation.

He checked a nail. "Statistics lie."

"Fine. Let's forget our highly anal worldwide crime stat work, the data upon which we allocate our JAGCs. How'd you come up with the mugging theory?"

"My experience, which you cannot touch."

"List your contacts in the search for Captain Buford."

He did. I noted them. A lot of ROK Army commanders.

"Sir, we deal in facts. Truth-telling. BS-removal." I scratched my head. "So tell me. Why are you so incredibly unbelievable?"

He leaned back. "That is so simple, even you can grasp it. Captain, you have no skills to assess others, much less to judge *me*." He crinkled his eyes. "So spare me your loyal-bulldog prosecutor routine. I must tell you. I am offended that One Leg Murray sent me a captain." He glanced around. "Yet, I don't want you feeling dejected. Not yet." He looked at me. "I have been a terrible host. What do you say? Before you go, how about cleaning under my desk?"

The two houseboys, men in their fifties, washed fatigues in the shower of the Ice Palace latrine and solemnly watched me change from Korean janitor to American officer. I unfolded the sheet of paper from the Wizard's floor. Simple correspondence paper, not a Form DD-320 CID sheet.

The M6A22 priming adapter is used to secure the blasting cap in a threaded fuze well. It is used with both electric and nonelectric blasting caps in detonating assemblies (Figure 1001-1) against a wide variety of targets. The M09 blasting cap holder is a metal clip used to attach and hold a blasting cap to sheet explosives. It is used with the MB11 sheet demolition charges or the M681 roll demolition charge and is shipped as a separate item of demolition support issue. Remember to use pressure-sensitive adhesive tape to join charges to dry, clean wood, steel or concrete, in 1/2 inch wide and 72 yard-long rolls. . . .

The file Colonel LeBlanc had thrown at Nagol was not a CID report. It was a sapper's demolitions tech manual—a controlled item with a strict distribution restriction—something that should never be floating around a lawyer's office.

It told people how to blow things up.

14

BETTER THAN MOST WAKING MEN

Eight A.M. Min and a ROK Army wireman had rebuilt the broken window and had given us an AUTOVON phone line into the U.S. military worldwide net. I thanked them. They stared at Levine.

"Secure now, *dae-wi*," said Min. He showed me a box full of muddy wires. "Micro-phonee in wall. To Wirra-bee room Q." We had been bugged. Min pointed. Willoughby knew IGs were after Buford, the Wizard and claims—and not racial equities.

I added unauthorized wiretap to Willoughby's conspiracy to commit multiple aggravated battery and interference.

"*Dae-wi*, Wirra-bee very mos' bad to other man, numbah-ten bad to Korean man. What 'Merican slang say him?"

"Asshole," I said.

"Ah ha. And for bad man, lie to people?"

"Cheat. Swindler. Fraud. Four-flusher." I had to explain that. Min repeated them. I couldn't find any other words. "Liar, liar, pants on fire—cheater, cheater, pumpkin eater."

Min repeated the words. GIs despised him as a lowly, groveling gook. I tried to like him, but I hated his driving.

"Corporal, stay with Captain Levine. Someone's following us." He nodded. I wondered if Min could help in an emergency.

"Figure it's one of the Wizard's boys?" she asked.

I said I didn't know. I described him. "Call Yongsan."

I left the sidearm with her. Sobered, she picked up the receiver. She had to yell into it, bellowing for Eighth Army.

The visit to Wizard Q had taken half an hour. Magrip had already checked the MP gate. Now he and I rode the unheated, springs-busted Casey bus in search of Jimmy. We checked units, barracks, aid stations, VD clinic, alcohol and drug abuse.

Casey was the forsaken, end-of-the-world, ramshackle home of our lost division, housing heavily armed, displaced fugitives from the world's richest cities and poorest farms. These underschooled, low-promise men had slid down the social totem pole to pit bottom.

Our Foreign Legion. Dropouts, drunks, dopers, delinquents, tattoo targets, alkies, riflemen, cannoneers and tankers pulling twelve-hour days. We saw tired NCOs we knew from prior assignments. I passed out Juicy Fruit, Doublemint, Marlboros, Camels, Luckies, Parliaments and Winstons to the two subsocieties: old hands who had been in Korea for years; and the majority, who counted days to get out of the Year in Hell. Many of the latter had bad teeth, lousy haircuts, lousier tattoos and hints of rickets. It was the modern Army in its post-Vietnam depression.

Most of the Eleven Bravo 11Bs—riflemen—were black. Most tank drivers were white. We saw three Korean hulk 76Ys—supply clerks—neckless, steroidal beasts averaging two hundred pounds, with maroon facial discolorations and stainless-steel dental work. They spoke English as if they had acquired it from matchbook covers. Most of the supply clerks were Koreans of more natural size. Many cooks were Hispanic. Some of the general population had larcenous hearts. Everyone was cold.

The driver of the jeep that had been following us for an hour was Asian. It was nearly noon. "Pincer him," I said. "You get behind. I'll force from the front."

We were at POL, the petroleum, oil and lubricants depot. "Screw it." Magrip yelled at the driver, forced open the door and got off the moving bus running. I punched out the emergency window on the bus driver's side and jumped to the ground, sprinting after Magrip in the direction of the jeep.

The jeep driver's mouth gaped as he skidded to a stop. Behind him, a platoon of M60A1 main battle tanks roared out of the petrol shop in single file, heavy with full fuel cells. The five tanks blocked the jeep's escape to the rear. We had him.

The noon base siren sounded. The jeep banged into reverse, weaving back at the second tank. The tank driver yelled soundlessly, then blew his air horn. The jeep kept coming at him and the tanker hit his brakes, the mammoth sixty tons of steel lurching and bouncing to a stop, its tracks chewing asphalt. The jeep scraped the tank, ripping off its own mirror and paint, narrowly avoiding a dramatic pancaking as the three trail tanks braked, bobbing like boats on an angry sea. The tank engines bellowed like ancient thunder lizards, blowing black diesel clouds. Magrip and I ran through the exhaust, around clanking tank treads and drawing more air horn blasts.

We came out of the smoke and the jeep was gone.

"See him?" snarled Magrip.

"Same guy. Korean. See the bumper stencils? Get any detail on the guy? You were closer."

"Jesus, they all look alike." He squeezed his grenade.

"Maybe Jimmy went down like this." I blew out air. "Now he'll back off. Gotta trap him next time. Encircle him. . . ."

"Kan, you squirrelly sonofabitch, you're talking to yourself."

"That happens to people who don't have anyone to talk to."

Magrip said to get off the bus. It was the mess hall for Second Battalion, First of the Thirty-eighth, Rock of the Marne.

"My unit after Nam." He didn't sound happy. I realized he had spent more of his adult life in Asia than I had.

If Levine were with us, she would incite a Stone Age riot over something more basic than creamed chipped beef over toast. She wasn't with us.

"Good chow here?" I asked. A Chinese question.

"It's dogshit. I'll treat." The mess hall was a factory of working mouths. It was too cold to talk. The ration clerk had seen sergeant's stripes four or five times and was now a private. "Room, atten-HUT!" he bellowed. "It's Butt Kicker Magrip!"

Old forks fell on cheap trays bearing the worst food in the U.S. Army as sixteen hundred wet, mildewing combat boots hit the wood floor. Magrip, Medal of Honor winner, had come home. A battalion of tired, grimy, half-frozen American riflemen saluted one of their own.

He smartly returned their salute. "NOW SIDDOWN!" he roared. He hated notoriety. He poked the food as if it might return the favor of an unwelcome bite. The food was ghastly but very hot.

Young troopers with scalp buzz cuts, cold sores and fingers at the edge of frostbite came to our table to salute and shake his hand, looking at a famous killer with affection and envy. Magrip eyeballed them and wished them well.

A short, broad-shouldered, square-faced, heavily scarred, ebony-black top sergeant named Reynolds was next. He looked down at Magrip. Magrip blinked and then stood.

"How goes it?" asked Top. He pointed to his own heart.

Magrip shrugged. "Shit. Hack, how the hell's yours?"

"Mighty fine, seeing you so squared away. Captain Luke, you're a jolt for sore eyes." He opened his arms and Magrip embraced him. They didn't hit each other's backs. They held on, heads down and eyes closed by a powerful clenching of brows, knuckles popping from the grip, chasing away demons.

"Hack," he whispered. "I got married."

"Hey, hey, Captain. Hey, hey."

We changed in the Q latrine. Having dry socks was like visiting Paris in spring. In the room, Magrip ignored Levine, who winced at the slimy beef ragout we had brought her in a pot. She offered it to Min. He looked at it with bared teeth.

"*Aniyo*, no, please, all for you," he said gallantly.

I stretched my bad back. "Trail Man risked killing himself to get away. He's dangerous."

"No shit," said Magrip. "He's a Korean in a jeep."

"Sorry, Min," I said. "Magrip is uncivilized. Uncouth."

Min nodded proudly. "*Neh*, he ass-hole, *dae-wi*."

Magrip laughed, probed his ear and studied his finger. "Min," he said, "you're okay. I checked gate traffic. One vehicle could've taken Buford out without a record: a ROK prison truck filled with GI inmates. MPs never check because it's an MP job to fill the truck. I tried to talk to the ROKs, but no speakee English. This should be Levine's crap detail." Briefly, he looked at her. Then he picked up a sock.

"The Wizard's trash," she said, "shows a lot of tobacco spit and five hundred claim payouts a month. Way over."

Magrip used the sock to clean his inter-toe spaces.

"That's unbelievably endearing," she said. "Kan?"

I described Wizard Q, the AA workbooks, the memorial to a SGM Patrick McCrail, the girl who fed LeBlanc from her knees, the concealed map with overlay behind the door, the DMZ map on the wall. I described the theatricality of Nagol's chastisement, the Wizard's knowledge of my janitorial disguise, his recitation of good faith, his theory that Jimmy had been jumped by Koreans. His invitation to clean his floor.

Magrip shook his head. "Kan, we play cute here, we get fucked. Screw your indirect method. Time to kick butt."

"You believe Nagol's arrest?" asked Levine.

"No." I told them about the bogus CID report, and that two CID agents seemed to work more for the Wizard than for the provost.

Levine nodded. "That's bad news. Why do you care about a map? And when do I interview Nagol at D Cell?"

"Lawyers," I said, "don't have tactical maps. And his is covered." I shook my head. "And I don't want you at D Cell."

Levine's eyes burned. Then her jaw flexed.

"Now I know why he's called the Wizard," said Magrip. "He gets the cellar of the Corps to re-up in Korea. And makes IGs run around in circles."

Levine snapped her fingers. "Magrip, you're right. He recruits friends of the grape here, to this cesspool. Cleans them with AA and old-time religion, max ratings and medals. He redeems them."

"Let's move on," I said. "Give me options."

"I punch Willoughby until he says where Buford is." Magrip.

"Macho Medal of Honor babble," said Levine. The heater whined down and Magrip booted it across the room. "Yeah, screw around like ruptured ducks. Give 'em the initiative."

"Magrip, we make like sitting ducks until they commit. Then I'll unleash you, throw the slab of meat and point."

Magrip leaped up. "You *asshole!* We did that in Nam! *Dammit!* There're only three principles of war. They already got initiative and mass. We can't give up surprise."

"We do a legal game plan to get Jimmy. The mission," I said slowly, "is to recover Buford alive. If we blow away every kidnapper in Asia, we will have failed if we do not restore James Buford to his family. There is no need to kill. Is that clear?"

Magrip said nothing, falling onto the complaining cot.

Levine studied me, thinking.

"Levine," I said, "is your Korean good enough for talking to ROK wardens about that GI prison truck that went out the gate?"

"Neh, honcho dae-wi," she said. "Magrip, you have any ROK phone numbers for me to follow up on?"

Magrip didn't answer. She leaned over him. "He's asleep."

Magrip snored in a leg-splayed sprawl, done in by a day of jet lag, bar fights, Arctic runs, short sleep, numbing cold, the angst of my tactics and the tension of Levine.

"My effect on men." She called post operator and was immediately placed on hold. "They collapse under my pressure."

"Let's be honest. You hit some of them with beer bottles."

Magrip snored as I opened his pocket and took his notepad. I read notes about flights, his MP interviews, convoy identifiers and ROK prison phone numbers, surrounded by meticulous notes. I found a long letter to Magrip's wife, Carole, written in classical, textbook cursive, almost female in its precision.

"So, Levine, you're hard on yourself."

"No, I'm pretty good to myself. Men are hard on me."

"You have a fondness for jerks?"

"Oh, like there's a choice?"

I smiled politely. I gave her the notepad with the ROK phone numbers. She hung up and began dialing.

Magrip lay in deep sleep. I envied his skills. The ice and snow outside radiated through the new window and sharpened the scent of fresh plywood. I had returned to Asia, older, sadder. Fatigue fell like a lead mantle. Levine was shouting in Korean. My eyes burned with fatigue. I closed them.

The room was green and the girl ran toward me. I tried to tell her to go back, but the muzzle came up. The rifle gave its small signature recoil as I emptied the magazine and she went down.

"Kamsamneeda," said Levine. Min giving her a box, bowing.

My legs spasmed. I shut my eyes, seeing dead flies marching across a white ceiling, my guts weak as if I had done murder. Levine touched my forehead. Snow was on the deck. I had a fever and Ma put cold cloths on my head as we headed for Dongting Lake and the shaman. I removed her hand and I cut it on the elephant grass. I awoke to Telemann's "Harlequinade." I thought it was in my head, but it was coming from a tape recorder near my wet pillow.

I was clammy. I sat up, head pounding. I looked at my watch. Three in the afternoon. I had been out almost three hours, dreaming of China, the boat, the girl. I looked at my hand and its scars. Magrip was still snoring, snuffling.

Levine put down the phone. "You need help," she said.

"I need a drink." I coughed, rummaging for a warm Diet Pepsi.

She stretched long legs. "You don't face your problems, they come after you. In your sleep or lack thereof. I'm old-fashioned; I think unconsciousness is the natural enemy of thought." A raised eyebrow. "To your credit, it's novel to hear a man cry. I like that, but I'm a voyeur. Never made a man cry, even when I've challenged one of your sacred stupidities. One of my *other* skills. But no points for doing it in your sleep."

I shook my head. Respecting inner problems only strengthened them.

"Don't feel bad. There are worse things than crying in front of a woman you're living with."

"I'm not living with you. It just looks that way."

She expelled air. "Don't flatter yourself. Although you do have jerk potential. Obviously, I love that." Musing. "What would Mom think? What a shame you're not a nice Jewish boy."

"Levine, we're Warsaw Jews. I follow the law, honor seder, eat kosher and weep for Jerusalem. You hurt me deep."

She smiled. "I'll call Mom with the good news. Just now, you once again reenacted 'Hamlet Laments Polonius.' " She held up a hand. "It was good stuff, Gielgud and Olivier. But I worry about a team leader who's more hung up on his past than he is on mission. Your past is playing you like a harp."

"What counts is the job. I get it done."

"Yes, that's your rep, isn't it? Work like a jackass and get an MSM a year." A medal. "You're on the same minority-showcase laundry line with TV coverage where I'm flapping. I saw you on *CBS Morning News*, talking about drug dealers and mutineers.

"I heard you followed Murray into the field in Vietnam. Sort of thing I would have done. And now, you hate to kill. Crying's normal. You ought to do it right. Talk about her to the chaplain and cry your heart out like a woman."

Men in pain cried out guts. "I did that." For a moment, I couldn't remember the girl's face, and was filled with a terror not unlike the moment in which I realized I had shot her.

"I doubt it! Men don't cry—they ulcerate and get strokes and male rage and beat women. Fine, trip out on it."

"Back off. It's my problem."

She stood. "No." She crossed her arms, leaning on the bunk. "You made it my problem with those pitiful noises. I couldn't sleep. One night with you and you got me worrying."

"Not the most flattering thing to say to a man."

"I've said worse."

Magrip moaned. Levine looked at him. "Can't imagine him married to a conscious woman. I'm grateful he doesn't spit tobacco, but that's probably coming."

"He writes love letters to his wife. Good handwriting."

She raised an eyebrow. "What, in blood? Do you know you scratch your crotches and adjust your equipment like this was a locker room? And you've covered the floor with dirty socks, jock straps and boots?" Her voice was going up; she lowered it, speaking lower, the anger gone into husky, disciplined military grooves.

"But what really gives me a case of the ass is your keeping me in the background, with Magrip as my nanny. That girls-in-the-back bull is over, Jackson Kan. I'm a member of this team. I know the law, I'm competent, I'm better asleep than most men awake, I bust butt, and you don't want me at D Cell? You're Third World and you're holding *me* down with chauvinistic preferences? How does *that* sell on Self-Determination Street? Don't give me that look!"

"What look?"

Her eyes blazed at me. "That 'this hurts my ears' look! God! Men scream and troops bang out 'Yes sir, three bags full!' A woman yells and men cringe like they're getting circumcised, crying pathetically about 'women's libbers'! Listen to me—men who can't deal with women and feelings are crippled. And they make really lousy managers and shitty boyfriends and intolerable husbands and useless fathers and they are turning our world to shit!"

"Don't be shy. Tell me what you think."

She drove her hands deep into her pockets, pacing angrily. "Screw your dismissive humor. God, I hate it that men can't cope emotionally! Drunks, drugheads, bummed by emotion. This isn't war, where you point your guns and kill people. We get Buford back if we *think* better than the opposing party—and if we're *prepared.*"

She pointed a slender finger at me. "That's *not* going to happen if you go psycho on us."

Her voice was a drill in my head. I rubbed my face. "Butt Kicker has combat fatigue. Used his youth in Vietnam. No flex left. Small things grind him down.

Can't cure him—not here. We trained him to kill Asians. He's not going to get well with me as team leader. Humor him. If it goes south on us, we'll need him. And let's be fair. I'm not psycho. I'm an insomniac."

"I used to like men who don't sleep." She fluffed her hair and pulled a metal chair. The noise made Magrip spasm. "Kill 'em—kill 'em now!"—his voice a desperate wheeze of an ancient man, twisting with old agonies.

She licked her lower lip. "It must have been bad over there."

"He did two tours." I had been undone by ten seconds.

She took a deep breath and picked up her notes. "The ROK prison led to a Sergeant Major Patrick McCrail—"

"Wait. Levine, end this argument."

"Monsieur Doggie Breath, this was *not* an argument. Not even a spat." She appraised me. "Listen, someday I'll show you an *argument*, and then there will be no doubt in your military mind."

I put up my hands. "I'll pass."

"The fragility of men."

"Ouch." The Q was a sty, but there were three of us, it was winter and my stuff was in discrete piles. It wasn't Monaco, but we were hostile, fragile, inexpressive, emotionally crippled males with one dresser, filled with *her* stuff.

I remembered clearing the footlockers of the dead. I imagined telling Murray that while chasing down Buford, Levine had been killed. I wondered if she was married or had kids. She wore no ring. I realized I was shivering.

"Levine, I'm old-fashioned too. I don't want you KIA, WIA, or MIA."

She stood. "Then don't screw around. Do it up front. Boot me 'cause women don't hold your confidence. Don't patronize me by tossing floor scraps and saying I'm a good little girl."

Droves of women were coming out of law school, and Levine was a TIG. There was a bill in Congress to admit women to the Academy and to Airborne School. Women in Beast Barracks, shower formations, getting hazed. I shook my head: no way. This was men's work. Casey was the global anus, plunked in the latrine of the DMZ, and when the balloon went up and the Grim Reaper went to work, the dead would be stacked like cordwood, the 57Fs, the Fifty-seven Foxtrots—graves registrars—facing a work glut and a shortage of leak-proof plastic bags in the zipper-tent morgues of the combat dead.

The new political creed declared males and females identical except in acculturation. I didn't think so.

I believed men's deaths were more endurable than women's. That wasn't Chinese; it was American, and I respected it. It confirmed Ma's value and made her the equal of anyone, regardless of gender, birth order, *guan shi*—face—connections, or wealth. In the China I knew, women were expendable, fungible, invisible.

In America, they could pretend to equality.

"Levine, Casey's a crap detail. You're giving me the evil eye, wanting to play in the dump." I waved at the camp. "This manure is for men. Crud on the floor, the toilet seats up." I shook my head. "If we die, we get zip bags with our names. You get killed, it'll be a national scandal and Carlos Murray's fault."

"Don't lay it on him. He made this IG team with a redneck, a Jewess, and a Chinese. Park your medieval courtesies. You use gallantry as license for bigotry."

A breath. "We're taking all the jobs we can, but surprise! Contrary to your castration fears, we don't want your silly little dicks. We want a shot—and not even a fair one. I took the same oath to the Republic you did. And you use all the latrines."

Silly little dicks. The potential weight of another dead woman. I hadn't known the dead girl and she was a blight on my life. I liked Levine and felt my brittle self, the absence of flex, my emotional reserves and youth spent. I'd probably lost Cara. I had no room to lose Levine to the Reaper. I looked at her, at her bright, shining will.

I saw BaBa's muscular face. He had come to America because it had no blood lords to wage war on the river. A *laoban*, an illiterate junkman, could see his firstborn son read books and sit freely on dry land.

"You ought to let a Chinaman keep you from being kidnapped. In a country where torture's legal."

"C'mon, Kan—the Wizard tried to get *me* in the Vegas. I'm in the fight. Once, Chinese guys couldn't vote, marry, testify, or own land, or protest your own lynching. Now it's your turn to make some big changes."

I started picking up my socks.

"I meant bigger changes." She sucked on the inside of her mouth.

"Okay. Here's your final citizenship test: look at me."

I did, rather sadly.

"What do you see, Kan? An officer? Or just a skirt?"

President Kennedy, in the bloom of his Army romance, had waived my lack of U.S. birth to appoint me, a naturalized citizen, to West Point. He was President and it was my *yeh*, cast by Fan *taitai*, to go, to pay off my family's debt to our new land. The Academy was a dark place of regimented duties and deadly honor, illuminated by his Boston Irish trust, his Celtic vigors. I studied her; I saw a competent officer, full of fervor.

Levine's fervor could cost her her life.

Her life. I was tired and she was wearing me down. "Okay, Levine. You're out of the law library. Go incite riots and bash men all over Korea. Make me wish I had become a pianist."

"Thanks, Kan." Her fires were banked. She looked at

me as if we were old friends, her eyes soft, and I knew she was going to ask me questions about myself.

I held up a hand. "And please. No more bad-mouthing Magrip's medal."

"Well, excuse me if I don't get misty-eyed over a chauvinist killer."

"He got the Medal of Honor for saving people."

Levine popped a candy. "Not people, Kan. Men."

15

Colony of Lost Souls

"I called the post NCO Academy. Found a master sergeant who knew McCrail when they were both Vietnam advisers. Said he was huge—six-five, two fifty, white hair and the biggest voice in the Army. Known for never leaving a man behind.

"McCrail was wounded in a second Vietnam tour, then got in some political hassle with the Pentagon. He became Far East recruiter, then, something of a dead-end assignment.

"Seven years ago, the ROKs arrested him for emptying one of their munitions trains down in Pusan on Buddha's birthday."

A sergeant major stealing on anyone's birthday made no sense. They *were* the Army, the icons of high conduct, the unforgettable marching repositories of killing arts and military courtesies.

"ROKs were no help. I called our embassy in Seoul— McCrail was busted for the train theft but never went to ROK custody. He deserted 24 April '66. Five days later, he was declared dead. And guess who reported his death by drowning, no body?"

"Don't tell me—Fast Freddy LeBlanc, counselor-at-law."

"*Maja-yo*—bingo! Then I found a grocery bill in the office garbage. To Major Nagol, from Suwon—a ROK prison for GIs." The wind howled at the rebuilt window, finding the cracks.

"Korea's a civil law system. It lays prison costs on the families of the con for food and clothing.

"So why would Nagol, a man without a hint of a human heart, pay for inmate meals? I called the Suwon grocery and got a woman."

"Meaning?" I asked.

"I had someone who'd talk to me. I asked if we owed for Sergeant Major McCrail. No hit. I asked about the huge man.

" 'You owe,' she said. 'Curadess ate big this quarter.'

"I asked her to describe Curadess. Hundred ninety-five centimeters, hundred twenty kilos. White-haired, six-foot-five Yankee with a big voice and a gut the size of Yoi-do Island.

"MILPERCEN said a Cabra Curadess got life for heroin dealing at Chinhae seven years ago. He died in a traffic accident on the MSR, 29 April '66, en route to Suwon Prison."

"The same day," I said, "the Wizard said McCrail drowned."

"You got it. The man named Curadess *isn't* Curadess."

"Curadess is in the Wizard's backyard under a sergeant major's flag. What's Curadess's description?"

"Five-seven, one thirty, DOB 1946. Kan, the big man in Suwon is Sergeant Major McCrail. He's filling Curadess's jacket. The Wizard slipped him in when Curadess checked out."

"The Wizard doesn't kill. He's a sorcerer—he makes

people disappear and switches them. Levine—Jimmy's alive. Maybe at Suwon."

"I don't think so, but you gotta see McCrail. He's been waiting nearly eight years in ROK solitary to fink on the Wizard. There's just one problem."

"Why am I not going to like this?"

"Inside Suwon is a maximum-security facility called Naktong Tower—a solitary-confinement block for Korean penal scum—spies, traitors, child killers and Korea's worst foreign prisoners. It's a colony of truly lost criminal souls. No Yankees allowed except as inmates. Min says it's pride; we've pushed big into Korean life. At Naktong they drew the line: Korean visitors only." Pause. "McCrail's in Naktong Tower."

She passed me ROK Army duds and underwear. "You tried janitor. Try being a Korean major in the ROK Airborne, courtesy of Min. And start eating." She gave me a carton.

"*Kim chi*—pickled, fermented cabbage in garlic, the national dish. It nukes colds, which, here, could kill you. Koreans take the scent in their pores for the health benefits. This is *kamdongjoh*, the king of all *kim chi*s. Octopus, roe, abalone, dropwort. Eat."

"I'm healthy as a horse," I said.

"You smell like an American. No more English Leather."

"Then why not just rub it into my skin?"

"Good idea. Kan, Curadess confessed before trial, under duress—a.k.a. torture. ROK national police were after his Korean drug network. They fried his privates; he gave names." She took an angry breath.

"Here's our scam. You are Major Hong, ROK Airborne. One of the innocent parties Curadess named is your beloved father, who we claim was crippled by the cops and, now, finally died after long suffering. Eat." She gave me chopsticks. I ate. It was hot.

"Major Hong wants to see the fat foreign circus beast. To tell him, as a good Confucian son, how foul he is, to spit at his big feet."

"That'll impress him." I picked up a pair of boxers. "Down to underwear level? Tell me they don't cavity-search visitors."

"Can't be sure. I don't think a big bad ROK major of paratroopers would put up with anything more than a pat-down."

"I could end up being McCrail's bunkie."

"Yes. At night, he'll hear all about the girl you cry about. Sorry. Why didn't you pass as a janitor? Keep eating."

I ate. "I'm too big. And I got caught by *Americans.* With Koreans, I'll be humming the no-paddle anthem up Poop Creek."

She came close. "Then we admit you're Chinese. Overseas Chinese are here. They're almost looked up to. It's just unusual for them to be career military."

Just like America.

She wrapped my head with a field dressing. "The problem is, you don't speak Korean. So we say your jaw was busted in an MSR crash. Who wouldn't believe that? With your jaw like this, you can't talk. We'll say your hearing was impaired." She remembered my ear and blushed. "And you already know some Korean. I'll give you more to go with your Chinese authoritarian first-son mentality. That works big here." She smoothed the bandage. She used a nice-smelling soap.

"I'd wear your tunic under the ROK overcoat and over ROK trousers. Show McCrail who you really are. After seven years, he may be paranoid, even schizoid. I'll sew the blouse to the overcoat, so if you have to take off the coat in front of guards, the greens will follow. Snip the thread to show McCrail your blouse. And I'd wear every ribbon you have."

That was something I did not do. I thought for a moment. "Levine, ROK majors don't ride in American jeeps. And ROKs wear shorter hair."

"Min will get a ROK jeep in Yongsan to drive you in. He's taking a chance; penalty for impersonation is life."

I disliked Min's taking chances, but Infantry officers rely on the valor of volunteers. Levine pulled out scissors and comb and pointed me into the chair. She started cutting.

"Kan, you know that Min is always asking me about you? He respects you—an Asian who's mastered the West."

She had a gentle, warm touch, removing big clumps.

"This haircut will change his opinion."

Later, she checked her work, her face close. She looked in my eyes. "Good." She licked her upper lip. "For someone going to the joint." She brushed hair from my face and neck, not looking at me. She fired a Polaroid. "For the ID."

It was a nice shot. I looked like a public enemy who had fought a lawn mower with his head.

She smeared *kim chi* on my neck, the garlic defeating all other scents. The peppers burned. "McCrail's an archive of the Wizard's tricks. *I'd* do it if I had a chance."

Hi, Warden. I'm a Korean major with the looks of a white devil foreign lady. Let me see the fat foreign person.

"Levine, I see why Carlos likes you."

"He doesn't like me. He thinks I'm a pain in the ass."

"Really?" I said flatly. The *kim chi* stung my throat. I finished the carton and held up the shorts. "Too small."

"Yes," she said lasciviously. "That's what all men say."

I looked around the room. Frowning, I checked

pockets. Levine also looked around the room. "What'd you lose?"

"My silly little dick. It was here a minute ago."

16

DRUMMING OF CUPS

Thursday, January 17

I dreamed of the girl and awoke at three, staying on watch and letting Magrip sleep. I wrote poetry to Cara. Some of it was John Donne. Most of it was Dr. Seuss. I couldn't mail it, because no one was to know an IG team was in Korea, running about like a collective headless chicken while exuding pungent *kim chi* vapors.

I used to awaken to look at Cara, reflecting on her full, robust personality, her expansive memory, her carnal laugh and healthy temper, now stilled by quiet sleep. She was resurrecting the man I had been before Vietnam, coaxing laughter, advocating mirth, uncritical of my patronage of street musicians and sad, broken panhandlers.

Cara had a vulnerability: a man performing an unannounced abandonment. Her father had done it. Now, so had I.

After a slogging run at dawn and *wu-shu* kicks and blocks, I phoned D cell to set Levine's visit with Major Nagol.

"Sir, I swear ta God Almighty ya can't see the man."

"Corporal Davis. Stop telling me I can't. Tell me why."

"Waal, sir, cuz he's croaked mostly dead. I mean we bed that man down with a shovel fer the last time. He's bumped off. Wolf meat. Whew, that sucker got a free ride from here on out. Sir, that old jasper's as dead as corned beef."

"Let me speak to the NCOIC": the noncommissioned officer in charge—the warden. It took a while.

"Staff Sergeant Scranton Plum, sir . . . Major Nagol, he's a deceased . . . Man was a juicer. Got DTs. Doc says he seizured and aspirated his vomit around Oh-Dark-Thirty . . . No, sir, Major Nagol made no statements. Well, 'cept, he kinda said, 'gaahcckkk!' " Sergeant Plum cackled happily.

I recalled Nagol's ghastly appearance, his ills, his cancerous temperament and bad manners, his disappointment that I had not been bashed in the Vegas. But I still felt the distantly metallic aftertaste of moral guilt. I also regretted losing a good source of information.

Min drove Levine and me down the wintery MSR to Seoul. No one was following us. Early Thursday, third day in-country. The traffic, in celebration of our MSR reprise, was worse.

I shut my eyes, choosing ruminations of Nagol and dreams of the girl over witnessing my own death. Min drove faster, causing my unhappy guts to bunch. But I wanted him to hurry; Naktong's gates closed at noon, and we were seven years late.

"Kan *dae-wi*," said Min, "you, me talk 'Merican try?"

"You bet," I said.

"Look at the bus coming at us," said Levine, yawning.

Min swerved as the bus blared at us, its air shaking the jeep.

"Kan *dae-wi*, you like Korea?"

"I admire its unity. I dislike the war-fear."

Min said nothing as we passed blocks of marching, white-uniformed factory workers, chanting and shaking fists in unison as they snaked in a six-man front into a massive white stadium. A workers' rally. It looked a little like Nuremburg.

"Your father, *dae-wi*, he want you be like white man?"

A huge question. BaBa wanted me to be loyal to his God.

The thought made me blink. I saw BaBa's flintlike eyes and cleared my throat. "He wants me to be like Jesus Christ."

A long silence. "Jesu Christ, he white man," said Min.

I heard BaBa's voice. "Jesu only man who hate no one, fear no one, love everyone. My God, your God, my son. He make earth, make night sky, make river, make *kwei-yu*, fish, you swim after. He hold your baby brothers in His arms, love them. Better father than me."

I had sensed BaBa's God in Muir Woods, Yosemite Falls, and the granite mountains of West Point. I felt Him during my baptism when I accepted the long-dead rabbi as my saviour. I had seen God in my life until 7 July 1967, when dawn broke at the river. In the bung of the Dong Nai I realized how alone man was on earth. There was no loving God, no saving Christ, no Holy Trinity, only human error multiplied insanely upon itself. I threw soil on the women. I told God His system was crud, a cruel deceit. Your world sucks and You're not here. I had been a good man and had helped others. I had always done my job. I jerked as my M-16 popped and the dead fell as green leaves fluttered, the echoes of grenades in the tall trees.

We passed a ring of mountains that Min called the Paegun-dae and entered Seoul, an immense sprawl of endless, hilled dun houses, temples, high-rises, rivers of smogging vehicles, covered in snow and brown soot.

"*Dae-wi*, your father, he honcho general?" asked Min.

"He was *laoban*. Boat boss-man. Now he owns a store. We borrowed two-percent money from our family association."

Min sucked in his breath. "Here, *pyon-hosa*, lawyer, only for *yangban* rich. Father farmer, his son also farmer. In 'Merica, seem all mix up."

U.S. Army Garrison Yongsan was north of the Han River, next to Itaewon's bustling shopping district.

Above Yongsan's gray skies was imposing, snow-covered Namsan, South Mountain. From there, the KCIA—the feared Korean Central Intelligence Agency—watched everything and everybody.

The streets were clogged with cars, bicycles and suicidal pedestrians. A smartly turned-out MP with white leggings and helmet saluted as we entered the secure HQ compound for the U.S. Army and United Nations Command. I returned salutes from British officers in brown uniforms and New Zealanders in berets, Gurkhas with curved daggers and Turks with shopping bags. Across the street was the massive, antennaed, ten-story stone structure of ROK Army Headquarters.

At Army HQ we got out and stretched. Levine would use the nearby Eighth Army computer center to print out Second Infantry claims disbursements, to check out the excessive payouts by the Wizard's staff. Good work, but we were being pulled away from Jimmy. Magrip would continue looking for him at Casey, doing another door-to-door. Min went to pick up a ROK jeep.

A young Korean woman opened the door of Eighth Army HQ, blinking as the wind whipped her long hair. "Captain Kan? Phone-a call. SJA, Casey. Mos' 'portant, sir."

Min drove up in a dark green ROK jeep with Hangul markings.

No time. I asked Levine to take it. I gave her my Academy class ring—something a ROK officer would not have—unwilling to part with my ID and dog tags. If Suwon busted me—illegitimately in the worst wrong place in Korea—I needed proof of U.S. citizenship. We wished each other luck.

Min and I lurched toward the Han River bridges. In an NKPA invasion, eight million residents would try to cross the Han's twelve bridges before the ROKs blew

them up to keep the Reds north of the river. Demolitions
and black all-weather detonation wires were visible on
piers above the half-frozen river. An air-raid drill siren
wailed hauntingly across the river, making me wonder
about the Wizard's interest in tac maps and explosives. I
remembered that whenever the sirens had wailed in
China, I had been hungry. I chewed gum.

The McCrail file described a big Bronx Catholic with
twenty-one Army years until the spring of 1966. Then,
as top Army recruiter, Far East, he had been busted
for ten counts of foreign grand theft. The evidence was
compelling.

"Under our Status of Forces Agreement," Levine had
said, "the ROKs give us all GIs except the drug dealers.
They give those guys life or execute them by firing
squad. It's a martial-law nation in a state of war with
Pukhan—North Korea—with no ban on torture."

McCrail had been arrested for making the Silla Sperry
rail computer siderail a ROK Army munitions train. It
went from Pusan railhead to a bandit spur built for the
theft. When the crew revived from a chloroform gassing,
the train's contents were gone.

The Republic of Korea was a strict, insular, Confucian-
Buddhist state under martial law. It took grand *baboe*,
foreigner guts, to take down one of its military trains on
Buddha's birthday.

The ROKs suspected the Inmingun, and the ROK
police had been brutal to its own people; officials and
staff had been questioned under duress and sacked en
masse.

The ROK *com-sa*, prosecutors, had security camera
photos and percipient witnesses to put McCrail in the
computer room at the point the train went off the program. Latents matched his prints.

A grainy black-and-white photo showed an immense
middle-aged man with a big nose and large lips, lighting
a fat cigar in a small automated room, looking directly

into the camera with hooded eyes. It was labeled "U.S. citizen criminal, Silla Rail Center Control Room. 0310 hours, 29 April 1966. Sony camera #One. Exposure 31." I looked at the copy of his arrest photo: same man. The train had gone off system at 3:25 A.M., 29 April 1966.

McCrail's 201 put him at six-five, two fifty, Military Occupational Specialty OOE, Double-Oh Echo, recruiter. An OOE would have no cause to mess with rail centers and ROK ammo trains.

His prior job had been rifleman, MOS 11B—Eleven Bravo, Infantry. He had earned two Silver Stars in Vietnam. Years before, in the Korean War, McCrail had won the Soldier's Medal for saving lives of fellow POWs in Manchuria. He had extended the lives of his comrades before their eventual deaths in a Chinese camp.

In an army of brothers, Soldier's Medal men were revered. Now, this savior of others had become a thief. Magrip had done two tours and was as friendly as a hemorrhoidal warthog. McCrail had done two wars and was for the second time a prisoner in the Orient. ROK penology was light in the giggle department, but being a POW in Manchuria was bottom-drawer foul luck. McCrail had lived the recipe for the creation of monsters. I closed the file for a while.

The jeep jerked as Min popped the clutch on a missed downshift. I resumed reading. The 201 said that McCrail had been trained in computers at Belvoir, including Sperry mainframes, one of which was, of course, the exact model in the ROK rail center.

The prosecutor could have convicted McCrail with one hand tied while taking clarinet lessons, doing stock deals and writing his memoirs. Worse, McCrail's counsel, one Fred LeBlanc, had reported him dead and sent him to Naktong under a drug dealer's alias.

I wondered if McCrail would tell the truth. Most of my

first clients had lied to me, richly and creatively. I had been lied to by experts and idiots, by men of different gods and by killers of children. McCrail was a professional soldier and a sergeant major, an exalted position in Army sociology. His background required intellectual breadth; his record bespoke competence, dedication, selflessness. If still sane, he would help us with Jimmy the Bee or he would lie through his teeth.

We reviewed the procedure at Suwon. "*Dae-wi*, you, me, American try. Naktong numbah-ten place. You *nakhasan pudae*—big honcho paratroop man. Guard say do, *I* do what he say. You honcho man, do what want. *Dae-wi*, say 'Uh-uuh.' "

"Uh-uuh," low and guttural.

"Numbah-one, *dae-wi*! You good ROK officer!" He smiled hugely.

We had left the highway for a snow-coated gravel road, passing through a farming village with whitewashed compounds, scrawny, winter-stricken scrub oak and screw pines. Ahead were long, gray medieval walls lined with snow-capped Japanese evergreens.

"Suwon," said Min.

"Stop." I stepped into deep snow, set the file on a rock, sprayed it with lighter fluid and lit it. I lifted the jeep hood and put my ID and dog tags under the air cleaner. Min pulled out a massive Bushmaster knife and slit his left small finger, letting it bleed into a first-aid compress. He bound the finger and bandaged my face with the compress. The blood soaked through.

"Should have used my blood," I said.

"You officer, *dae-wi*, I sogging enlisted man." He removed my gloves and rubbed garlic into my neck and hands. The ashes of McCrail's file fluttered away like black, broken butterflies.

"Sorry I touch you, *dae-wi*. Wife take off my sock at night. Put on in morning. Wash me, dry me. Serve me dinner, watch me eat before she eat. You wife, she do same-same?"

"No." Cara, I got these great ideas over in Korea.

I put on Ray-Ban sunglasses and buckled up; Min peeled out, jerking my neck. We passed through the open arch of an outer stone wall and entered the gray, shadowed courtyard of Suwon Prison. We were accelerating.

Corporal Min pumped his leg. We were doing forty miles an hour. "Slow down!" I shouted as we skidded familiarly on ice.

"Aeguuu!" he cried. I winced as we sideswiped the gray steel guard kiosk, tipping it and dumping heavily armed sentries into the snow. Min grunted, pumping his leg without effect. I pulled the emergency and we swerved toward the wall and dunked hard into a depression, smashing us into the dash and rattling my teeth.

A mind-warping prison-break klaxon screeched like a mutilated beast. Our doors were pulled open and muzzles of M-16s and Browning automatic rifles intruded. In a way, I was flattered.

A flushed pink face appeared at the windshield, disappeared, reappeared, then thrust itself close to me inside the windswept cab. It saw a ROK paratroop major with a busted head and sensed an alien at the gate. I was too big. It scanned me, smelling my skin. I pretended to ignore it.

"Uuhh." I intoned. The guard backed up. Min said I was Major Hong, *nakhasan pudae*, injured in the line of duty. Honor him.

"Ip dakk chuh!" snapped the guard, a cocked Smith & Wesson service .38 revolver in his trembling gloved hand. Levine had taught me that one. It meant "Shut up!"

He shouted. Min exited the jeep. The guards backed up as I stood in the deep snow. They wore surplus U.S. Army World War II uniforms and gear with Arctic flap forage hats. Some shouted. Someone popped the hood as the jeep was searched. Two new guards pointed bayoneted M-1 carbines at me while Pink Face waved his revolver, shouting an order. Min raised his arms.

No ROK paratroop major would raise his. "Uh-uuh."

A guards officer came from the arched, stone entrance, jumping the steps two at a time. He churned through the snow, thick-bodied, with a fat, pockmarked face. He saluted. I returned it.

He spoke. I pointed at Min, who delivered the fable: In 1966, the fat foreign pig Curadess dishonored the major's father by saying he was a drug dealer. The major's father was beaten many times during questioning. Now, after seven years of crippled suffering, he has died. The major is here without authorization, risking a brilliant military career to fulfill his filial duty by reprimanding the foreigner. His hearing is permanently impaired. He cannot speak. Please help my major.

The officer looked critically at me, at my ear, wanting proof. To ask more questions would be rude; to ask none would be negligent. Yet the story explained my bizarre visit. He asked Min if I was half-Chinese. Min said yes. He asked me for ID.

He took the counterfeit ID with a bow. He glanced at it, then spoke rapidly, gutturally, but without anger, directing a frisk of Min and then personally frisking me. He removed my sunglasses to examine them. My heart stopped when he felt the contours of my Combat Infantryman Badge, a unique metal decoration; he noticed it, but passed on to my lower body. The captain nodded, his breath white, pointing me to the gate. Min was taken away. My sunglasses were returned.

I looked at the guards. They saluted. I returned it. I was escorted into a compound formed by ageless, inward-canting, Japanese stone walls. No guard towers. Long, squat, windowless concrete blocks—the prison cells.

The granite became an untamed, painful stone quarry

that tore my boots. Ahead was a three-story concrete structure. Naktong.

The doors were six inches thick, a half-ton of Japanese steel moving on slow gimbals opening into a series of baffled and well-lit entrances emitting a terrible odor.

When the last double doors opened, the revolting stink hit me like a clean right cross that drew painless tears and a grunt. My senses rebelled at the living stench which rose from a frigid, cavernous concrete shaft, six or seven vertical stories into the earth. From this pit rose the repulsive miasma of human waste, unwashed men and nightmarish sewers.

Naktong was not a tower. It was a mine shaft, rich with veins of refuse, free-floating, unrestrained, organic and human. Guards held perfumed handkerchiefs over noses. One was offered to me. I wanted it but shook my head.

Someone clanged a cup against a steel bar. He was joined by others as some crowed hoarsely, the noise accumulating, encouraged by the echoes of a concrete-and-steel chorus, the curiously youthful music of old prisoners. The clanging became a discernible two-beat, and then evolved into a deep four-beat rhythm, *ba-ba-bom-bom*, a redundant drumming of hundreds of steel cups. This was not a chorus of inmate requests for food or rights; it was a hopeless complaint against stink and boredom, tuned up for the oddity of a ROK officer come to Naktong Tower. The guards looked at me warily.

The beat was compelling, mesmerizing, a sound of early tribes defeated by nature and by stronger warriors, drumming now for blood and vengeance by noise or any means, a syncopated metallic Korean marimba driven by hard lockdown, orchestrated in dead man's air and performed at the appearance of a single stranger.

I looked at the music men as I followed the guard down the stairs, breathing tersely, boots echoing on the hollow steel stairs in time to the four-beat drums. A thin, sad man in yellow utilities tried to join the band with his cup, but atrophied muscles and a slowed mind permitted only an occasional silent clang. On the fifth level down I had to take a breath and almost threw up because the stink was worse. I hesitated as an Australian voice seemed to say, "Mate, can you talk English? Call my pop will ya!" A long, pale, European face, wild eyes searching mine for solace. Foreign prisoner.

I am a ROK major whose father was sullied by foreigners. I am not who I am. I looked away and felt like a traitor.

"Gan-bang myunhae shill," said the guard. The lawyers' interview cell in Naktong's dank security basement. Dark sludge flowed from a wall crack and covered the floor. I removed my sunglasses and closed my eyes to adjust to the low light, breathing through a mothballed sleeve.

Bugs slithered over my boots and the green floor. A guard entered. He lit an incense stick and blew it out, freeing the sweet paste. Hands joined in the center of his chest, he bowed, smiling as men will who devoutly believe in God. His smile warmed the cell, but I ignored him. I was a ROK paratroop field grade officer with an injured and mummified face, come to do a solemn Confucian duty.

Rats scurried in pipes and scratched at the walls, excited by the incense. Cons screamed down at me while banging metal. A cup fell down the steel steps, making lonely notes of descending loss. The drumming of the cups slowed, became chaotic, started up again, then died. Later, in the fetid silence, the beat continued, unbidden, in my brain. Men wailed while others barked and screamed, exciting echoes of dying troops waiting for medevacs. The floor thickly oozed with brown and bright-green flying roaches.

There were lyrics to the tune: Don't break the law in the ROK, where punishments would hurt and food was below imagination. The collective fear soaked into my bones. I felt like a caged dog.

I rubbed my hands together, sniffing the red, glinting incense head and watching for rats. An inmate screamed, the object of a beating. Claustrophobia teased me.

I had left Cara for Jimmy and was here, playing out Murray's mission and Levine's instincts. I wondered what Levine's first name was. I remembered how she had looked into my eyes. I brushed roaches from my legs. I was in Asia, but this did not remind me of China.

BaBa shook me as I slept. BaBa's voice, husky and urgent, smelling of ginger and black tea, his big hand shaking me.

Hu-chin! Open eyes, Little Tiger, moon watch. The wind is up and a storm comes fast. It will tear the sateen sail.

Do not be *don ko budong sho*, a boy who moves mouth and not hands. You have job to do. Show your little brothers how a man does work.

His strong hand lifted me from my cotton pad. I stood on the quickly yawing deck, stretching and yawning and he laughed, rubbing the hair on my head.

He held little Hu-hau, Good Tiger, in a thick, rope-scarred arm. Good Tiger giggled at me, bright-eyed like Wen Ch'ang, the scholarship god who sat high in the night's north sky, and rubbed my head as our father had, his tiny hand pulling my hair.

17

PATRICK TREATY McCRAIL

Three guards escorted him. It was McCrail, an immense three hundred pounds on a big-boned frame, older than his years. He was a sergeant major, a special station in the Army, and he was *so-yang saram*, a white foreign prisoner in Asia, which was such a vast misfortune that it nullified all the good in one's past.

McCrail matched the gray, grunge-sweat walls, his face crachin, the color of drizzly days in Nam, the product of bad food, no sun, vitamin deficiencies, a Western beard meeting a Far Eastern coldwater shave with a solitary convict's dull razor.

The sergeant major had a rocklike head, snow-white brows and a broad, angry fissure of a mouth formed by full, indignant lips. Coarse cut of white hair. Jowls of muscle and fat. Red, deep-shadowed eye sockets. Deep creases punctuating heavy brows. A slab of nose with generous nostrils. A massive man undiminished by the big trouble that had turned all the hair on his body white. His face was a terrain map where the weather never gave a break.

Shackles ran groin-neck-ankles, glinting against ill-fitting yellow utilities. The thud of the boots on crackling bugs and cold concrete and the clink of his steel made a mournful soundtrack to a hanging.

I had seen bad prisons, sad jails and cannibals, but he was a spectacle beyond experience. I would've paid to see him. He saw me and laughed, high and girlishly, a white sound in a shadowed world, his torso undulating in fresh corpulence.

The guard cracked McCrail in the mouth with a big baton.

"Aniyo!" No! I blocked another blow with my upper arm and booted McCrail behind the knee as I shouldered him away from the guards. He fell and slid like a bag of cement thrown from a fast truck, kicking up a wake of scuttling insects. Hot pain sizzled up my arm from the baton, my hand numb.

I faced the guards, crushing roaches, and they backed up. McCrail spat out a brown tooth and shook away the blow, a mastiff in the rain, his leash complaining, blood on the bugs and the weeping floor.

Master Wong had taught me pain, but McCrail had taken a postdoctorate in anguish, going summa cum laude to the grunts of enemies and the mournful call of Army bugles.

Manchus would have feared the killer in him, doing as the Koreans did—beating the crap out of this big, antagonistic *gwailo*, foreign running dog, trying to make him complacent with frequent personal pain. His lined face documented the pallor of torture, the feral scars of agony. The slide into inert emptiness, a Buddhist absence. For a middle-aged con back in stir, the new brutality reawakened old rages and drew lost regimens from dusty memory. It made his eyes beam red and silent in a dark cell, surveying me, measuring my meaning.

My face had its own dents.

"Tae don hee jaesong hameeneeda, yukkun soryong." So sorry, major. The guards bowed, backing away. They couldn't lift McCrail. I helped; we dropped him in a concrete chair. They hauled on his chains to crush his testicles and left, their boots respectfully quiet. The steel door clanged shut, the echoes cold and full of dark promises.

We silently surveyed each other. Then he gratingly spoke

Korean. He had brushed his teeth and stank of old-man fear. The guards were gone. "I am Captain Jackson Kan. I am a JAGC IG. Who are you?"

He exhaled, looking old. "Ah, hell. Shoulda seen it. Friggin' Wizard." He spat. "Shoulda killed me years ago."

"The Wizard disappeared one of our IGs. I need your help to find him. The Army may owe you, depending on who you are."

It didn't register. The big boulder head nodded, features crinkling. He muttered both sides of a foul chat centering on my corporeal reality. He blinked; I was still here. He showed big yellow teeth as half-crushed roaches struggled on his body.

"TIG, huh? The hell you are. You look chink army to me. What the hell happened to your face?" Sandpaper on plate glass.

No guards. I popped the threads and removed the overcoat, showing the U.S. blouse with Indian-head patch, French braid fourragère, Presidential Unit Citation and my decorations. I had gotten a Silver Star for the river ambushes, a red, white and blue silk ribbon painted in a child's blood. I had slid them on the four-tier chest-decoration rack for McCrail/Curadess. Otherwise I did not wear the award I had gotten at the Dong Nai. I had suspected that Carlos had put me in for it to confirm my judgment that day.

"I don't speak Korean. The bandages are a cover for silence."

He spat thickly on the cold floor. The red spit sizzled. He raised snowy brows, white portcullises on an ancient castle. "Cap'n, you're the cat's pajamas. No sir, *never* seen no Chinese Airborne Ranger IG with a DSC, Silver Star, Bronze Star, Purple Heart. Hell if I don't feel the Lord's grin in a shitty place."

He giggled. "*Damn*, you fooled me. Hell, you fooled them! I see it. Big even for an American, but I seen your type. North Chinese. *Ni hau ma.* Same chink stock that blew me the hell outa my hole and walked me into Manchuland. Damn—an American officer! You found me. With so much Chinese face, they let you in here and gave you a joss stick. Hell, you're probably West Point. Tell me if I'm wrong."

He let coils of incense undulate under his nose. "That smells good," saying it like James Brown, stretching the second word with a voice that had given orders above the screams of dying men and the earth-shaking crunch of guns, a voice that made the stink back off.

His voice was a combat NCO's big vulgar fist, the gruff call of a warrior slayer, Irish in manner, black in speech and Army in blood. He had Richard Boone's deep, imperative rasp, spiced with Harlem and Kilkenny and Tennessee-hill-country drawl, full of wry mischief, fattened on other men's blood and busted bones, textured with a history of silent injuries. I put on the overcoat.

"I don't know how much time we have. Tell me who you are."

"A kick to hear American. Used to practice it in Tangyuan. Don't, you lose it and go chink. Knock the roaches off my back."

I looked interested, my remaining hairs standing up in the dungeon, my intent blunted by his circus nature. I brushed off the bugs and stitched my coats together with cold fingers. He cursed all insects. "I eat food raw, like a bug."

"You keep playing games with me, I'll end up having chow with all of you."

"Tee hee. I'd like that! Patrick Treaty McCrail, sergeant major, U.S. Army, RA5666838, DOB 26 October 1927."

It was him. I recorded his service number and DOB. The lilt reminded me of Academy days, full of tough, red-faced Irishmen with hard fists and big bellies.

"May I?" He nodded. I huffed on my sunglasses and

cleaned them with a handkerchief, put them next to his
shackles and pressed his fat, spatulate fingers onto the
lenses. "I'm looking for a missing captain. Tall, thin,
brown hair."

McCrail's hooded eyes were gray and deep, red-
flecked, lined with yellow fatigue and shaded in anger
gone brown. He grunted like a fattened ox, wet, tired, his
flanks immense, his slow breathing the bellows of a
mammal larger than man, a beast who had lived in
Manchuria, in weather colder than this tubercular cell.

"Cap'n, I been in solitary. I don't see crap. No—crap
is *all* I see. No officers here. Just enlisted pukes. Aussies,
Turks and Korean political types. Child killers. How long
he been gone?"

No Jimmy. I hated to say, "This is the ninth day."

He tried to point. His face went to crinkles as he guffawed like a monolithic jackass. Once, I sensed, he had
laughed for the pleasure of a soft glade. For years, that
gift had been denied him. Now he laughed at life's absur-
dities, because an Asian man let him roar and slobber
without bashing out his teeth. He choked on his laughter.
He hawked and spat. "Ah, that's rich. Dirty, tight officers. Forgettin' your men. If you knew how—oh, hell."

He glowered, stopping himself. "Sir, they gave me
the big one—life," the last word a paragraph. The cackle.
He closed gray cat-eyes, licking the cut in his mouth.
The joss smoked in retreat from bad smells, roaches
scrabbling to reach the stick. Rats scurried in broken
sewer lines. Prisoners screamed. Fluids snaked down
dark walls. The humid cold was in my bones. I felt like
killing bugs.

"McCrail, tell me about your JAGC."

"That bastard gave evidence to the ROK prosecutors."

I exhaled. The Wizard had not only sent McCrail here
for life; he had convicted him while serving as his
defense lawyer.

Reassessing me: "You any good at this legal crap?"

"I'll do all I can for you. Tell me your lawyer's name."

McCrail leaned his ample form toward me, chains complaining. He motioned. I leaned forward. He smelled of new sweat squeezed from old pores and of long pacing on ammonia-treated concrete. His stomach growled like low thunder in a black summer sky.

"Need to unass this pit, Captain," he whispered, jackboots on rock. "Monkey the wires and get me out. For ten lousy days. I need to be in Hong Kong."

Preposterous. "Perry Mason with a crowbar couldn't get you there."

Chains clanked. He leaned back. "Then figure it out."

I had no clue how to sneak a chained three-hundred-pound foreign prisoner out of maximum security without using military force. I had a Richelieu letter, but down here it was toilet paper with black print. I could start a habeas today, but here, it would move with the speed of the dead.

Footfalls. A guard. I crouched, faking a quick, hard body blow to McCrail's ribs. He recoiled and the guard left laughing.

I asked why his JAGC had cheated him into prison.

Ten seconds had passed and I hadn't busted him out. "Well, Captain, maybe he wasn't as good as you."

"Tell me about the train. Give me something I can work on."

"Drop it. I'm dead meat on that damned train. Got me on film and wired for sound." The big white head, the hard, pained eyes.

"Knocked out *four stinkin' cameras.* Found one screwed into main power. If I cut it, I couldn't play the program. Pried out the film canister. Like openin' a crab." He paused, thinking.

"What the hell. I was on the road to an Article 32 hearing for recruiting fraud and black-marketing." An Army grand jury investigation.

"That's a lot of badness for a sergeant major."

He sniffed. "Did it. Had me a good plan. Broke the schemes down to my lawyer—Fast Freddy C. LeBlanc."

Got him. I wrote, "McCrail's JAGC: Fast Freddy C. LeBlanc, 1125 hours, 17 Jan 74, Naktong, Suwon ROK."

"Gave Freddy the rail center film. Quick-like, *com-sa*—DA—has crime scene photos. Freddy says, 'Sign papers.' I read Hangul; the damn thing was a confession. Tore that sucker up, but the court gets it anyway. My crimes pull thirty years with a confession—and I get life. They did me good, sir, without no Vaseline or hand towel, later.

"I wrote the CG, Congress, President Lyndon B. Johnson. Bolo. All I get is a jackcrap JAGC with the clap."

"Major Thomas Nagol, a thin syphilitic?"

His eyes burned. An iron voice, cold as ice. "*Him.* He kicks my green butt out of Suwon and clangs me in the Naktong Forget-It Hole. Me, a nut for high ground and clean air, bein' stuck down here. Teach me to speak out. My mail don't go out. Don't get food. I scarf it raw when it comes. I write the UN commander, bulls beat me with sticks." He puckered on a gum hole and shrugged. Chains clinked. "I seen worse.

"Nothin' personal, but I think this kinda gives lawyers a bad name, or you think I'm just bein' an asshole pessimist?"

"You're a pessimist. How much time we got?"

He cackled. It was good that I liked it, because he laughed at me a lot that day. "Nagol goes *straight* to Hell when *he* dies."

"He may be there. He choked on his own vomit last night."

He looked upward. He closed his eyes, his great mouth open. The great brows bunched in either agony or ecstasy. "Thank you, Lord. Two damn prayers answered on the same damn day." He did a double take at me. "Nagol dead on his upchuck. Christ." He giggled, again and again, higher and higher, crazy as a latrine rat. "You know, they get pissed, they do us with sump hoses from the shitters."

"I can see why you want to leave."

"No you can't. This place ain't hard. Stink don't kill."

"I'm not so sure."

His eyes narrowed as he studied me, a bluish tongue coming out to test the air for predators. McCrail's big, swollen eyeballs ran over me like a tongue over an old wound.

"You got a debt on you." He smiled, happy.

Damn all old sergeants, weighing men's pains, sniffing out drinkers, wife beaters, barracks thieves, rapists, pot-heads, bed wetters and physical cowards at ten meters.

I was inches away, making it easy for him to set the hook.

"Sir, what'd you do?" The girl was dead and the rounds ripped her lungs and the women were dead and there was no changing any of it except that their deaths were growing larger with time. The girl would be about sixteen now. The grass cut my hand and I shot her and the baby, the memory loop out of order but visually clear. Wanting to protect Asian women, leaving one alive long enough to call me Ba. I was ill, my gorge rising. I put my head down, slowly hating him.

"You got a load. Nam." A goofy grin. "You were in some bad crap to get those medals. Lost some guys. Made a bad tac move and now dead boys play flag foot-ball in your sleep. Hey, no sweatee-da. Five, six years, you get used to most of it. All blind luck, anyway, who gets blowed away, who doesn't. You know that, lad."

Then he smiled, as if a bright halo were growing on his head.

"Dammit—*God* sent you here! Seven damn years and I get the word, and here you are! You got a marker on you a mile wide and you owe *big*. You're the best damned soldier who ever crapped between two boots I *ever* seen! Cap'n, *you* go for me."

I fought my guts. A guy in this place, with his foul luck, believing in God? Go to Hong Kong? I didn't think so. "Why?"

"Sir, just go. No college debate." His eyes lit up. "I see it now. Thought He'd left me in a bad place but He was *testing* me. *God* sent you to me in the desert. Dammit! You believe me?"

"I don't even understand you. This here is God's favor?"

"Tee hee. God's here, lad. You learn that when you're without the regiment and its laws, the work, the boys. The noise in your head stops and it gets clear." He looked up, like a lunatic.

I wasn't buying it. His face dropped. "Okay, sir, you're a fine, cynical, college-boy sonofabitch, hooked to your dead. I'm *asking* you," he snapped in his gruff, avalanching command voice, "to *trust me*. Look at my record. It'll tell you something. Ask why a good ole Regular Army lifer NCO like me would rip off something wasn't his and *not* kill people who by God's law oughta die hard." His gray eyes burned with inner fires, unimpeded by past error and driven by a just future.

I had known idiot generals and idiot lieutenants but not a single stupid sergeant major. Piercing screams; guards beat a prisoner above us. Dante was no poet; he was a reporter.

"Cap'n, I'm real sorry for your tragic past. You lemme know if you're going to help or just look pretty." He exhaled. "Gotta say now. LeBlanc knows you're here sure as monkeys shit from trees. You come and ask law-school questions and waltz out to stick your nose back in a law book? Sir, you crossed the line of departure into enemy country. We got hours before LeBlanc quotes scripture the wrong way and puts rat killer in my rice—or yours. You asshole officer. I got a mission. Do you?"

My visit had put him in deeper jeopardy. Keep him and Levine alive. Find Jimmy. Follow the law. He had a good voice. The call to action. My job was getting Jimmy. "McCrail, I'm not going to break the law for you. I am not going to play with your illegal businesses. That's black-letter gospel."

He shook his big head. "You know, they're right? Talking to a lawyer *is* like passing a hair ball right through your dick."

"Well. I always lived for endorsements."

He looked away, shrouding his disappointment. "No problem." He chewed on a big, chapped lower lip. "You're not for real, so what? You gotta see I don't give a good hoot and a holler about myself. Had a *fine* wife, *good* friends, and Nagol's dead as a French doornail." His eyes were down and he was talking to himself. He lowered his head to pick his nose, forgetting I was there. Then he saw me and jerked.

"I got a mission I ain't accomplished. Sticks in my craw every day here in paradise." He leaned back, chains clinking.

"What's your mission, Sergeant Major?"

"Hong Kong," he growled, an animal in a cage.

I hit the concrete table with the flat of my hand, making the sound of a gun. *"What do you have on LeBlanc!"*

He didn't blink. He shook his head. I heard moans and tin cups on steel bars. He looked down and tears ran down his cheeks. "I'm gettin' old and fat and some weeks I don't eat and my heart hurts and I'm not done with my job. Am I talking to myself? You hear me, mister? Am I in the room with you, or am I freakin' out in a funny farm?"

"I'm here with you, Sergeant Major."

He bared yellowed teeth. "Chinks made me. Ain't no train thief." He snorted. "Not good with books like you, West Point. But I worked at it. I did the train, clumsy, no touch, like shooting a commie fifty-one-caliber. That damn camera. Funny Koreans, working on Buddha's birthday. Pulling Freddy for my lawyer. Who'd a guessed?"

I told him that LeBlanc had already buried him in his backyard. "As long as you hold on to the secret, LeBlanc has cause to kill you. Once it's out, killing you has no purpose."

He closed his eyes, his face wonderful in its strengths and terrible in its visible costs. He was going into his murky past, a tangled labyrinth of old roads and buckets of bad-smelling years. I saw his closed eyeballs pick out dimming trail signs.

"Seven years, eight months, two weeks and two days ago, not that I'm countin', I was in ROK lockup. This JAGC—really, a beautiful-lookin' man—comes in. God's smile. Sweet Mary, I thought he was an angel. Some men have that look." He shook his immense head.

"I told him everything—the recruitin' plan, the black-market gizmo—laid out the whole nine yards like he was my priest.

" 'Thank you, brother,' he says. 'Be all you can be,' he says. He says, 'You know what it is that you can be?'

"I said, 'No, sir.' I looked at him, a kid at his daddy. I had a problem; he was gonna fix it, put on the Band-Aid.

"He says, 'You're a damned thief and a filthy disgrace to your uniform. You have broken so many laws for what you pretend to be a noble purpose. It's all your selfishness, and arrogance, and your eternal soul will burn like fat in unholy hell.' His words.

"You know how it is. ROKs woulda treated me square, but they saw an American light colonel treating me like dog crap. So here I am, hounded like a bullshit life-term drug dealer."

"Wizard's a full colonel now. And that's what Curadess was—a life-term drug dealer. You're doing his time."

McCrail grunted, moving like an athletic combat sergeant. "What the hell does that mean? What does 'cura-dess' mean?"

I told him he was serving Cabra Curadess's jacket. His face filled with surprise and then he laughed high. "Thought it was a new Korean cuss word! Hell, I had *no* idea it was my name! Who the hell was Curadess?" I told him.

He flashed his big, square teeth. "Captain, you nail the Wizard's skinny butt to the floor an' rip his head off so the devil can crap down his neck!" He was experiencing pleasure. I let it rush through him, let old nerves tingle with the once familiar.

"Here I am in solitary gook lockup and it's the flamin' Wizard who's deservin' a final verdict—without an appeal." Giggle. "Laddie, will ya go to Hong Kong for me?" Pure brogue.

"You do fraud and tell the wrong JAGC and end up here. Now you got a JAGC you can trust and you won't say squat. I'd say you're a stubborn sonofabitch." I was swearing, a bad sign.

"Aye, lad, I see your fires. Smell the smoke a your work against the enemy. Aren't ya thinkin', laddie, it takes one to know one? You're holdin' onta somethin'. With both hands, tight."

"Nice try. We're sweating *your* problems, not mine."

His bright gray eyes gleamed over dull teeth. "Think hard on Hong Kong, lad. And be thinking too on this man who'll kill us, once he hears we shared a tot in this kind, cozy green tavern, talkin' of Fahey, McConnaughay, and McLaughlin."

He grimaced. "No man ever bested me. He came damn close. But now I got 'im. The filthy, stinkin', connivin' sonofabitch! I'm gonna drop a verdict on his wee piggy head."

He winked, Uncle Patrick to little Nephew Jackson. "With a pinch a your help. You're me lawyer. An angel with the Uniform Code in your ammo pouch, death in your beautiful black eyes, able ta give the Wizard a dose a his own rotten medicines.

"He screwed me good, sir. Made me live with roaches again. Fouled me pa's name, the flag, the lads, my stripes, and every unit I served. He did my family and he puts the slam on God Himself." He bared his yellowed teeth.

"Goddammit! He's not to do it again!"

It was an order.

18

A Cry to Heaven

The joss was burning down and the foxhole clock said it was time to move out. TIG existed to correct wrongs, but Carlos Murray hadn't sent me to break the law.

Axiom: Lawyers can only represent a client's interests; they cannot become involved in a client's business. But no JAGC had ever done to a client what LeBlanc had done to McCrail. I was the JAGC-in-the-box, looking at the results of justice gone to hell.

Under American law, all parties were theoretically equal, making Jimmy no more valuable than McCrail. But small men struggled to find legal aid while corporations hauled in the best attorneys like BaBa used to net fish. Whites who killed whites got stir, and blacks who killed whites got the chair. That's why it was a theory.

I had done 7 July 1967 and had nothing more to lose. Soldiers serve, and I was looking at a man who had been sodomized by jurisprudence. I saw my job. I could also smell it. Whatever drove McCrail was not petty profits. He had a cause.

"What do you want?" I said quietly.

His face collapsed on itself. Tears leaked from tightly shut eyes. Later, he opened them. With a grunt, he hauled on his chains, crushing himself, his hand out.

"Shake my hand," he said, strangled, voice comically high.

It was like shaking hands with Ohio. Never get involved in the personal affairs of clients. He wasn't even supposed to be my client. Shake hands with *yeh*, karma.

His needs had overwhelmed my education and training and my clean chance to get Jimmy. Tears ran down his craggy face. I had seen men and boys cry for dead comrades and lost causes. He wept Achilles' tears for Patroclus, the salts older than most soldiers in a youthful army, shed by a man who was no proponent of weeping.

I used tissues to swab his face. "They were just hot-rod kids in the Bronx." The porridge voice. "Then the draft calls. Korea." The summer of 1950. "First of the Twenty-fourth. *Good* regiment. You went to West Point. You know what that means."

He had been in MacArthur's march to the Yalu in a bitter Manchu winter. Peking had said: Go back or we will fight you. MacArthur had laughed, split Eighth Army from X Corps so they couldn't support each other, and walked them north into the worst defeat in Army history, losing ground we would never see again.

"Friday, 24 November 1950. The Chongchon River. Too cold to dig foxholes." His eyes begged. "You'd like it, sir; we dug good in high ground. You could smell fires or bird breath. Full moon. The wind cut to the bone. MacArthur in Japan, he kinda forgot to send winter gear.

Sniffed something. My hair stood up. I unsafetied. So did the squad." Nothing.

The cold was deadly. The scent was wet wool.

He had yawned and the Chinese had come out of the snow. They overran the regiment with bayonets and burp guns, blowing whistles as guys MacArthur's staff called "Chinaman laundrymen" cut off the companies. Five of his rifle squad survived because they had dug in and faced front, firing at the first wave. They survived to become POWs and were marched into Manchurian winter with their injuries.

Shot, blown up and bayoneted on the night of the full moon, McCrail carried his buddies to the camp. Half-dead, they reached Tangyuan Public Enemy Prison, north of the Songhua, where the Reds tortured Chinese Nationalist and ROK officers.

"This," waving his head at Naktong, "is seventh heaven, garden spot of Asia, Copacabana. In Manchuria, they beat our dicks to sign confessions. Killed most of the Oriental POWs."

Three years later, in the summer of 1953, the Panmunjŏm cease-fire was signed and prisoner exchanges began. Only McCrail and a Canadian were strong enough. McCrail's buddies would come in the September exchange.

McCrail left his pals in the huts of Tangyuan. Walter Twigs, Joseph Two-Toes, Cal Siguera, Seb Delasanto, without a diploma among them, and the old Chinese Nationalist General Fu Tse-hsu.

"Sir, I promised I'd get them out." He sighed and looked around. Naktong seemed deserted. "Come September, commies said my boys died. But no white boxes. I said: They're alive."

McCrail asked futilely for help from the War and State departments, the White House and the UN. They grew to hate him.

He wiggled his nose at me. "Cap'n, maybe you can

scratch my nose with your pen. Yeah, like that. Then I found out." His boys had signed confessions to the Reds.

He glared. "Don't give a crap how tough you are. Your Red brothers up in Manchu land are hard boys. They break people. Do your dick, ears, teeth." He spat. "My boys said we did hot-dog germ warfare for a Howard Johnson's in Peking. Bogus." He grimaced. "And the War Department gave 'em up for 'confessing.' It was Joe McCarthy time. They hosed POW patriots."

He put his head down and talked to himself, rapidly. Then McCrail had gone to Vietnam twice, to be shot four times at Chu Pong massif. He survived a two-hour dustoff and rehabbed in Formosa.

There, a black-dress lady visited him. She was the daughter of General Fu Tse-hsu, his Tangyuan mate. She informed him that her father had died and that the four Yanks were still alive. She had read about McCrail's POW efforts. She said that governments can't help—she used Chinese gangsters.

She used the San Ho Hui—the old Triads. She mentioned the White Lotus, the Black Flags—syndicates, smugglers, Chinese gangs. Sergeants major were the sons of systems, but America had abandoned his men. He gave the Black Flags twenty grand in crisp, newly printed U.S. currency drawn from sixteen American Legion posts with GI survivors of the 24 November Chinese offensive along the overstretched American lines.

"Black Flags said our boys were in Manchuria. No proof, no photos, for twenty grand. Others dropped out." Head shake. "Left me and a buncha chinks, last kind of goddammed people I *ever* wanted to see. For half a million U.S., they'd get four POWs to Hong Kong. Half a million. *Half a goddamn million!* I'd have to be an oil tycoon."

"So you did recruiter fraud. And became a black-marketeer."

"Oh, hell no, sir. I'm *it*. *The* black-marketeer—Mr. Max. *My* show. Hell, I shouldn't say that. God gave it to me, He did. See, South Koreans'd join our army in a heartbeat. Families pool money and buy a fake ID to get the youngest son in. He comes out a U.S. citizen and ships in the family. Instant Americans—add hot water and stir." He shrugged. "Korean kids are educated. Enough English to answer the ASVAB." Military entrance exam. "They work like hell in the Army, put our boys to shame. Good workers. Family men."

I shook my head. "That's a lot of cheating and rule breaking."

"Yeah, West Point. Well, excuse me. I got buddies in Dutch."

Enlistees had to be U.S. citizens or holders of alien resident green cards. McCrail made bogus green cards and sold them to his Korean enlistees at five thousand a copy. Supply clerks get minimum security checks, so he enlisted them as Seventy-six Yankees, company supply clerks. He only took clean applicants. Seventy-six Yankees, MOS 76Y. It rang a bell. He was talking fast.

After basic, they returned to Korea, buying immense quantities of controlled American products with McCrail's capital and selling them on the black market for five to ten times the purchase prices.

"They scraped off the top, gave me a quarter-mil a year clear. Had warehouses in Taegu, Tongducheon, Kwangju."

He had beaten the Yongsan GE225 computer, which should have rung the alarm. "Got me a cyclic program, Fortran V. Made Yongsan read my boys' purchases as a binary zero. No hits, no arrests. Got my half-mil in two years, shut it down, and gave the earnings to the Flags."

"But it wasn't enough."

"You got that right. 'So sorry, Mr. Max'—they can't

say 'McCrail'—'your boy not in Manchuria. They in Russia.' Russia! Crap, *that* made me pucker! My men, toys for the fucking Russkies." His eyes distant, the chains slack.

He peered at me. "They wanted *ammo*—old seventy-five-mike-mike Willy Peter, white phos, moldy ordnance. Ain't made anymore. Chinks swore a family oath in a Confucius temple it was goin' to Iraq and Iran. Bet on a war out there, dollars to donuts. Now guess who has depots full of that crap."

"ROK Army," I said. "In container cars."

"Four-oh, time on target."

"So you wired the program to load the Willy Peter on a munitions train and rerouted it and the Black Flags took it."

"Used my market boys to load. Last job together. They're all Yanks now, selling Corvettes, real estate and photocopiers in L.A."

"The Flags got your men and are moving them to Hong Kong—after nearly what? Eight years?"

"See, that's chinks for you," he said admiringly, eyes bright. "Loyal to a fucking fault. Chinks and Russkies don't get along, so they circle-jerked. But Asiatics don't give up. Last week, this bull comes in my cell, beats the crap out of me and says if I want the POWs, be in the backyard of Kwan Tai Temple at Shek Wu Hui, New Territories, two weeks from today, the last Thursday in January.

"I said, what's the rush? Turns out the Flags're spooked by the new Year of the Tiger. In their heads, it's a bad year. They cast their bones and their horoscope shit to get the date. No changing it.

"Fine, I said. You go for me and I'll give you more money than you can count. He split. Now how the hell was I supposed to get to Hong Kong—or get someone else to go—from here, anus of the world? Then *you* showed up. Christ!"

He took a breath. "After twenty-four years, the boys'll be on our side a the Bamboo Curtain. On high ground, old and full a fish phlegm and rickets and that amoebic shit that grows in Manchuria. Gets in your skin." He glared at the bugs. "Like the fucking Wizard." Whispering, almost inaudible. I strained my good ear. "See, Captain, he sent a man to rape my wife. Nagol."

Bug legs scraped our shoes. I felt a moral chill.

"Sir, bring 'em out." He studied the cell. "Not here. Don't you *ever* bring 'em to Korea. Frisco. The Huntington, with clean sheets. No guards or flying, biting roaches. T-bones and Lucky Lagers. Laugh at everything, Captain. They'll look like cow dung, but tell 'em they look good. Even old Two-Toes would like to hear that. Twigs is ugly as sin, but he don't care."

Go to Kwan Tai Temple, an old monastery dedicated to the war god, to deal with Chinese bandits. I had seen bandits on the Yangtze, coming onto our boat, BaBa and Master Wong silent: the bandoleered *duchun*, bandits, the throat-slitters. BaBa believed God favored me and Ma believed in my tiger sign; it was my job to welcome them.

I stood stock-still, trying to inflate myself into mansize, ignoring the crying of my baby brothers. The *duchun* were smelly and ate our food from hatchets. I thought the sharp-knives were gone with Shanghai *dongshi*, singsong girls, frail, curved-backed gentlemen in long blue gowns, turquoise-garbed Chinese male opera divas, and thick-necked Muslim Chinese warlords eating lamb from their fingers.

"Do it!" he barked. "Finish my job! Do the best thing of your life! You're a good officer. You won't do me like Uncle Sam. A big Northern Chinese with face to take the boys from the Black Flags, just like I was there. You'll take no crap, kick butt, and get the boys out. They follow orders. You're a West Point Airborne Ranger and they'll follow you through hell itself.

"You're chink, patient when the thing turns on you—which, as sure as God made little green apples, it will." He grinned. "With Oriental blood, you won't crap out. You have debt on you bigger'n me." He liked the idea so much in that fetid cell that I liked it. But I was out of my lane and moving away from Jimmy.

"Captain, you screwed up once. Been looking for a way to patch it with something good. This is it, son. You get points in heaven for pullin' out POWs. What you clean-cut West Point sonsofbitches are built for—shit details to save good men."

He took a shuddering breath, chains rattling. The huge chest inflated, face beet red, wheezing. His heart hurt—I moved for him.

He lifted his chin and crowed in a wailing, ear-busting, bottom-lung cry to unseen clouds, the sergeant in the field, bellowing mastery over the battlefield, telling all to screw off as the cups drummed, crying triumphantly to heaven. The guards were returning. I reattached my bandage.

In time, Patrick McCrail stopped bellowing gratitude for the change in fate. Chest heaving, wet from spit and tears, he launched a smile that made old, dry skin crackle from the newness of it.

"You're a beautiful man, Captain. A fine-bred Irishman and a credit to the green." An old man feeling pleasure when none was expected. "I love following tall elephant turds on a long march. Ain't seen sky for seven years plus, but it's a helluva good day in Heaven."

"Sergeant Major, where's your wife? Can I help her?"

He shut his eyes, a child with an old man's facial tic. "She killed herself. Her family understood. I sure as hell didn't." Clenched jaws, a small voice. "Never took to Jesus; she's buried on a Korean holy mountain. Move on."

I exhaled. "I'm sorry. What drives the Wizard?"

"That's a dumb question, sir. He's trying to get rich."

"I don't think so. He has other motives. Maps of the DMZ, fantasies about arming Korea. He didn't kill you. I hope he didn't kill my buddy. Where would he hide him?"

McCrail nodded. "Ya know, guns to him were entertainment. Asked how to use *plastique*. I told him. A bloody mistake, I'm sure. Wizard likes to save people so he can use 'em like toilet paper later. Back then, he was tryin' to turn the provost marshal and his MPs.

"Look for your buddy in a hooker hooch in Southside Ville, shot full a scag and probably dead. I'm sorry, lad. What else?"

"Okay." I rubbed my face. "What can I get you?"

It was a hard question. He raised his great head and let tears flow freely while he picked his nose. No social pretenses.

"I'd sure like to touch a Bible." He looked up. "I hear You, Lord," he whispered, weeping. "I praise You from the bottom of my black, shitty heart for sending him. You are great. I owe You big."

I stilled my face. Fate had hammered on this man every time he had stepped foot in Asia. America had forsaken him, his comrades and his cause, and what he missed was touching a book no one thought much of anymore. But anyone would go nuts down here. "Roger that, Sergeant Major."

"You ought to read it. Unload that crap *you're* carrying around. I owe you one, Cap'n. I just hope no one's gonna cheat us."

He spoke liltingly in brogue. "What am I sayin'? You're the bloody Inspector General and a JAGC to boot and ya can make birds sing in spring." He smiled crookedly, eyes bright, teeth yellow.

"My boys deserve a fuckin' day in the sun." The great white brows at parade rest, his devils appeased. He winked. "Go get it for 'em. They're waitin' for me cuz I said I'd come. You understand a promise like that, don't you, Captain?" The tower was silent.

He glared. "You know we got eighty-one hundred sixty-eight Korean War MIAs? Yes, sir! It's like ten fucking regiments unaccounted for. Well, shit, sir. Four a them bastards are comin' home."

Eight thousand men, missing for a quarter of a century.

He took a breath. I expected him to crow. He sang a deep-voiced melody that came from his heart and played with the muscles in my eyes. He was singing me a wish.

May the road come to meet my step, may the wind be at my back, may a soft rain fall on my fields, might I always be in the palm of his God's hand. It was a song of Chinese rivers.

"Michael Patrick Murphy's Irish blessin'," he said, breathing hard. "Benediction for a parish before it took to its horses." He grinned almost boyishly. "Poetic, ain't it. Tell me, lad. Tell me true. What's the sun like?"

I thought of spring days on the Plain of West Point, the broad Hudson a cut of blue paradise through the dark rock. "Hot, round and steady. Soft and easy in San Francisco, angry as hornets in Georgia. The clouds in fall, up the Hudson, are like pillows for the gods, and grass lawns smile upward."

His eyes were closed. "God, lad, yes. God bless ya." He cleared his throat. "Here's to ya comin' back to me fine green tavern to share another tot." His eyes popped open and he shuddered.

"Afore ya leave, can ya be killin' that fat bug that's feedin' on me neck. God knows, I hate 'em. Ate those little wee cracklin' bastards for dinner at Tangyuan. Now they're payin' me back, they are."

19

HOGACIDE

City lights of all skylines remind me of San Francisco. Driving through Seoul made me miss Cara. The City bore her indelible impression. I saw her profile, loving her face.

Her laughter merged with the fall of artificial rain inside the tropical bar in the Tonga Room's indoor pool on the downslope of Nob Hill. The band played mercilessly nostalgic slow tunes. "Our Winter Love," "Stranger on the Shore," "Theme from *A Summer Place*," "Perfidia."

I could not dance with her without feeling the deliberate need to take her to bed. It was how she fit against me, the warmth of her breath, her scent, her beguiling eyes, her own desire.

"You're too much." I kissed her ear, her slender neck. "Too beautiful, too sexy, too wonderful. Too stunning."

"Oh, baby." She held me tightly, uncaring of the world. "You're crazy. And smart. I only know law and the trivia." Her lips on my ear. "You're idealistic. You know the significata."

"I'm perfect for you. 'Significata'?"

Her face on mine. Arousal tempered by agitation. "*Caro*, I want you to be the last man in my life."

I smiled. "I accept. But we need sleep." I held her tighter. "Think of it, Cara: four hours' sleep, all in a row."

"We sleep enough, *Caro*. I love to talk all night."

"I thought I charmed you in other ways."

"Oh, baby, I love that, too. But I love your brain. Your fidelity. Your stability. And your wonderful, sweet butt."

It was dusk, my wonderful, sweet butt hurt. Chindo hounds howled all over camp, and my uniform smelled like the Naktong sewer system, overpowering the pharmaceutical garlic.

I had left my sunglasses with Major Foss for fingerprinting.

"It was Patrick McCrail," I said. "We got a new client. He says Jimmy may be in the Ville in an area called Southside."

Levine was pale, eyes red. Magrip killed beers. Pabst cans littered the floor. He didn't like the warm bottom of a can and probably stiffed rude waitresses.

Levine bit out the words. "James Buford is dead. Jeep accident last night on east post."

Magrip crushed a can and threw it, opening another with a savage punch of a church key. "Bullshit. They killed him."

"That was Willoughby on the phone in Yongsan," said Levine, "as you left with Min. Said Jimmy was being buried. I came back by taxi. It was held at Casey's post chapel."

I was on the river at Chingshan, watching China burn. Peasants buried unboxed dead on high ground in a black dawn. The high, sad wailing of children crossed the brown water as it lapped the hull, laughing rhythmically at bad-luck Chinese sailors.

I was a boy, but I felt the souls of my dead brothers, struggling in the soft, loess mud. *Dzai jian*, see you again, Hu-chien, Strong Tiger. *Dzai jian*, Hu-hau, Good Tiger. I was seven, holding the tiller so Ma and BaBa could weep.

"A ROK Army doctor," she said, "found him in an irrigation ditch off Pusan Alley. He estimated death to be near midnight. Cause was spinal fracture, traumatic head injuries, smoke inhalation, and burns. The med called

Bethanne Buford. I talked to Carlos Murray. Burial will
be at Arlington."

My heart sputtered. I saw him, heard him, the slow,
courtly cavalier, imagined him slipping my watch from
my wrist with a laugh that would make the devil pause. I
had a premonitory flash that he was alive. I shook my
head and exhaled: denial. Carlos and his wife would be
with Bethanne. Beth would tell the kids.

Boys, Uncle Jack tried real hard, but Daddy's dead.

"I'm very sorry, Jackson," said Levine.

I had just inherited three sons. A small white box.
Inside was a brass urn with Jimmy's name, DOB, and
DOD, along with the death cert. I tried to read it, but my
eyes glazed over. I touched the urn.

Ah, Jimmy, the bastards got you before I could
find you.

Out of respect, I tried to say a silent prayer for him and
his family, using his words of faith. They rang hollow
without mystic choirs and cherubim gliding into pink
sunsets. The room was tropically hot, memories sweated
out by the pressure of the urn, his big personality inside a
jar, the hideous, blood-sucking, carrion insects exultant,
his little boys weeping.

Our efforts were futile. The devil owned the deck, ran
law offices and killed innocent children. I felt the host of
ancient Chinese gods, ranked by petty human needs,
answering to incense and paper offerings, amused by our
suffering, making us bend down to them in weakness,
bathing in our fears.

Well, screw all of you.

"Where's my ring?" Levine passed it to me. I put
it on.

"I go now, *dae-wi*," said Min softly. "So sorry."

Prove that Jimmy's death was murder. The Wizard had
done this to Jimmy. Get evidence. Support McCrail's
verdict on him.

I took a breath. "Stand fast. What'd the computers say?"

"I didn't run it." She saw my face. "I should have stayed."

"Yes, you should have," I snapped. "Need me for anything?"

"Nothing," said Levine, looking at me as if I were far away.

I took overcoat and briefcase. "Min. Let's go."

I released the magazine of the Browning. A round in the chamber and a full load. I slammed it home and safetied it, comforted by its metallic coldness, and put it in my belt. We drove east. I turned on Min's headlights. I tried to think, brains swimming in tangled emotions, rampant with sour, fogging pain. Think. Don't feel.

Pusan Alley was a lonely country gravel road used by perimeter patrols at the Siberian end of a wasteland camp. The ground sloped south into an irrigation ditch which served a dead, ugly field.

The mountains were cold and dark, witnesses to war. This was deep in Korean soul, shaman country.

We got out with big flashlights and unfolded entrenching tools. Snow covered any skid marks. Min found a cracked tree and hints of a boxed burn area on a snowy hill. The road turned hard above it. The jeep had lost the turn in the ice, gone off the road, hit the slope toward the ditch, struck the tree—and burst into flame.

Min held the flashlights as I carefully shoveled snow.

No wide, digging, swerving treads. No sharp rock or steel rebar to puncture the tank or gas line or rip a hot wire. And Jimmy didn't smoke. He had small kids and drove like Don Knotts. He had died here, near midnight in the Korean winter. He could've been meeting or following someone. Or been chased. A jeep flying off the road would have shattered the tree; it was cracked. I studied the trunk: axe marks. The light glared on the snow. Burn patterns on the ground revealed carelessly tossed accelerants. I walked the hillside. This was no accident scene; it was theatrics.

Jimmy had been killed and dumped on an arson stage. I was a JAGC, but I had learned in the ultimate human courtroom that God pretends to appear only when you're dying, and not when you kill. Murder chases out all deities. Jimmy was my proof.

Min fired up the heater. I tried to read the ROK doctor's signature on the Death Cert. "Can you read this?"

"*Dae-wi*, this fake-oo." He made a face. "Cheatah cheatah punkin eatah." He paused. "Liar liar pant burn big-oo-time."

"You're saying this was forged?"

He nodded emphatically.

Second Med Battalion was at north camp, close to the water reservoir and the support services helipad, hard-standed with portable, perforated steel plank flooring for winter. Huey medevac rotors were tied down, tarped and dusted in snow. This was a full division facility with smoothed plywood surgical suites, ample lights, backup batteries, and reserve generators. I stepped into a camou-flaged GPL—general purpose, large—tent with a thou-sand cots, crates of body bags and two thousand olive drab stretchers in stacks. This was 57F graves registrars, undertaker country.

A quiet night in emergency: two stabbings, six contusions and a broken wrist from Ville brawls, and fifty-three troopers who suspected they had clap. The stab victims moaned, the bruised complained about MP brutality, the clap paranoids whined, and old medics muttered, "Aw, quit yur bitchin'—this ain't the Nam.

"And chump, didn't I *tell* you not to Savoy? Bro, those girls got VD." Behind him, on a board, was a bar graph showing VD rates by the clubs. Savoy was the big leader;

Vegas was the tail. The bars were represented by red condoms.

"Where'd you get this?" asked a tall, lean doc named Purvis with a nearly beautiful face and flawless black skin. He read the certificate through metal-rimmed reading glasses. Behind him worked a small, stetho-scoped ROK Army major. Casually, Major Purvis sprayed me with a can of air freshener. "What," he asked, "hit a fertilizer truck on the MSR?"

I blinked in the mist. "Something like that."

The Inmingun invasion was projected to produce sev-enty percent line casualties. While diplomats traded manly insults, ROK and Yank doctors worked together daily in preparation for hard times. Army physicians of all nations were realists.

I told him the document's history. "I need to talk to the ROK doc who signed this certificate last night."

Purvis showed it to his colleague.

"I Major Koo, number-two surgeon, First Brigade, White Horse Division." He saw my ROK trousers from the Naktong masquerade. He sniffed, shrugging. I bowed to the modest national standard. The Japanese occupation had required low bows. "Captain Kan, IG."

Major Koo, respecting authority, bowed again, lower. I returned it and introduced Min. Major Koo ignored him, studying the paper.

"Captain Kan, this paper is bolo—fake. ROK doctors not sign death paper on U.S. soldier. Only U.S. doctor do this. Slicky boy can steal paper. Next door, have thou-sand blank DC. This," holding it up, "is not a signature. Is a mark, not name."

He waved his hand, looking to Purvis for help.

"Graffiti," said Purvis.

Major Koo nodded. "Graffiti."

"Thank you. You have a Captain James Thurber Buford, DOA? Or a John Doe casualty? Buford is thirty, white male, six-three, one ninety, blue eyes, brown hair. No scars or marks."

They checked the logs. No record. "Chaplain did a memorial service for Captain Buford today at post chapel. Maybe a DOA went someplace else? A battalion aid station. Somewhere."

Dr. Purvis used the eraser end of a pencil to dial a number, the rotary face clicking erratically.

"Zipper, this is Sam Purvis at the med. . . . Yes, Zip," he said slowly, "it's cold enough for me." Purvis asked about a Captain Buford, or an unknown soldier, or anyone going through graves registration since 6 January, eleven days ago. Zipper the mortician said he'd check it out.

Jimmy's death might be as fake as the certificate. Time slowed while Purvis and Koo cleared patients. They were both good. Filled with hope, I thought of Beth and the boys.

An hour passed. Zipper Man phoned Purvis. No hits, no deaths, no cremations, no tags, no Captain Buford in any UN shop.

The Q echoed with combat between country music and Motown. I knocked. Major Foss, the burly, thick-necked cop, stepped into the hall in grayed thermals, brown socks, and watchman's cap. "Shit. You again."

Horny troops went to the Ville; high achievers hit the sack. It was eight P.M., and the number-two cop in town was asleep in his work cap. His roommates snored, one industriously, the other pitifully, like a dying asthmatic. Foss closed the door on a socked foot and swore for a while.

"Ooh," intoned Min, recording the oaths in a notepad.

Foss belched. He smelled of chaw. A lot of troops on the Z never brushed their teeth, violating a local regulation.

"Sir, you remember a jeep accident last night?"

He tried to think. He nodded again, swaying like a drunk hippo in the red aura of the Q emergency light, eyes half-closed.

"I need to see that jeep now, sir."

He smelled my clothes and leaned back. He squinted at his watch. His head came back into two-inch glaring range. "You do, huh? Gonna help me run at reveille, too?"

"You find me the jeep, sir, I'll get you out of it."

"I hate running." He exhaled. "Prints on the sunglass lenses belong to Patrick McCrail, a sergeant major who drowned back in '66. But the prints were fresh." He looked at me. I said nothing.

Min drove us to the DX yard, the elephant grave for dead equipment. We skidded into the dark compound, rammed two wood barriers that used to say Stop, and shot into the junkyard, headlights bright and eager for another hapless target.

The major awoke with a jolt. "God crap a brick! You drive like Oh Shit Min! Christ Jesus—it's *you*!"

"Neh, yukkun soryong." Yes, Major, gasped Min.

"STOP THIS JEEP!" We lurched to a stop, throwing snow and skidding on ice and banging me into the dashboard. "Craphead KATUSA! Asshole! You filled the yard with half the junk! Oh, man! Great blotter report: 'Foss killed by Oh Shit Min Andretti.' Man, what a wreck you caused at Armor Crossroads!"

Min had shrunk to the size of a Chihuahua.

"Hey—forget it, son. Didn't mean to ruin your opinion of yourself. Hell, I can brag I rode with you and lived."

Min coughed, hissing through his teeth, head down.

A dark yard filled with two-and-a-half-ton trucks which had been caught in floods, fires, or MSR wrecks or had driven too close to Min. There were stacks of flattened jeeps, a dead armored personnel carrier.

Foss stuffed Red Man in his bulging left cheek, chewed, and spat a glob. He got out and churned through the snow to a hut. He turned on a line of low yellow lights. The yard was immense. Most of this wasn't Min's work—it was the Korean MSR 3, the suicide alley between Seoul and the DMZ. Foss returned, spitting in the snow, admiring his dark marks while he glanced at a DX manifest.

"Top of stack sixty-one." Jimmy's jeep sat on top of five other crushed sisters in a numbered pile. I heard a chopper.

Even in the cold air in a snow-filled hulk, the high-hydrocarbon, metallic stench persisted from a petroleum fire that had taken rubber and steel in its search for fuel.

I scooped out the snow and switched on the flashlight. Something had burned and spattered in the driver's seat and my guts turned. I sat on the chassis where the passenger seat once was, staring at the smear of former humanity, my stomach acidic. "Thanks, Jimmy," I said. "I needed this."

Foss and Min climbed in after me, shifting the jeep. Foss spat, dribbling on his field jacket. I was going to say something about preserving crime scenes, but this was Korea. I saw the chopper lights. It was coming in low and fast from the west.

"What we looking for here?" asked Foss, sitting on a pile of snow and ice in the back. His jeep radio below squawked.

"ID of the deceased. You worried about that chopper?"

"Cap'n, no fatal wrecks come to DX. Got them in my yard."

"Sir, you have any vehicle fatalities since 6 January?"

He shook his head. The wind burst over us. Junk rattled, snow blew, and metal clanged against coiled barbed wire. Min put his nose into the driver's seat. "What smell?" he asked.

"Petroleum fire," I said above the chopper rotors.

"*Aniyo, dae-wi.* Is *twae-ji.* Hog-oo. Big pig-oo."

Foss put his nose into the seat, the cop in him emerging. "Oh Shit Min's right. Smells like pork rind."

It was like seared *chujou*, pork, absent the sickening stench of flesh fires pushed by gas accelerants, when bodies were torched by napalm and burned in helo crashes. I cleaned the Randall knife and scraped the burned matter into an envelope, glued it shut, and time/dated it across the seal.

The chopper banked around us, bursting with noise and light, a hundred meters out. Its thumping rotors raised my heartbeat. Vietnamese country music, an indelible association with bad days.

The chopper whipped snow as its hot searchlight hit us. I saw a door gunner, gun post, ammo, and no barrel, meaning that the M-60 machine-gun muzzle was pointing at me. I sensed the gunner's nervousness, adrenaline warming his frigid door position. Fear rang through me; I remembered dusk engagements when gunships had seen my Asian features as a bull's-eye. I froze.

"Do not move. Identify," said a bullhorn.

The light caught Foss. He pointed at his MP arm brassard.

"Call us next time, Major," came the echoing voice. The light was doused and the gunship whumped off low across the yard, blowing ground snow. I exhaled.

Min looked at his watch. He had timed the helo response.

"Captain Shawn," shouted Foss. "Good man with good eyes."

"Think a man died in this fire, Major?" I yelled.

"Oh, hell no!" he bellowed, the rotors still loud. "This was arson—lots of gas thrown in the compartment. Completely blew away the jeep." He smiled like Groucho Marx. "And committed a hogacide."

I began to laugh. Foss hit me and we laughed harder.

The Wizard didn't kill. He roasted barn animals,

torched jeeps, and incarcerated sergeants major in foreign lockups.

"You okay?" asked Foss.

"Oh, hell, I'm fine. You sure?"

He pointed his flashlight. "Someone burned the crap
out of something, imprinting bacon, rind and small
animal skeleton into the floor. Spread that on bread with
some cheddar and you got yourself a ham-and-cheese
sammich."

I saw it. "Major, this wreck goes with a comprehensive
chain of custody to Evidence." That meant each MP
effecting the jeep's transfer from DX into evidence
would document time and action, without any breaks
in time.

"Then tie it back to the wreck at Pusan Alley. I want to
know everyone who even saw this jeep." He nodded.

I showed him the death cert. He read it under a flashlight. "Bogus. A two-dollar whore offerin' a Rolex. No
ROK doc in his right mind would sign a death C on an
American." He squinted at me. "Mind telling me what
the hell is going on?"

"Major, if you wanted to disappear an IG captain,
where would you stow him?"

He huffed breath and looked at me flatly. "I got a
good idea. Go screw yourself *and* the horse you rode in
on." He climbed down and strode through the snow,
talking to himself, getting angrier. "*I'm* the straight cop
and the asshole IG rousts me. And Oh Shit Min's his
driver. Hauls my butt to DX to study a kitchen fire and
don't tell me crap." He turned to me. "Captain, you go
jump high and wide. I hate to see what happens when
you get higher rank." He spat ferociously. "Which you
probably will."

We were driving back to his Q with the heater fan
coughing, Foss's long, thick leg stuck between our front
seats, the missing engine rockers competing with his
ceaseless spitting.

"Major, someone kidnapped an IG and faked his death in that jeep. I'm sorry for stiffing you. I could use your help."

The studded tires plowed snow. He sighed. "I'd fly 'im to Japan. Shoot 'im full a scag and drop 'im on the Shimonoseki ferry back to Korea. Heroin addict docks on Korean soil becomes instant dead meat. ROKs don't play games and ain't half nice. Got a craphole called Naktong Tower south of the Han in Suwon country. American boys melt down in there with stick beatings and then get blown away by firing squad."

"Where would you stow him around here?"

He shrugged. "Probably Southside Ville. Old Japanese industrial park, survived the war cuz both sides used the warehouses as hospitals. Ville changed hands between us and the Inmingun seventeen times. Villagers took it in the shorts. Now the oogliest whores in the Orient work there. ROKs don't hassle 'em—go figure."

That's where McCrail had said Jimmy would be, half-dead: Southside. "Maybe you can draw me a map." I gave him my notepad.

He drew it. "Park at the canal and walk. Southsiders are retreads and vampires; sleep in the day and work at night. Wait till dusk or they'll freak and, if your boy's there, they'll crapcan him. We got no jurisdiction there." He rubbed his nose. "Guess if you asked pretty I'd give you some sidearms. I sure as hell wouldn't go into Southside with just good looks."

"What would you use as a rally point?"

He studied his own map, then drew an X on the northwest corner where the alley that led to the warehouses met the main Southside road. "Leather shop. Only red sign on the block."

I nodded. "Major, we could sure use some guns."

He blew out air, then passed me his service automatic with two magazines. "Armorer competition model. Hits what you aim at." He pulled an S&W Airweight five-shot .38 from an ankle holster and a speed loader from his jacket. From his armpit he removed a leather-banded concussion grenade. He opened the glove box and extracted a massive S&W .44 magnum revolver with a speed loader.

"Kan, this is some of my personal stuff. I want it back."

I had trouble stowing it. "Roger that. You bare?"

He pulled a nickel-plated S&W .357 Python from a shoulder holster. "Don't ask ROK cops for help. South-side's a parking lot for two-bit whores and fugitives from justice." The brakes screeched and I banged into the dash. We got out. "You owe me one, Captain."

"Yes, sir, I do." I looked at him. "What happened to the law here?"

He holstered the pistol, worked the chaw, and spat on his chin, where it began to freeze. "We trash evidence. Drink too much *mokkli* and write bad reports. We don't chase perps—we pull guard duty on claims payouts." He wiped his chin. "GIs are usin' AK-47s to dust comfort girls who piss 'em off in fee disputes. I got a direct order not to find out where the guns came from. I gotta tell you, *that's bullshit*." He picked up a rock and hurled it. It landed and a dog howled.

"Think the old man's on the take. Wizard covers for him while they play grab-ass with claims and recruiting and let bad cops lie. Never thought I'd say that about the top MP or the SJA." He shook his head. "Goddamn Korea, oink, oink. I don't like it. But the odds out here are the shits." He pushed the wad into his left cheek. "I didn't even use to curse."

"Sir, you keep holding the line."

He studied me, chewing. "Why in hell should I do that?"

"It's your job, Major."

"Yeah, so should everyone. Where's our heat? Chow?

Fresh wire? New winter gear?" He snorted. "No one does their damn job. It's colder than blue crap and I wouldn't know a head a lettuce if it bit me. I'm the best cop here and I think I'm going sideways."

Dr. Purvis awoke sharply, accustomed to living in an ongoing emergency. Rumpled and sleepy, he inspected the contents of the envelope. He sniffed. He put it under a microscope on his desk, tweezing a burned hair under the glass. "*Suidae* family. Porcine. Pig, swine, hog. NHI—no humans involved. Want a report?"

"Please." When drug dealers blew each other away in retail debates, cops said it went down NHI. No Humans.

"I'm about to call the jeep accident deceased's wife and inform her that she's not a widow. You see a problem with that?"

"These are not human remains. Use my phone, Counselor."

Noon yesterday in Silver Spring. The phone rang six times. "Beth, this is Jackson." I had to wait three seconds for my voice to get there and three more for hers. I said I had proof Jimmy didn't die in the wreck, that I believed he was alive but didn't know where he was, that Carlos had sent a team to find him.

She cried. She had always had control, her voice softer than Charlotte lemonade. "Oh, God—oh, God! Oh, the kids. Kids! David! Rick! Brian! Come here! Come here now! Oh, my God, thank you, Jackson, thank you. God love you! I *knew* you'd do it! Jackson, does Carlos know? I'll call him. Kisses from us. Jackson—I love you! Oh, sweetheart, find him! Oh, God bless you! Oh God! Oh my God! Boys, oh my boys! Your daddy's alive! Daddy's alive! Yes! Honest to God, cross my heart! It's Jackson on the phone and he's not dead!"

Their weeping rang in my head, even though they had cried in joy. Jimmy was a lucky man. If I could find him.

I wanted to call Cara and tell her I had not left her, that I was doing something I had to and would soon be home.

"Want some sedatives?" asked Purvis.

I shook my head.

"Come in the three-to-eleven. See Doc Dwaine Dean. You're labile, emotionally in flux, with sleep deprivation and delayed, chronic recurring combat fatigue. You're treating it by clenching your teeth, which is like fighting fire with your hair. You don't respect it, and treat it, you'll embarrass us for another failure to exercise preventive medicine."

"This a masked comment about my ROK Army haircut?"

Later, I thanked Corporal Min. "You should be a general."

"*Dae-wi* too muchee kind!" He bowed, baring teeth and scraping. I regretted saying anything. He saluted horribly. I returned it.

I took a military shower but nearly emptied the tank.

Magrip was supposed to be on duty. He slouched like a dead man in the chair, sounding like a garbage disposal dispatching artichokes. I had left him without a weapon.

Levine was breathing easy. I put down the firearms, opened the box and urn, clicked on the flashlight. I stirred with my knife. Pure, fine silica, no bone.

I turned on the bright ceiling light.

Magrip fell out of the chair. "Whatthafug?"

Levine grumbled into her pillow. Her makeshift curtain had fallen. I found one of her candies. I popped it in my mouth. I preferred Chinese sour plums.

I cleared my throat. "I'd like your attention, please." Sock-clad feet dragged under covers, the groveling, sordid, sour grumping of overworked cadets at dawn.

"Listen up! I have the murder of an innocent pig to report."

20

No Deals

Friday, January 18

It took only ten minutes to reach the Pentagon exchanges and Carlos Murray on the second floor of the D Ring. I heard him sip coffee, black. Eleven-thirty yesterday morning his time, one-thirty A.M. ours. Beth Buford had called him with the good news. I gave him the details. His sense of relief brought out his supportive nature.

"You waiting to find Jimmy next year? This year too soon?"

"Been working on my tan." I told him we needed to free a ROK inmate named Curadess, explaining McCrail. I said a habeas would take too long; we needed a ROK presidential release. I suggested new staffs for damage control on Casey's legal woes.

"*Cholo*, I send you to get Jimmy and you decide to become an interior decorator."

"Yeah, well I once had a Chicano professor who said, 'Research all options, exhaust all remedies, and exercise unlimited zealousness for your client.' "

"You should not believe everything you hear in college."

"That wasn't college. Carlos, let me deal McCrail for Jimmy."

Give the Wizard immunity for McCrail in return for our getting Jimmy intact; the Wizard would fall to a host of other charges.

Carlos bristled. "No way we forgive an SJA for Curadess and McCrail and let him retire with an attaboy. *Jesús Cristo*, what are you thinking?"

I told him he was wrong. Then I told him about the POWs.

"*Culero!* A crazy con in ROK stir might not even know his name anymore. Forget Hong Kong. You get back on track, Captain Jack."

"My job," I said, "is getting Jimmy. Don't get greedy. We got to bring our boys in. Not only Jimmy, but McCrail. Carlos, he said there are *eight thousand* Korean War MIAs."

He exhaled. "Urchin, get Jimmy. Stop being creative, stop ghost chases, at ease with further slop thought and *stay in your damned lane!*"

"The Wizard drips with evidence. Pig Breath's here. Carlos, we owe McCrail." Pause. "I told him I'd go."

"No way. Pig's a loose cannon. Wizard hangs with our rope, so it's done right, not as a religious exercise by a half-fascist who'd convict his mother had God issued him one. Get the Bee, avoid Pig, and trap the rats. I didn't send you out there to do a missionary dance. No deals for the Wizard and no Chinese gangs."

He was excited to the point of contractions.

I said nothing.

"Crap, *pendejo*, you're sticking it to me! You're the one guy in the Corps who always remembers the job, and you do this, to me, your old *patrón*?" He cleared his throat. "You piss me off."

I knew that. *Pendejo* was a kind word for "stupid."

"Let me deal McCrail so LeBlanc'll give us Jimmy. Ten years—" Murray had hung up.

The phone rang at four A.M. I snapped on a flashlight and jumped out. Levine squealed and leaped behind her curtain, pulling sheets like a deckhand smothered in sail. She had probably showered and been dressing in one of her isolated moments of relative privacy, putting on underwear while one man snored fitfully, the other chewed on his pillow—and the phone rang. Her long johns lay lonely on the floor. I picked up the phone and passed her the thermals. I hung her curtain, hiding her. "Yes," I said. No courtesies, only anonymity.

Levine's legs were lean and corded in striated muscle.

"Urchin," came the echoing voice. "McCrail checks out. He's who he says he is—a black-marketer. But Al Haig and the White House want the PR angle on him." He let that sink in. "So Al called President Park."

Park Chung-hee, the former ROK officer who had become the president of the Republic of Korea by a military coup. He was a short, stern, hard-faced man whose military austerity was thought to be offset by a smart, calmly elegant wife.

"So now we wait." He paused. "*Hombre*, listen—we *do* have eighty-one hundred, sixty-eight Korean War MIAs. The President was shocked. He wants McCrail released, then Jimmy."

"Dammit, forget Nixon. We're not doing politics."

"I thought you didn't swear, *culero*. Do not blame him; if he brings POWs home from *any* war, he gets points. Right now, he is way down. Con Law, *chico*. He is *commandante*.

"Today, Kicker Magrip goes to Naktong to extract McCrail."

"By that time, Jimmy could be dead."

"My friend, you got hooked by the sergeant major. It was the right call, so live with it. Levine to the embassy to help the ambassador smooth McCrail's exit. Kicker takes McCrail to the 121st Evac for med clearance before he goes to Hong Kong.

"Urchin, your job is to get LeBlanc to give you Jimmy."

"The man has no incentives. Give me something to deal."

"Use your charm."

"Why didn't I think of that?"

I told Levine and Magrip the plan. I told them to take the Wizard's map and overlay from his Q and to leave convincing copies in their place.

They looked at each other. Kan busting the law.

"No warrant?" asked Levine. "It won't be admissible."

"The Wizard's up to something bigger than kidnapping. I need to know how he thinks, and I don't expect the map to taint any other evidence we find. Okay? You have Murray's plan down? Good—dump it. I have a different one."

I laid Foss's arsenal on the desk. They looked at me; they looked at each other.

"A fine mess you've gotten me into," said Levine.

"Fuckin' A," said Magrip, taking the S&W Model 29 .44 magnum with the eight-inch barrel and the speed loader; Levine rolled her eyes. "Phallic, don't you think?" She pointed. "What's that?"

"Concussion grenade," I said. "Foss's. Straighten the pin, pull it and throw. It incapacitates at three meters and stuns at five."

Levine took it and the Airweight. Magrip took the competition .45 Colt and magazines, his clothes sagging with metal.

"Big enough, Magrip?" asked Levine.

We left before dawn to avoid the rush of seventeen thousand troops on road runs. We stopped at the provost marshal's Q. I owed Foss for finding the hogacide jeep. The senior officer Q had fresh paint—probably applied as recently as 1955.

I knocked hard on the top cop's door. He was a thick-bellied, balding, red-faced beast with small ferret eyes, short arms, and an unhappy Korean woman in his bunk. "Sir, I'm Captain Kan, IG. Major Foss is excused from the reveille run. You have a real nice day."

"What?" he said. I repeated myself. "What?" he said.

We exited remote Gate 2 to the north. It was desolate country, filled with concertina wire to deter NKPA infiltrators. The twisting, narrow road was snowblocked, but tanks had been out last night and had cut a deep trail through the side pack. I nodded and Min turned off the road to follow the deep track trails.

I told Min to stop as I switched off headlamps. Something was moving off road. I got out. Here, the wind blew harder.

Below the ridge on the military crest, two fire-team-sized squads ran at a pace far faster than the eight-minute-mile rifleman shuffle. They ran in the fast lope of long-distance runners. They were huge men in jump boots, carrying big rucks. I pulled cold field glasses from the glove box, focusing fast.

"Come on, Kan, let's go," said Levine. "It's freezing."

I knew one group. Dr. Death and his happy steroidal fools with the exclusive private gym and exotic weapons.

The second group had equally immense runners, headed by a skinny officer. Henry Jubala, Army marathon champ, my fellow passenger from Japan. They reversed field, sprinting like they had left explosives on a short fuse. Flankers ran with Uzis and grenade launchers. They had seen us first.

Min stared, barely breathing.

"Sappers," said Magrip. "The packs." Explosives engineers, Twelve Bravos. "Never seen such big guys. You?" Saps were the diagonal ditch parallels engineers dug to besiege a fort in medieval Europe, packing gunpowder under its walls.

"No." Sappers were runts who crawled tunnels and scooched under bridge trusses, slapping on plastic C-4 explosives and stringing green det cord.

"Can we go now?" asked Levine. This wasn't like her.

I was looking at a piece to a puzzle I felt I recognized.

Sapolu had told me not to think. Jubala had concealed his job. Big runners who ate steroids for Uncle Sam meant—

"Kan." Levine. "Dawn's going to catch us. Let's go. This is none of our business, and they're better armed than we are."

She was right. I was out of my lane again. It was time to feed the team. We drove out of Casey into Tongducheon.

A rooster crowed, dogs howled, and we turned into a district of single-storied clothing and sundries shops. Korean signs sat above the doors, like flipped-up brims on a row of baseball caps.

The street curved and hiccupped; the angles deflected bad luck and brought good *feng shui*, geomancy.

"Happiness Cafe, numbah one." Min made a thumbs-up.

The cook, in a stained, padded jacket, worked over a smoking grill, cigarette dangling. I went in. The warmth was like a hug from Mother. He stared as I pounded the snow from my boots. We were deep in Tongducheon. The others entered.

"No *pulgoki*!" shouted Magrip. *Pulgoki* was barbecued dog.

"No goddam *pulgoki*!" shouted the cook. "No cook damn dog!"

"Hate this goddammed country. It eats dogs and snakes."

"Magrip," I said, "you would hate Heaven."

The browned vinyl in the last booth had once been red. The table had been abused by people who had known Moses. It was like the cafes of my youth—no menus. You ate what the cook prepared and watched for dogs at your feet, hoping none were on your plate.

The cook threw plates, the scarred table surface braking their slide. He brought Chinese tea as Min described the meal.

"*Bulgoki*—barbecue beef. *Kalbitong*—soup. *Kim chi*—ferment cabbage." Levine knew chopsticks; Magrip used a Gerber killing knife to sharpen a stick into a skewer. The tender *bulgoki* was a marvel of strong, sweet flavors and scents.

"What's the plan?" asked Magrip, meat dangling.

"First," I said, "Carlos is for equal opportunity."

Magrip nodded happily at me. "That explains you."

"Yes," said Levine. "A woman, a Chinese, a Korean—and an idiot."

Magrip paused in mid-bite, then laughed. "Levine, you're okay."

"Levine," I said, "go to the embassy in a motor-pool sedan. Then get McCrail out of Naktong and get him to the docs."

"You're really busting Carlos's orders. ROKs don't groove on women. What impresses them is the size of your dick."

"They haven't met you. Corporal Min and Magrip, recon Southside. Magrip, don't blow anything up. Around dusk, you and I will go in and look for Jimmy." He nodded.

I showed them Foss's map. "Find doors. Check security. Find the entry point. The X is a leather shop with a red sign. Our rally point. Sixteen hundred hours. Brush your teeth, turn in your library books, and bring your grenades.

"Magrip, you're a JAGC. *Save* evidence, don't blow it up. We hurt others only if we have to. The objectives are to rescue Jimmy and accrue evidence against the perps."

"And while I recon?" asked Magrip, his mouth full.

"I go see the Wizard and wow him with my charm."

"You have a better chance to fart to the moon."

"Something to which I have always aspired."

"Kan," she said. "I want to go with you into Southside."

Magrip blew out air. "That'd be cute. Reach into an

ammo pouch and pull out a pair of panties—nothing personal."

Levine arched an eyebrow. "From you, Magrip, nothing's personal. Monsieur Idiot, I wasn't talking to you."

"Levine," I said, "you make it back with McCrail before 1600 hours, come to the rally point. Stow McCrail on post first."

"Christ, you're shitting me!" said Magrip, swelling. "What's this, some sort of minority, female-lib revenge party? She can't go in! You're taking *her* as our reserve over a sergeant major?"

I lowered my voice. "Magrip, you should know the truth. We're actually working for Gloria Steinem, Betty Friedan and Bella Abzug. I held back, knowing how you take bad news."

Levine laughed. Magrip dropped his skewer. Min said that if so many other people—"Stinnim, Abbug and Freeman"—were going, could he come as well?

21

SONG SAE MOON

Thus inspired, they left the Happiness Cafe. It was six-thirty A.M., and patrons trickled in. I had an hour before entering the Wizard's court with the moral high ground, a weak opening statement, little evidence, and a closing argument to match. I had to make him give me Jimmy before Jimmy became bacon.

Colonel, give us Captain Buford so we can convict you on your confession, bust and disbar you, and drop you for a life term in Leavenworth. You could become the Rasputin of the legal profession. People would talk about you and then spit.

I could hear Jimmy Buford say, "Son, that dog won't hunt."

A woman had entered the cafe and was looking at me.

"*Annyonghasheemneeka, dae-wi.*" The woman in white from the Las Vegas, now in a brown coat. A white fur cap above a captivating oval face. Madame Cho had said she was *michaso*, crazy.

I returned the greeting. I gestured to the seat.

"Thank you. You are most kind." The coat opened to a form-fitting white turtleneck and black pants with high boots. The voice was high, pretty and melodic, tremulous with anticipation.

Thick coal-black hair hung like heavy summer fruit over her shoulders and cascaded across a high forehead. She was formally rouged. Widely spaced dark eyes, attentive and feline. A man she studied would be the object of an analysis of unknown purposes. The eyes were messengers from another time, dominating a well-defined nose and a small, precise rosebud mouth, artfully red. Her small eyebrows were dark to the point of bright-ness, the eyelashes long and black.

I wondered whose side she was on.

She removed gloves. Her fingers were twisted and gnarled, as if they belonged to an old Chinese boxer who had spent a lifetime hitting hard objects until the pain went away.

She angled her head and brushed back her hair, the regal Ice Queen. Her gaze had projected a superstitious light into my nervous system, setting off Chinese warning lights.

"I am Jackson Hu-chin Kan."

"I know. I am Song Sae Moon," she said in her musical voice, haunting big-cat eyes scanning my body. "Thank you for your politeness." Her words lingered, sweet notes on a warm day, a voice that leaned deliberately on its dancing, feminine qualities.

"You are a smart Chinese firstborn son. A man with *ch'ilgo chiak*, ancient Confucian doctrine and culture. You are what every girl in Korea prays to Buddha for."

She was like thin Mrs. Fan, the Chinatown oracle, foretelling by guesswork, using flattery in place of insight.

"*Dae-wi*, the *wang mansin mudang* needs to see you for the health of her village. Do you understand '*mudang*'?"

Mudangs were female shamans, sorceresses. Mediums who healed and spoke for the dead. Spirit dancers, drum beaters, spiritual snake-oil merchants, peasant manipulators.

When I was six, I had met a *wu*, a shaman, at Jinsha Monastery on Dongting Lake. My parents had taken me to him to cure the fever from drinking the river when the whirlpool had taken me. BaBa, who could barely swim, had saved me. The *wu* stood at the gate, looking at me with furrowed brows and hard eyes, spitting on the black stone path.

BaBa had growled. He spat at the diagnosis that I had a demon in me, scaring the *wu*. Ma argued openly with BaBa and not the shaman. I was a Taoist believer, and could feel the *wu*'s judgment on my *yeh*, my karma, something a father's anger or a mother's imprecations could not wash away. I felt the hollowness of his medicine that day, offered more to placate Ma than to cure me.

The feeling about the shaman did not leave my nights until we came to America, the wide Eastern Sea swallowing the *wu*'s opinion of me. When I lay in the medevac, Moms Bell next to me, his life bleeding out, the company still in the bush waiting for extraction, I thought of rivers and remembered the *wu* spitting at me, and saw the dead girl, calling me Father, feeling all the luck in my life change from good to bad. I had been hit twice and thought I was going to die, accepting the equitable judgment of God for my error. I recovered and saw that the atheists were right.

Now, those feelings returned, radiating like low bass from a radio on the other side of a long-forgotten, distant wall.

The mission memo had said that North Koreans believed in male shamans, that *paksu* accompanied Inmingun strike teams for good luck and to assist in operational decisions. Kim Il Sung, the Great Leader of North Korea, was regarded as a *paksu* who could harmonize Lenin's material dialectic and Asian palm reading.

"'Shaman,'" I said.

She had waited patiently. "I enjoy how you respect and remember your past. The *wu* at the lake, your little brothers crying for you. Yes, 'shaman,' a pretty word. I am *kidae*, her helper for music and ritual.

"*Dae-wi*, may I?" She took my hands, her inwardly smooth fingers tingling my palm lines. Signals ran up goose-bumped arms.

Her touch was personal, clinical, familiar and foreign. She inspected my hands in the same manner I would study a new power drill. "You are a complicated person." She smiled innocently and it reminded me of the days before I had killed anyone. I concealed my low estimation of her occupation, my disrespect for her powers. She would know that Chinese *wu* could be found at the shores of lakes, and could guess that I would have younger brothers.

"You work with pens. Your hands have killed. You are firstborn but not married. God favors you, saving your life many times, but taking your brothers."

My heart stopped.

"You are not Buddhist and are empty of faith. Your *ki-bun*, harmony, is good to others, bad for you. You are

American and you are Chinese, happy and sad, and not in balance.

"Harmony is what all people seek. The *wang man-sin*, the chief *mudang*, works for the village's *ki-bun*, what the Chinese call *ho*"—synchronicity, peace, harmony. Zen.

"You are loyal to one who cannot love you. A woman you hurt very deeply. For this, *dae-wi*, you feel great and deep shame."

Cara. I saw Mrs. Fan, who had forecast my life, sitting in her threadbare chair smoking a clove cigarette in a shadowy, mildewed room full of old, dry women. Pigeons cooed and a block away, a cable car bell rang. Mrs. Fan waited for me to get her hot tea from the old stove, never looking in the eyes of the boy who never smiled, the boy she had declared to be the future soldier, the killer.

"I am right. Someone said you would meet me. Remember?"

"Hu-ah," my mother had said on Monday, four days ago, "Fan *taitai* say you go far-away mountain, meet *wu* lady in Korea. She give all answer, help you get *jen* back"—benevolence, my high Confucian virtue, which had died in Vietnam.

A shudder, full of tangled seaweed, sour currents and infant fevers, ran up my spine. She spoke of my hands as if she and they were old intimates from years of easy clasping on long autumn strolls, their histories cemented with shoeboxes of meaningful, admissive correspondence, free of secrets and empty of lies. She frowned, smiled, closed her eyes, mining imaginary messages in my hands. She traced scars. "Here cut by plant, burned with blood."

She closed her eyes in pain. A tremor ran through me. I wanted my hands back.

She closed them as one would close books, her fingers warm and almost moist from effort, her cheeks flushed, her chest rising. My fingers tingled with an acupuncture-like residual ring. Maybe Jimmy went this way, following a lovely woman to the local witch doctor.

"*Dae-wi*, I only wish you well. I was a teacher at Ewha Haktong, Pear Blossom Institute, for two years. Child development. Ewha Haktong is a very prestige college, for women only. We spoke perfect academic English, for scholarship. Now, I talk with Vegas girls—stinko." She pinched her nose. She turned her head, looking at me carefully, somewhat from the side.

The cook brought a brown china teacup. He cleared the table and poured for Song Sae Moon, which surprised me.

She smiled. *"Chosumneeda*, Chun *shee."* He took the smoke from his lip, bowed low, held it, and left.

She wrapped her damaged hands about the small cup, tasting the bland, earthy barley tea, looking at me over the steam. "Some people think I am a crazy person." Customers entered and Chun yelled hoarsely at his wife. She screamed back. Chun muttered to himself and Song Sae smiled.

"I was twenty-four when meat made me ill. I could not sleep. I was outside Ewha teacher dormitory. In a nightgown." She pulled up her sleeve; her forearms were welted with purple scars. "I had torn skin from my arms. Friends said I danced as if I had no bones. Then I hit trees, walls, breaking my fingers. I spoke in the voice of an old man who had died.

"These things happened many times. Last year, I came to Jungsan, black holy mountain, to write on a paper lantern my strong wish to be free. I hung it on a tall tree, near Heaven, asking the Buddha a favor on his birthday. Then, I had *ggum*, a dream of babies of *kong ch'ang*, prostitutes who sell their bodies to GIs. Half-Korean, half-American babies, most very lost in both worlds." She looked at me. "I cried for them. I still cry for them."

Bui doi, dust of life. I remembered the Amerasian orphans of Vietnam.

"*Dae-wi,* we are the same. I have a returning dream every night. I understood my dream.

"My job is to find parents for these babies."

"That would be a hard job. Are you having any success?"

She shook her head. "Too many babies. I had to stop Blue Hearts from selling their bodies and having babies—so sad."

"Go to the source," I said.

Dark eyes flared. "Oh, yes, *dae-wi,* you are right! The good Chinese words. To the source. I go to the clubs and talk about Buddha. Some bad people try to hurt me." She lifted a hand. "But they see I have the signs, the voice, of the medium.

"When I sit in the clubs and pray, some of the Blue Hearts stop. But few change inside, wanting American cash too much. I have told so many Americans that I am not a *kong ch'ang,* but they do not believe me. They call me Ice Queen. What does this mean?"

"A woman who is romantically cold. A rude term."

"Ah." She nodded. "With the *mudang*'s help I have started an orphanage at the base of Jungsan. I can take only a few street children. I try to feed the others. But I need fathers."

She brushed back her hair, looking at me solemnly. "Men with the attitude of the kind farmer to his children, the way it was before foreign factories and corporations. This kindness from men is worth all the *won* in the world. *Dae-wi,* I had a dream about you. You are the answer. How, I do not know. I want you to see the *mudang*! She wants to see you. This is a most high honor. When I came here, the *mudang* said I had *sin-byong,* *mudang* possession sickness. To tear our flesh lets us hear the dead, to connect Heaven and Earth.

"It is stronger than the *gut*, the trance to talk to the dead."

I nodded politely.

"To have *her* call for you is most special! She is a magic lady. She hears cries and can descend into hell to save us. She rescued me from darkness and explained my life to me."

The grill sizzled; patrons argued in loud voices. I felt the old drowning ghosts of the Long River's whirlpools, moaning in humid winds, trying to increase their tribe by swallowing young sailors. Ma cried to the river gods in winter storms, the moonlit, nightmare winds howling in the mast. I took a breath; she was seducing me from my job. I smiled. She smiled. "So how's Captain Buford?"

She frowned in genuine incomprehension. "Who?" she asked.

"Nothing." The *mudang* wanted to see me for the health of her village. Why me? I sounded like Magrip.

"*Dae-wi*, she can help you with your *ki-bun*. Evil spirits and lost souls weigh down our days. The *mudang* smoothes our path."

"My *ki-bun* is my own business. Why does she want to see me?"

"*Dae-wi*, our harmony comes from her knowing all. She cannot advise when there is a hole in her knowledge. Terrible things are happening, and you are part of the future of this valley. *Dae-wi*, you are going to change this small village."

Villagers confessed to the shaman, and she used the knowledge to settle disputes.

"I can't now. What can you tell me about Southside?"

She drew in breath. "*O wa.* Is a very bad place, *dae-wi.* Is most dangerous for girls. Southside girls do not come back."

I looked at my watch. "I'm sorry. I must go."

Overcoats on, we stepped into the street. "My room,

dae-wi, is six alleys past Second Market, this side of the canal. Go and face Jungsan." She pointed to the barely visible, fog-ridden black peak as it rose above the flat-roofed village and the valley mist. A high-cliffed peak, morning sunlight gleaming on its snow.

"Say my name and children will show you where I live. My babies. I work at the orphanage at the bottom of Jungsan Peak. But I will stay home, and wait for you."

"Miss Moon, what if I don't come?"

"*Dae-wi*, the *wang mansin* calls for you. You will come."

Men led horse-drawn barley and rice carts to market. She took my arm as if we were old high-school chums, pressing innocently, smiling happily. "Please, call me Song Sae." She licked her upper lip. "It gives me pleasure to hear a man say my name. Villagers call me by who I am, *kidae*, spirit helper."

Like a tour guide, she said, "Tongducheon has fifty thousand people. With good soil but poor harmony in wind and water, what Chinese call *feng shui*. Here, men grow war."

We passed fish mongers offering live clams from truck-tired carts. Stockmen moved fat water buffalo, and we followed muddied roadmen bearing ten-foot loads of winter hay on A-frames.

I was little, running after BaBa in Chapei above the Whangpu, happy to plant my feet on the great deck of dry land.

"*Chi-ge,*" she said. A-frames. We passed a residence bursting with people, a clothesline over the doorway, draped with brilliant red peppers. Her grip tightened. "New baby boy." Like a Chinese red-egg, one-month party for newborn boys.

A woman pulled Song Sae inside. It was a gathering for women only. I waited impatiently. When she emerged, her eyes were wet with tears as she gazed, over her shoulder, at their happiness.

"I am sorry." She dried her eyes. "I feel everyone's emotions. *Dae-wi*, Korea is hard; winters, very cruel. People work and try to live correctly. We are pessimists who laugh quickly. The winds are from God. I think you know this."

Second Market's smells were wonderful, primitive. Overeager jar, pan and pot stallkeepers cried *"Tan-ji! Nam-bi! Chu-chon-ja!"* with hot, condensed breath while fishermen bragged on yellow and red squid, warming my memory. Once, I had smelled of salt water and its fish. I remembered Yangtze merchants calling *"Man-TOHHHH! Do shao bao!"* Red bean paste dumplings!

Urchins played with pebbles and rusted cotter pins in the margins of alleys. As firstborn, I had not played; I had worked, envying Hu-hua and Hu-chien as they romped with ropes and nets.

They yelled after us. Song Sae touched them, using their names. Some literally jumped for joy.

"They say you are 'Chinese giant man.' " The small girls clustered around her, looking up at me, gingerly touching me. I tried to smile. I had to shut my eyes.

"Kwenchanayo, dae-wi—it's okay," she whispered.

Black-hatted elders, *haroboji*, with unlaced tennis shoes and ankle-bound pants, sat on short stools, nodding at the village *kidae*. A gong-beating red-jacketed man stood in the middle of the street. He chanted in a high, operatic voice.

"Paksu—man *mudang*. Not as smart as women; charges too many *won* for a *gut*—dance with drums and cymbals, where he talks to the dead and tells the family what the dead say to them."

Paksu. Advisers for Inmingun raiders. He saw me and spat.

"Dae-wi, this eel, this pig's cheek. *Choggye*, clam. This *mandu*. I make for you." It was like *kuotieh*, a

potsticker. The merchant offered her a bottle. Song Sae blushed and passed it to me.

"Bacchus-B, ginseng extract, *dae-wi*. Good for . . . husband love his wife." She rubbed her fingertips together, as if she had touched something hot.

Officious blue-coated security police scanned roof-tops. I followed their gaze.

"Last summer, *dae-wi*, Northmen here." She imitated an explosion. "*Bghooo!* They exploded the police station."

"Do you think the Northmen will invade?"

"The *mudang* says Northmen are already here, in the valley."

"How can I tell a Northman from a South Korean?"

"Not easy. We are brothers. They speak with a dif-ferent sound. Their hands and faces are very rough. Northmen are hunters and sad poets who live in the winds. We are farmers and musicians. We live in the sun. You will see in spring, the white-flower buckwheat fields, the soft streams, the bulrushes and foxtail weeds, taller than any Korean man." She smiled for warmer days. "I love to see mushrooms growing on the roofs of old farmhouses, the moss in rain ponds, the songs of thrushes and starlings, the flights of white egret." She sighed.

"But Korea was always one country, since Tangun founded Korea. Until America and Russia cut us into two countries, which was so very sad."

A hundred and thirty thousand Americans had paid the price for our thoughtlessly splitting Korea with the Soviet Union. We figured we were cutting a cake, but we had halved an interdependent society, separat-ing northern industry from southern agriculture and dividing great clans with the DMZ, making both parts suffer and inviting poverty, terror, war and the threat of world war.

"We didn't know," I said. "We thought Korea was a little place, where dividing the country wouldn't matter."

She nodded. "Yes, *dae-wi*, you are right. I hear your words. The harm did not come from the heart. You think you are American."

"I am."

Song Sae looked into my eyes. "You are loyal to America. But a Chinese firstborn son can only be what he already is."

We were at the taxi stand, not far from the Casey gate.

"Goodbye, *dae-wi*. I will wait. Remember that the *wang mansin* too waits. It would be rude to be late, and you must see her today." She touched my face with the soft palms of her broken hands, her eyes lingering on my face with an unreadable look.

As she walked through the crowd, some of the girls ran after her and villagers bowed. The boys gathered around me, staring, chattering, feeling my arms and pulling on my fingers.

A drum. The *paksu* was coming and the children ran to him. At the end of the street was a Korean man in his thirties, about five-nine with short military hair, wearing an old green coat. He saw me looking at him and disappeared into the crowd.

22

UNCOMMON DECEITS

The flagpole outside the SJA office was at half-mast, but the SJA office seemed upbeat in the wake of Nagol's death. The door draft hit Muldoon, the big Howdy Doody sentry. He saw my IG brass, tried to stand and fell out of his chair. I helped him up. Typing stopped and I took jeep keys from the vehicle control board.

"Put on your field jacket." I gave him his crutches.

"Yeah—I mean, yessir!" he croaked. I held the door and he crutched out. Snow swirled. His freckles turned green: the dumb gook janitor, the guy he had tried to thump in the Vegas who had destroyed his knee, and today's IG, were all the same man.

"Aw, crap!" he squawked, grimacing, waiting for the blow.

"Specialist Muldoon, Koreans are not your servants. Never call anyone 'slicky boy' again. Get your own java. Get in."

I drove to Wizard Q. Muldoon's traumatized Adam's apple bobbed as he tried to swallow dry spit.

"Who's acting deputy now?"

"Ain't got one, sir. Hard ta replace ole Count Dracula."

"How long you been in-country?"

"Sir, I'm a Double-Digit Midget, down to ten days and a wake-up. Not like some officers, here till hell makes ice. DEROS"—Date Estimated Return Overseas—"to Bliss, Texas." He smiled like the boy he was. He coughed painfully. "Sir, I'm short as a bug dick."

"Why the sidearm?"

"Sir, we got bo-coo cash. SOP is sidearms. Oink, oink."

"Remember Captain Buford, the IG who came in last week?"

"Yessir. The officer got toasted in the jeep."

I parked. "You know, you're not a fighter. You ought to give up bullying."

He spoke quietly. "Sir, my fightin' days are over."

"Muldoon, who arranged our Vegas welcome party?"

He gulped painfully. "Count Dracula and Willoughby."

I made the note. "How you likee java, boss-man?"

Muldoon blushed. I winked at him and helped him out. The guard looked up, stiffened, and picked up the phone. He punched the intercom button. "Sir, visitor. . . . Yes, sir, it's him. With Muldoon." He hung up and stood, smoothing his fatigue blouse.

"Coffee, sir?" He smiled unhappily. I shook my head, helped Muldoon sit, and got him a cup of java. I removed my field jacket and sat under a poster of the television *M*A*S*H* cast; pretending to study a new magazine called *People*. The guard straightened his desk. Muldoon stared at his java. I thought about the Wizard's map.

Prosecutors rely on fair courts and good hands. I was in a crooked court facing a stacked deck. I had one ace: McCrail.

And playing it would jeopardize the sergeant major and his long campaign to free old comrades. But McCrail was hard to kill, and the Wizard seemed a cheat but not a murderer. Since I did not know Nagol's prior influence on the Wizard, I could not calculate the effect of his death. I sensed an improvement.

The intercom buzzer sounded. "Send him in." I passed the fountain. It looked very clean. Now to face an elder.

Giving this man gum would probably not help.

"Sit," said the Wizard, the dentist to the patient. I closed the door, looking at the covered map on its back. He glanced up from his big Bible. I hoped the girl wasn't behind the desk. She was. He saw me notice her. I did not sit.

"Captain, we both have suffered losses. Thomas Nagol fell victim to the vanity of my anger." His eyes narrowed. "I have lost a good friend. And I am sorry about Captain Buford."

Yesterday, I had played my role. Subtlety had its uses.

"Colonel, forensics indicate Buford did not die in the jeep. So TIG salutes you for not killing him, since Jimmy can wear out his welcome with some people. Usually suspects. We'll take him back and save you his ration bill. Hand him over. Please."

The Wizard closed the heavy, gold-leaf Bible with manicured pink hands. He found dust on his desk and brushed it off.

"Captain, your friend is dead."

"Wrong," I intoned like an Academy formation buzzer. "You wasted a pig, a fake death cert, and a jeep in a bogus crash. No human remains. No ROK doc, no 57F cremation, no dead man in a jar, no accident. Just bacon, beach sand, and a plant urn.

"It's a no-brainer. Give me Buford. That's the offer. You know how it works. The longer you wait, the worse it gets."

"Are you a man of God, Captain Kan?"

"Irrelevant. The probative inquiry is: Are you a man of the law?"

"I obey God's commandments. I see your confusion between my sins and yours. Pray with me for your friend's soul?"

I wanted to break his desk and tell him to stop making winter flatus. "You waste time. Invite Buford and we'll pray together."

The Wizard bowed. " 'The Lord is my shepherd,' " he said in a voice that could stop war, using words from an abandoned past. " 'I shall not want. He maketh me lie down in green pastures. He leadeth me beside still waters; he restoreth my soul.' " I stopped breathing, the orange wall shading into deep, dark green.

The words pulled like claws, drawing me by my skin toward the Equator, the tropics of the Eleventh Parallel, into the hot, wet, verdant vortex of the Dong Nai and the three rivers. I smelled incense in the Presbyterian chapel in Chapei and heard my father sing songs to the kind, forgiving, mythical Christian God in Chinese river slang full of salt talk and fish anatomy.

LeBlanc's voice filled the room. I had said the Twenty-third Psalm when I faced death—three hundred iterations with organs tight and jaws crushing molars in that moment before enemy contact when I knew the exact dimensions of my fears and made sweat like a hot grapefruit in a press. I had used the old words until the Dong Nai, when they became empty sounds in a cold jungle.

I didn't believe in it anymore, but I disliked his use of the old words. My hand was wet and I opened my fist, looking for blood. She ran to me and the slugs tore her chest. Her small, weightless head was in my palm, the large, luminous eyes looking at me with love and hope, her lips moving soundlessly, her cries screeching in my mind. Go away, baby. Don't play here. Blood came from her mouth.

"Jesus," I said. I was in Korea. In the Wizard's den.

"These words mean something to you," he said.

I tried to blank out my past. I coughed. "Don't con me, Colonel. That was pig matter in the jeep."

"Son, I am sorry, but your friend is dead. This is Korea. Perhaps you have listened to Brother Foss, the village idiot with a fool's cap. Forgive the crudity, but Major Foss is a brick shy of a full load and perhaps the worst policeman since Inspector Clouseau. He couldn't differentiate the fatal jeep wreck from his own dop kit. No doubt you found a dead pig, but Foss led you to the wrong wreck. His shop prepares accident reports the way it would make sausages." He raised a hand. "Of course, it is not his fault. It is Asia."

His words slowed me. It was like listening to BaBa or Carlos, with the volume up, without the honesty.

"You know, sir, you're right. That's why the CID report you threw at Major Nagol was a sapper's manual." I waited.

"Captain Kan, we are at danger's door, at the threshold of godless communism, to do His work under these pitiful conditions. Here." He pointed at the floor. "Where the rubber meets the road."

I nodded. "With plastic explosives under the asphalt."

He cleared his throat. "A tragedy that a brother Christian came to die a useless death." He smiled. "By the way, Jackson Kan, who does my housegirl remind you of?"

I paused. "She reminds me of Major Dogface Nagol. But I think everyone who kisses your rear end bears a family resemblance."

LeBlanc grimaced. He leaned forward. "She represents your worst pain, am I correct?"

I shrugged, my heart slugging. "I don't know her. But someone I *do* know just left Naktong Tower. Sergeant Major Patrick Treaty McCrail, free courtesy of the White House. McCrail remembers your lawyerly advice. His case has been briefed to TIG, the Chief of Staff, the President and TJAG"—The Judge Advocate General of the Army. "Soon, it'll be in the Washington *Post*." The Wizard seemed unperturbed.

"And by the way, yourself, Colonel, if McCrail gets the flu, I'll take you down for attempted One-Eighteen-Murder." No blink of an eye, no quiver, no digital fidget, not a pop of sweat. No satisfying thunk of a steel shaft piercing a soft-centered bull's-eye, the defendant sagging in moral defeat in the witness chair. Instead, my eye flinched, the girl's fingers closing around my heart in a red-speckled green rain forest. I coughed.

"I'm the IG on your case. Carlos Murray wants your nuts in a small evidence pouch. If I get Buford and everyone else gets home free, I'll defy TIG to protect you." I saw Carlos's fine anger for so many disobediences in the field. I didn't care.

No more deaths.

"You're lucky today. It's a good offer. Going once."

"I'm lucky?" He laughed. "Well, aren't you the ever-admirable number one son, representing all the fools in town."

"Who I am doesn't matter. What matters is what you do." I leaned on his desk. "Colonel, your fly's open. It's Buford or a murder charge. Hangmen are ready. The knot's in the noose."

His eyes burned. "You punk. Am I under arrest?"

I smiled. "Sir, we're just two boys talking."

The Wizard rubbed his nose. He didn't like being in a group of which I was a member. "McCrail died in 1966. If you have met someone of his description, it is not he. My Patrick was a Catholic boor pig, a fat, unschooled slob of a man who could no more string two thoughts together than see the queen for tea." He inhaled. "To Patrick, 'uh' was an Irish soliloquy."

I tried to look convinced. This man offended everyone.

I thought of the map and had an unbidden image of Jimmy coming through the door. "Jackson, how are ya?" I'd bear-hug him and I could forgive all, from the Wizard to myself, and winter would end.

I moved closer to the map, seeing the edges of the clear acetate overlay covered by the decorative silk banner. The overlay would show some of the Wizard's inner workings.

"Cap—" said LeBlanc, anxious about my proximity to the map. I pretended not to have seen it. I peered at him.

"Sir, where do you stow an IG in Korea?"

He exhaled. "Sit, Captain Kan. Let us focus on you. God calls you to place your injuries in the past. It's what draws you to me."

The girl moved, rustling silk, changing the beat of my heart.

"Colonel, give me Buford and I'll sing 'Day by Day, Dear Lord' in the key of your choice." I smiled.

He smiled, doing it better. "I know of your resoluteness. It is your Chinese blood that drives you. A DSC and Silver Star, an MSM every year. Given our current

taste in coloreds, you're a future general officer. Your
very difference from Americans makes you earnest." He
smiled. "You're such hard little workers."

No one thought I was an American. "Yes, it's genetic."

He pursed his lips, wondering at my sincerity. "Of
course it is. I admire both your notoriety and your ambition." He checked a cuticle. "I know of the Dong Nai
River ambush. I subpoenaed your Letterman psychiatric
file." He steepled hands. "You could see Doc Benton for
ten years, and you would still need chloral hydrate to
sleep in the darkness of night.

"Captain. Confess to me." He looked at me. "I'll help
you carry it. This is no light offer." The wind gusted.

He knew my deepest pains and greatest fears,
expressed to a quiet man in Letterman's west wing, over-
looking the Bay and the bridge. The small, poorly managed sailboats undulated as I sought clinical help for a
hopeless event. I had taken Doc Benton into the Dong
Nai and I was still lost with night sweats. LeBlanc knew
my weakness as if I had told him.

I chose my words carefully. "That pisses me off."

"Your confidences are safe with me." He was
sweating. He snapped his fingers. The girl stood and
came to him stiffly. My mind superimposed the dead girl
onto her face and blood seeped from the corner of her
mouth and soaked her sleeve. I closed my eyes, my world
red, humid, riveted with error and blood.

I opened my eyes. The girl looked at me. A small, oval
face, overlarge eyes, a wide mouth and the tight, beaten
aspect of a serf. Her thick hair made her seem older.
Blood soaked the sleeve of her pink sweater; I tried to
blink away the image.

"Hoon Jae-woo, thirteen, orphaned, brought to
Jungsan for healing." He smiled. "I adopted her. She
thinks I'm a *paksu*, a wizard. Whenever anger is directed
at me, she punishes herself.

"Captain, you came here uninvited, filling my house

with your noise, your dislike for me. Look at what you have wrought." He pulled up her sleeve and I blanched as I saw the bright bleeding, open tears on her flesh, blood running thinly. Her face remained passive.

I frowned and the girl dug her nails into open flesh.

I sat down and lowered my face, blanking it. I was panting, bright hatred drilling holes in me wherever it wished. The Wizard had found a girl with *sin-byong* and turned her self-flagellation into a weapon, eerily, painfully, tailor-made for my weaknesses.

I saw the evil-eyed man slash his wife at the Wuhan docks. It was autumn on the Changjiang, summer markets thrived and we sold fish in barter. The woman fell onto our junk and BaBa stopped the husband, but it was too late; she was dead.

"You," screamed my father, shielding us, his three tiger sons, our mouths open, "are the tears of Jesu Christ! You have money and power and you cut the skin of the weak!"

I expected BaBa to kill him. But Master Wong took the rich man's knife, pulled the man's hand out, and cut it off at the wrist.

Now I took a breath. I forced a smile. I forced a chuckle, then a laugh. The girl smiled as I looked at LeBlanc, laughing uproariously. "You're the sickest sonofabitch I ever met!" I slapped my thighs, laughing louder. "Know what? I'm going to lock you up *forever!*"

She backed away happily to kneel. I laughed with relief.

His eyes narrowed. "Captain, I am a lawyer. I disapprove of threats and I condemn killing. I am sorry you do not."

He swallowed. "What is the military truth of Korea?"

There are mountains. Then, more mountains.

"Korea," he said, "is an unarmed society, without the blessings of the Second Amendment. No armed citizenry, as are we. The Korean has no gun and the Inmingun is on the border."

He stood and looked out his window. He opened his door so the hidden map was further concealed against the wall.

"Seventeen thousand U.S. infantrymen cannot stop a million yellow savages armed with Russian and Chinese automatic weapons."

Hands behind his back. "The invasion scenario: The Reds breach the DMZ in force under rolling barrages, cross the Imjin, crush Casey on D One, occupy Seoul on D Plus Four. In 1950, it took them four days. Now it will take them five.

"ROKs blow the Han bridges, pinning a million Inmingun in Seoul. The Reds burn the city, savaging ten million civilians, with great harm to the women and no regard for the children, while their engineers throw pontoon bridges over the Han.

"Do you agree?" His fist was militant. I nodded. I did.

"Captain, what if South Korean civilians could be armed? Here, in Tongducheon, in Seoul, Taegu, Kwangju, Inch'on, Pusan. Then, when the NKPA arrived, there would be a cleansing war.

"A modern crusade for a grail of American freedom. I tell you this." He took a breath. "I go to the Imjin. I stand at the Z and look across the great wire and I *want them to come.*"

The words echoed in the room. His fingers fidgeted.

"Civilians," I said, "would be slaughtered by Red armor."

"Details. I'm working with ROK legislators to allow citizens to be freedom fighters against a Red horde invasion. Captain, you take that message to your Pentagon handlers."

I looked at his own self-belief. "Sir, TIG worried that long service on the border had impaired your judgment. It's worse than they feared. You've become a lobbyist."

He snorted. "Imagine the expression on the face of a Korean when someone hands him a firearm to defend his nation."

Streets, homes and schoolyards could become automatic weapon shooting galleries. "Gratitude?" I asked.

"Absolutely! Heathen slaying heathen, pagan killing pagan, useless trees burned in holy fire."

The chant of the Inquisition. Death to Jews, Gypsies, Muslims, unbelievers, the slow and the halt. The tragic misinterpretation. The bloodied so-called followers of the Prince of Peace would inherit all the good parking places.

"Death to non-Christians?"

"Those who do not accept Jesus Christ are dead already."

"Aha." Why wait for technical details. Kill them all now.

"I have trouble imagining Christ carrying an assault rifle. Wasn't He the one who advocated for those who were different?"

"Your minority background limits your knowledge. Not your fault." He held up his hands. "I do not advocate killing. Only patriotism. Captain, God gave us the Korean people as a buffer, a shield for America, letting them go in harm's way."

"We did it when we divided their country."

The once-kind eyes piqued. "Oh, please. Do not feed me revisionist history. The small are sacrificed for the great. The Canaanite was fodder for the tribes of Israel; Indians, Africans, and Mexicans are our groundskeepers. Our pickers."

I had gotten him to talk without the gum, but it was all propaganda, with bigoted cant and nightmarish child torture.

He shook his head. "Vietnam is about to fall like rotten

fruit. Kim Il Sung is desperate to reunify the peninsula. He must strike now, while America is heartsick over Vietnam, before our wounds can heal and our own citizens recover the resolve to fight."

I remembered his map. "What should we do about it?"

"Cross the border. Put Kim Il Sung out of his misery."

I growled, "I thought you didn't approve of killing."

The girl stood, eyes stretched by fear, drawn by my tone. She looked at my face and reached for her wounded forearm.

"Aniyo," no, I said softly. She glanced at LeBlanc in fear, then looked at me. I picked up a chair and moved it to her. She sat, trembling; I stood close. Her hand reached tentatively and I took it, her small fingers closing around mine.

The Wizard saw my face; no inscrutability—I couldn't pretend to be romanced. The small social chat was over. "Captain Kan, I do not endorse illegality."

"Only larceny, fraud, graft and uncommon deceits."

His brows came down. "Innuendo, libel, slander. And rude."

"Where's Jimmy Buford?"

He coughed. "Do I sense a failure in my evangelism?"

"Deeper than that." I needed to get the girl out and study the map, to imprison this man and prepare against bogus appeals.

He cleared his throat. "How badly do you want Buford?"

"More than I value my career. More than I value yours. Today, I can be had; make me an offer." My heart lifted with his larcenous question.

"Focus on the real issues." He pointed. "We're on the same side. I wear the white hat. You should be routing out spies and agents provocateur. North Koreans are everywhere and you are wasting your time and taxpayer money on me."

"Sir, the IG's on you. You're big, bright, and blue

on TIG's radar screens. We're talking real world. Headquarters, U.S. Army is about to stick a UCMJ baseball
bat up your back. For Buford, I'll do all I can for you.
But do it now. And pull that Korean dandy off my
trail."

LeBlanc blinked. The comment had surprised him. "I
don't know what you're talking about." He glanced at the
girl.

"Colonel, she leaves with me, one way or another."

LeBlanc picked up a number-one wood. I gently
pulled the girl from the chair and put her behind me. He
set himself and did a smooth practice swing.

"Captain, kind of you to visit." He took another
swing. The girl found my hand and squeezed it with
both of hers, palms wet. I squeezed back. The imposi-
tion of a pale blood mask on her young face was familiarly bearable. I felt her true pulse, sensed vibrant
emotions, and I was as happy as I had been all week.
My face was still, showing no triumph to watching,
jealous gods.

"Feeling a little dumb, Captain? A little useless here
on the cutting edge of Communist invasion and Satan's
slope-head whores, offering their bodies to good
American white men?" He set himself.

"Isn't it ironic that we send an Oriental to West Point,
and when he arrives here, fully trained, when he could
deal communism a death blow, he's as useful as teats on
a bull."

He swung, smooth and true.

"You cannot help it. The Oriental personality is passive, unable to make good decisions. Take the girl. She
intrigued me—the pagan's infantile mind—but she was
becoming a burden. And frankly, she smells like Korean
dirt; her roots will not wash. I tried to teach her, but she's
a peasant to the wool.

"And now you enter my world, a West Point graduate
doing a fool's dance, offering the persuasions of clowns

in the theater of the absurd. Mister, you don't believe in God, and you're trying to raise dead pigs from jeep wrecks."

He smiled warmly. "Tell me, Captain, just between the two of us. Who can help you now?" He laughed, mimicking precisely the artificial sound I had made when I vowed to lock him away.

23

HWAN YONGSA

Doc Purvis had pulled graveyard and had been asleep for two hours. As a proponent of sleep deprivation, I knocked hard.

He slept in scrubs and looked like a honeymoon bedsheet. I apologized. "It's okay, I was asleep, anyway."

The room was cool, his roommates out. He padded back toward his bunk. "How you sleeping?" he mumbled.

"Not my skill. This is Hoon Jae-woo. Miss Hoon, this is Dr. Purvis."

She bowed. He bowed, saw his boxer shorts and got a robe. "She's the Wizard's adopted daughter," I said. "Self-inflicted scratches, left forearm. Maybe elsewhere."

Purvis opened a cabinet and produced antiseptics, antibiotics, gauze and bandages. He yawned. "I heard of her. How'd you get her away from the Wizard?"

"I'm a lawyer."

"You're a comic." He washed up and seated her, checked her nails, cleaned the wounds and dressed them.

She accepted his work. He asked her questions in Korean. She answered, looking at me.

"Doc, tell me everything you know about the *mudang*."

"*Mudang*'s the shaman witch doctor. She's also the *wang mansin*, a top, hereditary *mudang*. Back in the world, abused girls booze and marry batterers to keep the cycle going. Here, some abused Korean females have violent psychotic episodes called *sin-byong*, possession illness. They dance and hit bricks. Tear their flesh. A hundred thousand of them." He yawned. "Honored savants, crazy with prophecy and insight.

"*Mudang* has a pharmacy that'd put Rexall out of business. Koreans are into ginseng, garlic and roots, antler horns, snake soup and eye of newt." He pulled back the sheets, covered himself and settled in. "Can't blame 'em. Pharmacological basis to their work. Three thousand years older than ours. Proof is, Koreans are a hell of a lot healthier than us. Half the division's sick, while the Ville is like a health spa."

"Doc, Foss thinks our missing officer might be in the Ville. Would the *mudang* know anything about that?"

"Yeah. She picks up vibes, bummers." Yawn. "Tuned in . . ."

I envied my effect on others. He had fallen asleep. But he had given me a couple of reasons to see a voodoo woman whom I would otherwise avoid like the plague. I didn't like *wu*.

I needed to look more Korean and wanted the girl to have gloves. We stopped and I paid 2,400 *won*, five bucks. Some of the gawkers questioned Jae-woo.

"*Aboji*," she said, pointing at me. Father.

Kids followed, trying to look into my bag. Jae-woo put her small gloved hand in mine. I had seen adult Korean friends of both genders walking hand in hand, but not a father with his daughter. It seemed right. I squeezed her hand and she trembled.

At Second Market I bought dried fish and *yakimandu*, potstickers. She pointed at clams, which she ate ferociously. She had probably been living on American rolfburgers.

We turned east, staying on the same side of the canal. A gaggle of dirty, raggedy Eurasian street orphans gathered in our trail. Children of the dust life. They screamed at each other and at me, as if my eclectic character contained an answer to their half-world fates. They cried *"Chung guk ko-een! Chung guk dtwae nom!"*—Chinese giant, bogeyman.

Gravel, slush, animal waste and wheel ruts defined the narrow alleys. I could stretch my arms and touch both walls.

Shoppers carrying winter melons and pale cabbages stopped to stare. We reached the sixth alley and turned to face Jungsan, the black mountain. When the children saw the direction of my gaze, they fell silent. Some touched my clothes, feeling American gloves, chattering to me in Korean. A few sucked red, soiled thumbs while staring goggle-eyed.

"Mei-guk," said one boy, pointing to himself. American.

"Chung-guk saram, mi-guk saramieyo," I said— Chinese man, American man—pointing to myself. They shouted. I was like them. Except I had two loyal parents, an old clan with many ancestors and a long river full of fat fish.

"Aboji," said Jae-woo, squeezing my hand.

"Song Sae Moon. *Chebal.*" Please. Jae-woo stared; I was calling on the *kidae.* The oldest boy took my glove in a small, bare, cracked hand, pulling me like a big dog, Jae-woo in trail. Down a crooked, stained alley, past junk and corrugated metal shanties into a small, snow-covered courtyard that smelled of seared vegetables, rice and an overly popular outhouse. A woman with a heavily wrapped baby bundled onto her chest ran water from a new brass spigot into a pot. The baby smiled, crinkling her face.

The boy pointed at a shack with robin's-egg-blue roof boards, rosy side slates, a frozen, electric-green hummingbird feeder and a brilliant gold television antenna. I heard a television and knocked on the rosy door. It opened.

"Buddha blesses me," said Song Sae, smiling and bowing low, her head to the side, her arms in a Chinese dancer's delicate pose, fingers steepled in front of her chest. "*Hwan yongsa*—you are most welcome," she said musically. "Come in, *dae-wi*." The children fell quiet. She wore the same snug turtleneck, thick ebony hair over her shoulders, catching the light.

"Song Sae, this is Hoon Jae-woo. She may have *sin-byong*."

The girl's flowing black hair blew in the cold wind. Song Sae put her hands out and the girl took them, entering the hooch. They spoke quickly, the girl bobbing her head in huge affirmations, almost prancing, communicating in ways beyond the power of men. Song Sae wept. The girl bowed to her, and then to me, weeping happily.

I gave Song Sae the *yakimandu*. She accepted with both hands and a bow. "*Dae-wi*, Korean gentlemen offer with the right hand while bowing; the left holds the cuff of the right sleeve. As if you were a court official in the Chinese style." I was the son of a sailor.

She demonstrated. I imitated. She smiled brightly. The girl also smiled, tears and hope in her eyes.

Her room was twelve feet square: a red bedroll with a small pillow, a portable stove with a simmering teapot, and mother-of-pearl black chest and dresser.

The girl sat in an open space. Rough pine walls. On them hung Chinese geomantic *feng shui*—wind and

water geomancy—good-luck mirrors with red tassels, a
Cheju Island calendar and posters depicting the *ba-kua*—
geomantic solid and broken-bar hexagrams of Chinese
prophecy and change. Broken toys filled a tall cardboard
box. The room was warm and private, and smelled of
her, of tea and children and a distant perfume. Filling the
room was the sound of a television.

"Who's the tall dark stranger there? . . . Maverick is
his name." She had been watching Armed Forces TV,
writing down the dialogue.

"Your deal," said a cowboy. "Five-card stud."

"Let's keep your hands on the table," said Bret
Maverick.

"I watch TV to learn more vocabulary. *Dae-wi*, it is a
miracle that you freed this girl from the Americans."

I was going to say that I was American, but the gun-
shot made me jerk as Jae-woo cried out. My heart
pumped; someone in Hollywood had not kept hands on
the table. On the television, a body fell heavily. I
straightened the furniture I had knocked over.

"I am so sorry, *dae-wi*. This is a naughty show, but the
words are very colorful. I am sorry that sounds are your
enemy. The same is true for this girl. You both need to
see the *wang mansin*." She touched my arm. "Oh, *dae-
wi*, is God not lovely, to bring help when help is
needed?"

24

TWELVE MEN

The mountain loomed. The taxi stopped near rusted Quonsets. In the snow, children played soccer and fought while old women gasped for breath in various imitations of cardiac arrest. Girls in discarded Army uniforms waved fans in the red faces of their teachers. The orphanage. It looked like a refugee camp, filled with the children of the world.

"I am proud of this place, *dae-wi*. Children are safe from GIs. We have built good bomb shelters. Perhaps you will visit and play father-teacher for me?" Her soft hand on mine.

The road was steep. A thousand feet above the valley floor and a hundred feet short of the near summit, the Pony taxi shuddered on the steep grade and died in the mountain air. We rolled backward until the parking brake held.

The driver refused payment; charging the *kidae* for a ride to the holiest site in the valley would, in the next world, cost him far more than the fare. At the edge, I looked south.

"Buddha temple of Soyasan," she said. The gold temple spires rose like candelabra from a lower peak. Casey was swallowed by the march of snow-capped ridges that crashed like endless waves of an angry, choppy sea on a small and innocent land.

"Can Jae-woo stay here, or at the temple?"

"Oh, most very yes. Will the Americans try to take her back?"

The Americans. "I don't think so. But there is legal work to do."

The sky was slate, storm clouds on the horizon. To the north was the Inmingun, Chinese Manchuria, and my past. Ma wanted me to get a gift for Fan *taitai* and to light joss for two baby boys. BaBa wanted me to buy three coffins, to fix the hasty wartime river burials of our family. And to pray.

Song Sae moved up the path, holding hands with the girl. We stopped at a rude, squat hut: windowless, flat-roofed, half-spackled stucco with exposed chicken wire, a weather-warped door and a worn, snowless path. She opened it to rickety shelves filled with cans, jars, produce, rice sacks and fish.

"*Sonmul*—present—for the *mudang*," said Song Sae. The Ville supported her. I put the dried fish from Second Market on a shelf, as if I were part of a village, a foreign feeling for a river man.

Footfalls. An approaching patrol file, careful, inter-valed, the soft tread of Asian men coming. I pulled Song Sae and Jae-woo into the hut, closing the door. The hinge creaked painfully. I made the universal sign for silence as I pulled out the Randall knife, smiling reassuringly at the terrified girl.

Through a crack I saw an Asian GI. Ethnic Korean, bald, hands pink from the cold, a red facial birthmark, about five-seven, one ninety, early thirties, his chest so big that the arms sprouted from it like thick branches from an old tree. In a field jacket without load-bearing equipment or weapons, he was a private dressed for lunch break, moving like a rifleman. He looked auto-matically for monofilament tripwire and ambush signs. Point man.

I recognized him: one of the immense 76Y supply clerks Magrip and I had seen on our search of post.

Some meters behind was another. In an American patrol, slack man.

He was about five-eight and wide, bow-legged, bald, bare-headed and ungloved. His shoulders advertised years of hard iron work in weight rooms and a steroid bloat that had pushed him over two hundred pounds. He coughed without apology and walked with the air of accountability that weighs heavily on battalion commanders, managers of eight hundred men on a confused battlefield full of fog, flying steel and ripped limbs. His face was sinew and high cheekbones, a sad mouth and the eyes of a hunting hawk. A Korean Magrip. He spat scarlet. A red splotch ran from his left ear to a deep left eye orbit. He was the honcho. I saw his rank: private.

Behind came other men in file. I was certain these were the big Asians who had caught the attention of Henry Jubala and Major Foss, and had made them wonder if we were all part of an Army Peregrine team. But Peregrines were a motley crew of many Asian tribes. All these men were Koreans.

Song Sae and Jae-woo were silent, their eyes agog at me. After a seven-meter interval came another man, a brother in build and rank to the others with a similar skin blotch. All had skin problems, and this man limped. He looked to the left, at the hut, checking the door and the ground.

The next looked above for aircraft. Sound Man, able to pick up enemy air activity at the periphery of air-vibrational sensitivity. Had he been point man, he might have heard the door hinge.

Trail man, twelfth in column, followed fifteen meters later, brushing and sanitizing the path with a pine branch.

Jubala had talked of "a million Inmingun led by thirteen-man Tiger Tails who'll slit our throats." These were twelve GIs.

Numerology was determinative in Asia; "four" in Chinese sounds like the word for "death" and is unlucky. "Eight" is round and good. Americans didn't care except for lucky seven and unlucky thirteen, and GIs knew to keep the magic five-meter interval on patrol; crowding invited slaughter.

Song Sae started to move; I froze her with an upheld palm. We waited ten minutes. I spat on the old hinges and opened it. Below us, I saw the twelve men entering three taxis.

"Who are they?"

"They are patients of the *mudang*.   Why are we speaking so quietly? You made us most afraid, how you looked."

"I'm sorry." I smiled and so did they. "Let's go."

I put the knife away. The girl stared. I tried to look at her with *jen*, benevolence, but now she looked Vietnamese.

The wind stiffened as we approached the last peak. Naked scrub oak gave way to winter ginkgos, stubborn, densely clustered snow-dusted Japanese evergreens in an artificial winter forest.

"The Japanese made us plant the forest in 1910. Their generals lived here. We brought valley soil to replace the rock, and cypress and ginkgo, pine and oak trees, from Cheju-do."

A two-story, snow-covered Japanese villa with high green winged arches, tiled roof and shoji-screened windows, flanked with white rock and a high pine fence above the roof, shielding it from the north wind. Small white winter birds bent the branches of the trees, their gentle fluttering dusting the ground with sparkling specks of snow.

At a stone shrine to the left of the high fence, Song Sae stopped. She said the *mudang* was past sixty years, deep into Chinese Second Life, that she was strong but suffered bad vision and back pain, for which she took viper wine and *saengkang cha*, ginger tea. The *mudang*, like herself, was a poor sleeper and dawn riser. Her face was old because she read Chinese winds in her skin. Song Sae was announcing credits.

"She is *kwanseum Bosa*—Prayer to Buddha. She is hearer of cries and singer to the dead. She dances for her people. She fools the *ag-wi*—devils at the gates of hell—plays the *chango*, the hourglass drum. She shields this village, its women. She knows the three Buddhist *Samsang* spirits—but relies on Sanshin, the tiger spirit who rules holy mountains.

"She knows all herbs, active and passive, the Five Primal Energies, the harmonies of female and male. She fears no medicine and wears the cinnabar necklace for nature, the mercury headband for *mi-gae*, destiny. She has surpassed the Three Realms of Desire.

"When she was a girl, her father drank *mokkli* and beat her. *Mudang* knows pain and knows we need men, but, being most honest, she does not appreciate them very much."

Levine would like her.

The girl rang the brass bell, making a silly, flat sound. Song Sae clapped her hands to draw the attention of the gods, and my two companions prayed, heads low.

Ma had bowed low in the seven-story Wen Feng riverside pagoda near Yangzhou on the Grand Canal, where we dropped cargoes and sold the carp to war-thinned farmers for a few measures of rice.

"River god," she had said, lighting joss, "your dry ground is good. I thank you for no Japanese soldiers or *duchun* today." She clapped for the god's closer attention, then squeezed my hand so tightly it hurt. "Ow," I said.

"Thank you," she whispered. "For our laughing happy firstborn son. I owe you much gold, forever!"

Later, she had wept for not thanking the Wen Feng river god for the lives of her two younger sons. Gods, she said to me, punish ingratitude. Owing tears, she cried for my little brothers whenever she saw a river, or a lake, or a picture of water. Crossing to America had cost Ma her good looks.

Song Sae opened the gate. We walked on a complaining, pure-white gravel path to a low portico upon which sat a dozen women in warm wraps. They bowed to Song Sae, who bowed back.

Petitioners. Women with ailing, abusive, drinking, smelly, unfaithful or indolent husbands, unmarried daughters, bad-luck beds, headaches, neuralgia, back pain, painful joints, stomach ills and vapors, all waiting to see the *wu*. I felt guilty; as a man, rich with Eastern status and special invitation, I had cut the line. I nodded to them as an American male, confusing them.

We removed our shoes. The pronounced hush of the peak, emphasized by the whispering of the pines, the Chinese wind and the shrines, reminded me that I was in the presence of forces I had not respected since childhood.

25

MUDANG

Song Sae opened the heavy oak door. She shouted, at the top of her lungs, "*HALMONI! SONG SAE!*" A woman shouted back from a corner of the warm house.

"*Halmoni* means 'Grandmother,'" she said. Then she spoke to the girl, who bowed and sat. Song Sae pointed at the floor. "Heated by *ondol*, charcoal bricks below the floor. We are home." She smiled serenely, removing her coat. Polished hardwood floors, two large, high-ceilinged rooms in a row.

A woman and her daughter, crying in what seemed to be relief, emerged from a third room and left. This room was even warmer and heavy with incense. Rugs of every description, dusted by dried flower petals. Purple, green, red and teal pillows colored a sea of over-sized white cushions. Pink and red accordion and box paper lanterns gilded high oak beams. Bright yellow candles in golden candelabra guttered on rosette tables. Rows of crimson hourglass drums. Stacks of bronze coins and snow-white ceremonial rice in glass jars. Smoke rose from brass incense burners. The scent of jasmine weaved through the pungency of joss and the aroma of flowers. Carmine Chinese calligraphy graced ivory walls.

Hesitate in heart, dream is gone. Tree prefers calm, wind does not care. Man remembers past, woman remembers all.

These were the idioms Mrs. Fan liked to recite.

The *mudang* sat among great white pillows. A brilliant white robe made her brown skin darker, her mien older, wiser. A bright red necklace encircled a thin neck; a silver headband restrained wild flights of thin gray hair. I bowed.

She ate, sitting in blossom *sutra*. On a warm day, she might have reached five feet in height. Small back and round shoulders, hands deformed by the pains of cathartic possession. Cataracts clouded feverish eyes that swept me with reptilian focus. The coarsened leather of high cheeks was creased deep, its fissures capturing candlelight like old ravines in a summer dusk.

Her face radiated wrinkles in all directions, for all emotions, from the hub of onyx eyes. She closed them and briefly smiled, the equivalent of a returning bow; she held no affection for men. With eerie eyes hooded, she looked less fantastic and more human. She was a female *wu* who embodied mystic powers in a harsh land of zephyrs and mortal snows. I sensed her examination of me by other senses. Song Sae sat in front of me and spoke.

"Here, the silence of holy women is bigger than the orders of all males. *Halmoni* has suffered *sin-byong*, illnesses of prophecy and pain that led her to a life of prayer and divination, above the world and beneath the heavens. She mediates people and spirits."

The shaman swallowed, burped and yelled at top volume toward the kitchen. A woman shouted back. Song Sae laughed. The *mudang* touched her and they spoke easily, communing with open, flowing emotion, their faces like theater, reminding me of the comforts to be found in the company of Chinese women.

The *mudang*'s infectious cackle and ever-changing face made me smile. It was a tuned device as specialized as a boxer's left hand.

"*Dae-wi*, I meet to you Madame Chae." Her voice quavered. "She cleaned her mouth with willow twigs and welcomes you.

"Please sit by *mudang, dae-wi*." I walked on pillows and sat. She considered me and measured my hands, my chest, my arms, with arthritic, baby-soft fingers. Song Sae gave me a stone cup of jasmine tea while the old woman examined, speaking softly in a gruff, used-up voice, as if she, like Janis Joplin, had torn her vocal cords while screaming, in beat at a demented world.

"She says you do not believe in her."

"I believe her information. I know medicinal prophets, the *wu*. They had the confessions of every fisherman on the river."

Song Sae translated. The *mudang* squeezed my left hand. Song Sae translated quickly as the old woman spoke.

"She says you were born Horse, but are Tiger with war in your belly. You miss your soldiers. Your *mi-gae* is to be with danger. You were a boy in the Tao water sign, eating salt fish you swam with to build your *yang* spirit. God favors you. You miss China, your baby brothers, your grandfather. You pretend at pens but you have death on your lips, bitterness under your tongue. Your *ki-bun* roams free, without a compass.

"*Mudang* says you are here because of the same forces that are eating her village. She heard your footsteps across the sea."

Her villa was a garage sale of icons from my past. Her analysis was shockingly accurate.

"Please thank her."

The *wu* spoke. "She says last year in Year of the Rat, three wives died and GIs killed six women in the bars.

"This, Ox year, forty-seven women were murdered, thirty-nine by the foreign soldiers, who beat a thousand other women. Sixteen children were shot through accidents. Guns are in her village."

I had come hoping for information. I had planned to give none, myself. I considered the repercussions, then told them of Colonel LeBlanc's plan to arm Korean civilians to fight North Koreans. That the American military police had noticed the results, but had been ordered to not take action.

"*Mudang* asks, are you here to stop the American *paksu*?"

I paused. "Yes."

The *mudang* smiled, leaned forward and caressed my cheek.

"*Halmoni* hopes this man will not be killed, only improved."

"Grandmother, I'm looking for an American kidnapped by other Americans. He may be in Southside. Can you help me get him back?"

The shaman spoke. "She knows of him and will help . . . on these conditions . . ." She spoke. "Take him from Osudong-yuk, what you call Southside, by tomorrow. His fate is in the air. He is on the third floor, first Japanese house.

"Enter through the first *tabang*, teahouse. She expects you not to harm anyone. Perhaps a little violence will occur."

I believed her and relief filled me. "What happens after tomorrow?"

"*Mudang* awaits your true question. From where you were near three rivers and bad fortune reached up from the muds of hell to take you by your throat, choking your life. As you know, this is where tigers kill their victims. It is where you, as a man with the tiger in his name, also died."

26

TIGER'S TAIL

In China, to doubt a *wu* outright would violate *ji hui*. To believe her now was to know that Jimmy was alive.

"*Mudang* asks if you know *kung-hap*, the Chinese horoscope."

In Chinese, the *badze*. My *badze* said it was time to get Jimmy. "Yes." Mine had been cast in the Year of the Horse, the fifth lunar month, the sixth day, in the fourth hour. Excellent year, good month, fair day, a dangerous time. The sexagenary calendar with its sixty permutations of meaning had been cast and my name selected to ward off evil, invite good, and throw my chances to the wind of *yeh*, karma, while invoking the tiger, travel, and danger.

"She asks you to go to the peak with her."

Song Sae opened shoji screens and we passed through the arbor, skirting a precipitously sheer cliff which provided a breathtaking view of the valley. We climbed a path toward the howling of mountain winds until we faced north.

Everything lay before us like a terrain mockup—the valley, the village and light-twinkling canal, rows of endless, dragon-spine mountains, the micro systems of fog, mist, clouds, rain and snow, the panorama of the DMZ and the loom of North Korea and Manchuria. The wind was from China, and the feel of it was like an old teacher's touch.

Two hundred thousand Inmingun lay within cannon shot. Behind them were eight hundred thousand more. I felt their weight, their great hunger to come south.

I stand at the Z and look across the great wire and I want them to come.

Observation helicopters ran along mountaintops. The sun was bright and cold, reflecting silver flashes from radar antennae. The *mudang* spoke as the winds whipped us. Song Sae shivered, smiling at her spirit mother as she spoke to the winds, as if we were all participants in a tea party where cats and playing cards might talk back and we would all dance the hokey-pokey. She pointed toward Casey, hidden between the third and fourth snow-capped ridges.

"*Mudang* says she stood here and knew you were coming, months ago. To the west, white tiger direction, is evil. It is in your camp. Very dangerous. Dark gods deep into Buddhist hell.

"She says geomantic forces will make something happen in three days, when Ox Year dies and the new year is born.

"The horoscope is full of death." The wind howled and my temperature was stripped. "The confluence of these forces is so terrible that it is like fire come upon the earth."

The *mudang* screamed to the wind, making my hair stand.

"She asks the wind to change the moon. It cannot. She faces the four winds. All she sees is flames on snow."

The shaman stood on rocks and held my face in small, cold, rugged hands, weeping. She spoke, her emotions bombarding me, making my cold skin crawl, her eyes too dark, too intense, her passions scorching my cold mind. I tried to frown and could not.

"She says violence has a way with you. To change your *in-yon*, your fate, you must ask your true question."

Gobbledegook. The howling wind cuffed my ear. Pine needles came like hail. Her incandescent eyes and high, palsied voice stirred deep, boyish fears of *wupo*, witches.

"She says a Chinese man who comes to work white man's deals must pay. He must know the cost will be in blood.

"You are a tiger on a lake, your stripes not making you safe, but unsafe. You must be prepared. You have injuries. More are coming. You must be strong. Not in body. In heart."

The *mudang* spoke gruffly in the wind.

"She says twelve men come to her for medicine. Twelve is a good Chinese number, a bad number for us. We like odd numbers.

"They have cast their *kung-hap*, geomantic futures, their eight characters and sixty chances. All signs cross on the lunar new year, in three days, when a bad year will be born."

Twelve GIs with Korean blood had cast their fates. The fates had told them to act on the lunar New Year. Chinese Hsien Nin, Vietnamese Tet, the traditional date for birthdays, for rebirth.

"She asks, what year comes with the new moon?"

"Tiger," I said. The year of change, of bold steps. To Mrs. Fan, a bad year, a year for war, the year the

Japanese invaded. My year, the year of my name. A year for soldiers.

In Asian parlance, America was the Tiger. So it was my American year, unified in pledges and the alignment of stars.

The last Tiger had been 1962, America's final blessed and innocent year, when Kennedy's hair seemed long and he was loved in Europe, when idealism outweighed money and "assassination" was almost a foreign word in the American dictionary. The Tiger Year before it was 1950, when the Inmingun had invaded South Korea and set the peninsula aflame in a war that had not yet ended.

We returned to the warmth of the villa and sat on the sea of pillows. Jae-woo served hot tea. I held the comforting warm stone cup in both hands. "What will these men do?"

Song Sae translated. "She does not know. They have a terrible disease such as she has never seen by any medicinal *mudang*. It is hungry and eats skin, hair, organs and inner *ko*, what you call inner spirit, *chi*. It is as if they have been in spiritual fire."

I asked her to describe the symptoms. I wrote them down. They sounded like cancer, a universal and far from exotic disease.

"*Mudang* wishes to tell you a story." My watch itched.

"It will reveal a truth. The truth will alarm you, but you must be Confucian, not Western, in understanding it. You must use your father's judgment and your inner heart. After hearing this story, you cannot call your police.

"You cannot cause questioning or arrests of her patients. *Dae-wi*, the *wang mansin* does not have to tell this story.

"You have been trained by the foreign long-nosed people to value power. Your father trained you to honor your duty, to be a man of *chinjol*—benevolence. The

wang mansin says because you do not humble yourself to
God, she wonders will you bend down to her, an old and
physically weak woman?"

Song Sae's eyes burned into me. Prosecutors
understand conditional disclosures. I wanted to question
the twelve men; my guts told me her story was worth
more. "I will."

Song Sae listened as the *wang mansin* told her story.
Madame Chae's hands depicted mountains, a fierce, ter-
rifying animal, a river, many men, fighting, loss, dismay,
surprise. It took only a few minutes before she spread her
hands. Finis.

Song Sae arched, her chest filling with air, a trumpeter
sitting on first note.

"When Heaven broke from Earth, when Tangun, the
founder of Korea, was young, a tiger came down Mount
Sohak to a village divided by a stream. The tiger ate
farmers who came to the water. People suffered and children cried at night.

"The farmers on one stream bank gave the tiger food
to befriend it. But food only made it stronger, bolder,
hungrier.

"The farmers on the other bank sent a hunting party
which attacked the great tiger with pitchforks." She
paused. "Wounded, the tiger killed most of the hunters
and destroyed that half of the village, making everyone
poorer than ever before."

This was not the ancient proverb of brave men pulling
the tiger's tail, a story of pluck and courage. It was a
Pyongyang Communist fairy tale. Kim Il Sung was the
great *paksu* of Korea. I wondered if southern *mudang*
answered to him.

I wanted to trust her. Just like Jimmy would. No—I
wanted to trust her more.

"*Dae-wi*, thirteen farmers survived the tiger's attack.
They tried a new plan, to torment it—to keep it from

sleeping—to make it leave. They pledged like Chinese brothers, promising their lives against the big, angry cat.

"At night, one farmer pulled the tiger's tail, awakening it. The tiger roared and ate the farmer. Now twelve remained. The next night, another pulled the tail. Each morning, the tiger was slower and more confused. Even so, it always managed to kill its tormentor.

"By New Year, only one Tiger Tail man remained. The tired tiger had won. But the survivor had made a pledge. He had to try.

"On New Year's morning, the tiger was gone. So were all thirteen of the Tiger Tails who had taken the pledge."

Song Sae bowed to Madame Chae. Both women looked at me.

The tiger was America. The stream that divided the village was the waters of the Imjin and the wire and minefields of the DMZ. The village half that had pulled the tiger's tail was called the People's Democratic Republic of North Korea. The village half that fed the tiger was the ROK, the Republic of Korea.

Thirteen men had pledged like brothers to pull the tiger's tail. Not to kill it, since this was impossible, but to torment and confuse it, and drive it from their home.

"If these men are North Korean, and twelve is an unlucky number here, why are there an unlucky twelve patients?"

She said, "*Mudang* does not say they are Northmen. She says the *kung-hap* does not change. Twelve will act in three days. One died two months ago. There were thirteen."

I looked at her. "Why did she tell me this story?"

Song Sae smiled, a little sadly. "She is a storyteller."

Three days. I wondered at a connection between the Wizard's desperate kidnapping of an IG and this worrisome fable.

These men might be Inmingun. Whatever they were, they planned an action seventy-two hours from now, and I had promised that they would not be questioned or arrested. Casey could not be alerted to a possible terrorist attack. I was to use Confucius, BaBa's brains and my inner heart in an unproven spiritual recipe against the unknown and the unknowable.

Today was Friday, 18 January. The lunar New Year was Monday, 21 January. I had committed this day to the rescue of Jimmy, leaving two days to arrest the Wizard, analyze his map, and protect Camp Casey with my hands tied behind me.

And something compelling and irreversible had made the Wizard take Jimmy.

Too much to accomplish, too many unknowns, not enough resources and time running like the sea into a broken hull.

Jimmy's life now had the weight of spit in the wind.

BaBa's voice. Hu-chin, work. One bucket at a time, fast as you can, hard as you can. You are *syau*, but you are firstborn and must work like a man. You have luck. Help us find the current that will take us from this place.

See here, you must show little Hu-hau and Hu-chien what work is. Work with me. Do not give in!

I stood and bowed to the women. *"Kamsahamneeda."*

Song Sae bowed: *"Komabsumnida chonmaneyo,"* she said regally. Madame Chae stared without expression. I began to leave.

The *wu* spoke. I stopped as Song Sae translated.

"She says you will remember her old-lady, wind-beaten face, marked so clearly by Chinese winds. And, you will remember her old voice." The *wu* pointed at me.

"Yes. I thought she might say that."

27

Southside

I scanned the line of *tabang*, teahouses, bordering the far side of the wide, empty street and the first of the Japanese warehouses. It seemed more seedy than foreboding.

I was going to get Jimmy. I cast away the thought: *ji hui*. I looked at the men who would cover my crossing.

Men loitered at the shops, lacking the fortitude to cross, harried by begging street orphans. Street kids panhandled for money and got none. One worker cuffed a persistent boy.

I knocked on the window and pointed at him: you're busted. The man spat angrily and left, his *in-sam*, harmony, disturbed.

The warehouses were dingy and the snow a crystalline white, the color of Chinese mourning. It was *ch'ing ming*, the shining bright day of reporting to ancestors.

I remembered asking Cara to join me. She had put on a white dress, fixed her hair, and helped my hands while I interfered with her work. Later, we strolled the western walkway of the Golden Gate Bridge, selfishly taking deep draughts of clean sea air on a day for ancestors.

The bridge connected the City to the Marin headlands and was the bright orange border between East and West. BaBa loved this bridge, and had brought me here until his arthritis stopped him.

"This is how I do it. I face China and the river, my back to America. It's my job to report to the old graves at

Chingshan along the Yangtze River. I report on the family's health, and our memory of them." The winds fluffed her long, dark red, sunlit hair as if it were a happily broken sail.

Silent while I made my report, she asked questions, trying to touch, to confirm, her own old-country roots.

I looked at her, full of happy and sad. I was the first-born son, replete with excessive rights and the duty to make sons, but made highly imperfect from an encounter with unforeseen evils. Now she had come, bringing me sheer pleasure to replace nagging anxieties, de-romancing my solitude.

"Jackson," she said softly. "How did your brothers die?"

I shook my head. "It's not right to talk about it."

She held my face and kissed my nose and my eyes, the winds from Asia whipping us, the bridge vibrating with fast Western cars. She stopped. "Can we always be in love?"

"I will be. It may not be that important."

"Oh, God, yes it is. I know people who are together, but not in love." She kissed me deeply. "I've been in love, each time thinking, this was it. I need this to last forever." She bit my neck. "Want to know how you can keep me?"

"No, thank you." I laughed. "Of course. Tell me."

"Always talk to me. And never leave. And, naturally, never touch another woman. For the rest of your life. I know you can do it." Her eyes teared. The wind. "I hope I can."

Magrip strode down the alley, pursued by orphans. He entered the leather shop. The shop proprietor, already worried about me, coughed nervously, seeing too many bad luck signs.

"Give me the sit," said Magrip, the old company commander. Part of his anger was not being in charge.

"Shaman says Jimmy's in that first big building. When

customers start crossing, I'll go with them. What's in there?"

Magrip squinted. "A whorehouse. They're *all* whore-houses and shooting galleries. So much bong weed over there you get a contact high." He pointed.

"Enter through the teahouses in front." He pointed again. "Hookers at tables. Customers pick 'em, pay the pimp, go out the back door up iron stairs to the rooms. Pimps are the only security. There are rumors of guns." A calm voice.

"Jimmy," I said, "might be on the top floor of that building."

He nodded and studied the top of the warehouse. "Kan, Levine called. She ran into some crap—McCrail won't leave Naktong without you. Bulls couldn't get him out of his cell. He thinks Levine works for the Wizard. Now they got her. Good move, sending a woman to a Korean pen."

"She's okay. I'm not going to sweat her more than I sweat you. And I worry about you all the time."

He smiled. "Believe that shaman? We rely on her over there?" He hitched his head toward the large, dark warehouses.

"She knew a lot." I told him of the men who would pull the tiger's tail, about the New Year and her condition precedent to telling me the story. He squinted at me. "Jesus, that's squirrelly."

I hit him on his shoulder. "I go down, you're in charge."

"To do what with that gaggle of Korean spooks?"

"Magrip, if I knew that, I wouldn't be cold in Korea, waiting for johns to give me cover to cross a street."

He nodded, frowning as orphans saw us in the window and stared. "Someone oughta get them gloves."

"The orphanage director says they need fathers."

"Don't hold your breath. Men are becoming crap-out artists." Johns began to cross the street.

"Magrip, I'll signal. Give me ten minutes. If I don't signal, get Min and send him in to find out what happened."

"You don't show, I'm coming after you."

"You'll follow orders. They snatch me, they'll be waiting for you and then we'll have dumped the mission. Point man goes down, slack man tries something else. Don't go down the same hole."

He nodded. "You buy it, who do I call?"

"My parents." I took his wrist and wrote on it Cara's phone number. "And her. I couldn't tell her I came here. The fable she got is that I went to Walter Reed for back surgery."

"Yeah, that's what Dirtbag Murray told Carole. For *my* back surgery." He shook his head. "If anything happens to Levine, I guess I call her mom and ex-husband."

Ex-husband. "Yeah," said Magrip, "the poor bastard."

I offered my hand. Black troops did daps and whites did high fives, which used to be black. Magrip took my wrist and pen and wrote a phone number on it. "Carole. Goddamn, I'll be pissed if I get killed." He slapped my palm. "Make it happen."

I took the pen back. "Be sure to write." I crossed and entered the *tabang*, the weight of the Browning a comforting ballast.

The teahouse was a cold slab with worn tables and bundled women sitting in hobble-legged wicker chairs, the walls postered with lewd and fading Asian women expressing unimaginable thoughts to cold camera lenses, the air thick with smoke.

Three women. They sat up, snuffing Virginia Slims in tin ashtrays. *"Yobo saeo"*: Hi; literally, "you listen." They removed caps, flaunting hair before they saw I was not a customer, swearing as they fought tresses back into caps.

A man limped through a tinkling yellow beaded curtain. Under my height, six-one, gaunt in a bulky red fiberfill jacket, old jeans and faded, vented jungle boots. His eyes were tired in a malarial sort of way. He was American, black and no longer young after pitching his adolescence into an Asian bog. He saw that I had not picked a dance partner.

"Igosee peeryohamneeka?" he asked.

"I don't speak Korean. My name's Kan."

He backed up, tired eyes sparking, matches in the night. "You the heat? Army fuzz? Whatchu want, Jack?" he barked harshly.

Lucky guess on the name. "I'm looking for a friend who might be in one of these hooches, dinky-dau sick and in trouble. If you have it, I'll take a Diet Pepsi."

He snorted. "'Diet Pepsi'? What the hell's that? An' you mean *dien cai dau*, right? What kinda dude come Southside lookin' for frien's? Mistah, this be Hanguk country. No white boys an' no frien's a white boys. You a big, rich damn fool, wearin' too much scratch to be dippin' wick in a numbah-ten BJ Alley girl. And I *know* what you Ornamentals think a black men. So don't crap *me*, Fu Manchu Jack."

"I'm not looking for a girl. I'm an old Squawking Duck rifleman. I need some help." He was Army and he was Vietnam, the imprint of the bush rising from his personality, his sharp, quarrelsome irritability clouding like steam from a generator, the proliferation of Asian faces and scents prohibiting recovery.

He kept narrowed eyes on me as he reached into his jeans and pulled out a Kool from one pocket. I lit it for him.

He exhaled. "Hunnerd-an'-first, Screamin' Eagles." He laughed. "Highlands an' the Iron Triangle. Tunnel rats and the three rivers? Yeah, you got down with the brothers.

"Me, I was wif the Psychedelic Cookie, Third Brigade, Tan Am, fought for Saigon during Tet." The Ninth

Infantry, with its cream-cookie insignia. "I was just a kid. Man, it sucked, big-time.

"Got my black butt half blowed away. Was easin' my pain in the Evac." He shook his head. "Shee-it! The Man got me on a Mary Jane use rap and sent my butt here to Ko-rea, Republic-of. Hey, I ruck up for an Imjin *gang* Z patrol an' the damn Inmingun shot me! Can you believe that shit?" He took a drag and shrugged. "Got fifty percent disability." He smiled with his teeth. "Guess I found me a home in the Far fuckin' East."

I offered my hand. He looked at it for a while. He dapped languidly. "Stubblefield. Manager."

"Jackson Kan, tourist." I pulled out a photo of Jimmy and gave it to him. "He was with us." I didn't add he was with the clerks and jerks, chowing Chinese food in Cholon, surfing on air-conditioning and sleeping in a dry, bedsheet cot every night.

He was going to say no.

"One question—he on the top floor?" The *mudang*'s tip. He closed his mouth. He opened it. "Yeah, man, he is."

"You protecting him?"

"Hey, chump, you said one question."

"That was the free one." I extracted my TDY, travel money, and gave it to him. Maybe four hundred dollars. He nodded as the bills unraveled. Like BaBa, I was never good at keeping them folded. The women stood. "Jack. You one rich dude."

"He's a buddy." I let that sit. "You paid to hold him down?"

"Got no part a that. I jus' guard the ladies."

"You're in charge and you let someone use your place like a jail, and you don't know who?"

He frowned. "Hey, man, you talk like a lawyer."

"No need to get personal."

"Fu, don't mind-fuck *me*, man. You were in the

Nam. Don't hassle me or be crappin' on me like a damn honky cop."

"Why not take me to him?"

He hesitated, thinking about business.

"We short here?"

He saw my ear. "Nah." He took the cash. "Vet discount. Blue-light special, holiday shoppers. Lunar New Year an' all that happy shit. Don't hammer me, I save you some bread."

I had a new friend. "Who's with him right now?"

"Man, you one pushy motha." Hands on hips, he looked down, then up, hard, ready to take a bite out of me. "Airborne Fu—you bein' *straight* wif me? You just here to take him out and that's it?"

"On my old, stinking ruck and my bad, smelly dogs."

He took a drag and exhaled through his nostrils. "Nam sure busted *my* damn feet. Your dude's hooked to the Queen a Scag. Ride them horses mos' every night. Promise you, man, it ain't pretty."

"Where's the security? What do I run into up there?"

He cocked his head. "Airborne Jack, *I'm* the security. Lissen, you a baby cherry here. You contain and be cool, Airborne, cuz there ain't gonna be *no* hurtin' the Scag Queen, or no girls, nohow, no way." A hard finger from a soft hand poked my chest. "Dig it?" He pulled on the smoke as if it were his last.

I held up my hands. "I'm a peace-loving man. I got a partner." I went to the door and pumped a fist. Magrip sprinted across, came in. Kids littered the street, afraid to come closer. The hookers pulled off caps and looked at Magrip hopefully.

He sneered like Elvis. "Forget it." No screams.

"Magrip, Mr. Stubblefield, once of the Ninth Infantry. Mr. Stubblefield, Mr. Magrip, once of the Twenty-fifth Infantry."

"What's this, Kan, a blind date?" They shook. Stubblefield led us through the back door to an external iron stairway that went three flights in a building airspace.

It smelled like a perfume factory, a noodle shop, and a truck stop. We stopped at the third floor. He hitched his head at the door and whispered, "That's it. Third door, left. Be cool."

"Only cuz you say so." A three-part dap. He left.

I pulled out the Browning and a mini-can of WD-40. I touched my jacket pockets for the extra magazines.

Magrip pulled out the long-barreled .44 magnum and the competition Colt .45.

"Sorry I couldn't get you bigger sidearms."

He shrugged. "I forgive you."

"I open, you look right, I look left. I go in left, you follow. Close the door. Keep your cannons out of sight."

The hinges looked good, but I sprayed WD-40. I opened the door; it parted silently. I looked left, he looked right. I stepped into the narrow wooden hallway, floorboards creaking. Empty. Down the hall came the music of a woman hollowly, eerily singing a soft Korean radio rock tune, "Chibee Chibee Chirum."

He clicked the hall door shut. The stairway behind was silent. Third door—locked, TV sounds. From somewhere, a woman laughed and another argued loudly. Someone was coming up the iron stairway behind us.

I pocketed the Browning, pulled the knife and stuck the blade into the panel and leveraged, cracking wood, chunking out a spacer, and splitting the lock lip from its strike. I yanked the old iron mechanism out of its well, pulled the gun and brought it up as the door swung open and we went in, Magrip closing the shattered door, wood splinters everywhere.

"Smooth technique, Godzilla," said Magrip.

I dropped the lock. Sour debris, human waste, stale cigarettes. A black-and-white TV flickered, horizontal control rolling. Magrip stood ready.

I scanned the room and my heart fell.

They had moved him. The arguing woman's voice was louder, more discordant through the wall. Voices in the hall. I glanced at Magrip; he shook his head: no sweat; they had passed our busted door.

Two beds were pushed together, covered with empty food cartons, cardboard boxes, Korean and Japanese beauty magazines, and weeks of old newspapers. Something was under them. Weapon up, I cleared them and found a body wrapped in a comforter.

I lifted the bedding, rolling the body. A slack-mouthed, tongue-floating woman, age indecipherable, comatose, face freshly bruised, arms tattooed with black injection sites, her body showing signs of all manner of earthly abuse. The Scag Queen.

"And, if she talks," said Magrip, "it'll be Korean."

I looked under the bed, clearing garbage. Nothing. A foul toilet closet. Empty. Magrip found a closet behind a tall cardboard carton. It was locked, so he tore the handle from the door and it swung open.

Inside the closet, a man was hanging from the ceiling, dangling from leather straps that held him in some sort of arcane bondage harness, not unlike a parachute rig. The man was Anglo and thin.

I lifted the chin—no mortis. It was Jimmy.

28

AN ANSWER TO PRAYER

I safetied and pocketed the Browning, cut the straps and carried him to the cots as Magrip rapidly burrowed space.

His chest was stone. I put fingertips to the heart. Nothing. Then a tremor like an uncertain soup under a weak fire. He was alive, the old spark protected somewhere within. I touched him, coaching him into breath, feeling blessed life in a faint pulse. His color was that of an old, forgotten porcelain doll, his arms blue.

"Bee," I said, compressing his chest. He had a beard and smelled like a dead goat. He was jaundiced, bruised and stirred into a ragged breath. He wore soiled thermal underwear, the arms cut off to allow easy injections. I took his pulse—42.

His forearms looked like beetle food. On the bed stand was a cop's dream sheet of paraphernalia: needles, bottles, spoons, coke dirt, grime and criminal abuse. I slapped him hard.

"Bee, you're in deep granola—you're grounded for a week." I massaged his heart. "Keep pumping."

I thought Naktong and its firing squads would be ample deterrent to drugs. I had underestimated the power of bad habits.

Magrip looked at Jimmy, one eye scrunched, jaw clenched, more somber than I had ever seen him. He was standing guard.

"Jimmy the Bee, you're beautiful. And you smell ter-

rific. Jackson's here to take you home. Let's go get some
Cholon Chinese food and convict some scag dealers,
what do you say? Talk to me, Jimmy. Wake up.
Reveille." I whistled it.

He moaned, trembling. He tried to lick his lips, white
with salt. The local water was unpotable. I gave him
Song Sae's bottle of Bacchus-B ginseng concentrate
from Second Market. I helped Jimmy suck it down,
almost gagging him.

Magrip crinkled his nose. "What the hell is that?"

"Ginseng. Improves your sex life."

A flat face. "Yeah, that's important right now."

"Jimmy, we gotta go."

He garbled something, trying. More Bacchus-B. I
lifted him off the bed, testing his legs. Rubber. He
mumbled, "Am I goin' through changes?" The voice
faint, a memory of him, the weakness, the confusion.

The TV played *Wanted—Dead or Alive*. Steve
McQueen spoke Korean without a hope of lip synch. I
put Jimmy down and found socks and a pair of running
shoes. Magrip came upon his fatigues and boots.

"Jimmy, who did this?" I repeated the question.
Nothing. I shook him and tried again. "Who, Jimmy?" I
hissed. Magrip put on the blouse; I did trousers and
socks. I repeated myself. I squeezed his cheeks as if I
were a Chinese mother with her first baby.

"Talk to me. Name the bad guys. For Carlos." I cross-
hatched his boot laces. "James, do it for the Tarheels."

That got him. He mumbled parts, then put it all
together.

"Wizard . . . Dogface. Dogface Nagol . . . bad boys,
Jackson. Police 'em up. . . . Get 'em, Jackson. . . ."
Moaning, "Sic 'em, boy."

I recorded it.

"I thought a guy named James Thurber would talk a
little different."

I wrapped his field cap around his head and put him

over my shoulder. He felt like a long blanket roll. His lack of weight made me ache. I held the Browning in my left.

Magrip entered the hallway and nodded. I led down the stairs into the *tabang*. Stubblefield was gone.

Magrip cursed and something hard bashed the automatic from my hand, leaving it numb. Our guns clattered to the floor. Two men in brown leather jackets crouched, backing away, eyes wild with fear. They had clubbed our hands with heavy steel rebars.

I should have put Magrip at point; he had no body occluding his vision. But I was team leader and the firstborn.

A dozen armed pimps and users, backed up by angry comfort girls, faced us. The crowd held several versions of police revolvers, two rusted service .45s, scarred, ancient fighting staffs, brooms and a baseball bat in jumpy, quivering hands. Two of them, after several tries, picked up our guns.

I lay Jimmy on the floor, stepping away from him.

Stubblefield appeared. "Sorry, man. Turns out, these dudes an' dudettes get premium pay for feedin' scag to your man. Man, I didn't know. But they scared an' they like their cash."

"We'll pay them," I said. With Magrip's TDY advance.

"*Told* 'em you had a purse. But they afraid of somethin'. You gonna hafta give your man back, Jack, and I ain't sure what happens after. They be on some bad high-octane Turkish shit."

Someone cocked a hammer, encouraging the same action in others. We were primed for a mass accidental shooting.

"*Aniyo,*" no, I said. One of the walking dead aimed his revolver at me and the hammer fell with a loud click. No explosion. He cursed and threw the gun. I ducked. It crashed into the only mirror in the shop as Magrip and I picked up tables to throw.

"*ANIYO!* STOP!" Song Sae Moon glared from the door, facing the mob. Their gazes, pop-eyed for the violence we offered and expanded by the wonders of drugs, enlarged. Muzzles and bats quivered, then lowered. I put down the table, adrenaline banging. Magrip, less trusting, remained in throwing position.

Song Sae approached. She spoke harshly, then softly. She lifted a big steel cooking pot and threw it on the floor, where it clattered loudly, right side up.

I winced as the Browning was dropped into it, followed by all the handguns. Incredibly, none went off. I wondered if any were loaded. Song Sae seemed to bless each donor, smiling at one, touching others. After each benediction, the penitent left.

The whorehouse militia was gone. Magrip dropped the table, picked up the pot, and retrieved ours and the one that had hit the mirror. He gave me the Browning. I safetied it, fingers unresponsive.

I put Jimmy over my shoulder. "Hello, Song Sae. *Mani kamsamneeda.*"

She bowed, smiling graciously. "I was happy to help. *Dae-wi*, can you not see that you are a believer? Did you not pray for help?" She looked at me expectantly, hopefully.

There had been no prayer. I had cursed my stupidity for taking point, had almost been shot, and had picked up a table. Her faith had small play in my reality. "Yes, of course."

"Song Sae, Magrip. Song Sae Moon. She runs a *bui doi* Amerasian orphanage. She helps the shaman. And saves lives."

She bowed. Magrip, intrigued, half-bowed.

Song Sae smiled, then saw Jimmy's inverted face. "Your *chingu*, your poor friend, is very ill. Please take him to Western doctor. *Mudang* cannot help this illness of drugs."

"I agree. Are you safe here? You said girls who come Southside do not come back."

"*Dae-wi*, I am not a girl. I am *kidae*. I felt your prayer, *dae-wi*. It is what brought me to this *tabang*. If I am true to *in-sam*, to harmony, and my karma, I have nothing to fear."

I nodded. "You take care," I said to Stubblefield.

"Back at you, man," he said. We went through the door, walking faster across the broad, open street in the moments before true dusk. We were surrounded immediately by kids. I put the Browning in a pocket. Magrip followed suit. Clouds were forming to the north.

I took a deep breath. Jimmy to a doc, Magrip to babysit him, and I to Naktong for Patrick McCrail and Levine.

Jimmy the Bee groaned. He sounded like a little boy.

"You made it out, buddy," I said.

"Gonna be sick," he moaned. I felt his abdomen spasm.

"Oh, man, Jimmy, not on my new coat. It cost me fifty cents."

Movement in the shadows caught my eye.

Acne Man, the busted-nosed thug from the Vegas, stepped into our path. Fleeg. He had an AK-47, the muzzle on us. Even without Jimmy on my shoulder and with a following wind, he was beyond the range of my best kick.

Fleeg, courtesy of our dance at the Vegas, had two blackened eyes, a busted cheek, a rebroken nose and a bright white bandage on the swollen bridge.

"Well, screw me to tears in the Navy," said Magrip. "What'd you do, Happy Face, shave with a rake?"

"You fucker," said Fleeg in a high nasal voice.

"We both go," whispered Magrip. I took a deep breath.

"I wouldn't." Willoughby came from behind, standing so his AK-47 held both of us within an inch of sweep. I looked at him. He stopped, then backed up. I felt Magrip try to close the distance, and Willoughby aimed his rifle at Song Sae.

"Keep coming and I blow her away."

Magrip stopped. We were in the kill zone, tin ducks in the arcade gallery. I stared, waiting for the clacks of Claymores, the crump of grenades, the high wheeze of automatic weapons. Sun Tzu said: Strike like the *shuai jan*, the snake.

I had been the tortoise. No Napoleon today.

I licked my lips. "Gee, guys, what kept you?"

"Screw you, jerkface," Fleeg hissed.

"Okay," I said, "have it your way. You're under arrest."

"Well, excuse the hell outa me, but you're dead meat," he growled, counting witnesses. The children began to melt away. He aimed the rifle at them. "Kneel or I blow them away. Now!"

We hesitated and he fired two rounds at the kids, kicking dirt and missing them, the 7.62mm rounds whining down the alley and breaking glass in the distance. Orphans scattered, the sound of panicked children making me want to cry.

We knelt. The kids were gone. Jimmy was my best weapon. I leaned forward.

"I can see you're stupid," offered Magrip. "But even you aren't dumb enough to murder three IGs and all those kids."

He had made Willoughby pause. He grinned. "I don't think so, Luke. Don't like me calling you 'Luke'? Luke, babes, we just caught two kidnappers with a GI. And those gook kids don't know anything. Hey, Luke, you're not so tall now, are you?"

"Jesus, Willow," said Fleeg with wonder, "it's the Ice Queen." He admired her while trying to keep his eyes on me.

Willoughby wasn't ready to kill a woman he hadn't

dated. He wanted to woo her with moonlight sonatas, long-stemmed red roses and a low purchase price.

I edged forward as he did the math of courtship, trying to squeeze in a date with the demands of multiple murder.

"Willow," said Fleeg, regretting his comment. "Plenty where that came from." He was nervous. "Do her first."

"Who?" I said. My best answer. I edged closer.

Willoughby wanted Song Sae alive, in round heels and a short skirt. He gathered himself, grimacing, and backed up. We didn't have a chance. Time to drop Jimmy and cover him.

A small black object bounced off Fleeg's leg. He looked at it stupidly and I went down, covering Jimmy as it exploded with a blast that erupted in my skull, fluttered cheeks, whipped my body with debris and began a shrill metallic ringing in my brain. Jimmy twitched. A great pocket of cosmic, heated space filled the world. I was stunned and there was no shrapnel.

Concussion grenade. I struggled up, head bursting, staggering, clawing the Browning from my jacket.

Fleeg was down, blood trickling from an ear. Willoughby twitched, and Magrip was struggling up, drawing the cannon. Willoughby managed to get up on all fours, slowly shaking his head, fingers feeling, reaching for the AK.

Magrip planted himself, then punted Willoughby in the head with his boot, knocking him into a backflip and making the kind of sound that makes the faint ill. I already felt ill. Magrip spat, then collapsed. My ears rang and I felt a tremendous urge to throw up, so I did.

I looked up. A woman officer in dress green slacks turned in a circle, a snub-nosed revolver at the end of both extended arms, her mouth and eyes wide open, exhaling condensed air as she looked for more renegade JAGCs. She wore marksmanship-competition ear covers.

It was Levine, thrower of concussion grenades.

Her lips were moving at me, but I couldn't hear. I shrugged. She made a face and shook her head and recovered the AK-47s, slinging them over her shoulder. For some reason, I couldn't stop staring at the creases caused by the straps.

She helped a dazed and trembling Song Sae stand. My ears rang like the bells of Notre Dame. With ferocious concentration, I was able to get Dentyne in my mouth. Chewing was harder.

Children began running to Song Sae. Automatically, both women embraced the returning children.

It took a while, but I picked up Jimmy. His chest moved in small sharp shudders. I had to hurry for him. There was another reason for urgency. My brain was fogged.

I shook my head, generating deep, dark inspirations of profound cranial pains and solicitations of dry-land nausea. A vibration in my throat: I was moaning. I stopped it.

I struggled to arrange my thinking, but the grenade had scrambled it, shuffled it and then tossed the remains into the solvent-stained street, where they blew away in a sour wind.

All I could remember was that something bad was going to happen. Something about tigers.

29

Fit for Womankind

According to habit, I led a disreputable band into camp, exuding swamp gases and worrying sentries. Min's reckless driving revived me. My ears ached with a high-band tone.

Somehow, the abbreviation of senses brought to me the sea air from Cara's balcony. I felt the sweet, aching acceleration of her, her pulsing irresistibility, the vision of her clearing fogs in my mind and giving light to failing day.

MPs did double takes at the two bodies roped onto the hood. We passed the gate and I felt an attachment to Cara with the militant belief of a survivor of catastrophe. It was a stupendous feeling, as bright as the August sun on the Long River, as fixed and enduring as a Chinese commitment. I loved her. I had made a remarkable and stunning discovery of the obvious. I felt stupid, happy, liable, labile, brilliant, mindless.

Magrip and I untied Willoughby and Fleeg at the stockade. Levine quietly held Jimmy's head in her lap.

I looked up. "It's a beautiful day."

Magrip squinted doubtfully at the dark sky. He got in the jeep. Min raced for Second Med.

McCrail, Levine had shouted, was still secure at Naktong.

The stockade bulls scooped the two men like street debris. Staff Sergeant Scranton Plum was the warden who had allowed Nagol to hang himself. He was smelly and sawed-off. He perused a *Playboy*, lips moving slowly as he listened to Buck Owens and the Buckaroos. He reeked of tobacco and rotgut and couldn't care less that a TIG had brought him business without a hint of paperwork. He took the prisoners with the consideration of a cow consuming grass.

"I'm deaf," I said to Plum. "Give me the paperwork and get a medic for them." I filled out forms, using question marks.

Plum kicked both men in the gut. Fleeg threw up.

"Don't need no medics, sir," mouthed Plum. "These boys are squared away."

"BULL!" I shouted. He and his men jumped, dropping cigarettes. "Do that again, I'll make you walk funny." My ears hummed. His eyes swelled. "Hold them in solitary. *No* contact with anyone but medics, whom you *will* search and pat down.

"You're not doing another Nagol on me. Sergeant, don't screw this up. The guys they'd call would put a bullet in your head and will not remember you on Veterans Day."

He had slid from gentlemanly reading to sweating his retirement to winning a hole in his skull. He looked at Fleeg and Willoughby without affection. "Full cavity search," he growled. I took names; stockade duty invites sloth. I left them Dentyne.

Major Foss's hut was warmer because I was getting used to Korea. I dropped the AK-47s on his desk. He looked at the rifles' tool-dye stamps, recognizing them as Chinese manufacture. "Wonderful. Now IGs are using these crappy guns." He sniffed their muzzles.

"Major, get your men to sit on the Wizard now. I'll do the paper to arrest him." I lifted his typewriter. "May I?"

"Sure. The only damn working typewriter in Korea. Take my desk. Want my jeep? How about my stinking job?"

I think that's what he said; my ears were still ringing. "Make the call, sir." He did, sending MPs to LeBlanc.

"Willoughby and a guy named Fleeg are in D Cell for attempt One-Eighteen on three officers and a ROK civilian, using these AKs. Can you print these, and can Plum hold them?"

Foss pulled latent print tags from his blouse, filled them out meticulously and tied them to the rifle straps. "Pit's got two months to retirement. He'll do it right."

"Sir, need you and an armed West Point O-3 at the Med."

"You're a piece a work. Heart attack on wheels." He went into a latrine. A Sergeant Myers stepped into the office and tied a chain of custody form to the rifles, signed them and bagged them.

From the latrine, Foss shouted, "Myers—do a chain of custody on those AKs!"

Myers bagged the rifles for printing and left with them. Foss came out and finished his coffee, burning himself.

"Damn! Get me Childers! And Myers—bag those rifles!"

Grumbling, his watch cap low, Foss drove fast up the main drive, talking to himself as he peeled around a convoy of mud-packed armored personnel carriers with bright red Live Ammo flags, dumping soil tracks like sick pachyderms.

I wrote a note for Childers as the jeep bounced.

I looked at Foss. "Sir, we got our boy back. Thank you. I owe you big."

Foss turned off the drive. "I figure you do. Thanks for getting me out of that reveille run. The PM, he don't like you. Says you woke him. He have a Blue Heart in his bunk?"

"That, or a very funny-looking GI."

He chuckled. "Never thought I'd see anyone take down the Wizard. When you gonna nail the PM?"

My hearing was making a rebound. "Soon."

Foss nodded and radioed. "Pit, this is Foss. If the old man tries to see the JAGC folk, he don't. No one but yours truly. . . ." He laughed. "Uh-huh. That chink captain who rang your bell is future Army Chief of Staff and he heard you say that. . . . No, he ain't deaf. . . . Pit, I don't give a damn what he said. He's the IG. Out here."

Levine stood under the med door light, her overcoat collar up. I wanted to hear about McCrail and how she had gotten out of Naktong. She took the typewriter from me. She put it down.

She put her arms around me, her face in my neck. I held her to give comfort. Her quivering inspired an image of Song Sae and the *bui doi* being shredded by AKs. I held her as she squeezed, and I saw Beth and the boys and felt the nearness of losing Jimmy, Magrip, Song Sae and Levine, in a single moment. I closed my eyes tight. We held each other with raw strength, the power of those who had survived a swarming of wolves.

In time, her breathing smoothed and her tremors stopped, reducing our need to hold each other. Now our touching, our closeness, meant something else. We sighed, our breathing one. A low voice. "Jackson, this is crazy."

"I told you," I said softly. "I'm an insomniac. You're crazy." I felt her every breath. I felt her legs. She was whispering.

"You know, when this mission is over, I could mature you. Make you emotively insightful. Fit for womankind. To be someone a woman would want to grow old with. Someone who'd talk, be attentive, not watch TV all the time. Love, and like, care and cry." She was talking into my neck. Her breath was warm. "You have the potential. You're evolved past the primary male emotion—anger. And you have good Jewish blood."

I shouldn't be holding her. Not like this. I thought of Cara.

"She dumped you, right?" she asked.

"Maybe. I haven't dumped her."

More emotionally advanced, Levine leaned back a little. Southside had loosened our emotions. Her mouth was near laughter, her eyes closer to tears. She was lovely. I wished I didn't think so. She licked her lips, tossing her short hair. "Do you love her?" The large dark eyes, the warmth of her.

"Yes."

"Super. I knew that. If you didn't love her, you'd bore me. Well. Table for one." She stepped back with a devastating smile, sardonic and sensual. "I'm so happy you're a good man." She pushed me. "Get out of here, Kan."

"I think I'll just stand here in the cold for a few minutes."

I did not watch her as she walked away. I thought of baseball. How about those Giants.

Magrip was sitting on the floor of ER. Medics, orderlies and doctors moved in methodical chaos. I felt the memory of Levine's legs, her great face. I had a headache.

My back hurt, but I sat on the floor. "Good evening." I put the typewriter between us.

"Everyone says that. No one means it anymore. What—now you want me to type for you? I already got a job."

"Son, the Army's not a job, it's an adventure."

"The Army's not a job," he said. "It's a blow job."

I laughed. "Magrip, you're as much fun as a truck hitting a dog."

He nodded. "We all got our strengths. Got Buford's wife on the horn. She said some crap about kissing you but I'll pass if that's okay."

"Please."

He yawned. Adrenaline dissipation. "Doc Purvis saw Buford. You treat heroin OD with intramuscular Narcan and methadone detox. Like food and sun and vitamins, not at Casey. They'll medevac him to Yongsan."

I glanced at him. He looked like I had ruined his life.

"Why don't you get out?" I asked.

He studied his hands. "Oughta. Get tired of being pissed. Miss cherry farms and fishing. Sturgeon Bay, Wisconsin. You knew everyone. Cops'd give you a ride home." He shook his head. "Miss it. Had hints of it at the Academy and in Nam." He picked at knuckle scabs. "Damn hard ways to get a community.

"Then I became a lawyer and learned the good old days maybe weren't. Families were screwed up, but quiet about it."

I rubbed my scalp. "I believe in the good old days."

Magrip sighed. "Oh, hell, so do I. They were a kick."

"You kicked Willoughby so good I threw up."

He smiled, happy, and the doors banged open and medics brought out Jimmy on a gurney with IVs, pallid under a wool OD blanket. He looked great: no sucking chest wound; no steel in his body; head, limbs, external organs intact; dog tags bright.

I took his cold hand. "Jimmy, this is Butt Kicker Magrip. He called Beth, so they know you're okay. Nothing personal, but all she talked about was kissing me."

James Thurber Buford showed some color. He nodded at Magrip. He squeezed in a weak grip. "She always lahked y'all more. Hey, Magrip, thanks, man."

Magrip coughed. "Get well, Buford."

"Bee, you gotta fly. Places to go."

"Thangs ta do, people ta see, thangs ta understand." He grinned and the sun came out, making me blink fast.

They took him into the cold and loaded him in the medevac on the illuminated pad. I yelled at the crew chief to wait as the turbine whined angrily. An MP jeep screeched around the med, throwing snow. An armed MP officer emerged, taking long strides. Captain Childers.

I pointed to Jimmy in the bay. "IG. Kidnapped and loaded with heroin by American officers. They want him dead. Stay close to him. Expect trouble. I'm Kan. No one but us sees him." I gave him the scrawled description of our IG team. "Keep him safe. Until relieved."

Childers jumped on board next to Jimmy and strapped in.

Magrip squinted in the rotor wash as the medevac pulled pitch and took a sharp attack angle on the wind, whumping thuddingly. It was a familiar sight. I remembered hot, bloody days, when angels were helicopters and tomorrow was a crap shoot.

I willed the light-flashing medevac to get out of the range of small arms fire, as if this were a jungle clearing and enemy guns could still claw it from the sky. Foss looked at his watch. I looked at mine; it was gone. I checked my pockets and laughed; Jimmy had slipped it off my wrist.

Purvis was in the hallway, writing charts. "Hey, Ludwig!" he greeted Foss.

"Hey, Doc," said Foss.

"'Ludwig'?" I asked Foss.

"Drop it," he snarled.

Purvis steered me away. "You're great for bringing me patients, but you need therapy yourself."

"If everyone followed your advice, you'd be unemployed."

He smiled. "Buford's febrile. May have hepatitis, has circ problems. Needs a week in detox with antibiotics. They'll medevac him to Walter Reed. Near his family."

I shook his hand, too hard. "Thanks. Where can I type?"

"My office. Got incoming inhalers. Q fire."

Foss and I stopped. "Where?" we asked.

Purvis was gone.

"Screw it," said Foss through thick chow. "Let the fire-fighters hack it. My ass is grass." He hitched his trousers. "You wear me out."

Purvis's office was, unlike our Q, orderly. Ludwig Foss spat in the waste can. Magrip collapsed in a chair. I rolled the Form 15-74 onto Foss's typewriter and hit the keys.

I named James T. Buford and Patrick T. McCrail as victims and witnesses for preferral of charges against COL Frederick C. LeBlanc, Judge Advocate General's Corps. I got him on Articles 84, 92(1), 92(3), 121, 128, and multiple Article 134 specifications—effecting fraudulent enlistments, black-marketing, dereliction of duty, larceny, graft, assault, battery with deadly force on an officer in execution of duties, kidnapping.

I would have charged more, but I was in a rush. I smelled smoke. Levine walked in, breathing hard. Magrip sniffed the air and nodded at Levine. "Hey," he said, making me smile.

"Hey, yourself," she said.

I ripped out the 15-74 and showed it to her.

"Typos," she offered.

"Hey, man, we're in the field."

"Jackson, you called me 'man.'" She arched an eyebrow.

I laughed. "I only meant well by it." I took back the form, signed and dated it, and gave it to Foss. He had been studying Levine and jerked. He read it and whistled.

I hammered out 15-74s for Willoughby and Fleeg. Battery, interference with investigation, attempted murder and kidnap, and charges on the other JAGCs for obstruction of justice with a wiretap on Willoughby. Levine read them, making corrections which I initialed. I signed, dated and gave them to Foss. "Major, the men in D Cell are incommunicado until lunar New Year. No rescues. Get LeBlanc."

Foss smiled at the report like it had kissed him. He winked at Levine and strode out, a cheerful bear, as Purvis came in.

I stretched my back. "We have a date in Suwon."

And twelve Inmingun running in our rear area.

"Oh, Jackson, no," said Levine, "not the MSR. Please."

"Forget it. You need rest," said Purvis. "People with unresolved combat fatigue need to get their jammies on. Now."

"No time." I looked at my wrist; my watch wasn't there.

"Horse pucky. Rest, or I'll order you quarantined."

"What, for bad manners?"

"For being a hazard on the road."

I laughed. "That won't work. We're in Korea."

"Levine, how'd you get out of Naktong?" asked Magrip.

She sighed. "I inspired a riot. By the staff."

"Fuck them," said Magrip. He liked her.

"Not a good idea," Levine said, turning to me. "Jackson. There's something I need to show you. Right now."

30

MAP

Our bare Q light glared. She handed me an accordion file with Asian rice-paper invoices: twenty thousand Chinese AK-47s, a ton of Soviet *plastique* with det cord, detonators, and Czech timing devices. Plastics. Stable, transportable, hard to detonate, and incredibly destructive when properly triggered.

LeBlanc loved automatic weapons. Why the *plastique*?

On our pocked desk, Levine unrolled a KAMS—Korean Army Map Service 1:50,000 map of the DMZ and North Korea. We pinned its corners with boots and a Lady Clairol hair dryer.

"This," she said, "is the Wizard's. I took his map and overlay and hung an identical KAMS sheet in its place. There was this fire. All I could grab was the accordion file." She rummaged her hair. "I smell like smoke. It destroyed my hair."

I looked at the map. "Very impressive."

"My hair or the map?"

"Both." It depicted the area above Casey—the pink DMZ and the dark North Korean mountains above. The ranges funneled toward Tongducheon, becoming the Valley of War.

She unrolled the clear acetate over the map and we reweighted the corners. I studied it; it told me nothing.

"This is his original overlay. For this, I committed larceny." She smiled. "Like it?"

The acetate was blank. Erased. I looked at the shiny surface.

I leaned close and huffed onto it, fogging it with condensation. Minute dents on the acetate surface held my breath like peaks hold mist and fog. Indentations in the plastic were highlighted. I huffed, seeing where pencils had made tracks.

"Grease pencils," I said. Levine gave me red and black. I softly marked red lines for movements, black circles for objectives and staging areas.

Lines ran from two circled towns in North Korea to our circled forward camps and Casey. They were named I'chon and T'osan. Where the advance lines crossed the DMZ into South Korea, they thickened.

Something was there, speaking to me. The phone rang. I picked it up. "Foss here. Wizard Q was torched. I figure the Wizard did it—used the smoke and confusion to hit the road. My guys lost him. The Wizard's loose and we're looking. . . . Don't hassle me—we know what he looks like. Hey, you didn't tell me why you want those boys in lockup until the lunar New Year."

Levine checked a set of olive drab rucksack straps. She casually put them in her pocket.

"Can't say, Major. But if I were you, I'd work that day."

"Hell, it's a dammed Monday. I gotta work anyway."

"Good, because something is going to happen then."

"Like what, Counselor?"

"Beats the hell out of me."

He slammed down his phone, making my ear ring.

31

NAKTONG BLUES

I contemplated a queasy burger while Magrip reviewed the evidence. He read like a lawyer, taking indented notes and making sucking sounds. He was bound for G-2 to see what they thought of LeBlanc's map work.

I had conspired to steal a map and had busted Carlos's orders. Stay in your lane, he had said, and I made McCrail our new mission; no deals for LeBlanc, and I offered the Wizard a way out; Levine was to go to the embassy and I sent her to Naktong; Magrip was to go to Naktong and I took him to Southside. So the hell with it; I was phoning Cara. What could Carlos do, send me to Korea? The lines to the U.S. were busy.

At the shower, I undressed and saw Cara, her brilliant, beautiful green eyes, the wonderful fluted space on her upper lip, the flood of her impetuous hair, the curve of her neck, the taste of her, her small, subvocal sounds, her soft, husky voice in the moonlight of her room. In the shower I couldn't remember the scent of peach, but the sense of her wouldn't leave me. I imagined her in the shower with me and closed my eyes. Cara, I love you. I forced myself to say the words aloud, to make them real.

"Aiguuuu!" Someone slipped and fell with a loud crash and painful groans. A cough. "*Dae-wi*, what *mudang* say?"

"Corporal, she said Captain Buford was in Southside."

"*Dae-wi*, that all she say?"

"Basically. Will they recognize me at Suwon?"

"Hope no, *dae-wi*. I changee. No glasses. Now I sergeant."

"Congratulations. I hope they don't catch *you*."

Levine was breathing behind her sheet, on the edge of a snore. I had a sense of how much energy it took for her to function in the male-dominated Army. Like being a cat in a cageless dog kennel while raw meat was constantly tossed onto the floor.

Min peeked at the exotic Western woman. Then he said goodnight. Time to try Cara again. I reached for the phone and it rang. I picked it up. "Yes," I said.

"Hello," came a lovely, distant voice. "Who is this?"

Our number and location were secure. "Wrong number."

"Jackson Kan? This is Carole Magrip. I kept after Colonel Murray until he gave me the number. You're Hu and he's Justicio. Did I say the secret password to get into the little boys' treehouse? I also have a secret decoder ring with a lot of Frosted Flakes sugar on it."

I chuckled. "In that case, let me get him."

"No. First, tell me if he's been . . . angry."

"Uh, no. Not exactly. He's fine. Cheerful. Like Goldie Hawn."

A laugh. "You're a liar and I can't trust you either."

I awoke Magrip, saying it was his wife before he bit me.

"Doll, is it you?" His voice sounded young and open.

I left. When Magrip left the Q, I went back in and dialed the access codes for Cara. It was three in the morning yesterday in Mill Valley. Cara, I love you. My heart pounded.

Magrip was sitting in the snow, his head in both hands.

The phone rang: not home or not answering. My stomach turned sour. I imagined her with other men. It was an evil thought and it was then I remembered the Wizard had sent Nagol to attack McCrail's wife.

I called Carlos and asked him to put security on our

families, including a Cara Milano on Morning Sun Drive in Mill Valley.

Dawn, Saturday, 19 January. Magrip and I ran at reveille and watched Levine stride away. Temperatures rose and birds sang as smoke rose from battalion mess halls all over camp.

Casey resembled a World War II Army post, only older. I considered breakfast until I thought of driving with Corporal Min and remembered the stench of Naktong.

Min drove up in a four-door GM sedan. I wasn't worried about getting McCrail out of Naktong; I worried about fitting him inside the car. "How did you sleep, Corporal?"

"Most very good, *dae-wi, kamsahamneeda.* And you, sir?"

"Fine." I had been on the phone for six hours until I was patched to the CID agents guarding each of our families. Cara, I was told, was now safely in her downtown office.

The jerking motion of the sedan put me to sleep. The girl ran to me. I tried to scream.

"*Dae-wi,* I am sorry, you believe in Heaven?"

Screw pines, a rural village. Suwon. He had asked me about Heaven. Did I believe. I looked at the sky. "No. You?"

"*Dae-wi,* I think Heaven and Hell here, in life."

I would agree; BaBa would not. "You married, Corporal?"

"*Neh*—good wife, two children, two girl."

"You still want a son?"

"Of course, *dae-wi.* I am a man."

"Slow down, Corporal. No hitting kiosks."

Min awkwardly slowed. The guard saluted. No guns. I gave him the ROK Ministry of Defense telex, signed by the ROK judge advocate general. It gave us Curadess by executive order.

We entered prison administration. I signed in and was fingerprinted and photographed. We were led down a long gray hallway, footfalls echoing. At dungeonlike doors, we waited.

Levine had come here yesterday to cause a riot and be evicted. Metal-tapped shoes echoed down the hall. The overweight, pockmarked guards captain who had frisked me on our first visit. With him, two bulls. At attention, he bowed. I bowed back.

He spoke in Korean.

"This man, *dae-wi*," said Min, "Honcho Deputy Numbah-Two Warden So. He say Curadess no leave cell without you. Sorry. He must frisk." Min, without glasses, squinted badly.

Assistant Deputy Warden So began at my ankles and moved up. He continued more thoroughly, touching the distinctive CIB as he had on my first visit. But no sunglasses. I breathed slowly and shallowly.

He asked questions harshly of Min, who answered. Again the captain studied me, his tongue pressing, searching his cheek.

The great door swung open and the shocking stink of Naktong overwhelmed us. Metal cups hit random rappadiddles while the cons stared at the Chinese man in an American uniform. Inmates yelled and cried at me, over and against each other in cacophonies of discordant screams. After false efforts, the prisoners found the four-part tribal beat.

Most of the screams were Korean. Some, I think, were Turkish; a few were American. "Hey, Cap'n!" came a voice. "You came for *me*!" cried another. "Goddamn, you fuckin' officer mothafucka, get me outa here!"

I walked down the stairs in the clanging rhythm, stopping where the Aussie had asked if I spoke English.

His cell was empty. "What happened to him?" I asked.

"Molla-yo," said the guard. I don't understand.

"WHAT HAPPENED TO HIM?" I shouted down.

"They shot the asshole!" came the answer.

Four guards led me onto the Chinese-unlucky fourth level down. The smells were worse. In the eighteenth cell stood a mountain of a man, huge mitts clutching the gray steel rods that had set the stage for seven years of his exposure to the arts, sunsets, sunrises, sunbathing, moon gazing and star watching.

"Hey, Captain. Damn, you look good."

"Morning, Sergeant Major. Sorry for the delay."

He giggled. "Hell, sir, you're way early for a lawyer."

The guards thunked him on the chest with batons. Unblinking, he backed up. They shouted. He turned his back at the rear of the tiny cell, hands locked behind his great white head.

A foul grate was his toilet, a reed mat his bed. His bean pillow was the size of a softball. Bright green cockroaches with hairy, scrabbling legs ran floor sprints. A thick-bodied brown spider dominated a ceiling corner, the web sagging with corpulent black bugs. I had disliked spiders until I learned to hate water snakes. I never had nightmares about spiders.

"Nice place."

The guards secured the cell and frisked McCrail.

"Just got everything Airborne and now I gotta leave." He looked at me, trying to be casual. "I *am* leaving. Right, sir?"

"Roger that, Sergeant Major." He made a grimace of faith. The bulls bowed; I returned it. A guard lifted his nightstick behind McCrail's head—he was simply being prepared. We walked down the floor and up the stairs, a march of free men in life's absolute counterpart to Fat City.

McCrail walked well without leg irons, rather like a magnificent ocean liner plowing heavy seas. He sported an enormous crap-eating grin, talking to himself. "Hey," he said amidst the din, "I can walk and talk and I'm gonna see the sun."

"It's Korea in winter out there," I said softly.

He blew out air. "It's okay, lad. Works for me."

The inmates saw one of their own being escorted out. The drumming became a murderous, crushing din as cups were thrown and men barked and wailed and threw their bodies at the bars, the roar of scraped, fading throats and imprisoned lungs, clanging steel and shaking bars, their lower-primate-like antics threatening to sweep my mind into the wash of their erupting emotions. They thought McCrail was going to be shot.

The higher we went, the more obvious became his doubts. He began panting, not from effort but from fear. "'Hail Mary full of grace the Lord is with thee' . . . Damn chink joke on a fat foreign devil's old mind. We get to the top, apes'll change their minds, you wait and see. . . . 'Blessed art thou among women . . .'"

The door closed behind us, sealing off the banging cups and screams, the contrasting silence causing a shudder. McCrail exhaled. I rubbed my nose. He sucked great, shuddering gusts of clean air as he looked furtively about him.

"Holy Mary Mother of God," he said. "God's sweet air."

The door opened again and McCrail flinched as pandemonium flooded our ears. He bared his teeth as fear took his old, glacial face. A guard emerged. The door closed. He shook.

"*Shit! That* made me pucker! Damned Naktong Blues. Won't miss it. No, sir. Not ever. Not till pigs fly and sing."

They led him away. It was an hour before McCrail returned. He and his utilities had been spray-painted dull black. He bled from a skull cut. He did a model's delicate pirouette, a thick-bodied hippo turning for the crowd.

"Clothes don't fit. That good chow. Bulls spray-painted me. Asked 'em to take the utilities off, but they're stupid little monkeys. Sprayed me in the wind. How do I look, lad? Like the regiment's squared away for parade and inspection?" He put his head back and roared, scaring the guards. He popped knuckles, the sound of breaking glass. The prison staff gawked.

"Look at 'em," said McCrail. "Apes don't know whether to shit or go blind."

"I vote for blind." I introduced McCrail to Min. McCrail shook hands with a sergeant major's dignity. He smelled of paint and a dying man's outhouse. I draped my overcoat over his shoulders. "Let's get you in the wind."

We walked down the long gray hall. A voice. Min turned around, grimacing. He stopped. So did I. "Sergeant Major, stand fast."

"Bleeding rectal crap," he muttered. Min, ever studious, tried to record it. The portly guards captain clicked down the hall with five guards. They were carrying body chains and military aid bandages.

The captain kept his eyes on me and spoke to Min.

"Deputy Numbah-Two Assistant Warden So want wrap your face, *dae-wi*. I say no can do. He say yes can do. I thinkee he do."

I shook my head. "No man touches my face."

The warden suspected I was the ROK *nakhasan pudae* major who had come to spit at Cabra Curadess's fat foreign body. Then Levine had come. Two foreigners in Naktong, and now he had someone to blame.

Warden So flashed all his teeth. He barked an order and the guards clamped irons on McCrail's neck and wrists. They tried to pull him back toward the tower. McCrail looked at me, his face reddening, his great legs planted on a slick floor, unmoving as they choked him.

"I'm sorry. Please wrap my face. Corporal, whisper to

the warden that if he wraps my face, his men will see that I tricked him. How can I fix this?"

Min tried to whisper to Warden So, who rudely pushed Min away as he wound the bandage about me with shaking hands. So's eyes bulged, forehead veins swelled. It was not the first time I thought that men prone to stress should avoid prison work.

Warden So studied me. "Sssss!" The ruse confirmed. His eyes watered in the fury of his glare, teeth bared, neck muscles straining, face turning red. Naktong was Korean land, where no American officials could come. During his watch, I had busted the rule and sullied his fine and pretty prison with my illegitimate foreign presence. My heart sank for McCrail.

The pressure built up until So exploded words, spittle and globally recognizable oaths. He shook his finger, his arm, his body at me, his mouth curled, then repeated it all with Min.

I had to ride the warden's anger and see what happened. I hoped he remembered who had fooled him. It hadn't been McCrail, unless they had figured out he wasn't Curadess. Warden So screamed orders and then screamed at Min. I stood in front of McCrail.

A guard approached, baton cocked, aiming at me. He trembled in fear of the warden and in terror of me. Korean guards do not strike Chinese superiors. I took air.

"Kwenchanayo," I said. It's okay. Hit me and we'll go. I'll take it, but if you go for my head, I'm breaking your stick, and we'll have to take it from there. Min whispering.

So shouted and the guard jerked, and drew back his arm. Min still whispered, but it was too late—the warden had lost face. I spread my feet and readied for the swing.

There was a silence that made the guard hesitate. Warden So spoke. The guard sighed and lowered his stick, sweating freely, chest heaving in sweet relief. He bowed to me and backed far away.

I was suddenly tired, but McCrail was getting out.

A red-faced Warden So bowed stiffly to Min. His face down, he snapped gutturally. The guards unshackled McCrail, bowed to him, to Min, and to the warden, and left, their heels echoing down the hallway. McCrail's face said: What the hell was *that* about?

I wondered too.

"We go now, *dae-wi*," said Corporal Min.

"Don't have to say *that* twice," I breathed.

"As you were, sir," growled McCrail. He cleared all his pipes, taking a long time, and hawked ferociously on the floor, his spit a living thing from the nightmares of children. Warden So looked at his floor, curling his lips and showing teeth.

McCrail smiled grandly. Maurice Chevalier. "*Now* we go."

We stood on the snowy steps, looking out. It was freezing and he wore short-sleeved, paint-coated cotton casual prisoner's utilities with my coat draped on his shoulders. I watched him suck in fresh air for a few minutes.

"God is great, laddie," he said in a breaking voice. "SWEET JESUS, I'M OUT! GOD BLESS ME AND MY FOUL DAMNED MOUTH!"

He belted me and knocked me off the steps into a snowdrift.

"Christ's blood, laddie!" He jumped down, hauled me up and brushed me off. "Oh, lad, I'm sorry. With me freedom and the bleedin' commotion o' that arsehole Korean hoosegow, I'm besides meself. I'm sorry, I am."

I tried to catch my breath. His brogue fell thickly, his chest swollen with the arousal of breathing free air, his personality shifting as he spun in the thick snow, looking at a world without walls. He threw snowballs at parked jeeps. He had popped his lid. He giggled like a girl, his great shoulders jitterbugging, and I laughed.

"Ahck, is that me limousine?" He howled. "An

American car! Screw me blue. I'm in heaven and I'll never fit."

He looked at the sedan as if it were a carnivore and he a morsel with a parsley sprig. "Can't be gettin' in there, lad. You'll have to grease me like a pig."

A deuce-and-a-half truck roared into the lot, spraying slush. The bumper said "2X DISCOM"—Second Infantry Division Support Command, the chow truck for GI inmates. The driver braked and parked. McCrail moved toward the driver.

"Son," he announced as if on parade, "I'm Sergeant Major P. McCrail. We'll be takin' your vehicle for your reckless drivin' and to give me a proper seat. Here's me captain. He has authority reachin' to Sergeant Major of the Army Jack Woolridge himself, so you'd best be behavin' and shuttin' your yappin' trap. Gimme your keys." SGMA Woolridge was the top NCO in the U.S. Army in 1966, when the driver had been about ten years old.

The driver was no fool, but he was terrified by this painted, oversized, brogue-spouting monstrosity. He saw courts-martial, angry officers, yelling sergeants, grease-pit assignments, perpetual punitive crap details, and endless paperwork. He opened his mouth to protest.

"Uh-uh-uh-uh!" admonished McCrail, waving a sausagelike finger in the driver's red face. "Shut your doggie mouth." With a hand the size of a football, McCrail took the man's keys. I dropped the bay gate and began unloading the boxes.

Prison staff retrieved them. One signed the manifest.

"Aye. Now there's a good little soldier."

"Listen, you big crazy loony, what in hell are—"

"Specialist," I said, "we're taking your truck. Corporal Min will drive you back to Casey. I will leave the truck in the MP yard at the Casey main gate, tomorrow by retreat, the keys under the passenger floor mat. Now say that back."

Staring pop-eyed at McCrail, he struggled to recite his instructions. I wrote a hand receipt for his vehicle on my notepad, tore it off, showed him my ID and the receipt: "2 ½-ton truck, 1 ea. 294,941 miles. /s/ CPT Jackson H.C. Kan, TIG."

The driver read the receipt four or five times, perhaps liking some parts more than others. "Sir, no way can I take this. You—"

McCrail tapped him with a right hook to the temple. The specialist flopped, arms and legs out scarecrow-style. McCrail picked him up, flipped him in the sedan and closed the door.

"Sergeant Major, what if an IG saw you do that?"

McCrail hauled himself into the cab, shaking the truck and reminding me of the birth of cetacea, a process I had never witnessed, in reverse. Min was leaving.

"Stand fast, Corporal, what'd you say to Warden So?"

He coughed. "*Dae-wi*, I say you numbah-one honcho *mi-guk saram*, 'Merican too-muchee big-shot. Say your father honcho *chingu* to Honcho President Nixon. Warden hurt you, he die."

"Wish I had thought of that."

I remembered the spider, the shiny green roaches with the science-fiction legs, good for crawling on inmates at night.

"Ah, it isn't such a bad place," said McCrail. He spat. "Tangyuan, Manchuria—now that's a bad place."

32

A FINE SENTIMENT

I drove. McCrail stared silently at Seoul. Its skyline had undergone radical change in the seven years of his imprisonment in the not-so-bad place. More Western high-rises and Han River bridges, vast developments on the south side of the river, a million more vehicles and smog-belching Myung Jin buses, all of it making me think of Cara.

Later, I described the Wizard's map of North Korea.

"Only the devil knows that man's mind. Talk about the States."

In the spring, Hank Aaron would chase Babe Ruth's home-run record. Kareem Abdul-Jabbar, a.k.a. Lew Alcindor, was the best player in the NBA, Julius Erving the best in the ABA, and O. J. Simpson was the NFL offensive player of the year. Whitey Ford had been elected to the Hall of Fame. Clothes were ugly, hair was voluminous, sideburns were massive, people used sex in lieu of afternoon matinees. Recent movies and songs were nostalgic—*The Sting*, *The Way We Were*, "Killing Me Softly," and "You Are the Sunshine of My Life." Big Koss headphones were in and people did their thing.

"I liked Mitch Miller and his band." McCrail stretched. "Captain, I'm so happy I feel like sex."

"Get you something better. Chinese food." I missed it; it had been five days without.

"You're a sick man, sir." The commanding deep voice, middle-American, Kansas, without a trace of brogue.

262

No Chinese good-luck long noodles. A bad sign.

I hoped Foss had caught LeBlanc. I could not presume that he had. "Sergeant Major, the Wizard's escaped. Where would we find him? Would he hide in Tongducheon or get out of the country?"

"Sir, gotta get you a first-class stogie. I don't leave for three days." He giggled. "I'm gonna get 'em out."

"The Wizard, Sergeant Major. Where would he go?"

"Son, he's going to Hell in a handbasket."

I smiled. "Thank you for your help."

The MSR was thick with vehicular menace, but we were safer in the truck. All drivers respect bulk.

"Open the briefcase."

He found the knife. "Pretty."

"That's not it. Keep looking."

He hauled out the Browning. "I like your style, Captain."

"No cigar. Keep looking." He found the airline tickets.

TWA, to Hong Kong and San Francisco, in his name. He studied them, then resumed looking. "A rosary." He kissed it.

"Faugus McFinnegan! Dammit, a Bible! Jesus, Captain Kan, you're a gift to man." Massive fingers touched the thin, fine parchment.

Bibles at the DMZ sold faster than beer. Looking at death across the wire invited scripture. He gently turned pages and found the small silver crucifix on a chain. He put it around his huge neck, slipping the rosary into his waistband as he read the inscription:

"'To Patrick T. McCrail, from his JAGC, CPT Jackson Kan, on his liberation.'"

He sniffed. Later, he said, "A fine sentiment, sir."

McCrail read to me from the Gospel of Luke. I was surprised that I recognized most of the stories. He read until the lulling of the truck's movement brought sleep, allowing him to miss some of the world's most horrific traffic accidents. The burning wrecks looked like war. His snoring was the work of lumber mills.

Two hours later we were in the Ville. Saturday, booze night for the division. I turned off the MSR and violently pumped the soft brakes until we stopped. I checked the Browning's action and dropped it in my coat pocket. I shook him. "Sergeant Major, time for a bath, hot meal, and dry socks. Got more water in the community baths than at Casey."

He stirred, panting, talking to himself. I told him three times who I was and where we were. He hit himself viciously, then saw the Bible, smiling when he was convinced he was awake and not in a dream. "That would be very nice. Really. All I could hope for." Everything he said was a surprise.

"Sergeant Major, where would the Wizard run?"

He laughed thinly, put the Bible down and flexed hands.

A gaggle of Amerasian boys jumped on the running boards, chattering as McCrail sat in the cab, looking at the old buildings. Opening the door, he hauled himself out, causing the children to scream and run. "Hell, we were here. Saw the bathhouse. We were going for the water and chink mortars hit us."

"Chinese mortars, Sergeant Major," I said.

"Ah, you're right, son. Sorry, lad. Bad manners I have."

He saw the community *pyon-so*, latrine, a low shack with a narrow fire walk. Below it was a pit filled with waste that could be smelled for two blocks. "Need the *pyon-so*."

Min and the dazed truck driver pulled up.

"Sergeant Major needs a bath." I told Min the evening's plans. The truck driver accepted my apologies for his headache. He was going to ask for money, then remembered I was an IG.

McCrail came out with a broomstick. He threw it in

the truck bay, where it clattered. "The stick to pull out the poor, miserable sonofabitch who falls in the trap. Five feet of shit in there." His eyes shone, inspired. "I'm puttin' the Wizard in there—with no stick to pull 'im out. Place smells like home, don't it?" He saw it all and giggled on the sharp edge of hysteria.

"You're not serious. That'd screw up Hong Kong."

McCrail stopped giggling, his teeth feral, his voice a push in the face. "I'm as serious as a chink guard. I don't get him in there, you do it. Push his face in it."

"I don't think I want to be your lawyer anymore."

He didn't laugh. "You throw him in headfirst. A verdict a crap. *Then* the mission's accomplished for my missus and for me. C'mon, for God's sake, don't crap law on me. Not now."

"You need a bath." We entered the bathhouse. A dozen people chatted in the office waiting area. Everyone stood, as citizens will when King Kong drops in for tea and crumpets. It was safe. He went in. I stood guard. He was in there a long time.

At the gate I told the guards that McCrail was a visiting California senator. They passed us. We waited in Purvis's office, where McCrail lay on the floor and promptly slept.

Purvis arrived. "Another victim of an unredeemed life? How many people does he represent?" He marveled at McCrail.

"ROK solitary for seven years, Korean War POW for three. His heart hurts." I shook him and introduced him to Purvis.

Magrip was in the hallway, sitting against the wall, long legs out straight. "G-2 says the Wizard's overlay made no sense. The objectives he circled have no military value. Inmingun isn't there; they're spread in advanced camps on the Z."

"So what does that overlay mean?"

He shrugged. "Nothin'. Guy's no tactician. He's a paranoiac, worrying about Reds in the night." He squinted. "Kan, after they get the Wizard, we done here?"

Monday, the lunar New Year, and twelve beefy Koreans. "No."

"Well, I'm number-one ready to get the fuck outa here." He looked up. "What're we doing to secure McCrail?"

"You got the duty. I didn't know you cared."

He shrugged. "Hell, I didn't at first."

"What changed your mind?" I sat next to him.

"It's so fucking cold I got stupid."

"And I thought it was my leadership skills."

"It was your pep talks. You know, LeBlanc really butt-hosed the sergeant major. He needs to be greased."

I felt the knife in my boot. "I'm not killing. Not anymore."

Magrip looked sadly at me. "Good thinking, Einstein. Too bad you're in the Army."

I hung up. "Carlos is calling our families to let them know we're coming home. A follow-on IG group is in the air, bound for Casey with replacements. Jimmy's airborne, outward bound for Walter Reed. His brains are intact. Beth and the kids will meet him at Andrews. Someone tell me the time."

"Seven P.M.," said Levine. "I hate the military clock." She sat next to me, took my hand, and poured M&Ms.

I looked at the candy. "Levine, you were right on."

"Of course," she said smiling. "About what?"

"Curadess *was* McCrail. And McCrail was a key. I thought claims would be the way to get the Wizard, but McCrail and Jimmy are prima facie felonies on him, and are easier to prove up than a claims paper case."

"We oughta throw LeBlanc in the *pyon-so*," said Magrip.

Levine honked. "Where'd you go to law school, Magrip? Gulag archipelago?"

Magrip threw his last underwear and socks into his bag. "LeBlanc ain't goin' down to a subpoena duces tecum or a general court. He's left the tribe. You think you can nail 'im with briefcases and charges and specifications." He zipped the bag and threw it near the door. "Kan, you oughta know better. Wizard's a punk who likes guns and explosives. Figure it out."

"So we just go shoot him?" asked Levine.

"Be the best fucking present you could give McCrail."

Patrick McCrail snored in my bunk. His girth overwhelmed it, stretching the springs. He had demanded a uniform. A gnomelike tailor near the tracks had a set of size-60 greens, tailor-made for a no-show customer years before. The tailor expanded them and gave them to McCrail for twenty dollars.

Levine researched McCrail's medals, racked the ribbons at the clothing store, and pinned them on his tunic. McCrail's regimental unit patch no longer existed, the Twenty-fourth Infantry having been deactivated after the Chinese slaughter.

I looked at McCrail and knew that Magrip was right; LeBlanc was less a West Point colonel and more a punk Chinese warlord. A warlord wouldn't care about courts-martial; he'd only want to run. Still, best to be careful.

"Where would LeBlanc expect us to be tonight?" I asked.

"Celebrating our asses off," said Magrip.

"At the CG's mess or the HQ O Club," said Levine. "I say we eat in the Ville. Pick a cafe at random."

"Great," said Magrip. "Barbecued dog meat."

I had to think of tigers and was honor-bound by the limits set by a drumbeating witch doctor. I needed a pacifist solution for what were probably twelve highly trained Inmingun terrorists—hard enemy soldiers who would happily slit the throat of every American while they

torched Casey. My brain turned on itself, making no
smoke. I felt pangs of panic.

God, I don't have a clue.

33

HAPPINESS CAFE

A Samsung stereo system played "Arirang" and other
richly sentimental, heavily stringed Korean folk songs,
full of hope, melancholy history, and hard separations. It
was a balmy night; a warm front had crossed Manchuria,
melting all frozen rivers. If the Inmingun came now,
they'd need bridging. U.S. Infantry officers all over town
were breathing easier.

I went outside the cafe into the darkness, listening to
drainpipes gurgling, observing foot traffic and worrying
about the Wizard. Magrip was checking the streets.

Min joined me. He wore unpressed fatigues. I was in
class As, dressed for dinner, the Browning in my waistband. He stood awkwardly, inclined his head, eyes down.
He spoke softly.

"*Dae-wi*, I very honored, work for you."

I returned the bow. "Corporal, it was my honor."

He straightened and went into the cafe.

A baby-blue Pony taxi rattled down the narrow,
unpaved street. Song Sae Moon opened the door. She
wore a purple, belted, form-fitting dress over black boots,
her neck wrapped in a thin white scarf, and she carried
her overcoat. Her eyes danced.

"I knew you would be here," she said. The cabbie
would take no fare. She stood close, loosening the scarf.

"I dislike uniforms, but you look most handsome. Please walk with me?"

I put out my arm. She took it and nestled close, leading me. I was unaccustomed to having different women so close to me this often. A dog whined. I missed Noah's tail whapping my leg. Men sat in warm courtyards sipping *soju*, smoking King Saejong cigarettes and arguing with neighbors. She stopped at a business doorway with tall steps. She stood on them, raising her face closer to mine. She gazed at Jungsan, the mountain of her life, and leaned against me, forearms between us in a posture of submission.

I kept my eyes on the strips of brilliant stars that unfolded as unseen clouds slowly drifted like great tattered kites in a dark night, blacking out the moon. I held her as I would hold a sister, and she clung to me as if I were a life raft, pressing her cheek against mine.

"If I had not gotten *sin-byong* and become *kidae*, I would want to hold you for a long time. My disease made me dream of you, and brought me to you. Now, the religion of my disease keeps me from you, from hoping your father will ask my father to give me to you."

It was as if all the lutes of China were playing, giving us license to proceed. She trembled, long lashes fluttering over closed eyes; she was beautiful, and I had no words.

"Kan *shee*, if you did not love her, could you care for me?" Her breathing was deeper and almost ragged. "I am a *kidae* who knows all emotions. But I cannot see your feelings for me. I have virtue, and should not be asking such a question, but I must know. Are your feelings a man's passion for any woman or for me?"

I leaned away; she followed. The moon came free of clouds and her face was from the dreams of men. I closed my eyes.

"Kan *shee*, it is written that I will never know the love of a man, and that you will leave Korea and never see me again.

"It is only a question. Only you and I will know of it."

I nodded and wet my lips. "I have enjoyed seeing your face. Watching you with children. You have a great gift of love, of *jen*, benevolence. You are good at a thing I cannot do easily."

Her lips parted, her fingers caressing my chest.

"You are a very good and wonderful woman. Because you are Asian, you remind me of my past, and of what, in China, I might have been. Of the family I might have had."

She closed her eyes and pressed against me, quivering at the edge of the unknown, making me aware of my westernization, my familiarity with women's bodies. In Song Sae's breathless embrace, I felt the Eastern sacredness of intimacy. I felt old and too wise.

"I am of two worlds. You make me feel my past and a connection, ancient and strong. You have the face, the personality, of the woman I was expected to bring to the *jia*."

Her eyes were sad. "This is true?"

"If I did not know the woman I already love, I would have been very happy to meet you." Without plan, I touched her face.

"To have children, Hu-chin?" My true name.

It would have been our job. She closed her eyes and kissed my throat, breathing on it, hands dancing on my neck.

"If I live to be an old man, I will always remember you."

"Oh, yes, please, I pray this is true," she whispered.

I separated from her caresses, my breathing controlled. She put her arms around herself, looking down.

"Hu-chin, do you find Western women pretty? I think their hair is thin and sad. Bodies, too full. But, I am curious."

I looked at the moon that seventeen hours ago had looked down on Cara and her balcony, her dog, her bedroom window. "Chinese women I know confirm me as a firstborn male. Western women challenge me. I don't always like that, but I respect it. I admire women who will raise confident daughters. Daughters who believe themselves the equals of their brothers."

Her eyes scanned me. "Hu-chin, you are a little *michaso*, crazy, no? This is an idea for paradise, not earth." She shivered and looked at the mountain. "Thank you for being honest. And also kind. I can tell you want to leave. We can go, now." Her arms still holding herself, she stepped down.

We entered the cafe, her eyes large and sad, her hair and lashes a hot ebony in the inelegant cafe light.

"Hu-chin, do you like my dress?"

"Enchanted," breathed Doc Purvis.

Everyone was in place. A waiter gave me a towel-covered serving platter. I put it before McCrail.

"Sergeant Major, take a whiff." I removed the towel.

"STEAK!" he roared. Diners in the next room dropped chopsticks and spilled teacups. McCrail beamed at two thick, rare T-bones, three fat baked potatoes with sour cream and butter, a row of cold bottled Miller's, and a lamentable, shriveled salad with orange Kraft's French, saved by the law of averages from the black market and framed by silverware from our own CG's mess. He emptied a beer and belched.

The steam from the potatoes rose like Western incense. He smiled, eyes moist. Perhaps I had never been happier for a client.

McCrail lowered his head. "Lord, thanks for everything. Bless this table and these good soldiers, amen." Sniffing loudly, he cleared his rheumy throat, and stood like Pan Ku, the Chinese world creator, his towering, oversized bulk and massive chest greater in uniform. His white brows dipped as he lifted a new bottle, the seasons of his hard life shading a lined face. He looked at us with brimming eyes and a fine, mournful mouth, seeing a wife, his missing mates and hundreds of slain comrades, remembering old battles and other military meals. It seemed the weight of them lay in his great, raised arm.

McCrail looked at me, gray eyes wet. He took a breath that was a scythe cutting wheat, filling swollen lungs.

"TO ABSENT COMRADES AND LOYAL WIVES!" The voice that could cause ships to crash on shore rang. We echoed it and drank, the saccharin in the Diet Pepsi burning like wood-still alcohol. He sat in a groaning sofa chair. The toasts went around for causes trite and true. Purvis, warm around the ears, toasted Song Sae with a romantic piece of Tang poetry: "The wind makes snow dance / Your face makes my heart float like clouds in blue sky."

Song Sae did not want to speak, but the table insisted. She slowly shook her head. "To *in-sam*, harmony, in your lives." Her delicate English winnowed into long-term memory. To harmony, borne on a voice to remember. She drank hot tea, looking at no one.

Magrip joined us, smiling perfunctorily: we were secure.

Chun *shee* and stern waiters arrived with the platters. Chun's cigarette pointing upward.

Fried kingfish, pan-fried beef, sauteed cuttlefish and vegetables, seasoned tripe and a pork and vegetable soup with highly spiced *kim chi* cabbage. The aromas mixed, grew and stimulated, and I wasn't hungry. I was bringing everyone home; I had one tac problem remaining. And it was big.

It was a small thing. When Chun had served Song Sae this morning, he had removed his cigarette to bow. Now he had not.

Maybe it was because Butt-Kicker Magrip, not following Emily Post, had put both of his big handguns on the table.

McCrail chomped steak while Magrip told him about the Oakland A's, Watergate, the new 55-mph national speed law, the Arab gas embargo, ethyl at fifty cents a gallon, and the entry of women into the professions.

"God, what's happening to the world? I was only locked up for seven years. It's gone to hell, it has."

I had twenty-six hours before midnight Sunday, the first hour of the New Year and the Year of the Tiger. I needed a solution without knowing the extent of the problem.

I pulled out my notepad.

"Kan, put a fork in it," snapped Magrip, unsure of the food, coveting the sergeant major's meal. "We're done."

The notes began with flights to Korea, six days ago, when I spent easy California nights in deep, untroubled sleep with a tall, very American woman who looked deep into my eyes before drifting off. I found the *mudang*'s description of her patients' symptoms.

Irritated, discolored skin with growing rashes on body and extremities; profusion of nose, gums, mouth and GI bleeds; unresolved phlegm production; diarrhea; night sweats; elevated pulses; weight loss; baldness and loss of hair in clumps; unresolvable dizziness and headaches.

These symptoms had killed one of the *mudang*'s thirteen bulky patients. It was hard to believe that they had suffered weight loss, but there had been a gaunt aspect to their mass.

Purvis was talking to Song Sae. Min was studying the ceiling. It took a few tries to get Purvis's attention.

"Doc, picture twelve Korean males, twenties to forties. Weight lifters who use anabolic steroids, with these symptoms."

I gave him the list. He put on metal-framed glasses. He read it twice—and I had good handwriting. He traded seats with Song Sae.

"You're in a sensitive area," he whispered. "Drop it."

I gave him the Richelieu letter. "Tell me what you know."

He read it, sighing from the trap of higher command. "Tell me everything, again," he whispered in my right ear.

I did. He rubbed his forehead. I took the letter back. The music seemed louder. Purvis whispered, "All twelve are Korean? See, I got fourteen guys I medicate and check once a month." He licked his lips. He looked at me, eyebrows inquisitive.

I waited. "What medications?"

"Androgenic masculinizing anabolic steroids. A somatic tissue builder. Thickens vocal cords, enlarges larynx, lowers body fat, raises muscle bulk, raises libido, aggression."

"Ethnic Koreans?" I asked.

"No. Standard-issue U.S. All colors, with a Samoan. Huge guys with a skinny commander who won't take steroids."

Henry Jubala, Dr. Death, and their steroidal troops. The men who, by my concurrence, I had never seen.

"Why?"

"I've wondered. You know the tune: I just follow orders."

"Doc, you check them monthly. For what?"

I could barely hear him: "Radiation levels."

"Rad badges? Why?" Nuke systems in Korea were too risky.

"I've wondered. These symptoms suggest systemic, occult cancers from massive ionized radiation."

"Like from nuclear reactor leaks?"

"No. Plutonium-based weapon detonation. Hiroshima. Big boom. But of course, that doesn't add up."

I looked at him for a while. "We got two Doppelgänger teams of steroidal weight lifters. One's American. The other ethnic Korean. The Koreans have been radiated. Right?"

"*Dae-wi*," said Song Sae softly, her brows knitted.

"Something is wrong." She touched me, wanting reassurance.

Table conversation had stopped.

"You asshole. You're finding another mission, right?" growled Magrip, banging down his beer.

"Jackson, bring it to the table," said Levine. "We cannot simultaneously eat and eavesdrop."

Outside, men were trying to walk quietly in the snow and slush. Magrip heard it, too. He picked up his handguns.

Min was gone.

I pulled the Browning from my belt, unsafetied, and moved to the window as Levine drew her snub .38. I moved around the waiter as he cleared plates, and stiffened as a cold steel muzzle pressed hard against the base of my skull.

34

A MATTER OF THICKNESS

"Drop gun." Two voices saying the same thing. I thought of Song Sae. I dropped. So did Magrip. When Levine dropped hers, the waiter called out. I turned. Five Korean men in dark suits rushed into the quiet cafe.

One of them was about five-eight, medium, athletic build. The fellow who had been trailing us since Kimpo.

He had sleepy, half-hooded eyes and the soft warmth of a Komodo dragon. He picked up the Browning and enjoyed taking my knife from my boot. I slowed my breathing and felt stupid as he handcuffed and blindfolded us. They frisked me thoroughly, taking wallet, spare magazines, gum, cigarettes and change.

"You funny," said Sleepy. "Chicken-feather-man! Crash! Chicken go all place! Feather go all place!" He pushed me.

We were placed in what seemed to be a Lincoln Town Car and driven through Tongducheon, across a bridge, and into the stink of old industry, decayed solvents and vice. Southside.

Sleepy hauled me out of the car and led us through a teahouse reeking of cigarette smoke and barley tea. Up iron stairs, through doors, down a well-carpeted hallway. A brightly lit room. He pitched me and I collapsed into a comfortably padded leather chair.

They could be Stubblefield's employers, a prostitution and drug syndicate unhappy about our raid. Or a Korean wing of the Black Flags, the Chinese smugglers and McCrail's criminal partners. The Wizard was a better guess. I hoped it wasn't the Inmingun.

"We unlock you. Promise no fight. We have gun. You not."

I said nothing. Someone spoke in Korean. My handcuffs were unlocked and I began to pull at the blindfold.

"*Aniyo!*" came the command. I pulled it down anyway and a blow exploded against the left side of my head, knocking me and the chair to the ground. I rolled up, vision blurred.

Sleepy smiled, licking his lips from corner to corner, pointing an S&W Model 41 .22 competition pistol at my eyes.

We were in a light-green conference room with French crystal chandeliers, facing a long black table, our backs to the door, with ten chairs along one side of the table and the five blue suits holding Model 41s.

Magrip was two chairs from me; two chairs from him was Levine, and four away was Song Sae Moon. They were still blindfolded. There were six scenarios for getting out of this and all of them required some of us to die.

"Kan—you okay?" demanded Magrip.

"Fine," I said.

"Promise no fight," said Sleepy. "You like my high kick?"

"It was very special. Who are you?"

"Kwenchaneyo," came a voice. An athletic, hard-faced Korean male with a short military haircut entered the room. He wore an off-season white linen suit, a crisp white dress shirt with gold cuff links perfectly presented and an aqua bow tie. He ran a hand through his hair and flexed his jaw. He snapped his fingers and pointed.

The others were freed. Levine and Magrip, angry, rubbed wrists, counting the enemy, their expressions surprisingly alike. Song Sae was calm.

Aqua Tie fixed us with brilliant and intense black eyes. He had a nervous habit of rolling his shoulders and neck while perpetually jutting his jaw, as if someone had punched him. He smiled like an old friend or a cold-blooded man about to do a job he enjoyed.

He turned his back and put on glasses. He pushed something into his mouth. Stooping, he turned, flashing great buckteeth.

He bowed awkwardly. He spoke in a comically high and familiar voice. "Kan *dae-wi*, you, me talk American try, big-time, *neh*?"

It was Min. Levine gasped.

"Screw me to tears in a leaky rowboat," said Magrip.

Min removed glasses and false teeth and sat at the head, nodding as a blue suit brought him a cup of tea. He considered our amazement with imperial calm as hot tea was served to us. Sleepy spilled some on my lap. He was enjoying himself.

"Ladies and gentlemen," said Min in a clipped, Commonwealth-cultured voice that suggested Canadian diction. "I am Colonel Min Oh-shik, Korean Central

Intelligence Agency. My apologies for evacuating you so abruptly from the cafe. It was wired to detonate, to kill you. I assume the work of Colonel LeBlanc. I know of no one else who would place old *plastique* in cafe ceilings." Min winked at me. "University of Alberta," he whispered. "Poli sci. Rugby."

"Liar, liar, pants on fire," I said.

Min smiled. He had worn false buckteeth, fright glasses and clown boots. He had banded his chest and shoulders to make them appear sunken and puny and scrunched his spine into a submissive curve, shortening his five-feet-eight by three inches. He outranked me by three grades, spoke English better than most lawyers and grasped political science better than I; he had the guns.

I saw it. After Kimpo, the man who trailed us never followed when Min was driving; we escaped Naktong after Min had said to the warden: "I am KCIA. Do as I say or your family becomes dog food."

"May I see your ID, Colonel?" I asked. Sleepy bristled.

Min gave me his ID, his features flat. I had no way of knowing its authenticity. Levine would; I slid it to her.

She studied it. "Colonel Min is senior officer present," she declared, giving it to me, a male, to return to Min.

"Where are Sergeant Major McCrail and Major Purvis?" I asked.

"Major Purvis is in the prostitution warehouse next door, treating VD patients. The prostitutes are our cover for being in Tongducheon. We just asked his help; he generously agreed. The sergeant major left moments before I did. I do not know where."

McCrail was after the Wizard, hoping to dump him in the public toilet by the baths. I was glad he wasn't here.

"You are here," said Min, "in my country. Please answer my questions. Not because we require it, but because you are our allies."

Two of his men unrolled the Wizard's map and

overlay, pinning the corners with teapots. Levine had taken them from the Wizard and Min had taken them from us.

"This," said Min, "shows advance lines from two North Korean villages. But there are no Inmingun in those villages. They cannot even support themselves, much less a military garrison. You have studied this map. What is its meaning?"

I saw what I had missed earlier. The breadth of the lines as they intersected the DMZ. It was a matter of thickness.

The advance lines did not identify direction of march—no helpful arrowheads.

"We've presumed an Inmingun invasion of the south." I traced a finger from north to south. "A logical presumption. The North Korean Army invaded before and is configured to do it again. But what if the line of march on this overlay is *northbound*?"

I looked at Min. Magrip rubbed his mouth.

"The lines could show *our* entry into North Korea." I traced north from Casey across the Z. "Planners draw advance lines from them *to* the objective. Basic human thought-processing. The base of an advance line is always stronger than the tail. If this shows a North Korean attack on us, the deepest impression by the pencil should be at I'chon and T'osan, where the artist began his line."

"Or *her* line," said Levine. "But you drew them."

"Lightly," I said. "I didn't disturb the original marks. Wherever it tails off is the objective."

I huffed breath on the map, again and again to make sure.

"It's deepest at Casey. Faintest in North Korea. These advance lines were drawn from us into North Korea."

"Why," asked Levine, "do the depressions thicken as they cross the DMZ?"

I darkened them, filling the depressions with black

grease. I looked at Min, who nodded. "They're tunnels,"
I said. A cheap way through the DMZ. No wire, no
mines, no interlocking fires.

"They're on *our* side of the Z," said Magrip. "ROKs
found Inmingun tunnels back in '71. I never figured *we'd*
dig our own."

"Why, *dae-wi*?" asked Min. "Why would an American
Army lawyer want to plan a raid into North Korea? To
meaningless villages?"

"The Wizard said to me, 'I stand at the Z and look
across the great wire and I *want them to come.*' At first, I
thought he wanted to assassinate Kim. But I think he's
planning his own war. Korea is one big tripwire. If he
toasts two North Korean villages, it's war. And he'll be
the avenging angel."

"Who the hell'd cross the border with him?" asked
Magrip.

"He has some couriers he enlisted. Not many.
Twenty?"

"Captain," said Min. "Five men with explosives at the
DMZ can trigger war. The ROK Army is not deployed in
depth. We are stacked on the DMZ to deliver an immediate, massive counterblow.

"And we have extremists in our own Army. Line commanders who have long militated to launch a preemptive
strike against North Korea before the Inmingun come. If
LeBlanc begins a military incursion across the Z, some
of my colleagues will follow him."

"On Wednesday," I said. "LeBlanc named ten I Corps
ROK commanders as his contacts in a purported search
for Buford."

It was Saturday, January 19, 1974. The Inmingun had
placed twelve broad-shouldered terrorists in our own
lines, perhaps to kill or to destroy. The Wizard, on the
other hand, wanted global war, making him tonight the
most dangerous man in the world.

Colonel Min phoned Namsan, KCIA HQ. Namsan

called nearby White Horse Division's Third Brigade and ordered search teams to find LeBlanc. Doors in Kyonggi Province would be broken tonight.

"Sit," said Min, rolling his shoulders. We sat. "You know Kim Il Sung wants to invade now, while your army withdraws from Vietnam. But Nixon will not fight another war to protect Asians." He took a breath. "We understand. Nixon cannot take Vietnam and Watergate and a new Korean War at the same time. Agreed?"

"No shit," said Magrip.

"We have indications," continued Min, "that President Nixon put atomic bombs in our country." He looked at me for confirmation.

The atomic bomb in Korea. It took a moment to sink in.

The rad badges. Nuclear war.

"*O wa,*" cried Song Sae, covering her delicate mouth with broken fingers.

"You must know this, *dae-wi,*" said Min.

A distant explosion rumbled, shaking the warehouse. The walls groaned. Min hissed. "Some of the *plastique* in the cafe. We apparently did not find all of it. I pray to Buddha no one was hurt."

I thought of the Chuns.

Levine stood. "Captain Kan doesn't know, Colonel. I do."

35

A FIRE IN THE SNOW

I understood Levine's improbable appearance on the Z. She was a nuclear expert. I have a special skill, she said.

The *mudang* had sensed a mysterious power of gods hidden between the third and fourth ridges in the view from Jungsan Peak.

The old woman had seen fire in the snow.

"Jackson," said Levine, "I'm about to disclose Top Class data. Murray said it was your call. Who goes?"

"Blue suits out." Sleepy had poor demeanor discipline; he made a face. Min gave an order. They left.

"Let's sum up," said Levine. "McCrail fraudulently enlisted Korean nationals to black-market half a million. Money to ransom fellow POWs held in China. When he bagged a ROK munitions train, he was arrested and explained his money-making schemes to his lawyer. The Wizard copied the scheme to buy munitions to start his own war. An MP captain got suspicious and Jimmy Buford came to Korea.

"When an IG disappears near nuclear munitions, the lights go on in the White House and the Joint Chiefs. They do not go out until resolution. Ergo, *moi.*" She took a breath.

"The bombs are at Camp Casey. They're not strategic; they're atomic munitions with thirty-two alphanumeric digits indicating restriction to topographical applications. To blast down mountains in the invasion route in the

Valley of War, filling the Ouijeongbu Corridor with boulders and gamma rays, keeping the Inmingun from flooding through the passes. The last tactical resort."

"Ike's AGTs," said Magrip. "His atomic grenade throwers." He shook his head. "Had no idea they were still operational."

"You cannot mean grenades," said Min. "Are they in cannon shells? Why are you telling me this?" He stared at Levine.

"I have disclosure authority if I think the bombs are compromised and I need help. I think they are. And I think I do."

The porcelain tiles in the mah-jongg game clacked. Jubala and Sapolu's men were part of an Army steroid superman program. When we saw them running, Magrip and I knew they were sappers. Levine had done her best to distract me, to maintain the secret.

The bombs weren't in artillery shells. They were in man-portable rucksacks. Those overbuilt, weight-lifting troops had been trained to carry atomic bombs on their backs, ruck them into the Ouijeongbu Corridor, screw in the detonators, and bring down parts of the Taebek Mountains on top of the Inmingun as it marched south.

I remembered the SGS's hesitation to let us shower in the CG's bomb-proof gym; the field tarps covering equipment in the weight room; the hyperalertness of the behemoths as they drew high-tech weapons and issued gulag threats for my mere appearance. Under the tarps were bombs. The nicknames—'Shroom and Dr. Death. Levine was a marathoner so she could run with the AGTs.

And now there were twelve remarkably overbuilt Koreans—a counterpart unit composed of men with deficient English and stainless-steel teeth.

I knew their mission: grab our tac atomics. Put them on their backs and run them to North Korea, probably with a submarine rendezvous in the Sea of Japan.

I looked at the Samsung watch Min had given me. We were running out of time. Twelve skin-splotched North Koreans were going to pull the tiger's tail. And yank it from its root.

"I apologize, Colonel," I said. "Seems we left your country out of the planning." It was a replay of the unilateral division of Korea and Dean Acheson's defense speech—setting up Korea for a nuke exchange without an RSVP.

"Again," said Min.

"Levine," I said, "give us the whole picture."

She looked at me. "Ninety-five Mikes—the MOS for atomic sappers, a.k.a. Iron Mikes—are field-deployed for security. But that exposes them to a well-planned raid. We currently have two six-man teams and two officers. Total, four devices.

"In each team, two men carry a SADM-909, Special Atomic Demolitions Munition/Field Series High Terrain, yield fourteen kiloton, weight 162 pounds not including steel ruck.

"The Mikes have sardonically nicknamed the SADM 'Pluto,' for the risk of plutonium contamination through constant disassembly drills. They wear radiation badges, which Dr. Purvis checks.

"Two other men carry ID-967 trigger fuse mate detonators, nicknamed 'Goofy,' forty-nine pounds. They carry a machine gun. The other men carry M-79, ammo, radio, food, and water. All alternate carrying the Plutos. Despite noninterchangeability of ammo, half the team carries lightweight 9mm Parabellum Uzis, the other half M-16s.

"In a contingency, one man alone can carry Pluto and Goofy to the target site, arm it into hot status and detonate it. These are real strong guys. They have to be. Ergo, anabolic steroids. The downside is that steroids invite irritability; they get in fights.

"That's why the Pentagon worried about the Wizard

and SADMs. Brawling Ninety-five Mikes would mean possible arrest—and a crooked SJA could bring untold trouble.

"Once the Inmingun attack," continued Levine, "the Iron Mikes ruck for the passes in the Ouijeongbu-Munsan attack corridors, ten to thirty klicks. Officers provide security and rucksack backup.

"They will detonate the SADMs without delayed-action fuses, dying with their Plutos to insure they do not fall to the Inmingun, one of two world armies that cannot ever have atomic weapons."

"*Aeigu,*" whispered Song Sae, saying something like "non-gay."

Levine seemed to understand her. "Mikes live in winter bivouac with ground radar. I think they're compromised for three reasons. One, we saw them running two days ago. That is impermissible. I have recommended the commander's immediate relief, which is imminent."

She glanced at me. "Two. You were allowed into a Mike area twice—once to shower, once to work out. Unforgivable.

"Three. When I was in Wizard Q during the fire, I found triple-stitch load straps and ruck locks. That is equipment tailor-made for SADM-909s. Ergo, the Wizard knows something about AGTs down to an extremely uncomfortable level of detail."

The cargo straps she was looking at in the Q when Foss called.

"I should have known this," I said.

Levine took a breath. "Wrong time to worry about ego and pride. Do you understand? The Wizard knows about the bomb. That's why I burned down his Q."

Magrip smiled approvingly. I looked at her: the Wizard could have his war with tac nukes. On lunar New Year. Min saw it, too.

"Are Inmingun close to your sappers?" asked Min of Levine.

"I don't know. It's time we figured that out."

"What's your mission, Colonel?" I asked.

Levine's generosity with top-secret information had intoxicated him. "Locate the bombs. Guard them. Your security is lamentable." He shook his head. "America is a foolish country!"

"Whose boys," said Magrip, "died for you on the Chongchon, the Imjin, the Naktong? Chosen Reservoir . . . Pork Chop Hill . . . Heartbreak Ridge?"

Min nodded. "Yes, Magrip *dae-wi*. But your past battles never seem to improve current security practices.

"Now, please listen. Colonel LeBlanc enlisted Korean nationals into your Army—1,415 since 1967. None met your Army's citizenship requirements."

Min rubbed his face. "Nearly a hundred were North Korean troops. Radio men. Intelligence officers. Photographers. Special Purpose troops." He peered at Magrip. "A ridiculous country!"

"A hundred?" That was a big problem.

"It is not that bad," said Min quietly. "We have kidnapped all of them, except for twelve very big men."

"Colonel," said Levine, "even bolos have American rights."

Min checked his nails. "Captain," he said slowly, "there are three things my organization does not do. We do not underestimate. We do not overlook questions. And we do not screw around."

We had trained its CIA. "How many KCIA enlisted in our ranks?"

The colonel bared his fine teeth, smiling like a plastic doll.

"Why didn't you kidnap the twelve big guys, the jumbos?"

Min took a breath. "I cannot tell you that."

"Bullshit," said Magrip.

" 'Bullshit, *sir*,' right, Captain Magrip? Yet I must insist on not telling you. I will simply say it involves only our security."

Impasse. Min nodded. "The twelve men—'jumbos'—were at Vlodverny Testing Fields, Soviet Union, summer 1968. The Soviet Red Army was experimenting with tactical nukes.

"The Russians were joining a low-yield tac atomic to its fuze mate when detonation occurred, dumping gamma and alpha particles.

"Soviet sappers and technical types were incinerated. The Inmingun Tiger Tails were at the periphery of the blast. They survived. Five years later, they have cancers. Kept alive by the *che chub*, pharmacology, of medicinal *mudang*s."

The *mudang*. I could not imagine dealing peacefully with an Inmingun terrorist squad, but this was the price she exacted. I saw her wind-coarsened face, and saw the plan that might work.

"Colonel, I can share information with you. On one condition." I described the *mudang*'s offer. Min tilted his head away from me.

"You," he said, "have been smoking hand-rolled joints, I think."

"Then we will act without you."

Min almost snarled. "Not in my country, Kan *dae-wi*."

Song Sae stood. "Please pardon me standing and speaking in public. Believe that the *pu-dok*, the virtue, of Jungsan is pure, despite my manners." She glanced at me, coloring.

"I am under the direction of the *wang mansin*, and her authority must be heard at this table." She cleared her throat.

"Colonel Min, you are a man with *ch'ilgo chiak*, ancient doctrine and culture reaching back before Kongja. Or you are not. You will pardon me for saying such an obvious thing."

She looked at me and bowed courteously. "Kan *dae-wi*
is a foreign man, twice removed. He has not one drop of
Korean blood, but he gave his word to the *wang mansin.*
She accepted his word as if it were from a Korean
yangban of long lineage."

She turned to Min. "Your honor cannot be anything
less. Do not think a woman is asking you about your
heart. You ask yourself." She drew herself up, as if she
were performing in a theater. "Min *yukgun taeryong*, do
you promise to obey the *wang mansin*'s request?" A loud
voice.

"Moon *kidae*, how can I help if I lose the power to
arrest?"

"It is not your power," she said. "It is Buddha's."

Min exhaled. Later, he pushed on a speakerphone.
Johnnie Walker Black, Glenfiddich, and Diet Pepsi were
brought to the table with cocktail glasses; Western
alcohol was used to solemnize Eastern agreements.

A woman in a long purple dress with elegantly long
hair poured. Min downed whiskey; Levine took the
scotch; Song Sae stuck with the tea. We all drank.

Min drummed fingers. Hand through hair. A hiss. "I
promise."

"*Mudang,*" she said, "cast the *kung-hap.* The geomancy means twelve men will take an unknown action
on the lunar New Year, according to the legend of brave
men pulling the tiger's tail."

"Uuohh!" Min barked questions; Song Sae answered
in her normal, sedate, melodic voice. Min sighed.
"Lunar New Year begins tomorrow. *Dae-wi*, I told the
mudang you were here—information she valued. She
knows me and told me nothing. Why is this?" He was
whispering.

I thought for a moment. I whispered back, "Maybe she
saw you drive."

"Ah ha," he said flatly.

"If the Tiger Tails act tomorrow," said Magrip, "it

could be the prelude to invasion. What are your intelligence estimates?"

Min nodded. "The Inmingun cannot attack within ninety hours. They need bridging and fuel moved up. Ninety hours' work. None have moved."

"Gentlemen and lady," said Song Sae, "the *wang mansin* cannot allow bloodshed. She knows you have the authority, Colonel, to slay in the name of the Korean state. That Magrip *dae-wi* is a killer. That Kan *dae-wi* has killed and does not wish to kill again.

"This is why she told the Chinese man. She wants to stop the Northmen without death." She turned to me. "Her information placed their lives in your hands." She bowed, hands peaked in Buddhist prayer for submission, humility, emptiness, invoking a dominion over the unknown.

"She revealed to you that courageous Korean hunters from old legend have come to this valley to pull the tiger's tail. These are poor men from farms that can only give two meals a day. They are frightened and shocked by the richness they have never before seen.

"Even so, in enemy country, they come to Jungsan unarmed to receive the *mudang*'s care. They respect *ch'ilgo chiak*, ancient doctrine and culture, faithful to the past. They are polite to fatherless children." She looked at Min.

"Do not confuse your desire to kill with *in-yon*, God's fate. Other men have done this, to their eternal regret."

36

ARABESQUE

Min looked like a serial killer composing a victim list. I missed the cheerful bumbler, suspecting he was gone forever.

Song Sae spoke. "The *mudang* treats the twelve at Jungsan every noon. They will come tomorrow as usual. The *kung-hap* shows they will probably act in darkness, sometime after midnight tomorrow.

"Colonel Min. If KCIA or ROK Army come to Jungsan tomorrow, the *mudang* and her responsibility will be destroyed. She will then kill herself, in the style of Non-gae, the *kisaeng* who embraced the Japanese general and pulled him to his death three hundred years ago." *Kisaeng* were courtesans, trained in the erotic arts.

"I, her *kidae*, will follow her, as will all the Jungsan women who work for the *in-sam* of this village. It is a sad truth. Male violence always creates tragedy for women." Levine nodded.

"Worse, men will have fought men on holy ground. The spirits will leave, forever. Our orphans have found women who, at Jungsan, are serving as their mothers. These women will all be dead."

"Sad, but women have died before," said Min. Levine glared.

We were in a whirlpool.

"What does the *mudang* recommend we do?" asked Levine.

Song Sae paused. "The *mudang* cannot recommend in

matters that belong to the political world of men. She only states what you cannot do. You must not bring violence to Jungsan."

Silence.

I knew the power of the *wu* over Eastern people. Kim Il Sung was a *paksu* shaman and even the KCIA, with good scotch, could bend down to promise great forbearance to a *mudang*.

Do not think like an American individual; this is Asia, where promises bind generations and clans with the strength of Confucian *gahng* and *lun*, bonds and relationships.

I emptied the Pepsi. I stood. "I have a proposal. Set aside normal presumptions." I presented it. The plan sat heavily in the room. Chair legs scraped, glasses were emptied. Magrip did not appear amused. Min would not look at me.

"An arabesque," said Levine.

Min hissed. "You cannot be serious. It is terrible." He searched for the word. "Unthinkable. Psychedelic. *Daewi*, how will you become a general if you side with your enemy?"

"Colonel, after this, I'll be lucky to be a civilian."

He stood. "*Dae-wi!* This is weak and unmilitary. I know your honorable father is a Christian, a follower of Jesu. If he wishes to love his enemies, it is his business, but you must keep him out of our security affairs." He hissed again, arms crossed on his chest. "You are in Hankguk, the Republic of Korea. My country. No religious fools trying to love communism will endanger us."

"The Inmingun is my enemy, and it'd be easier to arrest them than try to dance with them. But I made a promise."

I looked at him. "Do you want SADM weapons out of Korea?"

Min took a sharp breath. "Take the bombs out. The bombs that would slow the Inmingun, allow UN reinforcements to fill the approaches south of the Han and save lives. Very daring, *dae-wi*."

"And real stupid," muttered Magrip, ever impressed with my tactical acuity.

It was a simple engineering problem: tac nukes, by definition, had to be positioned close to the enemy. If the enemy has nukes, their value is diminished. If the enemy doesn't have nukes, he'll try to take them from you. And if *this* enemy got them, the whole world could pucker and count its dead.

"*Neh*—yes." Min nodded. "They are far more risk than gain. Particularly in your hands. Your man-portable tactical nukes are too close to the Inmingun, too vulnerable to capture. If Kim Il Sung gets them, he will use them as fuel to burn the world." He chuckled. "American security. Oxymoron. Do you like my English?"

I nodded. "What do you want to do with the Inmingun sappers?"

"Death by firing squad," he snapped. "Or hanging. Gaah!" He brushed us away. "Why waste words? Your idea is dung on a carpet. How will a young Chinese captain in the American Army make nukes disappear? I know your country. Minority men are not leaders."

"No, but our boss is a member of the high command. And he's a member of two minority groups. Colonel, if he advises removal of the weapons, they'll go."

Colonel Oh-shik Min weighed my words. "The famous one-legged Colonel Carlos Murray." Thinking, he reached for a pack of cigarettes. I reached for my array of American smokes. Gone. Sleepy had them and my wallet. Min pointed the cigarette at me. "If Kim Il Sung captures your nukes, would that end Nixon? And if he refuses impeachment, will the American Army defend him?"

Magrip emptied his drink. "Listen, if North Korea gets our nukes, Nixon's political future won't be the issue."

"But it would be his political end," said Levine.

"The Army won't help him," I said. "Colonel Min. The Pentagon will evacuate the weapons immediately because they have been compromised. The bombs can be removed with immediate effect. The time it takes to make phone calls, to lift aircraft."

He took a slow drag. "I want to believe this." He leaned forward. Behind the anthracite gaze was a cruel interrogator. Once he was in pursuit of something he wanted, no blood was sacrosanct. He reminded me of the Wizard.

He pointed at my face. "Why do you care what happens to twelve Inmingun? They are like the North Vietnamese you fought. If these Tiger Tails knew you were after them, you would now be a dead man."

"I agree. But I don't need to kill anyone to fulfill my mission. I want to bring everyone home."

Min's eyes narrowed. "War has made you very sensitive."

"Like it's made the KCIA a democratic agency?"

He almost spat. "I fight a few individuals—for my people. The Reds suffocate all in the name of freedom. Do not confuse my patriotism for the evils of Marxist destruction! *Dae-wi*, you are a Chinese idealist, a scary and dangerous thing. What ideals does this female *yin* Jesu Christ plan serve?"

"The independence of your country."

"Ha! You sound like an American propagandist, citing my freedom as your license. So now, in my country, you lie to me?!"

"In 1945, you should have had full independence. But the Cold War was on. We divided you with Russia, making both Koreas crazy maniacs for military security, spending all your money on guns and tanks and propaganda. In January 1950, we said we wouldn't defend you against Red aggression.

"Six months later, Kim Il Sung invaded you using page one of the Soviet armor attack playbook. Now we've put bombs here. Bombs to delay an invasion that also invite a global thermonuclear war that would erase Korea. I'm not an idealist. Gave that up. I'm a historian."

Silence. He exhaled. "What you say is very reasonable," he said insincerely, his look glacial. "*Dae-wi*, why do you care?"

"Your country holds a marker on us. I pay my debts."

He looked into my eyes like a Chinese *wu*, as if all the answers he needed were to be divined within. His eyes narrowed and he nodded. "So. You are still Chinese."

"I pay my debts, and that is Chinese. I have individual beliefs. That is American." A long silence.

He weighed my words. "If you get the SADMs out of my country, you may negotiate with the Inmingun at Jungsan. But they cannot go back to the North. You need to know we have a no-hostage policy. If they capture you, we will not bargain; we will presume you dead."

"I understand."

"He negotiates with the *mudang*'s blessing," said Song Sae. "On Jungsan, it is her word, not yours, that sways trees."

Min smiled thinly. "Yes, of course, Moon *kidae*."

"Kan," said Levine, "Iron Mikes have an emergency field extraction sequence. I need PRC-77s to talk to them and to you. On 59.35 megahertz. And I need a DTOC hookup, right now." Division Tactical Ops Center, with the big radios to talk anywhere. "Then physically get me to the Mikes."

"Levine, you're translating at Jungsan tomorrow A.M. Send Magrip to find the Mikes."

She considered it. "The Mikes would shoot him for his mood."

Magrip emptied his glass. "How do I find them?" he asked.

"You don't," she said. "You can come with me, under my command."

He was going to curse, but Song Sae raised a finger. He stopped, giving Levine what Asians call the stink-eye.

"Colonel," I said, "I need two 77s."

"Come with me." We left Levine and Magrip to work out the command structure. Song Sae sipped tea. He led me to an adjoining office.

Min sat, gesturing at our wallets and papers in a pile; no cigarettes or gum. I retrieved them as he picked up the phone and gave orders. Photos showed he was a tae kwon do black belt. He canted his head at the door; I closed it. "I tricked you quite well, yes?"

I nodded. "Perfectly."

"I thought I played the fool too hard. But you bought it."

Which was particularly embarrassing. "I fell for it. Why'd you ram the kiosk at Suwon?"

He barked a nervous laugh. "I wore big boots to be awkward. At Suwon, the jump boot wedged between the accelerator and the fire wall. I could not stop. I scared even myself."

A knock at the door. Sleepy, another blue suit, and the woman in the purple dress entered with two dual-band, 920-channel AN/PRC-77 field radios in olive drab manpack frames. Seeing them generated memories. The woman brought a tray of more alcohol and a Pepsi. She set it down, bowed, and stood by the door.

I vented hydrogen vapor from the magnesium batteries, freed the preset lever and dialed in 35 on the kHz low band, 59 on the MHz high band, and locked them. I powered them up, checked antennas, waited two minutes for full power crank, halved the volume and keyed the hand mikes to squelch. The loud, crisp rasp of static filled the room.

"Colonel, what channel is radio station KCIA?"

"Thirty-nine point seventy," he said. I dialed it in.

Min squinted at the girl and tapped an empty glass

with a pen. She jumped and poured him two inches of Johnnie Walker, her face red.

I wondered if I could master that look, that tapping. Sleepy was smirking at me. He said something beneath his breath.

"Colonel, you order your guys to kick us?"

Min shook his head. "No. Why?"

I shouted hard and spun-kicked at Sleepy's head, stopping my kick an inch from his nose. He cried, "Uuohh!" and lost his balance, falling backwards. The door burst open and smashed him in the back of the head and he went down like a sack of rocks. Magrip was in the room, a bottle of Johnnie Walker cocked and upside down in his hand, the contents gurgling. He looked for the fight.

"What?!" he demanded.

I turned to Colonel Min. "Sir, we free to go?"

"The rug is Persian. Whiskey is hard on its nap."

Magrip nodded. He righted the bottle.

"My men," said the colonel, "should accompany Captain Levine. Provide her security."

"No need, sir. We'll call. I have your number."

Min looked at me coldly. "*Dae-wi*, you are in my country."

"And they are our bombs." Magrip picked up a radio, keeping the bottle, and I took the other.

"It's been real, Colonel," I said. "Let's get together again sometime." I stepped over Sleepy and took my smokes and gum from his pockets. I straightened and raised an eyebrow. "I guess this means we don't have a driver anymore."

Min snorted, lips tight. "No. You do not."

"Whaddya know," said Magrip, looking upward. "There *is* a God."

The north wind blew striations of ghostly snow across the headlight-illuminated road in writhing, otherworldly patterns.

Magrip drove a ROK jeep. "Fucking unbelievable. Min yanking our chain all this time. That whole thing, a shtick."

"I knew who he was all along," I said.

"Right!" said Levine. "You're not even sure who *you* are."

"Pissed her off, huh, Kan?" asked Magrip.

"Magrip," said Levine, "you should know I reserve such comments for men I like."

Magrip blew out air. "Woe to those other poor sons a bitches."

Song Sae gave directions to Magrip. When we stopped to let her out, Purvis also dismounted. "Don't wait," he said. "I'll walk back. Don't worry. I don't think the Inmingun are after doctors."

Eleven P.M. Saturday was nine A.M. Friday in the Beltway and six A.M. in Mill Valley. Murray was in the office. Cara would be in deep sleep, her stubbornly curly hair adorning a lucky pillow. I hoped it was hers. I hoped no one was next to her, and that her guards were good.

37

Extraction

Foss, Levine, Magrip and I were in the red-light DTOC, Ops Center's, third trailer, seated at the relief team com table. It was a radio room with vertical transparent mapping walls and a data center for ground, air, sea and weather. Dark hours on weekends were the hot shifts; it was then our enemies liked to drop off calling cards with armor and razored bayonets. Fans hummed, but the trailer was warm with bodies and electronics.

I hung up; G-2, intelligence, would research my questions on the big Asian GIs. Levine was going to call the Ninety-five Mikes.

DTOC gave me immediate access to AUTOVON. I rang Carlos Murray's office.

"Justicio, Hu. Buckle up." He scrambled. "The Wizard knows about our Plutos. So do the KCIA and the Inmingun. An NKPA special-purpose team that's already in our Army, wearing our uniforms, is going to hit the Iron Mikes some time after midnight tomorrow."

I held the phone away from my ear.

Levine was on the 95M emergency channel on a command radio. She broke squelch five times and waited. No answer. One minute later, she tried again. Carlos Murray was still cursing loudly.

I said the Wizard planned to start a world war. That the Plutos had to be extracted immediately to beat tomorrow's strike date and that Levine was sending the sapper extraction order.

I looked at her; she shook her head. No acknowledgment. I said I had promised a shaman, in return for learning about the enemy raiding party, that I would not arrest or harm the Inmingun.

Murray took a breath. "This is a joke, right?"

I said it wasn't.

"Urchin, what the hell you going to do with them?"

The North Koreans, I said, were Communists but also profoundly shamanistic. If the *mudang* would take their oath to stay at Jungsan until they died, I wouldn't have to kill them.

"I get it. *This* part is the joke, right?" I said it wasn't.

"I don't have time for this, Jackson."

"You got that right, sir. Out here." Murray had to get the Joint Chiefs to agree. And Nixon.

Ten minutes later, Levine began talking. "Five-Five

Zulu, this is Annette of the Mickey Mouse Club. Join the talent roundup now. I say again, join the talent roundup now. RSVP, over." She sent the identical message three times at one-minute intervals, then stopped. She flipped to a new tab in her ops binder.

She called the Nuclear Surety Agency and announced a red alert 95M extraction protocol in the Republic of Korea, 37° 65' North, 127° 5' East, grid 42103220 on sheet L 752/3121, NE Camp Casey.

Nuclear Surety would call the extraction op order to the Seventh U.S. Fleet elements in the Yellow Sea and Tac Air Command in Osan Air Force Base, a hundred klicks southwest of us.

Levine put a green headband around her short hair, pulled a face paint can from her fatigue blouse and greased her face, neck, back of hands and throat, doing it faster than most men. She pulled her trou from her jump boots, strapped on the ankle holster for the snub .38, inserted the revolver and bloused the trou with a boot garter. She completed her accessories with a cartridge belt bearing a canteen, first aid pouch, magazine ammo pouch and a service .45.

Outside, vehicles gunned cold engines and Eleven Charlies, heavy infantrymen, moved mortar tubes and base plates.

The door opened. Major General Michael Peters and Brigadier General M. John Mann, his ADC-M, Assistant Division Commander, Maneuver, entered. They wore helmets and sidearms.

The DTOC shift commander greeted them. The staff ignored them as they had ignored us. Levine showed them what I guessed was a DA nuclear authority letter and briefed them. BG Mann was the officer who had direct tactical authority over the 95M bombs. The CG had authority over BG Mann, Casey, DTOC, the bombs and, potentially, Levine and me.

"Captain Levine," said the CG, "you're telling me this

is a joint extraction operation run by the Navy. That members of my command are probably Inmingun but we're going to *negotiate* with them and not do anything so decisive as, say, *arrest* them."

"Roger that, sir," said Levine.

The CG and his deputy exchanged a glance. "Pentagon," sighed the CG.

"The Navy," said Levine, "supplies top cover for air superiority and AWACS to control the air show and coordinate the extraction helos. Air Force provides outer perimeter close ground support. Your air battalion provides interior ground support. And Ike's atomic grenade throwers end up in Navy billets on the USS *Coral Sea* Battle Group. Effective now, you are without tactical nukes."

"Michael John," said the CG to the ADC-M, "step up our tac readiness profile, clear the air, commit the gunships needed. Get us out of her way. Then get chief of staff to call an emergency commanders' conference."

BG Mann held up two fingers; the shift commander called for a DTOC backup team, hung up and pulled his top NCOs from chairs. BG Mann made phone calls, then began briefing them, everyone taking notes. Still no answer from the Mikes.

Levine looked at her watch and pointed at the radio operator, who began another ten minutes of one-minute-intervaled five-squelch breaks.

The backup team filed in, tense and shaking off sleep.

The CG stood near, making entries in a notepad. BG Mann watched the shift commander brief the backups while the G-3, Operations officer, asked questions and wrote the extraction timetable.

Levine looked at me and then briefed Magrip and Foss.

"Lemme get this straight," said Foss when she was done. He chomped on a decrepit cigar, his eyeballs flitting between Magrip and Levine. Levine stared at his stogie. "The lady's in charge." He coughed. "Two squelch breaks on freq forty-two point forty-two means we found the Ninety-five Mikes, and they are deploying to the landing zone."

Levine nodded. "Roger." Magrip said, "Check."

"We break squelch three times, it means the helos took all team members and their ordnance and lifted off clean.

"But if we squelch four long ones, it means Tiger Tails got us in deep *kim chi* and I need help *mos tic.* Then we switch to channel 2, the KCIA frequency, and send them four long ones, too. Then I dial you back and send details in an open transmission." Levine nodded.

"Now, if Kan squelches us four, it means he couldn't contain the Tiger Tails on Jungsan and they're after us."

"*Maja-yo*, Major," said Levine. "We'll make a fine team."

"Lady," said Foss, "I'm just a cop. I don't have high-grade Infantry crew-served crap to fight a buncha Tiger Tails."

"Major Foss," said BG Mann, "Captain Levine has op con"—operational command—"of a cavalry squadron, a Ranger company and a heavy-weapons platoon." That meant a scouting force, a strike force and portable artillery.

"DivArty, gunships and slicks, are on call." Meaning division artillery—the big guns—as well as attack helicopters, helo transports and dustoffs were standing by. "Captain Levine, you will have control in the field."

Levine nodded. BG Mann added, "Once you find our boys, we will have Navy, Marines and Air Force on the scene with more firepower than the Inmingun can handle."

"Levine, what about the ROKs?" asked General Peters.

"Sir," said Levine, "they're on our side, but we're not playing with them tonight."

"Is that from the top, or your call?" asked the CG.

"My call, sir, under the protocol. Major Foss," said Levine, "the ROKs are not to even *see* the bombs. And KCIA thinks the Iron Mikes are on freq fifty-nine point three-five.

"They don't know Iron Mike channel one, forty-two point forty-two. We get the ROKs on the hook only if we're hurting. Given this firepower, I can't imagine why that would be."

MG Peters nodded. "I'll have hell to pay at the I Corps conference with ROK Army. This is no way to treat our host."

"No, sir," said Levine. Foss chewed, made ready to spit and stopped. "Kan, you're Asian. Don't you trust the ROKs?"

"I trust everyone not involved in murder, drugs or atomic bombs. You guys okay with the command arrangement?"

"It's too dark," said Foss as he and Magrip began applying face paint, "for any of them to see they're being led by a skirt."

"Stow it," said Magrip. "She's in charge; back her up."

Foss blew out air, studying Magrip. "Okay."

"If you see the Wizard," I said to Levine, "take him down. You find McCrail, give him a ride home."

She nodded and put on her helmet.

"Levine." She looked up. "Compared to Niagara, this is nothing." She smiled. The generals saluted Magrip, who wiped his hands on his trou and nodded. I watched them leave and noted the time: 0100 hours, Sunday, 19 January, Lunar New Year's eve.

I had set a Sunday breakfast meeting at the CG's Mess at 0800 in the morning. Magrip, Levine, Purvis, Song Sae and I would plan the meeting at Jungsan with the *mudang*'s twelve patients at their medicinal tea. Song Sae would be key.

By then, the Ninety-five Mikes should be having

breakfast with the Navy. An hour passed. A line flashed. Carlos.

"Urchin, we will extract the Plutos according to the protocol. I am recommending the SADMs stay out of the Korean Peninsula forever, but things are a little *loco* in Washington right now. Hard to get straight answers. But I am optimistic."

"You always are."

"Now, Urchin, am I to assume the Wizard is in custody, and that you've tied up all legal loose ends? Urchin? Hello?"

38

ALL YOU CAN BE

Sunday, January 20

I prescribed class A as uniform of the day. We looked official but not hostile. The PRC-77 radio sat silently by my chair.

Seven hours had passed. No one had called in, and here I sat, having breakfast with a radio at a tableclothed table in the CG's mess, rich with the scents of cooking eggs, sausages, waffles, pancakes and bacon. The coffee was strong. I was the only captain in a field-grade mess, and I was an IG; I had the table to myself.

Somewhere out there in the snow were Sergeant Major Patrick T. McCrail and Colonel Frederick C. LeBlanc and practically everyone else I knew in Korea.

I was about to negotiate with twelve North Koreans and Song Sae and Purvis were late.

I dialed Purvis. No answer at his quarters. The gate

said neither a Purvis or a Moon had entered post. I called the med. Purvis was there as a patient.

I called Foss, who sent me a jeep with a working heater. I drove to the Ville, the Browning in my belt.

No one answered at Song Sae's hooch. The families were at the community water faucet. I pointed at her door. The women looked to an elder; she made the universal shrugging of shoulders.

I drove to the Strip. It was a little after eight on a Sunday morning. The Vegas was dark, silent and smelling like human regret. A Blue Heart looked at me blearily and tried to adjust ruined hair.

I asked for Mrs. Cho. She waved toward the back. Mrs. Cho sat at a table, working a ledger and smoking. I greeted her. She took my arms, feeling lucky.

"Ah, *dae-wi*, you wakee up this morning, think of my girls!"

"I need a translator. I will pay."

She cackled. "Of course you pay."

I had no cash left. "Will you take a check with ID?"

"Chinese men all bankers. *Neh*, take check. You wait." I looked at my Samsung watch. Time passed slowly. I paced.

A clatter of heels and protests. Onto the floor came a bevy of puffy-eyed, hung-over, unhappy women in an assortment of frayed Frederick's of Hollywood presentations. They looked like bruised fruit. They stood shoulder to shoulder with the enthusiasm of mafiosi in a dawn lineup. I felt sorry for them.

Mrs. Cho barked, making them stir. "You talkee best!"

"Hi, big boy," said the first one absently.

"I love you too muchee, honcho man," intoned the second.

"I give best hum job, make you feel so happy. I speakee English best, numbah-one," said the third vapidly, smoking.

"Oh, the hell she does," said the fourth, chewing gum.

"I need you now," I said. "Dressed for church. Fast."

"Kinky, dude!" She was Miss Oh, code-named Catalina, and she looked like a starlet gone wrong. She returned in a black leather coat, tight, plunging black sweater, microskirt, black fishnet stockings with heels and a cigarette, chewing gum.

"This far-out? This numbah-one threads."

"They're fine. Can you ditch the smoke? Let's go."

She dropped it. "Gum's okay, right? Takee away bad taste. You know, is most groovy right-on. Cool have job, use English." She ran after me. "You in big-time damn hurry, yes?"

"Yes. Fasten the seat belt. Where'd you learn English?"

"All my *yobo* AFKN disc jockey, talk good, deep voice like you, big boy. But they breakee my sad heart and give me big ugly turd downer. Get too muchee sick tired, ask GI if married! They all lie through teeth, yes?" She studied me. "So, honcho *dae-wi* most big boy, you married Stateside, have rug rat?"

"Six kids." I drove hard, like Min.

"Oh! You like play hide salami! You want sweet-time with me?"

I told her what was going to happen at Jungsan. I asked her to translate *and* interpret what the *mudang* and the twelve big Korean men said. "First, say what they said. Then tell me what you think it means. For a hundred bucks."

"I can dig it!"

I asked her to wait in the jeep.

Purvis's head was bandaged. He lacked the attentive presence of the gravely concerned and slept deeply. The chart said, "Concussion. Frostbite. Needs rest. *Do not disturb.*"

I poked him. His eyes opened. He grimaced. "He took Song Sae."

My heart sank. "Who took her?" Notepad out.

"Don't know. American. Senior officer. I told CID. Six feet, one ninety, about forty-eight, silver hair, at her hooch."

"You ever meet the Wizard?"

"Oh, man—was that him? You mean a *lawyer* did this to me?" The realization seemed to worsen his injury. "Said I'd get the clap running with a harlot. He said, Is that all you can be? A whoremonger? He pulled out an M-16 with a short barrel." A CAR-15, an Armalite cousin to the M-16, prone to jams.

"Told him Song Sae was a religious assistant who worked for a holy lady. Not a Blue Heart.

"He said he knew she was the *kidae*, that she worked the 'pagan sciences' during the day and seduced Blue Hearts at night.

"I said something clever like 'You can't talk like that.' He butt-stroked me. I dodged. He was after my eyes." A pause. "Had four Korean GIs with him. When I came to, she was gone. Saw snow trails—they dragged her."

I could've arrested him. I had waited to do the paperwork.

"Maybe," I said, "she won't be in immediate danger. He knows the *mudang*'s *kidae* is a shield, a free ride into any rural village in Korea." He knew her rank but had called her a whore.

"I'm checking you out of here," I said. "We're going to need doctors up on Jungsan."

39

INMINGUN

Only a ROK Army lieutenant colonel in arctic white fatigues emerged from the tree line.

He checked our IDs and looked disfavorably at Catalina and the head-bandaged Purvis. I asked questions.

"*Aniyo, dae-wi.* Have not heard from Colonel Min. But the Tiger Tails are at Jungsan. He order me to watch road for you." He looked down the road. "Your men not come back?"

"No." With the Iron Mikes not yet alerted, it was a relief to know that the Inmingun were isolated on the mountain. "Sir, you sure all twelve are there?"

"*Dae-wi,* I very good at counting."

"Sir, you secure the base of this mountain?"

"*Aniyo, dae-wi. Wang mansin* say no can do." He hissed. "My troops, they Korean farmers. Fear her. When you go up the mountain, I go leave away. And no gun up there."

"I'll be unarmed." The Browning was in the map box.

He nodded. I strapped on the radio.

It was ten and the Inmingun were already at Jungsan. There would be no pretrial conference with the *mudang* to insure the meeting would proceed under American control. A lawyer should never enter court with an unzipped fly; this was going in without pants.

The sun glinted on the gold spires of the temple of Soyasan. The ridges ran like waves in an angry sea.

"What are you looking at?" asked Purvis.

"Smoke."

From the valley floor, in a distant, fog-obscured corner of south Tongducheon, streamed a thin pillar of red smoke, a harmless pop of military marker smoke. Then the red disappeared in a mushroom of blacks and browns and the air moved with the vibrating crump of explosives, rolling sequentially atop each other like a summer storm: no muttering or timber-splitting cracks of artillery but the sound of two thousand pounds of demolitions, simultaneously initiated, bursting the air.

Dark winged birds took flight below as finches erupted from bushes. The deep vibrations shook the ground and knocked snow from trees. Dry smoke billowed from the carcass of the explosions, the radiated, insulted air, agitated by the alien wind, and deep, angry crackling thundered rumbling across the valleys.

Purvis closed his opened mouth. "What the hell was that?"

"Someone just remodeled Southside, using the military method."

I was sure it was McCrail. The sergeant major had found the Wizard's *plastique*. No invasion of North Korea today, Mr. Wizard.

Catalina's small shoulders shook. Born in the Korean War.

"It's not war. Just some explosions. Let's go."

We continued up the path, the wind whistling through the trees of the transplanted forest, the detonations echoing. Snow blew from the winged roof of the villa.

I touched the brass bell to the stone shrine where Song Sae had prayed. I saw we could reach the backyard by climbing over bushes on the side. No shoes on the porch. We removed ours.

I opened the door to the thump and crash of drums, flutes and high-note cymbals. It was the music of the *wu* at Dongting Lake, and I knew this was the trance-inducing music of the *gut*, the *mudang*'s invitation to the dead to confer with her.

"Bring shoes." We removed hats and entered the incense and drumming. Good omens. On the sea of white pillows, below lanterns and amidst smoking incense and burning candles, sat the *mudang* in a ceremonial red-and-yellow robe, a queen of *yin*.

Along the left wall, nine adolescent girls wearing bright, multicolored, sash-waisted traditional dresses, long hair piled above heavily pancaked faces, beat red *chango*, hourglass drums. They drummed looking upward, inviting the spirits of the valley's dead with strong music, rich color, sanctified food and the signs of ancient purity.

Along the right wall, nine more girls played brass cymbals and flutes in the four-part underbeat. There was no thinking in this music, only transportation.

The *wang mansin* was using her tools to invite harmony. Her eyes were closed. She was humming a flat tune, again and again.

Catalina stared at the girls. I looked for Inmingun. Purvis embraced it all, staring at the *wang mansin*, the great physician in the Valley of War, his silent partner in community medicine.

I took off the radio and put it down with my shoes. She saw me. I bowed. *"Anyahashameeka, Halmoni."*

"Anyahashameeka, Kan dae-wi," she said, a throaty Janis Joplin. The music dropped. She hummed. She opened her clouded, feverish eyes as she spoke.

I looked at Catalina, who nodded and said, "The old lady says, 'What's happenin'?' to the doc and says, 'Where's Moon *kidae*?' to you."

I told her. Catalina translated. The *mudang* shut her eyes, raised her chin and cried painfully into the high registers, the incense twisting like a small snake. She stopped and stood, panting, tears streaking her brown face.

She spoke with great animation. Catalina listened, her mouth open, nodding. She blinked. "Oh, wow. She like knew bad shit was going to come down on her *kidae.*"

"Thanks." This wasn't going to work. The *mudang* dried her eyes on flowing silk sleeves. I turned to face the noise at the door as the drumming faltered for a moment.

Levine, in soiled fatigues and muddy socks, carrying her boots and looking as if she had been down a long road without sleep. They must have found the Iron Mikes. I looked at the silent radio and made introductions.

"This is Captain Levine, Dr. Purvis and Miss Oh." Catalina translated. The shaman nodded. Levine looked at me and barely shook her head. No joy. They had not found the Iron Mikes.

Levine bowed to the *wang mansin* and greeted her. Purvis did the same. The *wang mansin* answered. Levine began translating. Catalina sighed loudly. "Groovy," she said.

". . . Song Sae's karma," said Levine, "is to know pain from men, but not to die because of them. Women and children are asked to bear the mistakes of men. She asks us to pray for Song Sae."

The *mudang* knelt, facedown. Purvis knelt on the pillows. Levine hesitated, then also knelt and prayed with her.

"Spot me a hundred." Levine opened an eye and gave me two fifties. I gave them to Catalina, quietly thanked her, and told her she could go. She stared at me and then at Levine at prayer. After a while, the shaman lifted her head and spoke.

"She asks," said Levine, amused, "if you fear little girls."

I looked into the shaman's eyes. I nodded. Levine cocked an eye, trying to understand. The *mudang* clapped her hands. The drumming hushed and the cymbals ended, the girls' heavy breathing making the great room humid, the sound of children coming from the back. The girls, bright with perspiration, collapsed on the pillows. The *mudang* stood and gestured us to follow. She motioned to Purvis to stay in the room. He looked disappointed.

We followed her toward the back and I read one of the sayings on the wall: "Tree prefers calm, wind does not care."

Catalina had not moved. "Please leave now," I said to her as I picked up the radio and my shoes.

"Be so cool to stay close with you," she said.

"Not here. It's not safe. Go." We left Purvis and Catalina surrounded by panting, fallen girls in beautiful colored robes. We passed through an immense kitchen lined with garlic-rich black iron woks on great wood stoves and a narrow hallway that smelled of Chinese rosewood and ginger.

Levine whispered, "Couldn't find them. Signs of a close-in firefight, shells, shrapnel. Blood trails in the snow. Too much for just wounds. The Mikes're E-and-E-ing"—evasion and escape. "They're off my map. Magrip knows what to do and has the talk codes for the Iron Mikes. I thought you might need me."

"I do." I put on my shoes, and lifted the PRC-77. "Tell the shaman I'm going outside." Levine spoke; the *mudang* nodded.

I opened the back door to hear the high, excited chatter of a crowded schoolyard. I stepped quietly onto an open porch formed by the green-tiled curved roof and thick green dragon pillars to overlook a Japanese garden the size of a basketball court.

I counted the Tiger Tails, distracted by little Asian girls who darted among beautiful trees and bonsai plants.

Asians in U.S. fatigues were in two groups. One was in the garden, sipping tea and taking pills from paper wrappers. They were huge, quiet, skin-splotched, tired and profoundly serious. I saw point man, trail man, leader, listener.

A second group had climbed the peak to watch the smoke from the Tongducheon explosions, pointing, arguing, debating.

Older women in blue parkas poured odorous, medicinal ginger tea for the men in a well-practiced routine.

I counted twelve men, then recounted. I saw the Wizard's slave-daughter, Hoon Jae-woo, as she played tag with a horde of children. Half-bare ginkgos and snow-dusted Japanese evergreens crowded white stone paths and a bouldered wall with a broken section that led to the sheer cliff.

Along the cliff were small white gravestones.

The children's faces were internationally half-American.

One of the men saw me and they all stood and separated, shooing children away. Their faces showed no reaction, but their feet were athletically spaced, bodies tactically intervaled. I felt their dismay at seeing an American officer on the eve of the lunar New Year.

Jae-woo wore an Army field jacket and mismatched lime-green, thirdhand pants. She was lovely in happiness and ran to me, her movement making me sweat. I sensed echoes of guns, wet boots humping ancient green hills.

Levine and the *wang mansin* moved onto the porch. The children saw the *mudang* and ran to her with excited cries, swarming, touching easily, happily looking for open hands like children in a beloved family, touching Levine, chattering and wondering at her. For many of them, she was the mysterious missing half from their complex anthropology—a Caucasian woman.

Jae-woo stood a foot away from me, hands behind her back, torso slowly twisting in the hope of my goodwill, of my finding a clan interest in her. She gazed with innocent eyes.

The garden was a cruel charade. There was too much danger to children. I couldn't smile. She misunderstood, and dropped her eyes, her face breaking in bitter disappointment.

One Korean—the patrol leader descending the mountain—signaled, and the others returned to their tea and herbs. He moved warily. He was barrel-chested, with a neck like the trunk of a redwood and a splotched, boulderlike head. His posture said that this was his country, his mountain, his faith—not ours. Near him stood a boy with light skin, almond eyes and brown hair, who looked up as the man coughed deeply.

He was in his early forties, looking like an Inmingun lieutenant colonel, outwardly calm while good cells fell to occult cancers, his thick, overly muscled body racing with carcinoma, steroids and the rich, organic *che chub*, medicines, of the *wang mansin*. He spat redly.

The soft garden air was poisoned by hard tension.

The *mudang* freed herself from the gathering of children. Small shoulders hunched, she glided across her garden with us and the children in her wake. She put a hand out to Levine and pulled her close, chatting with her. Levine, head lowered, nodded.

The man who could be a senior officer from North Korea in an American private's uniform stood warily. The shaman said, "Chang Duk-kyo." Levine spoke to him, introducing us.

"Sir." A stiff voice, a stiff salute.

I returned it. His intensity reduced the sound of girls' voices in the garden. We stood politely, each imagining the death of the other. I recognized the *wang mansin*'s genius in bringing children to this meeting.

The wind in the pines, blowing snow from branches, the blood pounding in ears with the invitation to kill each other. There was no doubt; he was the enemy.

I felt his scorn for an Asian who had gone to the side of the big-nosed, running-dog imperialists. A large vein in his bald skull pulsed thickly like a blue worm avoiding a hook. Absent brows exposed large, bulging, bloodshot eyes as they ran across my face, asking: Do you want to die?

I smiled and removed my overcoat to show him my TIG brass. It meant we were not Infantry to fight them, or military police to arrest them.

"Please," I said, indicating a picnic table. "Bring your medicine. I would like to talk to you."

He nodded solemnly at my English. It made me more interesting to him. I put down the radio and sat. He nodded and joined me.

Chang sipped tea, pressing the powdered medications into his mouth with thick, reddened hands, roughened by a lifetime of Korean winters, swallowing the concoction with obvious discomfort.

I regarded him as the Asian elder and made no eye contact. "A beautiful day in a beautiful country. I am honored by your company," I said. Levine translated.

"*Neh.*" A gruff voice, accustomed to giving orders.

"A day to live with *in-sam* and *Fu'che*." Korean harmony and North Korean Communist doctrinal independence. "A life full of family and clan and home country. Children. No killing."

His large, liquid, bloodshot eyes darted over my face, trying to see which of my two cultures was talking to him. I was being polite. My Chinese face and American voice confused him and made him anxious. To him, I was an American, a renegade Asian, an ethnic trickster. Time for Yankee directness.

I smiled. He blinked. I winked. "You are Inmingun."

He inhaled through his nose, one nostril compressing. He grimly smiled, exposing stainless-steel teeth. "No," he said. "Silly saying." He coughed gently, then spastically.

I made my guess. "You have northern *bando* speech and Soviet dentistry. You patrol with seven-meter intervals, which is Inmingun doctrine. You are a senior officer, not a PFC. Anyone can see this."

Levine translated. He found something of intense interest in one of his nails.

"Sir, your men are Tiger Tails. Six years ago, your team was at Vlodverny Fields in the Soviet Union, where you were exposed to a massive burst of ionized radiation."

He sat as still as the statues at West Point.

"We know your target: the American atomic sappers."

He looked at the silent radio. His jaw tightened.

"We know your plan. Our sappers are gone."

Levine translated. Something flickered across his dark eyes. I didn't like it; he knew something we did not.

Calmly, he finished his meds. "Sir," he said in the injured voice of a chronic smoker, "you wrong. We good 'Merican sojer."

"You probably are," said Levine.

His eyes flickered between Levine's physiognomy and me. He blinked once, then shook a Camel from a pack and lit it with a one-handed snap of the matchbook. He exhaled to the side. "Ohh?" Chang hunched a massive shoulder. My gut rumbled with his private knowledge. I wondered if there was another Tiger Tail team. The thought made me dizzy. Then I had another thought.

I needed to eyeball each of the Tiger Tails. I stood. He stood. So did Levine. I began walking among the playing children. Chang tried to remain nonchalant as he walked with me. I recounted his men. One, two, three, four, five.

He puffed. "So, talk!" he barked. He looked at his watch.

"Sir, your mission is over. There are no bombs for you to take." Six, seven, eight, nine. Chang was ten.

Chang shook his head slowly. "Mean nothings."

"MILPERCEN-K"—Military Personnel Center, Korea—"printed out all Korean-born Seventy-six

Yankee supply clerks with maximum scores in the Combat Physical Proficiency Test."

Suddenly, his men began moving all over the garden. He had scrambled them and undone my count.

I smiled. "You all have unusual body strength."

Levine handed me her notes. I read, "Private First Class Duk-kyo Chang, DOB 2 May 1953. Which makes you—a man in his forties—twenty. Born, Seoul. You're not in the Kyoggi-do birth registry."

Levine translated and he coughed horribly. A woman ran and poured him more tea. He slurped it, red-faced, spilling on his chin.

"You talkee wrong man. Paper mistake. Happen any style, Army. Many Chang, Korea. Many strong Korean man."

"Your 201 says you graduated from West Central High School, Los Angeles, California, June 1971. So did all your men, between the years 1969 and 1972. West Central burned down in the 1965 Watts riots and was never rebuilt." I began recounting. One, two, three, four ... five ...

"You makee mistake!" shouted Chang. "*My* school." He blocked me, his swollen arms folded across his chest. His troops were still moving all over the garden. I moved around him, taking long steps.

"KCIA won't agree. You cannot fight us on a holy mountain. You cannot take us hostage, because the KCIA has a no-hostage policy and they do not negotiate. But there is a way to have life and honor."

Chang coughed badly, sat down and crossed his legs. His combat boot pumped nervously while Levine translated and I counted. He saw her notice, and he stopped. The wind was light in the protected pocket of the garden, framed by the peak and the great villa. Thin bright sweat glistened on his brow as I counted eight, nine, ten.

Two missing men.

Chang looked at the unseen peak, to the north. He tapped the cigarette ash into a big, square, reddened palm. "How?"

"You pledge your family and *Fu'che* honor to the *wang mansin.* You work for her, here on the mountain. You become fathers to the children in her orphanage.

"You work the fields, the kitchens. On your sacred honor to Korea, you promise to stay here. You teach the boys tae kwon do. How to be men. Worthy and honest, true to their word and full of *Fu'che*, independent spirit, free from Americans, Russians, Chinese, Japanese, Communists, capitalists, soldiers."

Levine translated. Chang peered at me, his big meaty hands flexing, the cigarette smoke wreathing his mottled, cold-pink face, trying to understand me, an inscrutable American.

"The *wang mansin* will care for you and your men. Give you medicine. We think you have a year or two to live. When you die, your bodies will be transferred to your delegates at Panmunjŏm for burial with your families in the north."

Chang laughed sardonically. He spoke gutturally in Korean.

"He says the pig manure you throw smells very bad."

"Then," I said, "your men can die Chinese deaths. If you do not want this offer, we leave you here. The KCIA will imprison you and your men. No *mudang che chub* medicines, but probably torture, which we cannot stop. A televised trial to embarrass your beloved leader Kim Il Sung and the Inmingun. Death by rope or firing squad, your bodies buried without memory or honorable cremation, your faces down, forever breaking your family lines from rituals and reports."

Levine looked at me and licked her lips. She translated.

"I sojer," said Chang. He had no fear.

Inside the house, the drums began again.

"Ask Chang what he wants." I stood and she spoke. Chang looked at her, studied her, thinking about an answer, then watching me.

I walked to the garden's blind area to the far right. Seated on a retaining wall were the two missing Korean GIs. Both were normal-sized men. They saw me and came to attention.

"Identify yourselves, please."

"Sir, PFC Arnold Kim, Ninety-eight Juliet, electronic warfare/signal intelligence interceptor, Second Intel." The other private was Private E2 Paek, Seventy-five Bravo, personnel admin specialist, HHC, First of the Seventy-second Armor Admin Center.

"What's your connection to these men?"

"Sir, they just invited us up here. Don't know why."

It meant two Tiger Tails were loose, running in the snow after Jubala and Dr. Death. The radio had not squelched; blood and shrapnel were in the snow of the Ninety-five Mike bivouac area; someone had died and the bombs were still out. The outcome in a fire-fight between two Tiger Tails and fourteen Iron Mikes should not be a matter of conjecture. But we had heard nothing.

Maybe there was another Tiger Tail team. Or two.

Levine and Chang were talking. The *mudang* was watching me. I took the radio into the villa. Under the cover of the drums and cymbals, I turned up the volume and squeezed the hand mike to break squelch four times, warning Foss and Magrip that bogeys were loose.

The radio was dead. I opened it—the mag batteries were gone, the terminals cut out. I swore, but it didn't help.

Levine. "*Mudang* asked me to come in. It's stalemate. Chang says it's a mistake, that if they were Inmingun, they wouldn't be clumped together. Says that if

Inmingun were here, they'd have several teams in the field. Jackson. These guys are going to die anyway. Think of it; they've given their lives to this mission. They're not afraid of the KCIA or of you."

I felt the truth of it. He was more committed. This was his country, and I was a foreign soldier of the hated tiger. His people would be the first to feel the nuclear fire that already devoured him. He had already sacrificed all that he had.

"That's the good news," I said. "Bad news is the radio's been tubed." I pointed. I told her that two Tiger Tails were loose. "Foss and Magrip have to know that already. They don't know that more Tiger teams might be out there. And division has to be told. You need to run for a radio."

Levine shook her head. "Leave it to you to ask a woman to run down a mountain in wet jump boots and without carbos."

"I'd do it, but I'm slow and it'd kill me."

She punched me on the chest and looked at the girls, hard at work, trying to influence events with percussion. She was looking at their feet; they wore tennis shoes.

I realized that Purvis was gone.

In a back room, I found him and Catalina trying unsuccessfully to wrap a huge man in a thick, quilted *yo*.

Patrick McCrail.

40

You Sent Him to Me

He looked like he had been run over by a tracked vehicle and dragged through a bog. He was upright against the wall, vast legs stretched along a small cot, his head separated from the wall by a stack of small bean *pegae*, bean pillows, his great, Promethean face slack, covered in sweat, soot, burns, and suppurating cuts, the sweat from his immense back staining the wall, his chest laboring rapidly, the blanket falling from him.

Purvis withdrew a needle from McCrail's arm. "Morphine, Sergeant Major, to relieve the chest and arm pain. You're having an acute anginal episode to go with exposure and hypothermia. We'll have you up in a few days." Purvis smiled warmly at him.

The sergeant major bore the elements of the earth. The rifleman, the mud soldier, imbedded in the fertile ecology of his profession. He smelled bad, premiering his own death.

"I need that radio," said Purvis.

"It's on the fritz."

He cursed. "I have an impending M.I. and no IV, and now no dustoff, medevac or ambulance. God!"

"I'll get it for you," said Levine, lacing tennis shoes.

"By running?"

"It's what I do." She moved to McCrail. He smiled at her. Levine knelt. She squeezed his great paw, stood and left.

Purvis leaned against the wall and held his bandaged

320

head as he looked at his immense, shuddering patient. "Sergeant Major, you smoked too many damn cigars. Had too many beatings and no exercise." He touched him. "Kan's here now."

McCrail nodded. He looked like the grandfather of all boonierats and the patron saint of lost men, at the edge of his own sad end. Catalina caressed McCrail's broad forehead.

"Gimme another pill," whispered McCrail.

Purvis shook a pill bottle. "You've had four sublingual nitros and you can't take any more. Your heart's under a load." He turned to me. "He made it up here on foot, dragging something. How are you doing out there?"

"Not worth a damn."

We considered the consequences of failure. I had to get back to Chang. "You get well, Sergeant Major," I said. "That's a direct order." He sighed. I stood. Catalina looked up at me.

"I lost him." It was a thin voice, never before heard from such cavernous lungs. McCrail, struggling to speak.

I leaned forward to listen, his chest laboring, slick sweat bright on his massive head. "Warehouse. Same one I used. Southside. Filled with Russkie guns. *Plastique.*" He rested, lips moving. "Wizard had green det cord. Yella time cord. Silver blastin' caps."

He closed his eyes. "Cut time cord, lit, timed it. Followed the book." He was reporting to me.

"Made a pyramid of his stash. Threw red marker smoke at Southside. Freaked all the hookers. Everyone bailed.

"I lit it. A fine, big blast." Exhalation. "Doncha think?"

"I saw your fire. They heard the detonations at Fort Belvoir. The Wizard knows he's lost his arsenal and his war."

"Ay, lad. 'Twas the idea." He fought for breath but it expired, hydrogen from a dirigible.

"Strange, bein' here. Of all places. Meant to bring her

flowers." His eyes closed. "In summer, we'd walk at Chinhae. She'd pick flowers. For me." A fat, hot tear. "I miss her, lad." He cleared his throat, his eyes clamped tightly shut, trying to stop the emotion. "Miss summer. Gotta see the sun."

I clasped his hand. "We'll get you there. Where'd the Wizard go?"

A savage grimace. "Hong Kong. But the rat, he goes there to hide. I'll catch 'im there. I know . . . his brand a cheese."

Purvis shook his head silently: no way.

I took a breath. "Sure is good to see you."

His smile was a shuddering rictus, the lips blue, his skin sweaty, thin, colorless, a sight to break hearts. "And ta lay eyes on you, lad. How I look? Are we . . . squared . . . away . . . for parade?"

He looked like plague death. "Sergeant Major, you look like autumn in New York, the sun on orange maples and the blue Hudson, the old Twenty-fourth Infantry singing 'Garry Owens' capably, to the shamrocks and to the green."

He nodded and faded, a great purple tongue lolling on slack lips, the chest heaving and shuddering at the same time. Saliva ran down his great chin, his snow-white hair gray, thin, and greasy with the final efforts of a prematurely ancient man. My head sank.

Purvis put the blood pressure cuff on him, barely able to close it around the great arm. He pumped it, read it, looked at his watch. He opened the sergeant major's mouth and slipped a small white pill under his tongue.

"How bad is he?" I whispered.

I had never seen Purvis angry. He bared his teeth. "Where the fuck's that medevac? Can't that woman run at all?"

I knew that tune. The drums deepened. I wanted them to stop, as if each beat stole a pump from McCrail's dying heart. But the drummers were working for a higher salvation. They were calling on their ancestors and the collective goodwill of their honored dead, trying to save their land and their people from nuclear fire.

Against this, a dying man's comfort could not be weighed.

I felt the desire to stay with him and the need to go.

McCrail mumbled. I leaned closer, bringing up my good ear.

"Can't hear you, Sergeant Major."

". . . world's got the lad by his curlies . . . he canna see you." He stopped to gasp unevenly. An eyelid fluttered above a blind eye. "Needed 'im. You sent 'im to me. Let the lad have his young life . . . ta save the squirts . . . and become a stinkin' general."

I had a job to do. I released his hand and placed it on his chest. I stood. Fingers scrabbled at my arm. I leaned over and he whispered. I nodded.

"Sergeant Major wants everyone out of this room, now," I said.

Purvis stood. He offered his hand to Catalina, who tenderly kissed McCrail's ashen cheek. They left.

McCrail's chest worked. He made the sounds of a little girl, humming aimlessly. I gritted teeth, looking at the Samsung watch.

Under the drums and cymbals, I heard the sounds of the distant upper Yangtze, felt the old deck and smelled fish. I saw the girl on the prow of a great red slipper Hung River oil boat with a hundred men, five fair cooks and a hundred tons of number-one cargo. BaBa was pointing at her.

"Third daughter of Merchant Wong Fa-gwo. Is arranged. She is your wife, Hu-chin. Very good deal. Good for the *jia*."

She was round-faced, pink-cheeked, pigtailed in a red satin jacket, ten years old. She looked at me solemnly. I tried to see a girl who could become Ma. I smiled at her and she smiled back, her shoulders twisting, pretty in the light.

My brothers ran on deck, chewing summer long bean. Hu-chien tripped and fell, and the girl laughed gaily behind small fingers as I helped him up, both of us looking at her, shading our eyes from the afternoon sun.

"Wongs," said BaBa, "Soochow, city of beautiful women. She will give good sons and docks on the Da Yuhe."

McCrail drew air, gathering faint strength. "We alone, lad?" he wheezed.

"Affirmative, Sergeant Major."

"Laddie," he whispered. "Got debts to pay. You'll do Hong Kong for me, if I can't, won't you? . . . take me boys into their day in the sun?" Pause. "Tickets are right next ta me. Say aye."

"Aye."

He smiled, then fought for breath. "Lad, he's gone sour, the Wizard has. In his ditty bag, I found a bloody surprise. Brought it with me." His chest spasmed and he licked his lips. "Outside . . . west wall, snug to a sharp boulder, under snow. . . . Secure it, lad."

Purvis and Catalina were on the back porch. I exited the front door. Along the west wall was a sharp boulder and uneven piles of crudely shoveled snow. I scraped the snow to find two customized, long-range, combat-load, steel-frame rucksacks. They had industrial-strength webbed support straps adorned with looped high-grade civilian nylon braided rappelling rope.

One pack held a big cargo. I lifted it, the snow falling from it; it was compact and ponderous, the weight of a male adult with a density that exceeded solid lead. My bad back spoke to me and I grounded it, using my legs. The second pack was lighter by a hundred pounds, and I knew what they were.

I moved slower, an apprentice touching a for-bidden textbook. Steel-rimmed pack flaps with a broken lock. With primitive fear, I opened the large pack, heart slugging in synchronization to solar flares and timeless superstitions.

The smooth steel container under the flap was snugged with field-stained Styrofoam and painted in flat naval gray.

The side bore a thirty-two-digit alphanumeric code in military black stencil. A quick take-off plate exposed what I presumed was the detonation shaft for the mate fuze. I looked into the narrow machined recess: the gate to hell.

My fingers trembled as I relocked the plate and closed the packs as red-and-white-faced Chinese ghosts ran sprints up and down my spine. The wind gusted through denuded trees, limbs moving in mockery of winter skeletons.

Pluto and Goofy, atomic death. I put my hands on the bomb as if it were a sentient alien, as if touching a cold container of an unimaginably fiery horror could rationalize the inexplicable and defuse its indiscriminate threat.

The Wizard had snatched a SADM tactical nuke from a highly trained, professional Ninety-five Mike sapper team. I felt like spitting. Lawyers who break the law can use the color of authority to generate havoc, sow disruption, spread misery, steal souls and even snatch the power of a small sun.

The sergeant major had toasted the Wizard's arsenal, liberating Pluto and Goofy, and dragging them up Jungsan, destroying his old and burdened heart.

A noise. Up, feet spread, hands out: nothing. I covered the packs with snow, taking time to do it right. The bomb and its detonator were safer here.

McCrail was breathing poorly, his color shot with broken blood. I thought of Doc. I remembered him shooting dextran blood expander into the dead girl on my orders; I saw Carlos as he looked at me in infinite sadness.

In the monsoon summer of 1967, two days before Doc's nineteenth birthday, he had been decapitated by mortar shrapnel, going down in a lump without pain.

Miss you, Doc. I shut my eyes. I was sweating.

I knelt by Patrick McCrail and wiped his forehead, a drop of my sweat staining his torn shirt, his vast chest thumping as he panted for cheap, shallow breaths.

Red, gray eyes opened.

I told him I had secured his packs. It took three tries for him to ask me for another little white pill.

"Don't have them. I'll send the doc."

"Nah," he wheezed. "Lad. Where'd that lass kiss me?"

He meant Catalina. "On the cheek."

Treacherous, whistling breaths. "Lad . . . which one."

"Your right."

He moved his burly arm to touch the cheek, and missed.

I guided his fingertips to the exact place, where they scrabbled at mottled skin. He sighed and tried to smile. I held them there, helping him revive the magic of a woman's kiss on his old and noble face.

41

KARMA

The garden was quiet. I stepped onto the porch, the smell of McCrail's effort and adhesive winter Korean mud in my nostrils. Purvis and Catalina stood by me.

I forced myself not to listen for the whumping of

the absent dustoff. It was now my job to save men I was supposed to kill, and to remove bombs that could do us all.

The kids were quiet, eating red-spiced vegetables and drinking black-market milk in gender-segregated clumps. Boys watched men. Girls looked at the *mudang*, seated at the picnic table. Hoon Jae-woo gazed at me. *Aboji*, father, she had said.

To the left, the ten Inmingun were in a patrol line in overcoats and hats beneath the trees, their medication procedure completed, ready for route march or for combat. The two other troops were several paces back, looking at watches, late for duty.

The little boy with brown hair gazed at Chang, who stood between the *mudang* and his men.

"Miss Oh, come with me." We walked to Private Chang.

He faced me, confident, buttoned-up, overbuilt and in no mood to talk. He frowned painfully at Catalina.

"Sir," I asked, "what are your plans?"

"I PFC, sir." (He said "Pee-Effee-Shee.") "We go Camp Kay-shee. Work." He looked at his watch. "Lunchee time gone. Inventory, must. Numbah-ten, late, have sergeant mad at Private Chang."

"You must stay here," I said. Catalina translated.

"No 'fraid KCIA," said Chang. Some of his men stirred. "KCIA know we no *kanchop*." Spy. Chang smiled, the victor.

The *mudang*, her bright yellow-and-red robe catching the winter sunlight, flowed toward us. The shaman took Chang's hand and spoke to him urgently, pointing to the children, the North Koreans and the sky.

Chang bristled, then feigned indifference, but the *mudang*'s voice was modulating, rising, deepening, controlling the environment and influencing emotion.

The children stopped eating to listen to the *wang mansin*'s powerful, rasping voice, the ancestors of Korea providing chorus. Catalina interpreted quietly, frowning in concentration.

"She say even dumbass *paksu* know *in-sam* bigger than biggest honcho man." *In-sam*, the natural law of harmony, inevitability, repayment. "Her medicine is same-same. Bigger than all big man. Chang, he hurt her *in-sam*—he say her kids not true Korean people—then her *in-sam che chub* medicines no can help him. She say his hate too muchee big for his pants."

I looked at Catalina. She nodded. The plan had not been rejected because the North Koreans did not trust us. It had failed because Chang did not want to help raise children who were not of pure Korean heritage, who were sullied with black, white and brown Western bloods.

It was the way of the world.

"Dude has the same problems we do," said Purvis.

"Small world," I said.

"Small minds," he corrected.

"She say," continued Catalina, "Chang hate her kids, then other men, they hate *his* kids." Her eyes were wide, her chest rising and falling. "She say his hatred eat his *in-sam* big time. Like, no leftovers, no style. She say, he catchee no hiding from *in-yon* up north."

I could hear Mrs. Fan saying, "*Yeh* has its way." In English, it was karma. The Koreans called it *in-yon*.

Chang, his jaw tight, crushed and field-stripped his cigarette, looking at the *mudang* as she spoke, his red eyes swollen with emotion, angry that she was in his decision-making cycle, making perfect theological sense against his military mission.

Still the *mudang* spoke, and Miss Catalina Oh of the Vegas translated more freely as the cigarette paper floated away.

"She say Buddha give her—old dry-bone-lady—orphan kids. Buddha also give her this twelve man. She say, Chang go down mountain, he crazy man, givee away *yang* power.

"Here, Jungsan, she give him life. Kids need father. Jungsan Korean boys need Chang. She askee his help." Catalina paused. "But, man, he stone cold dude."

Chang donned his military flap cap, covering his bald head and looking less menacing. He paced, his face compressed with argument, conflict, confusion. Yes, I thought, think it out. Jae-woo waited for my look, smiling bravely against all my fears. My presence endangered her, and I felt an exhaustion that went beyond the body. I struggled to remain a player on the mountain. Part of me wanted to leave everything, Jungsan and the bomb, to close my eyes and take McCrail down the mountain to the med. My innards were sour.

Chang studied me, looking for the lie.

"Nuke stay?"

A chance for resolution. I imagined what would happen to negotiations if these Inmingun knew the bomb was a hundred meters away. "We're taking them out. I do not know if they will stay out. We have recommended it."

Catalina started to translate. "*Kwenchanayo*, is okay," said Chang. "I understand." He turned and asked the *mudang* a question.

"He askee to hide here," said Catalina. "Old lady, she say no. Aeigu! She say his men be monks." Catalina shuddered, rubbing her arms as if feeling the cold for the first time. "She say he workee for kids. Teachee Kong-ja manners."

Silently, I urged him: Take the current. Ride it out.

Chang looked at me. He looked at Catalina Oh and spat. He would take no cards, the decision scrawled across his hard face, rejecting holy offerings because they came with American manners and Western fishnet stockings.

"Wait," I said. "What if, at first, you only took care of Korean orphans?" Catalina translated.

Chang's eyes narrowed. He spoke. "How long?"

A teacup fell and shattered. One of the older attending women screamed and children moaned in terror, their vocalized fear stopping my heart.

The Wizard was on the porch with Song Sae and Levine. They were roped to him. He entered the garden.

42

A Day in the Sun

Song Sae was soiled and worn, the shining vitality of her dramatic features blunted by exhaustion and fear. Levine seethed, her left cheek bleeding from a deep cut. They had come through the house and he was armed.

LeBlanc was the aristocrat standing on his veranda, waiting for mint juleps, flanked by his unhappy women. No one else knew he was here.

He wore a GI winter white parka. He held a cheesy CAR-15 in his right hand, the muzzle on the *mudang* and two extra banana clips taped to the one locked into the rifle. The selector switch was at full automatic, safety off. Ninety rounds of 5.56mm ammo that would tumble after entry, ripping organs.

A .45 service automatic was in his left, the hammer back and the muzzle at Levine's throat. Song Sae's black wool overcoat, purple dress and black boots were drenched and spattered with mud and ice.

Two rappelling ropes ran from their abraded necks to the Wizard's cartridge belt. Song Sae was fighting deep fatigue and fear; Levine was looking for an opportunity, glancing at me. I wondered if he had found McCrail and the bomb. I closed my eyes.

God, we're in deep shit.

He dragged the women. He seemed agitated. "Captain Kan, you are under arrest for consorting with the enemy and the devil itself." The beguiling voice. "For all your exposure to Christianity, to West Point, to find you plea-bargaining with filthy Reds and offending the Christ . . ."

I saw Colonel LeBlanc through BaBa's eyes. "I think you're taking the Lord's name in vain."

The Wizard recoiled. Song Sae and Levine slipped away from LeBlanc and his handgun. Slowly, panting, shaking, her gnarled fingers refusing to cooperate, Song Sae tried to loosen the tight noose about her neck. Levine also loosened hers.

The Wizard's emotions surged nakedly through his features. It had been a long night. He blinked, struggled for words. "You—you—stupid, uppity tree monkey! You *Red lover*! Quote scripture to *me*! God, I'm not surprised . . . truly. . . . America faded from perfection when they let in people like you."

"They didn't let me in," said Levine. "I was born here."

"I'M NOT TALKING ABOUT YOU!" he cried, spittle flying, the guns shaking, making children stir and moan in fear, the elder women crying again.

The Wizard stepped backwards, his distant infantry skills gone, pulling Levine and not noticing that Song Sae had freed herself. He tripped on a stone marker at the edge, lost his balance and recovered. LeBlanc kicked the marker in anger. Mud fell from him onto its Hangul and English characters.

MRS. KIM PAEK MCCRAIL 1934–1966

He sighed. "Darkies running the Army, women wearing brass, giving orders! IGs running with whores. *My God!*"

"Yo, Freddy *paksu*," said Catalina flatly. "Long time no see, hey? No like do handy-cuff kinky sweet time no more?"

He winced and turned to me, talking fast. "Whores and darkies multiplying faster than whites, taking our power, attacking our race. Now, even West Point's gone to hell!" He blinked, looking at the snow-covered ginkgos, then at Purvis, sad that the only non-Asian male he could look at was a black man he had bashed in the head with a rifle stock.

"Cadet Choir has niggers and chinks and spics, singing to God." He laughed, low and almost happily. "That would be the day, right? God hearing niggers sing to get into Heaven." He snickered.

"Sir, I've always wanted to know," said Purvis, "if you're a true sociopath, or if you're just deliberately confusing us with multiple pathological options."

"Gotta be drugs," said Levine.

I edged closer.

"Trying to provoke me, you bitch?" He shook his head in anger, the mouth bitter and dejected, eyes unfocused. I was getting closer. "None of you see it, do you? Why I came here, into Asia?" Wet, red, fatigued eyes, seeing the end of dreams.

"America's gone to the niggers, to the servants. Now they go to West Point." A glance at Purvis. "They go to *medical school* and learn how to become lords while the Reds get stronger." He looked at him with contempt. "Well, God brought me here to do something about this."

"Not drugs," whispered Purvis.

It was the Southside problem all over again. Except for the atomic bomb in the garden, we were without Levine's grenade or weapons. Levine was ready to pull the rope and I was edging to where I could do something.

LeBlanc saw Levine, instantly yanking the rope with all his weight, dropping her to the ground. He put the muzzle on me and slipped her rope from his D ring. He backed up, chest heaving.

"Captain Levine, join your coloreds. Go." He pointed with the muzzle. Slowly, she joined us, the slack rope following, making snake tracks in the wet, thinning snow.

"Now I want the witch doctor. Come here right now, *chogi mos tic,*" he said to the *wang mansin.*

Song Sae spoke to the *mudang,* who backed up slowly, the wind of the precipice billowing the flowing silk sleeves of her ceremonial dress.

They were his passports through the Bando. "Madam witch doctor, don't be stupid. God, you come right now, or I kill you."

Song Sae spoke to the *mudang,* her voice quivering. She said, "Non-gae."

The *mudang* glided to the cliff's edge, the back of her dress whipping her hair. She took a sailor's wide stance.

"Please," she said pitifully to the Wizard. "No hurt *mudang.*" The dismay in her voice caused the girls to burst into tears.

Anger filled the Wizard's face. Hatefully, he looked at the girls. My heart ached as he saw Jae-woo, who was tearing wildly at her arm. He wanted her dead.

"You old bitch," he muttered tiredly at the *wu.* He faced Levine, admiring her looks and disliking her ethnicity.

"You. Get those ugly half-breed bastards out of here. Keep the little breeding bitches here."

Chang quietly sighed.

"And the Commies stand fast," added LeBlanc.

Levine asked the boys to move into the house. They

froze. The *wang mansin* repeated the order, and they
moved, their eyes flitting between the *mudang*, the
Wizard and Levine.

LeBlanc backed up as I inched forward. He aimed
at me.

"Edge closer, I'll blow away the breeders. Now back
up. All the way." He pointed the assault rifle at the girls.
We backed up.

Song Sae stood with the *mudang* on the cliff's edge.
The afternoon wind rippled across her partially opened
overcoat and purple dress and rustled the branches,
blowing a fine mist of pure white snow across the pallid
gray sky.

"I didn't tell you to untie," said LeBlanc, his eyes
on me.

"I am sorry," whispered Song Sae. "The rope hurt my
neck."

LeBlanc gauged distances. The persuasiveness in his
eyes was gone, replaced by the cold mechanics of murder
one. The man who had gone to great lengths not to kill
McCrail or Jimmy Buford was, today, going to take the
bomb and slay everyone.

He had cleared his soul of its remaining conscience.

LeBlanc kept his eyes on me and went to the cliff, the
distance making him safe from me.

He looked at the two women, both pretending to
ignore him, their knees flexed, their breathing ragged.
He laughed at them, the guns on us. I could take him
down. I wanted to take him down. I remembered my
seventh winter, full of bitter winds. The junk had
canted and I had slid overboard near a Red Gorge
whirlpool. I swallowed water, struggled and felt the
slimy river fiends take me, soothing me. I came to
on the deck, vomiting out the demons, BaBa, dripping wet, shivering, pushing on my back while the
rain fell. In Vietnam, for a moment, I had welcomed
eternity.

Now I felt the same soothing. Death was not so formidable.

He pointed the rifle at the girls. "I said back up. I mean *way* back. To those trees." We backed up, my heart dropping.

"Let's see, Chinaman. You were an engineer at West Point, even if you look like the slanty kitchen help. Listen up, Cadet."

Humor him. "Yes, sir."

"I have a smoothed sear. My cyclic rate of fire is twelve hundred rounds a minute, but the thirty rounds in the first magazine'll be out in a fraction over one tick. Two seconds to reload. You're thirty meters from me. With a dead start, it'll take you four ticks. I'll have killed all of you twice by then." He would enjoy watching fish die, flopping on the deck.

"Now for the witch doctors. I weigh one ninety. What do you think the little one weighs—eighty pounds wet? The whore, she's one ten." He laughed again. "And I know they're coming.

"They want to copy that old Korean *kisaeng* harlot, Non-gae, heroine of Korea. All she did was jump a little Jap general and roll him down a hill.

"Well, now. I'm a little larger than that, aren't I?"

His face contorted. "Come here, both of you. Now."

No body block: he was expecting it. To make sure, it'd take a bear hug off the cliff. To die with him. The wind blew in the low shrubs as the women inched toward him. It was not their job. It was mine.

The Wizard thought of something, grinning with the inspiration of new torture. "You idiots know we have atomic bombs in Korea?" He nodded to himself, fortified. "Gentlemen, I got one of them! Funny, isn't it, how everyone trusts a lawyer. I mocked a bomb copy and switched them. Now it's good to go—into the north. Look behind me, people. You can see the mushroom cloud from here. Tonight, it's over for P'yongyang and beloved leader Kim Il Sung. The shit's in the fan."

Did McCrail get the real one, or a mock? I was sure it was real. I silently edged forward.

"You're stupid for a chink, aren't you? Simon says take two big steps back."

I took two small steps back, flexing leg muscles, tightening them with the need to release. Under a rush, he would move to the left, away from the precipice. I aimed for that, gathering breath, needing to explode at him out of the blocks. I felt Chang prepare, both of us counting on the Wizard's shooting us before he killed the women and the girls. Don't think of the great, distant *jia* or Cara. Do your job.

A breath of ground noise and a hand seized my ankle and held on. Slowly I looked down.

Patrick McCrail. Bleeding and wheezing in the bush, on all fours, a trembling swamp creature, sprouting twigs, sludge and snow. He said something, very softly.

It was a wind in soft spring's false grass, bugs scraping tropical leaves, eyelashes fluttering on a silent night.

"Say again," I said through my teeth.

"Remember your promise, lad. And put flowers on her grave."

"Let go," I said through my teeth. "I got a plan."

He almost giggled. "Me too, lad." A wheeze. "Light a cigar for me." He seized my tunic and yanked me. I went down as he pulled himself up and dropped me in the bushes. With a great expulsion of air, McCrail shot out of the low shrubs and sprinted head-down for the Wizard, sobbing and bending to his left. I jumped up in a flurry of snow and sprinted after him, following his canted, twisted torso, a gargantuan, charging Quasimodo, his left side in paralysis, the air whooshing in and out of failing lungs, moving by sheer will, rushing like a wounded, galloping rhino at the hunter of his species, the great shoulders and arms driving him, Chang, Levine, and I only steps behind. I was closing and running out of real estate.

LeBlanc froze at the sight of McCrail's craggy face and his huge, fast rush. I roared a tiger's hunting cry at the Wizard and he jerked and the explosive, staccato gunfire echoed, the lead plucking at my jacket and singing past my head. Girls screamed as he sprayed and bullets ripped and tore into the sergeant major's massive, barreling hulk, the big body recoiling from the blows, left, right, staggering, his breath whimpering. The Wizard backed up.

McCrail's great body silently smothered the rifle, a cloud taking a hill, his burly arms engulfing the Wizard, his thick legs driving, his dress shoes kicking divots as he catapulted both of them over the edge of the cliff.

I stopped at the edge.

Below us, the bodies were a single projectile, McCrail's shirttails flapping like small, ineffectual wings. LeBlanc screamed, a hand clutching at air.

They shrank to dots and made a small, tight impact on snow, limbs askew near a winter oak. The snow and rocks beneath me slipped.

Song Sae seized the *mudang* and pulled her back. Shakily, they knelt at the edge, sobbing. Girls and women wailed the lyrics of my nightmares. Snow sprinkled from me down the cliff. Catalina joined us, panting. She spat at the memory of the Wizard.

I looked over the edge, disbelieving McCrail's mortality. He was too large to die. I was too good a runner to have allowed him to get to the Wizard before me. I stared, my mind in cold riot. Please, let this be a dream.

The cliff beneath gave way.

"Aigu!" cried Chang, grabbing my arm and my tunic, buttons and ribbons popping into space as the edge collapsed down the cliff toward the dead. He struggled to pull me back to solid ground, and two of his men grabbed me and hauled.

Children were crying and running. They ran for the house, for escape, for adults. Levine and Catalina began collecting kids. My only client in Korea was dead. I heard the weeping of children.

The girl, dark hair flowing like a black banner, ran for me, her arms out, crying, and I picked her up and held her. She was breathing and unbleeding, her tears the proof of life.

"O ba," she cried, her face in my neck, her thin arms clutching me in desperate, unanswered and unspoken needs.

I hadn't killed her; she lived.

It's okay, I said. You're good and strong and God loves you. I was speaking Vietnamese, and the young bamboo shoots were soft under my boots, the humidity of copper muds in my lungs, the steam rising from the dead.

I walked her away from the cliff, her arms small and vital.

I looked at her. It was not the girl. It was Jae-woo, the adolescent in a field jacket. She did the hugging for both of us. I blinked at the nature of us, the fine natural wonder of a man holding a frightened child. I marveled that of all the humans I had held, this one seemed the noblest, the most graceful.

I let her see me smile with great *jen*, benevolence, and her small, tear-flooded face illuminated as she pressed her forehead against mine, sniffing and shuddering as she clutched me again, holding not only me but her idea of me, a girl's dream of a mythical loving father, constantly safe, forever caring, eternally approving, never angry or too busy or drunk. Her body calmed my broken heart.

I held her tight, my arms not mine but the warm, embracing limbs of all Eastern families, all great *jia*, welcoming home a lost daughter whose own warm, breathing presence worked like a sweet antidote on my aging ills.

The sun broke from behind clouds, casting long, languorous beams of brilliant light onto the white valley.

"*O ba, o ba,*" a girl said in my deaf ear, making me feel all my injuries, physical and psychic.

"*Kwenchanayo*, it's okay. You're fine," I said. "You're safe. All is well. Nothing to fear."

43

To Laugh Whenever You Can

Noon, Sunday

Silently, the white-parka Ninety-five Mike team set a perimeter around Jungsan. A thin Henry Jubala and an immense RTO, radio-telephone operator, with a point man's Winchester 870 pump, sat next to me near the sharp boulder.

"Now," said Jubala, "did I, or did I not, know you were up to some bad shit?"

He looked around him, Uzi at the ready. "I take Pluto and the damned Inmingun'll come outa the ground. Assholes already did us."

Jubala and Magrip should've opened on Broadway together, doing light comedy and slapstick.

Jubala checked the packs with wiry hands, his blue snake-head tattoo flexing jaws and tongue, his eyes still bug-eyed.

"Tell me this is the genuine nuke," I said.

"Technically, that's a negative. Just a puny garden-variety atomic, a baby 'shroom. Fission device. Not fission-fusion-fission, your true duck-tailed all-American nuke. This here's a little plutonium SADM Niner-Ought-Niner. A hundred-meter fireball to make Mother Nature move some rocks. Six thousand rems, 120,000 calories per square centimeter of thermal rad blast, five-PSI overpressure with hundred-and-twenty-mile-per-hour winds, blow us to hell." He enjoyed talking about his Pluto. I imagined he had few chances.

The munition checked out. He caressed the pack's flap. "Asshole LeBlanc broke my lock." He snapped his fingers and two sappers ran forward. Each assisted the other to load, Pluto first.

"Okay, Mushroom Man," said Jubala, squaring away straps and slapping both rucks. "Good to go." The big men moved out.

"Good luck, Henry, wherever you're going."

"Time to unass Easy Street on the DMZ." Jubala put out his hand. The RTO passed him the hand mike, and Henry made his call. The Ninety-five Mikes faded fast down the mountainside. The LZ—Landing Zone—was the orphanage. The children had been evacuated.

Magrip, Levine and I followed at intervals, guarding the Mikes' rear until Rangers came out of the trees to bring up the trail.

Jet engines. A squadron of warpaint A-10 Warthogs fanned over the valley. Above them, in the unusually clear sky, were the racetrack contrails of F-14 Navy Tomcats. Somewhere above them was an AWACS— Airborne Warning and Control System—directing traffic.

The air vibrated from massed rotors. Fast Loach choppers searched the hills, then cleared. A squadron of Cobra gunships flying NOE, nape of the earth, flared on wide perimeter around the valley. A second Cobra squadron hovered inside the perimeter, then moved out as a trio of big Navy transport Sea Stallion CH-53 helos thundered in from different vectors.

The helos circled the LZ, blasting snow, bending and breaking trees. They landed, and Marines deployed fast to establish a ground perimeter as white-parkaed troops jumped into the three Stallions with their rucks; the Marines reboarded and the helos lifted off, the Cobras on station to suppress possible enemy ground fire.

The Ninety-five Mikes were taking their little mushroom-headed cartoon characters out of Korea via the U.S. Seventh Fleet. I watched the air fleet deploy to the sea. I felt all of Korea could again take a deep, collective breath.

It was my job to go to Hong Kong. Underneath the pillows in the villa's side room, I found the tickets. Ramos Travel Agencies, Seoul. I opened the flap and checked the KAL flights. A thick wad of U.S. currency lay behind the tickets.

The forced, uneven scrawl on the accompanying note said,

Captain.
Found dough in the warehouse. Couldn't burn it, could I. Light one for me. See you in Heaven.

Your comrade,
SGM Patrick T. McCrail

Chang and one of his men had gone down the mountain on rope belay. The sergeant major's great, stilled body was paradoxically intact; the Wizard's had been broken in extensive and hideous distortions.

Magrip and I recovered the Wizard's effects; there were none to be found on McCrail except a purloined cardiac nitro prescription bottle, rosary and fragments of cut det cord. We belayed the bodies up the cliff.

In the small room where he had struggled for breath, I held the rosary, disbelieving that I would never again hear his giggle, his great Irish voice, that he would miss his long-awaited mission to Hong Kong.

"Kan, it's been a helluva week. You did good." Magrip had been as talkative as Buster Keaton in a silent movie. Now he jabbered like Walter Brennan with a hundred pages of script.

He belched. "You missed a helluva firefight out there in the snow. Those Inmingun were good. Hell, there were only two of 'em, and they fired our asses up." Magrip had killed both of them. And McCrail was dead.

I knew Magrip was trying to help. His goodwill was a Long River Western freighter, blowing smoke from afar.

"Soon as we get stateside, I'm unassing the Army. You?"

Butt Kicker and his Medal of Honor leaving the Army.

"I'm going to sleep for a week."

"Job-First Jackson Kan—sleeping. Now, that'd be something. That's the one thing you don't do worth shit."

I saw Cara in bed and wondered if the Wizard had actually sent someone to harm her. I wondered if I'd leave the service for her, if I would propose to her principally because of her wonderful body, and if she had slept with anyone else this week. I knew I would welcome daughters, and wondered how I would feel having sons. Job-First Jackson. I wondered if I had been doing the wrong job.

We got out of the jeeps at the turnaround and walked up the hill, the cold mountain wind painful to skin and lungs.

"*Mudang* wants to see you," said Magrip. "Alone."

The drums and cymbals were back at work. The scents of sweet incense and fertile barley tea filled the thick air, the trance of music a living thing. I found a bathroom and washed my hands and face with the same vigor I had used after meeting Dogface Nagol in the CG's mess. I looked at my scarred arms and hands, as if I could see the plutonium, as if soap could wash out McCrail's death.

Song Sae sat in lotus. She wore an elaborate multicolored silk robe with a white headband, a diva in a satin bed. She was wonderful, unreachable, unearthly, fantastic, barely familiar, her neck still red and violated.

Her eyes danced happily. *"Annyonghashamneeka, dae-wi."*

"Anyahashameeka, Moon-kidae."

"Dae-wi, the *wang mansin* offered to you an answer to your true question. She will hear your question now."

The *mudang* stepped across the sea of pillows to sit beside me.

"I have no question." The drums seemed to argue.

"Dae-wi, who is this woman you love, who cannot love you? The woman who shamed you?"

"She didn't shame me. Her name is Cara Milano."

Song Sae and the *mudang* spoke. *"Dae-wi,* this cannot be. The woman is an Eastern female and looks like Hoon Jae-woo. It is why you have such a strong reaction to her."

The girl at the Dong Nai.

I shook my head and cleared my throat. "I don't love her."

"Dae-wi, English has a flaw. Only one word for 'love.' For romance, for being crazy for music—or loyal to parents, hungry for special food, heartsick for children, enjoying vacations, thrilled by soccer, no? Americans love hamburgers, mothers and women and their country and rock and roll with the same word, but not, I think, with same style. In some style, you love this girl. Not romantically, but she is in the heart."

I closed my tired eyes, heavy and injured by the sergeant major's death. The drums and brass cymbals were like goads and crucifixes, whips and lubricants. I had talked about the six dead females to Doc Benton at Letterman Hospital, to no effect. Telling the *wu* about it would not help. I would do my next job, in Hong Kong, and feel better.

My heart was being squeezed by the brass and beaten by the drums. Song Sae sat next to me, silks rustling.

"Give her up. Relieve the pain. Tell us, who listen and understand. When men are sad, they are silent. You must cry out pain while someone listens." She caressed my inert hands.

Give her up. She waited patiently. The drums were moving me and I spoke.

"I killed her." My voice not my own but BaBa's voice when he sold our boat for passage out of China. "And her baby sister. Probably her mother and her grandmother and maybe some aunts. Six people." My chest ached. The girl ran toward me. I willed it to be Jae-woo, the teenager in the *mudang*'s garden, but it was the girl with no name, her body waiting for the slugs, and I couldn't watch, flinching in my soul, trying to flip the channel, knowing every program in my skull was set to receive the same grotesque horror show, frozen in constant reruns, prosperous and full in tragic endings.

"*O wa, dae-wi!* It had to be an accident! You are not a murderer." The *mudang* asked what I had said. Song Sae explained.

The M-16 gave its small, squirrelly recoil and I jerked as the *wang mansin* tickled my face with a goose feather, smiling like a secretive witch. I brushed it away and it returned, tickling.

"She wants you not to be serious, *dae-wi*," said Song Sae. "Laughing is a very big part of life. You are supposed to live."

I was going crazy and the world was going to hell. America was becoming a pleasure island without an admission charge. The President's going to be impeached, the races can't live with each other, Cara's not home at three A.M., McCrail's dead, and I killed girls and women and buried men without rituals. I have no sons to give the *jia*, and my mother weeps for her lost, unsmiling, childless son because her babies died in China.

The feather tickled.

Song Sae nodded, her eyes tearing. "Yes, it is so. But did you not dive into the river to swim with the fish that look like Chinese officials? Did you not try to save your baby brothers? Did you not embrace a holy woman who cannot give physical love? Did you not laugh once at death? Did you not look like a wet chicken with flying feathers? Are not so many things we do silly? Did not Colonel Min fall down stairs like a drunk man?" She laughed, rich, musically, from the stomach, filling the room with a delicious, ridiculous, earthy cackle that forced from me a chuckle. Her laugh was joviality itself.

Her pretty shoulders shook as she guffawed, her head back, losing her balance and somersaulting backwards as she squealed. She laughed and laughed, hiccupped, hitting the pillows and shaking her head. She laughed contagiously.

I chuckled, then I laughed. I laughed because she was funny and nothing was funny, because my mind was being cleared of thought and static and I was being ushered into a realm of hilarity with the power of narcotics. I laughed stupidly, a fool in an absurd world, a stranger in Asia, an American, trying to help everyone.

It sounded like crying and tears ran down my face and I sobbed, drowning out the drums and cymbals as I wept in racking, chest-aching sobs for the girl, for her family, for that damned bloody day, my tears flowing parallel to unknown tides, the salt of Vietnamese waters pouring from my eyes and choking me, choking my life, making everything I did meaningless and late.

The *mudang* pulled my head into her lap while I wept, my head rocking, my torso, my heart, my inner Chinese organs in agony, her gown wet with me. She narrated over my tears, her voice hoarse and low, speaking in step with the drums, the echoes of a hyenalike hysteria still in my head. I sobbed, the tears flowing like rainwater across bright, broad-leaved Indochinese palms.

"Kan Hu-chin, firstborn son, can you hear?" She said it again.

"Hu-chin, you have a big, muscular body, and *yang* power in the world. But you have the innocence of a small boy. Open your heart, boy, to our words. We are wiser than you."

The *wu* spoke.

"She says, 'You think God should not allow little boys and little girls to die. That nothing justifies God's cruelty. Listen to me:

" 'You treasure the girl's death. It is your proof of God's error. You keep your bond with her, to protect a Chinese misery.' "

The drums kept beat with my heart.

" 'There are greater things that deserve your loyalty.' "

Candles flickered. Light reflected in golden sparks from candelabra. The *wu*'s voice softened and I cried for the sergeant major, for his never having seen the sun since the very spring in which I had reported to Vietnam.

"She says, we are part of the universe, a dot of people, ocean and trees, swept clean by winds from the moon and sun. Under these stars and winds, Hu-chin, we have roles to play, using births, lives and deaths for good or for bad."

The *mudang*'s voice rose an octave. So did Song Sae's.

"She says, life is hard and it is good. The winds bring us news and tell us truth, changing us.

"It is sad that some trees are too proud to listen, to take the life lessons of the winds as shaping, as changing. You know, Kan Hu-chin, trees that do not bend to the wind are broken."

The shaman's fingers ran lightly through my hair, her

touch felt in my fingertips and toes, as if she were Cara and not an ancient *haroboji* with a bent back.

"Men are trees. Tall, proud, confident to know all things, and too strong to bend. They take. They do not submit to anyone.

"The world breaks these men and their bodies. Hearts, livers, stomachs, backs, brains, sex organs. No *che chub* herbs can fix it.

"The Wizard thought he was the wind, that he could bring change and mold humans, to use us. He named God every hour, but submitted to no one, seeing himself as the God he named."

I was breathing, short and choppy. I started to sit up.

"Submit," said Song Sae. I exhaled. I lay back.

"That was his *in-yon*, his fate, to see Heaven while living in Hell, giving words to God while spiting Him."

Song Sae spoke crisply. "Your true question, Hu-chin, when you were in war, was whether God was dead. Am I right?"

Seven years ago, dripping Indochinese mud and the blood of children, I had looked up to see an empty sky, a vacant Heaven. Eighty-nine well-trained, disciplined, heavily armed American men, muzzles up, standing over dead babies, girls and women.

Under my command. The little dead girl resembled the Wong family's third daughter, my betrothed. The little baby looked like my infant brother, Hu-chien, Strong Tiger.

I had looked up through the thick foliate canopy, praying to God to make my error a bad dream. Please, Lord, make it a dream. Into that prayer I had poured my soul and the blood of innocents.

I had gotten my wish.

"*Dae-wi*, you say you do not believe in God. But you are so angry at God, He is most real to you." I recoiled as the *mudang* began to rub me as if I were a cat. I held her hand and she stopped. I let go and she began caressing me again, focusing on my face, the temples, the scalp. Her hands, the incense, were opiates.

"You feel the magic of her hands. You cannot study it; only feel them, and it is more than you expect to feel, more than you can understand." Currents ran through me. I had a sensation of being a fish, my muscles dropping away in a wind-whipped sea of female pillows.

"Her care for you is not because you are powerful, smart or beautiful, but because you are in need.

"*Dae-wi*, whose God tells her to behave so, to care for you because you need, and not because you deserve?"

Grace. I shook my head. I whispered: Your God, BaBa.

"She says, 'Remember the stars above your boat in China. Above your men in a forest war. Men cannot create such things. Think of your mother's face and tell me if God is so uncaring, so cruel. You see the girl in your sleep and when you are awake. Think of her now." I shut my eyes tightly, trying to hold on to stars.

"God made her. God made your brothers. Men killed them. We cannot know why. God gives sky and stars. He gives choices, but He always takes back our dead.

"It is we who make human war. Men kill. God only makes war in our hearts. We cannot know all that God knows. If we knew all, we would not be human beings. If we do not recognize mystery, we are only animals."

I took a great breath. "She means *Bosa*, Buddha?"

"Hu-chin, she means the God of your father. *Wang mansin* says, the girl died for her own reasons. You did not intend to harm her.

"You were in battle. She was with a war party and would have killed you and all your men without shedding a tear, laughing over your bones and blood, gaining face for killing a Chinese warrior.

"You know the history of your people. For a thousand years, Chinese men rode into Vietnam, causing war, killing men and making women cry. Oh, Hu-chin, your tears are ancient tears for ancient debts. The *wu* cares for you, because you are a soldier crying for women not of your tribe."

A long silence of drums and brass. She had been a runner for a long-range strike team, fighting me, an old enemy. I had felt the creases in her blouse caused by the strap of an AK-47. I had smoothed them while I blew breath into her. I ached for her, her hard days, her sad end, her life bleeding out, calling for her father.

The shaman spoke.

"She says you made the girl a martyr. A Vietnamese *liet sy*. Killing a girl was so horrible that it suspended your spirit. The horror was not yours; it is the old horror of war.

"When you wear her death as your skin, you become like the Wizard. He thought he had God-like powers, and both you and the *paksu* Wizard focused on the dark world.

"His evil was hating nonwhites. Your evil is blaming God for the guilts of people. You have made carrying this girl your most important duty.

"There are other jobs for you to do. The girl served her purpose. She cared for her family. She did what her father asked of her. She died a death that means something in her life. Your brothers are in Heaven with the God of their father."

The *mudang* smiled with her bad teeth. She spoke.

Song Sae said, "Your purpose is to remain in the world of stars, sunrises, new moons. She says, 'You have helped my village. You took the fire of hell and the guns from the Valley of War.'

"Your *mi-gae* is to serve others. To make a firstborn son. To help other clans by protecting children. To honor females as true equals to men.

"To help all people who still need. To show humility and honor God for your life. To laugh, whenever you can.

"She says, you tried to breath life into the girl when she was dead. The bitterness of her death passed into you. It lives below your tongue and impairs your *ki-bun*, your harmony.

"Empty your mouth of bad *mi-gae*, of your anger at God. Do not blame God for the pains of males. Clean your mouth with willow branch, for you have six female lives to give up."

Song Sae handed me a teacup, a bowl and a branch.

I sat up and took the cup, bowl and branch, placing them carefully on the flat top of a great pillow. My hands trembled, the overrelaxed muscles responding slowly.

My mouth was bitter. Death, misery, angry wounds in my mouth. I saw the rain forest, felt my absorption in it, my inability to control war. I was firstborn and loved the power of my self-blame. I saw the dead baby, the dead girl, the women.

Perhaps I was not so weak against Chinese fate if the Dong Nai had been my personal fault. I was not so useless and hateful if I felt profound and everlasting guilt from the death of children.

I heard the *mudang*'s words. We cannot know all that God knows.

I rinsed with tea. I rubbed my mouth with the soft branch. The taste it left was neither sour nor sweet. Neutral, inert, open to possibilities. I remembered McCrail.

I removed the envelope from my pocket. I bowed and offered the envelope with the right hand, my left holding the sleeve of the right, as Song Sae had taught me.

"For the orphanage, from McCrail *shee*. Open it later."

Inside was over $150,000 U.S. It had belonged to a wizard. With it was my check for the Chun's Happiness Cafe, which had been blown up for our sake.

Legally, the Wizard's black-market and recruitment money belonged to both America and Korea. But the place where the true debts of those two nations met was the Jungsan Orphanage, where children with the faces of both lands waited for angels.

I had returned to Asia, rescued a friend, lost a comrade, practiced history and become a sitting magistrate, trying to dispense monetary and equitable judgments.

Song Sae nodded, eyes moist, her hands in Buddhist prayer. She accepted it with a low bow, her hands mirroring my offer. She spoke softly to the *mudang*, who showed no surprise.

Jae-woo entered and sat next to me, gently resting her head on my shoulder. *"Aboji,"* she whispered. Slowly, my body feeling apart from me, I put an arm around her small frame, and she breathed as cats purr. Song Sae smiled.

Time passed without measure, the drums and cymbals beating, something unseen and heavy leaving me, something invisible and sweet in my breath.

They spoke softly. I was content to listen without comprehension. When Jae-woo laughed, I smiled. When Song Sae wept, I closed my eyes, and felt Ma's warm smile from across the Eastern Sea, joining the warmth of this society of women.

Later, Song Sae held the willow branch to a burning candle until it ignited.

Gracefully, she took it outside in a trail of smoke, toward the courtyard where Patrick McCrail was to be buried.

44

FAREWELL

The report of the rifles echoed across the valley, the smoke of the salute dissipating like fleeing Chinese spirits in the high morning wind. Frightened birds fluttered down the mountain. The M-14 rounds cracked like the iron hammers of Norse gods, proclaiming that the soldier was dead. I remembered funerals at West Point, the widows recoiling, stabbed by the harsh finality of rifle fire. Let there be no doubt: This man was loved and is now dead. Move on.

The seven-man honor guard ordered arms at the last echo. They attempted precision, but they were distracted by the crowd of silent Amerasian orphans, the ten unusually overbuilt Korean men in peasant work clothes, the weeping women, the mysterious nature of the man they had honored. Their manual of arms was ragged, some of the older troops wincing in recognition of glaring imperfections.

The young bugler loosened the chin strap of his dress cap, took a lungful of cold mountain air and played taps flawlessly, the sad minor key lingering on the hillside, passing into the frigid winter fog that hugged the lower peaks, hinting at the hills of Eire. The sergeant major would have approved.

The honor guard commander gave me McCrail's folded flag with the spent cartridges within. With soft commands, he marched the guard out of the garden at subdued route step. The big, burly Korean men observed silently. Then they began the long walk down the mountain to the orphanage.

I thanked the padre, a Catholic chaplain little older than me.

He had delivered a service fit for a man who had sinned and been redeemed, whose ample good deeds had swelled his memory beyond the marks left by ordinary mortals. I was proud to have known this great sergeant, whose old bones had finally won repose, to stand in the place of a long-absent family of soldiers and kin.

The padre descended the path, following the men of the tiger.

Song Sae bowed to me, and I to her. "Thank you," I said.

"We did very little, *dae-wi*. It was your *chingu*, McCrail *shee*, who took the Wizard from the Valley of War and burned his guns in the village. You are the Chinese man who brought McCrail *shee* to us, to make the sacrifice of Non-gae on Jungsan Peak. It was you who marked the Wizard for the man he was, who drew his fire to allow the American giant to kill the evil in this valley." Her large, feline eyes glittered at me. "It is a story that will join the folklore of our sad country."

"The sergeant major would like that. Stories of soldiers saving children. Please thank the *wang mansin* for her help."

She surveyed my face. "Hu-chin," she whispered, using my true name. "I will pray for you, deep in my heart, every day of my life, in this garden. I will pray through all the seasons Buddha gives me. And I will wave to you, as if we were still close."

The wind rustled branches. "Soon, Hu-chin, the ginkgos will turn green, and the petals of many-colored flowers will make this garden the most beautiful place in all the world. I am sorry you did not see Korea in spring. The air becomes warm. Birds sing day and night. The fields are green, the sun shines on the rice paddies.

"My dear *chingu*, in this garden, every day, I will face east, toward America. Toward you. And pray.

"Hu-chin, I ask you to do the same for me in Mi-guk, in America. The money is a fine gift, but it is nothing compared to the love that children need. So pray for my orphans. Hu-chin, you are a tiger man, round and full with Korean *Sanshin*, tiger spirit, and your God loves you very much."

She smiled with her own sadness, touching my face. "This is very strong luck. If you shared it with me, through your prayers to your God, I would be very happy."

It was a heavy request, beyond my habits. Her eyes moved me, and the words fell: "Then I will do it."

Her eyes were moist. "Thank you, Hu-chin." She stood on her toes and softly kissed my cheek, letting her smooth face touch mine for an instant, her eyelashes leaving an indelible trace.

She walked into the villa, the children following her. Someone closed the door, and I cried without logic or anguish, for having been touched by so much selflessness, so much mystic love, by a woman of my fading past, a woman I would only know henceforth in prayer.

All the chapters of a second, alternative life had walked away, and I knew, regardless of the jobs, the joys, the pitfalls and the promises that might await me, I would always wonder about what I had left on this mountain.

It was not my *yeh* to be here; I had pledged to the land of my father, the land which had saved us and to which I owed an enduring Chinese debt, and that was to the east. I looked at the old, closed door and thought of the woman behind it with wonder. I held out my hand, as if we were still close.

Goodbye. *Manmanlai*, I whispered. Go softly.

Levine wore snug jeans and a bulky parka, her hair under a fuzzy white ski cap. I took a breath.

"Let's see, Levine. You found McCrail, got Jimmy out of the Ville, burned down a Q, stole the key map, negotiated ten Tiger Tails into a monastery, ate a pound of candy, helped avoid world war, and made me pick up my socks. Now what?"

"And I mouthed off." She looked down at her black high-topped civilian boots. "I always do that."

"Levine, we're the same rank."

"You're team leader. Men, senior or not, hate it."

"They shouldn't. You're unnaturally smart, honest and tough. And at times," I nodded, "a colossal pain in the ass."

"And that's all, to a fine, well-educated, polite Jewish boy from Warsaw who likes kugel and can roll matzoh balls."

I nodded. "That's all, for comedy teams in the field. By the way—what's your first name? Maybe, someday, we can evolve into a first-name relationship."

She put out her hand. She smiled sweetly as we shook. "Screw you, Kan. Call me if you get a dangerous mission."

Major Purvis, M.D., studied the headstone. It had taken petitions, permits, the CG, four lawyers and a shaman to inter Mr. Max on holy Korean ground.

"I'm extending my tour," he said. "Orphanage needs a doctor. Jackson, are you . . . interested . . . in Song Sae Moon?"

"No."

He rubbed his jaw. "I think she's hung up on you. Think I have a chance?"

I had been uninvolved with women for years. In the space of six months, I was brimming with prospects. Up and down the river, my ancestors had to be smiling and blessing Guan Yin.

"Absolutely. If you're very patient. Asian patient. Years."

He laughed. "Well, I'm that. Maybe Jae-woo, or some other girl, will pop up in the Ville with *sin byong* and strut the stuff to be the next *mudang*. And that'll be my chance to retire Song Sae and take her to Brownsburg, Indiana."

I smiled with the image. It could happen. "Good luck, Doc."

"You, too, partner." We shook hands and he left.

Magrip and Levine had the seven-digit port-of-call codes for seats on tonight's military charter, category A, Tiger Airlines. No more first class on foreign flag carriers.

I wouldn't miss it; I was flying coach to Hong Kong. My three team members—Magrip, Levine and Min— had survived.

"The Army'll miss you, Magrip."

"Oh, horseshit. The Army misses no one."

"I'll miss you."

He looked at me. "God, why? When the hell would you miss *me*?"

"Every time I see a chicken."

It was seven P.M. in San Francisco. I dialed the access code for her office, my pulse elevated. It rang twice.

"This is Cara Milano. Wait one minute, please."

My heart tripped on the sound of her smooth voice, full of sensual secrets and the steady workings of a conscious mind. I slowed my breathing. She returned. "Thank you for waiting."

"Ms. Milano, this is Art Fleming from the television game show *Jeopardy*, coming to you from the Republic of Korea. We were required to move the program without notice to our sponsors . . .

"Ms. Milano, we're in Final Jeopardy and the category is Romance. You are the leader. How much are you willing to risk?"

The pause was more than three seconds. "Everything."

My heart played dodge ball with my blood. "The answer, for the game, is 'He loves you more than anyone else in the world.'"

Three-second delay. "There was this toadlike fellow who romanced me with slow dancing and big talk of eternal families, but he never said he loved me. Then he left, I think, a little dishonestly. So, Art, this is a wild guess." Pause. "'Who is Jackson Hu-chin Kan?'"

"You win, Cara." I said "Cara" with an Italian trill. Softly, slowly. "I love you."

She laughed. "Mr. Fleming, you must be kidding. Don't you mean you *might* love me?"

"No mights. . . . Cara, I'm sorry I left you without a word. Part of my job. God, I love your voice. I love you. Isn't that a gas?"

She exhaled through her pretty nose. "You jerk. You toad. You're driving me crazy."

"I knew I was a jerk. I didn't know I was a toad. Cara, enough with the flattery. How are you?" Meaning, how are we?

"Oh, Jackson, Jackson . . . I'm wonderful. I love you— oh—I love you so much! Damn, you *are* such a *jerk*. Urrhhh! When are you coming home?"

"Three days. As soon as I can. I miss my pillow."

"Oh?" She laughed heartily, and bells rang and midnight was no more. "Baby, is that all you miss?"

"Some other things." I laughed, the delays of distance placing them on top of each other. "The smell of espresso. Your eyes. The smell of you. Your nose, the flute above your lips. Your mouth. Kissing you. I ache for you. More than black-bean *chow fun*."

"Well, then, it must be love. Hurry home, sweetheart. And be careful. I'll *kill* you if anything happens to you." A breath. "Baby, you are not off the hook. You've been holding out on me."

"I know. I'm going to tell you. Now."

I did, leaving nothing out, as if the sense of forgiveness I had experienced in the villa were a Confucian axiom, as if I merited her earlier fearlessness about me. I told her I was going to pray every day for a Korean holy woman. That I wanted to pay for the college education of a fourteen-year-old girl named Jae-woo.

"Do you love them, *caro*?"

"Like family."

"Then they are my family, too. *Caro*, it'll hurt, I know, but you should tell me. What happened to your baby brothers?"

I had to find the words. "They were in the Presbyterian church at Chingshan, on the Yangtze while BaBa and Ma shopped. I was supposed to stay with my brothers, but I went outside. I was throwing rocks. Shells began exploding in the town. I ran for the church. Hu-chien was four and he was scared and saw me coming and waved to Hu-Hau to come. A grenade hit me on the shoulder, knocking me down just as they came to the door. It rolled to them and blew up."

"Oh, God." She wept. "Tell me you didn't blame yourself. That your parents didn't blame you. Oh, baby."

"If I had been inside, the grenade couldn't have hit me. But it was civil war. Both Communists and Nationalists shelled the church that day. They had no affection for Christians. BaBa said that if I had been inside, he would have lost all his sons."

She exhaled. "And you became a soldier?"

"It was my *yeh*, my karma, and my *badze*, my horoscope."

A longer pause. "*Caro*, do you still believe in that?"

I thought of BaBa's durability after the death of his sons, his immeasurable spiritual strength, his expectations of me, the magic that still somehow ran through me.

"No."

"Good, *caro*." She blew her nose. "I'll make you a Catholic, yet."

"I can't wait." A silence.

Her voice became smaller, finer, more physically distant, more emotive, more personal. "Baby, I have a confession to make. You won't like it. It may cost us everything." She sighed, then made it. It felt like knives. I was silent for a while, taking controlled breaths.

"Baby?" she asked. "Talk to me."

"God, I hate it that you did that. Why did you have to do that? Couldn't you trust me?"

"Trust? Trust someone who never said he loved me? Who disappeared without a word? Who I thought was dead until your boss called to say you were at Walter Reed but never called me back—'cause you weren't there? Trust you to do what? To leave me like a mean, low-down son-of-a-bitch?"

She had been in bed with another man, a man I could deal a Chinese death and bury facedown in the mud, my knife in his throat. I held my head. I touched the knife like a crucifix.

"*Caro*, he meant nothing to me. It was so stupid. Horrible. I'll tell you anything you want, but he's not worth our time." She whispered, "Please forgive me. I was so lonely without you. You left me! Oh God, I hated you!"

We all had lonely needs. I thought of what I had done in a rain forest seven years ago. I felt the grenade bounce off my shoulder. I nodded.

"*Caro?*" she asked. I took my hand from the knife hilt.

I cleared my throat. "I forgive you. Don't ever do that again. It hurts too much."

"I won't, honey." She kissed into the phone. "Tell me you love me. That you miss me. That you can't live without me. That you'll never leave me."

"I do, I do, I do."

"Jackson, I love it when you talk suggestively, but that doesn't work. You have to say the words."

I did.

She took a breath. "Would you leave the Army for me?"

"I don't know. Would you leave the firm to have babies?"

"You're going too fast. I just want you out of uniform." And then she laughed. Cara's voice took me like a following sea to a calm harbor. I imagined her in a bridal gown. I imagined her out of a bridal gown.

I replayed her words of love for me, leaving out a part. I remembered the ruin I had caused others, the anonymous lives I had truncated, the men who had died with me. I saw her face, and reexperienced the lifting of burdens at Jungsan. I felt what it was like to love my life.

By dusk, the team had left Korea. I was alone in the garden. After cleaning Mrs. McCrail's mud-spattered grave, I laid a colorful, dried wildflower bouquet against it.

Da-ma, Auntie, I am sorry for the pain the Army caused you. McCrail's fresh white military marker was next to hers. This, unlike the bogus edition in the Wizard's yard, held the high ground, from the Valley of War, the Z and the Imjin to the MSR to Ouijeongbu in the south.

He had a good view and would always experience strong, clean, fresh mountain winds. He could smell the enemy and unsafety weapons before the enemy crested the ridge in their wet cotton-twill uniforms. It was an ideal site for a fine Chinese grave. Song Sae had said that their dead were interred on high ground. "We call it Happy Mountain, for the end of pain."

I looked to the east and the New Territories of Hong Kong.

His body was beneath me, the big hands holding his Bible and rosary, a straight, regimented squad of expensive cigars breaking the smooth contour of his heavily beribboned blouse, a sheen of British Sterling cologne on his cheeks and thick Irish neck.

I had bought him a Chinese thousand-piece-of-silver ironwood casket, the kind my grandfather, the man who had named me for the tiger and danger, had always deserved but had never seen.

The kind my brothers will have, someday, when Chinese sons from America can return home. This is for you, *didi*, my little brothers. And you, *Gung-gung*. This big man we buried, he, too, is a man of clans and long memory.

Perhaps, someday, my son will find your graves in China, and get you three fine, smooth red caskets. We will not forget you, for you are our ancestor and you are my brothers.

The Fifty-seven Foxtrots announced him to be the sweetest-smelling corpse in Korea. Even the dead would never guess he had spent seven years in a sewer and three in Manchuria without a bath.

I wondered where the rest of him, the uncorporeal part, was.

I thought I knew.

I put down my briefcase and rested the triangular-folded American flag atop the stone and pulled out two long cigars.

I stuffed the cellophane in my pocket and bit off the ends. I lit both, superstitiously inhaling the smoke of each to dignify the moment. I felt his big gray cat-eyes on me.

Aye, laddie. Give me one.

I stuck one of them into the soft ground above the sergeant major's body and puffed on the other, letting the wind build the ash on both. With it, I put an assortment of chewing gums and cigarettes so heavily favored by the men he had once led.

I looked across the valley. I stepped to the edge, where the wind gusted, whispering a keening reminder that we were all subject to change, to bending, to submitting.

Even men. Even American men. Even Chinese first-born sons.

Tree prefers calm, said the calligraphy in the villa.

Wind does not care. I heard BaBa's coda: God loves us all.

I faced his grave. "Sergeant Major," I said.

"I'll get your boys their day in the sun. I'll tell them how you saved some people. The innocents." I was knocking rocks down the cliff. The north wind shifted the cotton strings of fog around me.

I looked toward the hidden Inmingun camps on the Z, at the shaman's Japanese green-tiled curved roof, at the black granite apex of Jungsan, at the emptiness of the winter garden's bare trees. I saw the promise of spring in its evergreens above an invasion valley, fertile with the bones of the dead.

Inmingun, don't come. Stay home. Let peace do its work.

I lit two joss sticks and stuck them in the ground when the paste began to burn. Hu-hau, Hu-chien, these are for you, for good fortune, from Ma and BaBa and your older brother.

I had a full life, round with luck, robust with good *yuing chi*. Against this, I had had only a few bad moments. I was a fortunate man who had made too much of his losses.

The joss smelled old and familiar. I remembered the joss in Naktong, and something made me lower my head.

I felt McCrail's faith, glowing from a condemned, putrid cell, fighting off the curse of a life term in a toilet. That memory filled my chest. I humbled myself and spoke as the son of a *laoban*, a boy without a man's false pride.

God, I'm sorry I killed the girl.

I'm sorry my brothers died and I lived.

The wind took the sound of tears. I looked up, just like McCrail. I give You the girl. I had her for seven years. My brothers, for twenty-four. It's Your turn. They were good kids who had to live in war. Please watch over the

McCrails. If you have flowers up there, let them pick them, together.

Winter finches called to each other in light clear song, flitting from branch to branch, dusting the air with snow.

I felt the Korean willow branches, my gift for Fan *taitai*, who had foretold my life and put me in uniform.

Something was above me. I cried for the beauty of the world. I felt the fine and preposterously supreme logic to all we did.

I pulled the Randall knife from my boot, hefting it as I clamped on the cigar, took a breath, stepped into the throw, grunting as I hurled it toward the place where the sergeant major had delivered a final, zero-appeal verdict on the Wizard.

It sailed and spun, catching failing light on its blade before distantly and silently striking the tree where the two men had died. I would miss the knife. I would miss the girl more.

I pulled the glowing cigar from the ground, took a deep draw and stubbed it into the soft soil, the last plume of smoke wafting into the slate Korean sky. I stood and slowly saluted the sergeant major. I walked to the cliff, facing north, the land of my memories and birth, of McCrail's heroic captivity. Only his body was in the ground. I took the cigar from my mouth and looked up.

I remembered him singing to me in the *gan-bang myunhae shill*, the interview cell in Naktong. I closed my eyes, hearing his voice, recalling the words of an Irish blessing.

"May the road rise to meet your step. May the wind be at your back, the rain fall softly on your fields. May God hold you in the palm of His hand." I puffed on the cigar. "Goodbye, Patrick."

Goodbye, lad.

A strong gust of Manchurian wind forced me back from the edge, pine needles rattling against me, my body bending in submission, pointing me toward the east, toward the future of the *jia* in far-off America.

When the wind stopped, I straightened. The wind had blown out my smoke. I looked up into the endless sky that encircled the world, into a heaven that was a deliberate gift, a reminder of kindnesses, universally owed.

A smile, full of *jen*, universal benevolence, curled around the corners of my mouth. I pulled the coat collar tightly around my neck, picked up the flag and walked slowly down the mountain.

EPILOGUE

On the morning of 8 August 1974, Colonel Carlos Justicio Murray, senior legal counsel to The Inspector General of the Army, issued a five-point press release.

Headquarters, U.S. Army, Washington.

On 19 January, three U.S. servicemen died in a live-fire exercise in South Korea during field maneuvers with the Second U.S. Infantry Division. CPT Christopher Sapolu of Honolulu, an Army weight lifter, and PV2 Paek Ok-kyu and PV2 Kim Chae-yon, company supply clerks, both of Los Angeles, were fatally wounded during field maneuvers with the Second U.S. Infantry Division. IG investigation has ruled the deaths accidental. New safety measures for live-fire exercises are in place.

In an unrelated incident at the DMZ in Korea on 20 January 1974, two U.S. servicemen died while mountain-climbing near the rural village of Tongducheon.

COL Frederick C. LeBlanc, Staff Judge Advocate for the Second U.S. Infantry, fell to his death while climbing Jungsan Peak in northern South Korea. COL LeBlanc left no kin. A serviceman attempting to save COL LeBlanc was also killed.

In unrelated legal proceedings, five Army lawyers in Korea were today sentenced to confinement at hard labor from two to fifteen years for effecting claims frauds.

Due to normalization of relations between Washington and Peking, four U.S. prisoners from the Korean War have been repatriated after twenty-four years of captivity.

The four servicemen, whose names are being withheld pending notification of kin, are at Walter Reed Army Hospital.

It is noted that Hong Kong newspaper accounts attributing the release of these four servicemen to the covert work of Chinese bandits and a Chinese-American soldier of fortune are untrue. Nor is there any truth to the rumor that these POWs had been held captive in Arsenyev, in the Russian Far East.

The press has published reports that North Korean military terrorists recently attempted the seizure of U.S. tactical nuclear weapons. We state unequivocally that these allegations are suppositional and irresponsible, since the United States has no tactical nuclear weapons in the Republic of Korea.

The press release drew little attention; on the same day, amidst a press storm of unprecedented dimensions, President Richard M. Nixon announced his resignation from the White House, effective the following day, Friday, 9 August.

On Thursday, 15 August 1974, Chang Duk-kyo, a burly worker at the Jungsan Mountain orphanage in Kyonggi Province, broke his pledge to the local shaman by abandoning his work.

Five days later, an Inmingun special purpose team attempted the assassination of South Korea's president, Park Chung Hee in the Blue House, the executive palace in Seoul.

The team assassinated his wife, the first lady, and deepened fears of an imminent North Korean invasion. Eleven members of the team were killed by ROK security forces.

United Nations Command Korea, Eighth U.S. Army and the U.S. Navy Pacific Fleet went on full invasion alert.

Three Inmingun soldiers survived to be executed and buried in low ground. One was an unnaturally large man.

Western reporters who scoured Korea for stories that summer heard rumors of a "Korean nuclear crisis" and accounts of North Korean spies, called Tiger Tails.

They heard descriptions of a suicide squad of steroidal mesomorphs in the American Army. No rationale for or proof of the existence of such men was found. In time, the stories faded into legend and innuendo.

One journalist persisted. Julie Wong of the *Sacramento Bee* settled in Tongducheon for two months, interviewing residents and taking pictures. She, the daughter of a man who used to ride the currents of the Yangtze River with a junkboat family, later won a Pulitzer for a photograph that seemed to typify a troublesome Year of the Tiger.

It depicted a long-haired woman and a teenaged girl kneeling at two petal-strewn graves in a green ginkgo garden, high on a windswept mountain in the far northern border country of South Korea. One gravestone is gray with age; the other is a bright white. Flowers adorn both stones.

In the photo, the woman lifts gnarled fingers to the sky. She has an oval, sunlit face marked by large, feline eyes.

The contrast between the old hand and the beautiful

face captures a boundary and paints a bridge between vast unknowns and seems proof of things invisible.

The woman smiles as she faces east, toward America.

HONOR AND DUTY
also by Gus Lee

As the war in Vietnam escalates, Kai Ting, a cadet at West Point, must confront dangerous preconceptions about Asians and struggle to maintain his Chinese and American identities.

The candidate buses unloaded, and my status of being the first was lost. The reminder, in echoing tones, of a five-year service obligation after graduation, induced a few to leave, beginning a process of attrition that would last for over three years. The grim words invited me to belong to something honorable; there was no going back. We were briefed on the oath of service and directed to Central Area. I was the only Chinese I saw.

As we left with our bags to meet our fates, the sergeants gazed at us as if we were boys instead of projections of parental ambition. The Negro janitor and I exchanged a glance. He was solemn, as if he were saying farewell to someone he knew. I nodded, appreciating his presence, wishing he knew that I had been raised as a Negro youth, knowing that, for an American, I always dipped my head too low in deference to China.

We stepped into the bright and angry flare of a day that was now alarmingly hot. The heat broiled my skin. I was entering a huge quadrangle filled with a deep, primitive roar of voices.

A breathtakingly immaculate cadet awaited me. He thrust his intensely focused features directly into my face and I jerked. Man—too close! "Hi," I gulped, "my name's Kai and—"

"DROP THAT BAG!" he roared, and I recoiled as my unguarded mind took his angry words like punches to the head. I gaped as my smarts fled before this *yu chao*, bad omen. I placed my luggage at my feet. Others began to drop their bags in small "whaps" across the Area.

"PICK IT UP!" the cadet screamed, then bellowed, "DROP THAT BAG!" I winced as the bag smashed onto the concrete: it contained my father's carefully preserved Colt super .38 automatic pistol. "PICK IT UP!" I picked it up, faster. "DROP THAT BAG!" I dropped it. "PICK IT UP!" I recovered it before the "UP!" I had become a human marionette, bobbing at my master, disarmed by the emotion.

"MISTER!" the cadet shouted. "YOU WILL IMMEDIATELY EXECUTE THE COMMAND GIVEN. DO YOU UNDERSTAND?!"

"Yes," I said, voice quavering, eardrums ringing.

"MISTER! You have THREE ANSWERS: 'YES, SIR,' 'NO, SIR,' AND 'NO EXCUSE, SIR.' DO YOU UNDERSTAND?!"

"Uh, yes, sir," I said, politely.

He was impeccable in a starched white shirt with blue, gold-striped shoulder epaulets; a bright, black-visored, snow-white cap; razor-sharp, black-striped gray pants; brilliant shoes; and advertising-quality white gloves. His name tag said "Rice," a name I liked. I had never seen anyone so marvelously perfect.

"I CANNOT HEAR YOU, SMACKHEAD!" he bellowed, as if I were back at the hotel rather than an inch from his clanging tonsils.

"Yes, sir," I said, pupils and testicles contracting.

"POP OFF, MISTER! KNOCK YOUR EQUIPMENT TOGETHER! YOU SOUND LIKE A WEEPING GIRL! DO YOU HEAR ME?! DROP THAT BAG!" he screamed.

"YES, SIR!" I cried, wincing at my own voice, the bag slapping the concrete. His face filled my vision. Uncle Shim believed that shouting was for thoughtless men. To my mother, shouting was a mortal sin. A street ditty inanely ran through my addled brain:

> *Step on a crack, break yo' momma's back.*
> *Yell at her face, lose all yo' grace.*

"BRACE, MISTER! You are CROOKED! PUSH that neck IN! KEEP YOUR EYES *UP—SQUASH* THAT NECK BACK! MAKE WRINKLES IN YOUR CHIN! CRAM IT IN! *ROLL* YOUR SHOULDERS BACK! *PUFF* OUT THAT PUNY, BIRDLIKE CHEST! HEELS TOGETHER, FEET AT FORTY-FIVE DEGREES! ELBOWS IN! THUMBS BEHIND THE SEAMS OF YOUR TROUSERS! KEEP YOUR HEAD STRAIGHT! ROLL YOUR HIPS UNDER! How old are you, SMACKHEAD!?"

I balked. He had almost spit in my face. "Se-seventeen," I said. Ten years in the ring spoke to me: take your stance, gloves high, and box this bully with the Godzilla voice. It was an old tune: China boy trips in and bingo from the jump, it's Fist City.

"*IRP!*—IMMEDIATE RESPONSE, PLEASE! 'SEVENTEEN, *SIR*,' *RIGHT?!* NOT 'Se-seventeen.'" The "*IRP!*" was the dark, sonorous belch of a thunder lizard; "*RIGHT?!*" was

369

the sound of silk being slit by a sharp butcher knife. The cadence and emphasis of his speech were almost Negro, but there was no comfort in it.

"Yessir, seventeen, SIR, YESSIR!!"

"CROTHEAD" he hissed, "I WANT *SEVENTEEN* WRINKLES! PICK UP THAT BAG! *BRACE! ROLL* YOUR SHOULDERS DOWN AND BACK! *LIFT* YOUR HEAD UP! *CRAM* YOUR NECK IN! BRACING IS THE MILITARY POSTURE FOR A MEMBER OF THE FOURTH CLASS! IF YOU SURVIVE BEAST, YOU WILL BRACE FOR ONE YEAR! DO YOU UNDERSTAND ME, DUMBJOHNWILLIE CROT!? SOUND-OFF!"

"YES, SIR!" I cried.

"*KEEP* YOUR BEADY LITTLE EYES STRAIGHT AHEAD! NEW CADETS ARE NOT AUTHORIZED TO GAZE AROUND! REPORT TO THE MAN IN THE RED SASH AND SAY, 'Sir, New Cadet X reports to the Man in the Red Sash as ordered.' PRESENT ARMS—SALUTE HIM. DO YOU UNDERSTAND, CROTWASTE!"

"YES, SIR!" I screamed, catching only the inner threat of his incomprehensible speech. I struggled with the seventeen parts of bracing while recovering my luggage and trying to breathe the bad air and survive the truly awful lack of *ho*, harmony, in this place.

"NEW CADETS DOUBLE-TIME WHEN THEY ARE ABOUT THEIR DUTIES. 'DOUBLE-TIME' MEANS YOU WILL RUN IN A MILITARY MANNER, FOREARMS PARALLEL TO THE GROUND, HEAD IN. *POST*, MISTER!" he bellowed, and I trembled isometrically in exaggerated rigidity, trying to simulate an American picket fence post, stiff, unbreathing, and white.

"*POST*, MISTER! DO NOT SPAZ ON ME! TAKE YOUR POST AND GET YOUR SORRY UNMILITARY WAYS OUT OF MY AREA! *MOVE IT!*"

HONOR AND DUTY
By Gus Lee

Published by Ivy Books.
Available in bookstores everywhere.

Diane Elliot-Lee

Gus Lee is the only American-born member of a Shanghai family. He attended West Point and received a law degree from King Hall, University of California at Davis. He has served as a drill sergeant, paratrooper, military criminal defense lawyer, command judge advocate, deputy director for the California District Attorney's Association, and senior executive for the State Bar of California. He is also the author of *China Boy* and *Honor and Duty*. He is married, has two children, and is now a full-time writer.

Printed in the United States
by Baker & Taylor Publisher Services